About the

After years of stifling her writer's muse and acquiring various uninspiring job titles, **Victoria Parker** finally surrendered to that persistent voice and penned her first Mills & Boon romance. Turns out, creating havoc for feisty heroines and devilish heroes truly is the best job in the world. In her spare time she dabbles in interior design, loves discovering far flung destinations and getting into mischief with her rather wonderful family.

Sophie Pembroke has been dreaming, reading and writing romance ever since she read her first Mills & Boon novel as a teen, so getting to write romance fiction for a living is a dream come true! Born in Abu Dhabi, Sophie grew up in Wales and now lives in Hertfordshire with her scientist husband, her incredibly imaginative daughter and her adventurous, adorable little boy. In Sophie's world, happy is for ever after, everything stops for tea and there's always time for one more page.

Maya Blake's writing dream started at thirteen. She eventually realised her dream when she received The Call in 2012. Maya lives in England with her husband, kids and an endless supply of books. Contact Maya: mayabauthor.blogspot.com, X @mayablake, Facebook @maya.blake.94

Sports Romance

December 2024
On The Stage

March 2025
In The Saddle

January 2025
On The Ice

April 2025
On The Pitch

February 2025
In The End Zone

May 2025
On The Track

Sports Romance:
On The Track

VICTORIA PARKER

SOPHIE PEMBROKE

MAYA BLAKE

MILLS & BOON

All rights reserved including the right of reproduction in whole or in part in any form. This edition is published by arrangement with Harlequin Enterprises ULC.

This is a work of fiction. Names, characters, places, locations and incidents are purely fictional and bear no relationship to any real life individuals, living or dead, or to any actual places, business establishments, locations, events or incidents. Any resemblance is entirely coincidental.

This book is sold subject to the condition that it shall not, by way of trade or otherwise, be lent, resold, hired out or otherwise circulated without the prior consent of the publisher in any form of binding or cover other than that in which it is published and without a similar condition including this condition being imposed on the subsequent purchaser.

® and ™ are trademarks owned and used by the trademark owner and/or its licensee. Trademarks marked with ® are registered with the United Kingdom Patent Office and/or the Office for Harmonisation in the Internal Market and in other countries.

First Published in Great Britain 2025
by Mills & Boon, an imprint of HarperCollins*Publishers* Ltd
1 London Bridge Street, London, SE1 9GF

www.harpercollins.co.uk

HarperCollins*Publishers*
Macken House, 39/40 Mayor Street Upper,
Dublin 1, D01 C9W8, Ireland

Sports Romance: On The Track © 2025 Harlequin Enterprises ULC.

The Woman Sent to Tame Him © 2014 Victoria Parker
The Princess and the Rebel Billionaire © 2021 Harlequin Enterprises ULC
The Price of Success © 2012 Maya Blake

Special thanks and acknowledgment are given to Sophie Pembroke for her contribution to the *Billion-Dollar Matches* series.

ISBN: 978-0-263-41731-9

MIX
Paper | Supporting
responsible forestry
FSC™ C007454

This book contains FSC™ certified paper and other controlled sources to ensure responsible forest management.

For more information visit: www.harpercollins.co.uk/green

Printed and Bound in the UK using 100% Renewable Electricity
at CPI Group (UK) Ltd, Croydon, CR0 4YY

THE WOMAN SENT TO TAME HIM

VICTORIA PARKER

For my Dad.
Always my anchor in the storm. I love you.

CHAPTER ONE

Monte Carlo, May

Hold on to your hearts, ladies, because racing driver Lothario Finn St George is back in the playground of the rich and famous.

After sailing into the Port of Monaco with a bevy of beauties only last eve, the man titled Most Beautiful in the World donned a custom-fit tux and his signature crooked smile and swaggered into the Casino Grand with all the flair of James Bond. Armed with his loaded arsenal of charismatic charm, the six-times World Champion then proceeded to beguile his way through the enamoured throng—despite the owner of Scott Lansing advising the playboy to 'calm his wild partying and tone down adverse publicity'.

Seems Michael Scott is still battling with threats from sponsors, who are considering pulling out of over forty million pounds' worth of support for the team.

True, Finn St George has always danced on the devilish side of life, but of late he seems to be pushing some of the more family-orientated sponsors a fraction too far. Indeed, only last week he was pictured living it up with not one but four women in a club in Barcelona—apparently variety really is the spice of his life!

Though, with only two days to go until the Prince of

Monaco launches this year's race, we suspect Finn's wicked social life is the least of Scott Lansing's worries, because clearly our favourite racer is off his game.

While Australia was a washout, earning him third place, St George barely managed to scrape a win in Malaysia and Bahrain, leaving Scott Lansing standing neck and neck with fierce rivals Nemesis Hart. But when he crashed spectacularly in Spain last month, and failed to finish, racing enthusiasts not only dubbed him 'the death-defyer', but he slipped back several points, leaving Nemesis Hart the leader for the first time in years.

Has St George really lost his edge? Or has the tragic boating accident of last September, involving his teammate Tom Scott, affected him so severely?

Usually dominating the grid, it appears our much-loved philanderer needs to up his game and clean up his act, or Scott Lansing may just find themselves in serious financial straits. One thing is certain: while Monaco waits with bated breath for the big race tomorrow Michael Scott is sure to be pacing the floors, hoping for a miracle.

A MIRACLE...

With a flick of her wrist, Serena Scott tossed the crumpled newspaper across her father's desk. 'Well, she was wrong about one thing. You're not pacing the floors.'

On a slow spin the black and white blur landed in front of him, hitting the glass with a soft smack. Then the only sound in the luxurious office on the Scott Lansing yacht was Serena's choppy breathing and the foreboding thump of her heart.

'No pacing. Yet,' he grated, dipping his chin to lock his sharp graphite eyes on hers.

Well, now... She had the uncanny notion that after hours of musing over the true genesis of her three a.m. wake-up call she was about to discover exactly why she'd been dragged from her warm bed in London to globetrot to the Côte d'Azur. And if the suspicion snaking up her spine was anything to go by she wasn't going to like it.

'I have no idea what you're worried about,' she said, perfectly amiable as she folded her arms across the creased apple-green T shrouding her chest. 'Finn is performing to his usual sybaritic standards, if you ask me. Fraternising with God-knows-who while he parties the night away, drinks, gambles, beds a few starlets and crashes a car for the grand finale. Nothing out of the ordinary. You knew this two years ago, when you signed him.'

'Back then he wasn't this bad,' came the wry reply. 'It's not only that. He's…'

That familiar brow furrowed and Serena's followed suit. 'He's what?'

'I can't even explain it. He goes on like *nothing's* happened but it's like he's got a death wish.'

She coughed out an incredulous laugh. 'He hasn't got a death wish. He's just so supremely arrogant he thinks he's indestructible.'

'It's more than that. There's something…dark about him all of a sudden.'

Dark? A sinister shiver crept over her skin as the past scratched at her psyche, picking at the scab of a raw wound. Until she realised just *who* they were talking about.

'Maybe he's been overdoing it on the sun deck.'

'You're being deliberately obtuse,' he ground out.

Yes, well, unfortunately Finn St George brought out the worst in her—had done since the first moment she'd locked eyes with him four years ago…

Serena flung her brain into neutral before it hit reverse and kicked up the dirt on one of the most humiliating experiences of her life. Best to say lesson learned. After that, what with her engineering degree, working alongside the team's world-famous car designer in London and Finn's thirst for media scintillation—which she avoided like the bubonic plague—face-to-face contact between them had been gratifyingly rare.

Until—*just her rotten luck*—their formal 'welcome to the team' introduction, when he'd struck at every self-preservation instinct she possessed, oozing sexual gravitas, with challenge and mockery stamped all over his face. *Hateful* man. She didn't need reminding she was no *femme fatale*—especially by a Casanova as shallow as a puddle.

Add in the fact that his morals, or lack thereof, turned her stomach to ice, from the outset they'd snarled and sparked and butted heads—and that had been *before* he'd stolen the most precious thing in the world from her.

A fierce rush of grief flooded through her, drenching her bones with sorrow, and she swayed on her feet.

'Look,' her father began, tugging at the cuff of his high-neck white team shirt. 'I know you two don't really get along...'

Wow, wasn't *that* an understatement?

'But I need your help here, Serena.'

With an incredulous huff she narrowed her eyes on the whipcord figure of Michael Scott, also known as Slick Mick to the ladies and Dad when in private, or when she was feeling particularly daughterly, as he rocked back in his black leather chair.

Nearing fifty, the former racing champion reminded her of a movie icon, with his unkempt salt and pepper hair, surrounding a chiselled face even more handsome than it had been at the peak of his career. The guy was seriously good-looking. Not exactly a father figure, but they were friends of the best kind. At least they usually were.

'This is your idea of a joke, right?' It was hard to sound teasing and only mildly put out when there was such a great lump in her throat. 'Because, let me tell you, I have more of a chance to be Finn St George's worst nightmare than his supposed...*saviour*.'

The idea was ridiculous!

Visibly deflating, he shook his head tiredly. 'I know. But I find myself wondering if you have a better chance of getting through to him. Because, honestly, I'm running out of ideas. And drivers. And cars.' Up came his arm in a wave of exasperation and the pen in his hand soared over the toppling towers of paperwork. 'Did you watch that crash last month? Zero self-preservation. The guy is going to get himself killed.'

'Let him.' The words flew out of her mouth Serena-style—that was before she could think better of it or lessen the blow. One of her not-so-good traits that landed her in trouble more often than not...

'You don't mean that,' he said, with the curt ring of a reprimand.

Closing her eyes, she breathed through the maelstrom of emotions warring in her chest. No, she didn't mean that. She might not like the man, but she didn't want anything bad to happen to him. Much.

'What's more, I refuse to lose another boy in this lifetime.'

The hot air circling behind her ribs gushed past her lips and her shoulders slumped. Then, for the first time since she'd barged in here twenty minutes ago, she took a good look at Michael Scott—a real look. Her dad might be all kinds of a playboy himself, but she'd missed him terribly.

Inspecting the grey shadows beneath his eyes, Serena almost asked how he was coping with the loss of his only son. Almost asked if he'd missed *her* while she'd been gone. But Serena and her father didn't go deep. Never had, never would. So she stuffed the love and the hurt right back down, behind the invisible walls she'd designed and built with the fierce power of a youthful mind.

Yeah, she was the tough cookie in the brood. She didn't grieve from her sleeve or wail at the world for the unfairness of it all. Truly, what was the point? She was this man's daughter, raised as one of the pack. No room for mushy emotions or feminine sentimentality spilling all over the place.

So, even though she now had a Tom-sized hole in her heart, she had to deal with it like a man—get up, get busy, move on.

It was a pity that plan wasn't working out so well. Some days her heart ached so badly she was barely holding it together. *Don't be ridiculous, Serena, you can hold up the world with one hand. Snap out of it!*

'Anyway, you can't stay in London all season, fiddling with the prototype. I thought it was ready.'

'It is. We're just running through the final testing this week.'

'Good, because I need you here. The design team can finish the trials.'

I need you. Wily—that was what he was. He knew exactly what to say and when.

'No. You need me to try and control your wild boy. Problem is I have absolutely no wish to ever set eyes on him again.'

'It wasn't his fault, Serena,' he said wearily.

'So you keep saying.'

But exactly which part of Finn taking Tom to Singapore on a bender and Finn coming back first-class on his twenty-million-pound jet whilst her brother returned in a box wasn't his fault? Which part of Finn taking him out on a boat when Tom couldn't swim and subsequently drowned wasn't his fault? He hadn't even had the decency to attend the funeral!

But she didn't bother to rehash old arguments that only led her down the rocky road to nowhere.

'So you want me to…what? *Forgive* him? Not a chance in hell. Make him feel better? I don't. So why should he?'

'Because this team is going down. Do you really want that?'

She let loose a sigh. 'You know I don't.' Team Scott Lansing was her family. Her entire life. A colourful, vibrant rabble of friends and adoptive uncles and she'd missed them all. But the entire scene just brought back too many memories she was ill-equipped to handle right now.

'So think of the bigger picture. Read my lips when I say, for the final time, it wasn't Finn's fault. It was an accident. Let it go. You are doing no one any favours quibbling about it—least of all me.'

He pinched the bridge of his nose as if to stem one of his killer migraines and guilt fisted her heart.

He was suffering. They were all suffering. In silence. *Let it go...*

But why was it every time they spoke of that tragic day, when the phone had shrilled ominously through their trailer, she was slapped with the perfidious feeling she was being kept in the dark? And she *loathed* the dark.

It didn't matter how many times she asked her father to elucidate he was forever cutting her off.

'Tom wouldn't want to see you like this,' he said, irritation inching his volume a decibel higher. 'Blaming Finn. Doing your moonlit flit routine. Holing up in London. Burying your head in work. You've done all you can at base—now it's time to get back in the field. Quit running and stop hiding.'

'I haven't been hiding!'

He snorted in disbelief.

Okay, maybe she'd been hiding. Licking her wounds was best attempted in peace, as far as she was concerned. But honestly...? How far was solitude getting her on the heart-healing scale?

Serena's heavy lids shuttered. God, she was tired.

She'd lost her brother, her best friend, and she kept forgetting she was supposed to carry on regardless. This was tough love and she'd been reared on it. Admittedly the vast majority of the time she'd appreciated Michael Scott's particular method of parentage. You needed skin as thick as cowhide to trail the world for ten months of the year in the company of men. Not the best way to raise two children, but she'd genuinely loved her life. Honest.

If she'd often stared at other children with their mothers, wondering what it would be like to have one of her own, to live in a normal house and walk to an actual brick-built, other-children-present school every morning, she'd just reminded herself that her life was exciting. And if she'd prayed for a mum all those years ago when her adolescence had been shattered, leaving her broken and torn, she'd comforted herself that she had Tom. Tom had been her rock.

But now he was gone. Nothing was exciting any more and there was no one to hold her hand in the dead of night when the shadows loomed. *You don't need your hand held. You're stronger than that. Snap out of it!*

She swallowed around the lump in her throat, forcing the overwhelming knot of grief to plunge into her chest. Buried so deep her stomach ached.

'*If* what you say is true and there *is* a problem,' she said dubiously, 'how can *I* possibly help?'

'Get him to take an interest in the prototype or work on your latest designs… I don't know—just get him to focus on something other than women or the bottom of a bottle.'

Impossible.

'*I'm* a woman.'

'Only in the technical sense.'

'Gee, thanks.' As if she needed reminding.

Then again, the last thing she wanted was to be like one of Finn's regulars. They were the skirt to Serena's jeans. The buxom bombshells to Serena's boyish figure. The strappy sandals to Serena's biker boots. The super-soft, twice-conditioned spiralling blonde locks to Serena's wild mane of a hue so bizarre it defied all colour charts.

Which was wonderful. Inordinately satisfying. Exactly the way she liked it.

'The last thing he needs is another bedmate,' he muttered wryly. 'He needs a kick up the backside. A challenge. And, let's face it, you two create enough spark to fire a twin-stroke. Therefore I am asking—no, you know what…? I am *telling* you to help. You're on my payroll. You move back in here and you chip in.'

Tough love.

Then his graphite gaze turned speculative. Calculating. An expression she didn't care for that nailed her to the wall.

'Or you can kiss the Silverstone launch of your prototype goodbye.'

A gasp of air hit the back of her throat. 'You wouldn't dare.'

'Wouldn't I?'

Yeah, he probably would. He didn't believe the racing car she'd designed would be anything special and she'd do anything to prove him wrong.

That prototype was her baby. Three years of hard work. Her and Tom's inspiration. Launching at Silverstone had been their dream. The only tangible thing she had left of him.

'Low, Dad,' she choked out. '*Really* low.'

Averting his eyes, he scrubbed a palm over his face. 'More like desperate.'

Serena sighed. Nailed. Every. Time.

'Fine. I'll try…something.'

Unease began to hammer at her heart—she had no idea how to handle the man. None.

'But I know Finn will make it up. He had a slow start last year. The sponsors will forgive and forget once he starts playing to his fans. Monaco is in the bag. He always wins here. What happened in qualifying sessions today? He's in pole position, right?'

Her father's expression turned thunderous—one that boded only ill. 'He screwed the engine.'

He blew the engine? 'So he's at the back tomorrow? In one of the slowest and hardest circuits in the world?'

'Yep.'

Pop! Up came a vision in her mind's eye—the scene she'd

bypassed as she'd hauled her motorbike along the harbour—and her stomach fired, anger swirling like a tornado. Sparking, ready to ignite.

Raising her arm, she pointed one trembling finger in the general direction of Finn's floating brothel. 'And he's along there, in that…that yacht of his. Engaging in some kind of… drunken debauched sex-fest to celebrate his latest cock-up?'

One weary hitch of those broad shoulders was all it took to light the fireball raging in the pit of her stomach.

'What in the blue blazes is he *doing*? Doesn't he care at all? In fact, don't answer that. I already know.'

The man cared for no one but himself! *And this was a newsflash?* Obligation and decency had clearly been disowned in that gene pool.

'I've had it with him.'

Bullet-like, Serena shot out through the door, her biker boots a clomp-clomp on the polished wooden floors as she raced through the galley. 'I'm gonna kill him. With my bare hands.'

'Serena! Watch your temper. I need him.'

Yeah, well, she needed her brother back—and that was about as impossible as keeping her mitts off Finn St George's pretty-boy face. She'd had enough of that man messing with her family. Her team. Her life. Her brother was dead, the championship was heading for the toilet, and her dad was aging by the second as Finn continued to yank at his fraying tether!

How selfish could one man be?

Well, she was stopping it all. She was taking control. Right now.

CHAPTER TWO

Serena ducked and dived around the loved-up couples milling on the harbour, her sole focus on the *Extasea*, rising from the water, formidable and majestic.

Even moored among some of the finest vessels in the world, Finn's super-yacht was in a class of her own—a one-hundred-and-sixty-foot, three-decker palace—reminding Serena of the resplendent seven-star hotels he favoured in Dubai and certainly more regal ocean liner than bordello.

Still, opulence aside, she had the acumen to know that appearances were deceptive, and the fact that she'd been lowered to this chafed her pride raw. But there was no backing out now. She was going to say her piece and he was going to listen.

The bravado felt wonderful. Freeing. Cleansing. She should have done this months ago, she realised—had it out with him instead of letting everyone sweep her under the carpet like some bothersome gnat, as if her feelings were of no importance. Her grief had been so all-consuming that she'd allowed it to happen. Well, not any more.

Closer to the yacht now, she felt the balmy air cling to her skin and the thud of her boots become drenched by the evocative beat of sultry music. As she marched up the gangway the splash of water from the hot tub on the sun deck followed by intimate squeals of sexual delight made her trip over her size fives.

Flailing, she gripped the rail on both sides. Then a tidal wave of apprehension crashed over her and she stood soaked with a keen embarrassment. She was about as comfortable with this scene as she would be treading water in the company of killer sharks.

You don't belong here, Serena. Surrounded by sex and women who exuded femininity. *Don't think about it. Just get in there, find Finn, and make him clean the decks himself!*

Hovering a few feet from the top, she inhaled a deep wave of saltwater air to reel back her bravado.

In every direction—whether it was left, towards the luxurious seating area abounding with plush gold chairs, or right, towards the outer dining suites—there were bodies, bodies and more bodies. Wearing as little clothing as possible.

She shivered, chilly just looking at them.

One step further and still no one seemed to notice the impromptu arrival of an uninvited guest. No ravaging lips ceased to kiss. No fervent hands slowed their bold caresses of sun-kissed flesh. No flutes of champagne paused on their way to open mouths and the laughter rolled on in barks of joyful humour that only served to remind her of the last time *she'd* laughed—which made a scream itch to peal up her throat.

Why should Finn and his entourage be laughing when she was still unable to cry? Unable to shed one solitary tear? *Because boys don't cry...*

Indignation launched her the final few feet and out of nowhere a sinister-looking figure loomed and grabbed her wrist in a manacled grip.

'Ow!' Pain shot up her arm and she flipped her hand in an attempt to dislodge the hold—even as she was flung back in time and any lingering panic was ramped up into bone-shattering fear. 'Get off me!'

Except the more she struggled, the tighter the hold became—until the knife-edge of terror scored her heart and her vision swam in the blackest waters...

A rough yet familiar voice shattered the obsidian glaze. 'Hey, let her go. She's okay.'

Mr Manacle released her so fast she stumbled backwards. Her only conscious thought was that she was taking up self-defence classes again. Pronto.

Righting her footing, she glanced at the owner of that masculine rumble.

'Thanks,' she murmured, her voice disgustingly fragile as she rubbed at her wrist to ease the throb of muscle and friction burn.

'You okay, Serena?'

Vision clearing, she focused on the handsome, boyish face of one uneasy chocolate-haired Jake Morgan. Scott Lansing protégé and an apparent star in the making. She'd never watched him drive. For some reason he always got a bit tongue-tied around her, and the fact that he was Tom's replacement gave her heart a pang every time she looked at him. *Not his fault, Serena. Let it go.*

'Peachy. Since when does Finn have security?'

'Had them on and off all season. Mainly for parties when there's a big crowd.'

Translation: when he needed to fend off gatecrashing bombshells.

'Where *is* your dissolute host?' she asked, somewhat surly and unable to care. She was shaking so hard she had to cross her arms over her chest to stop her bones rattling.

'Not sure.' Jake's Adam's apple bobbed and his eyes jerked to a door leading to what she guessed was the main salon. 'I haven't seen him for a while.'

Oh, wonderful. He was covering for Finn. 'Forget it. I'll find him myself.'

The sensation of copious eyes poring over her wild mane and crumpled clothing made her flesh crawl and she had to fight the instinct to race across the polished deck. Ironically, the door to the devil's lair suddenly seemed very appealing and she slipped inside with a bizarre sense of relief.

The lavishness of the place was staggering, and way too gold-filigree-and-fussy for her. She might have a DNA glitch but it didn't even suit Finn. Granted, he'd purchased the mega-yacht from some billionaire, but at least a year had passed since.

After ten minutes of being creeped out by cherub wall sconces she was standing in a corridor surrounded by more doors. It was all like a bad dream…

Moaning, purring, steamy and impassioned noises drifted from the room at the far end of the panelled hallway, licking her stomach into a slow, laborious roll.

Pound-pound went her heart as she edged further towards the sounds, her gaze locked on the source as if drawn by some powerful magnetic force.

Her hand to the handle now, a wisp of a thought passed through her brain: did she *really* want to catch Finn the notorious womaniser *in flagrante* with his recent squeeze? She had enough nightmares to contend with at the best of times. Except…she could hardly roam around here all night, could she? If he was in a drunken stupor she only had sixteen hours to clean him up, and she was *not* leaving this place without some answers!

Astounded at what she was about to do, she pressed her ear up against the door panel in an effort to decipher voices.

Rustle went the sheets and *creak* went the muffled bounce of springs, as if bodies were interlocked and undulating in an amorous embrace. Cries of rapturous passion bloomed in the air and her blood flushed hotly, madly, deeply, in an odd concoction of mortification, inquisitiveness and warmth.

Jeepers, what was *wrong* with her?

Focus.

Ignoring the anxious thump in her chest warning that exposure was imminent, she leaned further in and relished the cool brush of wood against her fevered flesh.

The woman, whoever she was, was clearly glorifying in what was being done to her. No subdued cries or awkward silences while she wished it were over. Just murmurs of encouragement in a deep velvet voice that made the damp softness between Serena's legs tighten.

Not Finn. She would recognise that seductive rasp of perfect Etonian English laced with the smattering of an American drawl any day. A distinct flavour from the time he spent in the off season, presenting a hugely popular car show in the States.

Not that she *liked* his testosterone-and-sex-drenched tone—not at all.

Edgy, she licked her arid lips and told herself to back away before she was nabbed. So why couldn't she move? Why did she strive to imagine what was happening behind this door? Wonder how, precisely, Mr Velvet Voice adored his lover's body for her to reach such hedonistic heights that she became paralysed, unable to do anything but scream in wanton pleasure and abandon—?

'Has she come yet?'

A voice, richly amused and lathered with sin, curled around her nape.

A squeak burst from her throat.

Her head shot upright.

Boom! Her heart vaulted from her chest and she pivoted clumsily, then spread herself against the door panel like strawberry jam on toast.

One look...

Oh. My. God. *No!*

Squeezing her eyes shut she began to pray. *This is not happening. Not again. I am not the unluckiest woman alive!*

'Good evening, Miss Seraphina Scott. Come to join the party?' he asked, with such unholy glee that she was fuelled with the urge to smack her head off the door. 'There's always room for one more.'

'When...' Oh, great—she couldn't even breathe. And her heart—God, her heart was still on the floor. 'When hell freezes.'

She wanted out of here. *Now.* Except the idea that she was

acting like a pansy made her root her feet to the floor like pesky weeds and she prised her eyes wide. Only to decide being a sissy wasn't so bad.

Leaning insolently against the polished panels, no more than two feet away, Finn St George smouldered like a banked fire and the heat spiralling through her veins burst into flames, seared through her blood. All she could think was that she must have done something atrocious in another life to deserve this.

After what he'd done, had it truly been too much to hope his mere presence would have stopped affecting her?

She hated him. *Hated* him! He hadn't changed one iota. Still the most debauched, moral-less creature on two legs. And clearly he intended to go on as if he *hadn't* taken a crowbar to her life and smashed it to smithereens. What had her father said? *'He goes on like nothing's happened...'*

Over her dead body.

Seraphina. No one was allowed to call her that. No one!

'This isn't a social call, I assure you,' she said, proud of her don't-mess-with-me voice as she restrained the urge to shiver before him. 'Any other time it would take an apocalypse to get me into this den of iniquity.'

His mouth—the very one that had been known to cause swooning and fever-pitch hysteria—kicked up into a crooked smile and one solitary indentation kissed his cheek. 'And yet here you are.'

Here she was. It was a pity, that for a moment, she couldn't remember why. All she could think was that that mouth of his was a loaded weapon.

'I do seem to find you in the most...*deliciously* compromising situations, Seraphina.' His prurient grin made his extraordinary eyes gleam in the dim light. 'Listening at doors? Bad, bad girl. I ought to take you over my knee.'

Thanking her lucky stars that she wasn't prone to blushing like a girl—because, let's face it, she'd never *been* one, and the fact that this man made her feel like one was probably the greatest insult on earth—she weighed up the intelligence of answering that symphony of innuendo. Meanwhile she returned his visual full-body inspection just as blatantly. Why he insisted on going through this rigmarole every time they met was a mystery. With one arching golden brow he arrogantly put her in her place—ensuring she understood that she was a duck among swans.

Unluckily for him intimidation didn't work on her. Not any more.

As she soaked up every inch of him she decided she didn't understand the man's appeal.

Obviously there had to be some basis for his being named the world's greatest lover, an erotic legend in the racing world. But, come on, plenty of men must be good in bed—right? Plenty had sexy dimples in lean jaws. Plenty had a mouth made for sin, lips that moved sensually and invitingly and downright suggestively, and eyes the colour of—

Ohhh, who was she kidding?

Finn St George was flat-out, drop-dead *insanely* gorgeous—an abundance of angelic male beauty.

Thick dirty-blond hair; cut short at the back and longer at the front to fall in a tousled tumble over his brow, gave him a sexy, roguish air. And that face…

Not only did he defy nature, he literally bent the laws of physics with his intriguingly wicked mouth and that downright depraved gleam in his cerulean eyes. Eyes that had catapulted him into the hearts and fantasies of women the world over.

Between his leading-man looks and his celebrated body—currently dressed in low-slung board shorts and an unbuttoned crisp white linen shirt, showcasing his magnificent torso—he was mouth-watering, picture-perfect in every single way.

It was a good thing she knew how well a polished chassis could hide an engine riddled with innumerable flaws.

'What do you think you're playing at, Lothario? Don't you

think drinking and partying the night away before a race is dangerous, even for you?'

'I have to find *some* way to work off the residual adrenaline rush from the qualifying session, Seraphina. Unless *you're* offering to relieve some of my more…physical tensions.'

Her lower abdomen clenched in reaction to that catastrophically sensual drawl, and as if he could sense it his lips twitched.

'I'd be quite happy to knock you out—would that help?'

There it was again. That smile. A dangerous and destructive weapon known to bring women to their knees. And the fact that it turned her own to hot rubber made her madder still. 'Then again,' she sniped, 'we wouldn't want to mar that *pretty-boy* face, would we?'

A trick of the light, maybe, but she'd swear he flinched, paled…before something dark and malevolent tightened the hard lines of his body until he positively seethed.

Whoa…

Her mind screaming, *Danger! Danger! Run!*, she backed up a step and nudged the door. She wanted to snarl and bite at him. It was as if her body knew he was the enemy and she was gearing up for a fight. The fight she'd once been incapable of.

Not any more.

Her blunt nails dug into her palms, but in the next breath he pursed that delectable mouth in suppressed amusement, as if it had all been some huge joke, and the change in him was so swift, so absolute, she floundered.

'There's something dark about him all of a sudden.' Or she could be hallucinating from an overdose of his pheromones.

'If you don't mind,' he drawled, 'I'd appreciate it if we kept my face out of it. After all, I wouldn't want to distress the ladies with some unsightly bruising.'

'Like you need any more ladies! Looks to me like you've had your fair share already this evening.'

He looked well-sexed, to be sure. Hair damp, with his glorious fresh water-mint scent flirting with her senses, she guessed he'd just stepped from beneath the assault of a shower.

'On the contrary, I was just about to indulge in a good workout.'

Disgust drove her tone wild. 'Yes, well, bedding the latest starlet or pit-lane queen is one thing—partying the night away before racing on the most dangerous circuit on the calendar is downright risky and inappropriate!'

He gave an elaborate sigh. 'Where is the fun in being *appropriate*? Even the word sounds dull, don't you agree?'

'No, I don't—and nor do our sponsors.' She rubbed her brow to pacify its exasperated throb. 'I swear to God, if you don't start pulling through for this team I will make you wish you'd never been born.'

'You know, I believe you would.'

'Good.'

He brushed the pad of his thumb from the corner of his mouth down over the soft flesh of his bottom lip. 'So if you haven't come to indulge in some heavy petting why are you here, beautiful?'

His voice, disturbingly low and smooth as cognac, was so potent she swayed, nigh on intoxicated.

For an infinitesimal moment his cerulean-blue eyes held hers and a riot of sensations tumbled down the length of her spine. Pooled. Pulled. Primal and magnetic. And she hated it. Hated it!

Beautiful?

'Don't mock me, Finn. I'm not in the mood for your games. I want this place cleared and you sober. How *dare* you party it up and put the team at risk while everyone sits around feeling sorry for your little soul?'

'You know as well as I do that sympathy is wasted on me.

Especially when there is a profusion of far more...*enjoyable* sensations to be experienced at my hands.'

Ugh.

Temper rising, implosion imminent, she felt her breasts begin to heave. 'For someone who blew up an engine this morning— and, hey, this is a *wild* idea—how about you start thinking of how to salvage the situation instead of screwing around? Have you been drinking? You could get banned from the race altogether!'

With a shake of his head he tsked at her. 'No drinking.'

'You swear?'

One blunt finger scraped over his honed left pec. 'Cross my heart.'

Time stilled as she walked headlong into another wall of grief and memories slammed into every corner of her mind. The games of two children. One voice: *'Cross my heart.'* The other: *'Hope to die.'*

There it was. The elephant in the room.

Tom.

Cold. Suddenly she was so very, very cold. Only wanting to leave. To get as far away from this man as she could before the emotion she'd balled up in her chest for months punched free and she screamed and railed and lashed out in a burst of feminine pique.

She'd tell her dad he was barking up the wrong tree. No way could she work with Finn. She felt unhinged, her body vibrating with conflicting emotions, all of them revving, striving for pole position. And that was nothing compared to the hot whirlpool of desire swirling like a dark storm inside of her. How was that even possible? How was that even fair?

Life isn't fair, Serena. You know that. But what doesn't kill you makes you stronger. Makes your heart beat harder and your will indestructible.

So before she left she was getting the answers she wanted if it was the last thing she did.

* * *

In all the times over the last eight months when Finn had imagined coming face-to-face with Seraphina Scott, he'd never once envisaged the tough, prickly and somewhat prissy tomboy with her ear smashed against a door panel, listening for the orgasmic finale sure to come.

How very...*intriguing*.

It had certainly made up his mind on how to handle her impromptu arrival. With one look his heart had paused and he'd stared at the sweet, subtle curve of her waist, battling with innumerable choices.

Apologise? Not here, not now. Wrong place, wrong time. The risk that his defences would splinter equalled the prospect that she wouldn't believe him.

Wrap her tight in his arms because for a fleeting moment he'd sensed a keen vulnerability in her? Far too risky. If he buried his face in that heavenly fall of fire he might never come up to breathe again.

Act the polite English gentleman? Despite popular opinion he was more than capable of executing that particular role. He could be anyone or anything any woman wanted, as long as it wasn't himself. The problem was that kind of outlandish behaviour would only make her suspicious and no doubt she'd hang around.

He might be responsible for the words *delectable*, *fickle* and *playboy* appearing in the dictionary, but he was far from stupid. Soon she'd start asking questions about her brother's death, and he had to ensure they never came to pass those gloriously full raspberry lips. Lips he'd become riveted upon. Lips he'd do anything to smother and crush. To make love to with every pent-up breath in his taut body until she yielded beneath his command.

Never.

So in the end he'd settled for their habitual sparring. The usual back and forth banter that was sure to spark her every nerve and induce the usual colourful dazzling firework display. Make her hate him even more. Followed by her departure, of course.

While a vast proportion of him had rebelled at the notion, some minuscule sensible part had won out. After all, if there were fairness and justice in the world *he* would be the man six feet under and not an innocent kid who'd always looked at him as if he were some kind of hero.

What a joke.

But death eluded him. No matter how many of life's obstacles he faced, and no matter how many cars he crashed. He was Finn St George—dashing, death-defying racing driver extraordinaire. Death took the good and left the bad to fester—he'd seen that time and time again. Not that he deserved any kind of peace. When it finally came and he met his maker he doubted he'd hear the sweet song of angels or bask in the pearly glow of heaven. No. What waited for him was far darker, far hotter. Far more suited to the true him.

Was he worried? Hell, no. Rather, he looked forward to heading down into fire and brimstone. It couldn't be much worse than what he'd lived with all day, every day, for the last eight months.

Ah, great. There he went again. Becoming ridiculously maudlin. Entirely too tedious. A crime in itself when faced with the delectable Miss Seraphina Scott, who never failed to coerce a rush of blood to speed past his ears.

Clink. The door behind her opened and a bikini-clad blonde shimmied past, trailing one French-tipped talon down Finn's bare forearm. A soap opera star, if he remembered correctly, and a welcome distraction that twisted his torso as he watched her saunter down the hall with a practised sway of her voluptuous hips.

What he couldn't quite discern was why his eyes were on one thing while his mind, his entire body, was attuned to another, riding another wavelength—one set on Seraphina's ultra-high frequency.

Typical. Because—come on—if there was ever a more

desirable time to regain some kind of sexual enthusiasm for his usual coterie of fanatics it was the precipitous return of Miss Scott.

'One of yours, I presume?'

Derision drizzled over that strawberry and cream voice making every word a tart, sweet bite.

'I don't believe I've had the pleasure.' Turning back to her, he licked his decadent mouth in a blatant taunt. 'Yet…'

Shunning her sneer of scorn, Finn gave an unconcerned shrug. Women had been flinging themselves in his direction since he'd hit puberty. What kind of man would he be to deny their every sensual wish? Anyway, he loved women—in all their soft, scented glory. Almost as much as he loved cars. It was a shame the current state of his healing body continued to deny him full access.

Not that he was concerned. It would fix itself. He just had to make sure he was a million miles away from *this* woman when it happened.

'Do you think you could refrain from thinking with your second head for one solitary minute?'

He pretended to think about that and in the silence of the hallway almost heard himself grin. 'I *could*. If you made it worth my while.'

Three. Two. One. *Snap*.

'You're a selfish bastard—you know that? Anyone else would try and focus on the good of the team after we lost Tom. Or should I say after *you* took Tom from us?'

Strike one. Straight to his heart.

'But not the consummate indestructible Finn St George. No, *no*. You think only of yourself and what slice of havoc you can cause next. If it isn't women, it's barely being able to keep a car horizontal.'

'While horizontal is one of my *preferred* positions, I admit it doesn't always work out that way.'

Grimacing, she moaned as if in pain. 'Don't you take

anything seriously? You crashed a multimillion-pound car last month. One I doubt will ever see the light of day again.'

He scrubbed a palm over a jaw that was in desperate need of a shave. 'That was unfortunate,' he drawled. 'I agree.'

'Is everything a joke to you?'

'Not in the least. I just find it tedious to focus on the depressing side of life. I'm more a cup half full kind of guy.'

'Unfortunately that cup of yours is going to run on vapour if you don't start winning some races.'

Yeah, well, he was having a teeny-tiny problem getting any shut-eye, thanks to the flashbacks visiting him far too often for his peace of mind. And, while his driving had always controlled the restless predator that lived and breathed inside him, of late that wildness had overtaken all else. Until even behind the wheel he felt outside of his own body. Detached. His famed control obliterated. Even as he wiped his mind he could still feel the tight scarred skin of his back rubbing against his driving suit—and then... *Hello, flashback*.

Luckily his body was healing. The memories would pass and he had all season to make it up to Michael Scott. Thirteen races to land the championship. Piece of cake.

'Don't worry about a thing, baby, the team is in safe hands with me.'

It was, of course, entirely possible Michael didn't think him capable of pulling them out of the quagmire. Hence this visit from Little Miss Spitfire.

'Now, why does that fail to ease my mind? Oh, yes—because these days, unlike Midas, everything you touch meets a rather gruelling end.'

Strike two, sending his heart crashing into the well of his stomach even as he managed to hide his wince with another kick of his lips. 'You need to trust me, baby.'

She snorted. 'When sheep fly and pigs bleat. I'm pretty sure the first step to trust is actually liking the person.'

He let his debauched mouth fire into a full-blown grin.

Finally—someone who loathed him instead of walking on

eggshells and spouting blatant lies to his face that it wasn't his fault. Michael Scott had a tendency to do just that. But Finn wasn't blind to the turmoil in the other man's eyes. The reality was his boss had a team to run and they were locked in a multimillion-pound contract, so Mick had no choice but to keep him around until the end of the season. The fact the man had to look at him every day left a bitter taste in Finn's mouth. Mick was a good guy. He deserved better.

After years of driving with the best teams in the world, constantly restless, his itchy feet begging to move on, he'd hoped he could settle with Scott Lansing for a while. It was more family than moneymaking machine, and respect ran both ways. Little chance of that now, but he'd win this season if it were the last thing he did.

As long as this woman stayed out of his way.

'Also, do me a favour, would you? Quit the *baby* thing. It suggests an intimacy I would rather die than pursue.'

Then again, he couldn't see close proximity being a problem, because—*oh, yeah*—she wanted to stamp on his foot good and proper. He could see it in those incredible eyes. Eyes that were a sensual feast of impossibly long dark lashes acting like a decadent frame around a mesmerising blend of the calmest grey with striations of yellow-gold as if to forewarn that there was no black and white with this woman— only mystifying shades of the unknown. Ensuring he was continually intrigued by her. Bewitched by her secrets. Yet at the same time they promised peace, true tranquillity—a stark, stunning contrast to that hair.

Her hair…

A shudder ripped through his body just from looking at it, inciting pure want to move through his bloodstream like a narcotic. Because that spectacular mane of fire told him she'd been burned and lived to tell the tale. A survivor.

Shameful, reprehensible; his eyes took a long, leisurely stroll down her lithe little body, soaking up her quirky ensemble.

Clumpy biker boots which, more often than not, made him instantly hard. Skin-tight denims and an apple-green T with the words 'It's All Good Under the Hood' stroking across her perfect C's.

Ohhh, yeah, she was delicious. Lickable. Biteable.

She leaned towards a serious tomboy bent and after multiple seasons of being faced with silicone inflation, Botoxed lips and an abundance of flesh on show, looking at Seraphina Scott was dangerous to say the least. Intrigue gave way to intoxication every time. Unfortunately he'd just have to suffer the side effects—because she was the one woman he could never, *ever* touch.

Not only was she the boss's daughter, and not only did that tough outer shell conceal an uncontrollable fiery response that lured the predator inside him to prowl to the surface and claw down those walls, but he'd also made a promise to her brother—and he'd stand by it even if it killed him...

'If I don't get out of this alive, Finn, promise me something?'

'Don't talk like that, kid. I'll get us out of here.'

'Whatever you do, don't tell Serena about this place. She's been through enough. She'll go looking for blood. You have to keep her safe. Promise me...'

His lungs drew up tight, crowding his chest until he could barely breathe. He would keep her safe. By getting her away from him.

Shuttering his eyes for a brief spell, he blocked her mesmeric pull. He'd dreaded this moment for months, he realised. Knowing she would come out fighting even as grief oozed from her very pores.

Where once she'd been a little bit curvy, now she was a little bit too thin. A stunning force of anger and sadness, beautiful and desolate. As if heartbreak had pulled the life force out of her and every morsel was tasteless.

Finn had done that to her.

Tom Scott...

Guilt lay like crude oil in the base of his stomach and every time he looked at her it churned violently, threatening to catch fire, making him ache. *Ache.* God, did she make him ache. Make the mourning suffocate his soul. As if it wasn't enough that the kid was still his constant companion even in death.

He didn't want her here. In fact he wanted her as far away from him as he could get her. Which begged the question: why was she back?

She who now eyed him expectantly and for the life of him he couldn't remember what she'd said.

Shifting gears, he asked, 'How's London?'

'Cold.'

'How's work?'

'Great. Thank you for asking,' she said, with such a guileless expression he didn't even see the freight train barrelling down the hallway. 'Why didn't you come to Tom's funeral? He worshipped you.'

His stomach gave a sickening twist.

'Sick.' He needed off this topic. *Right. Now.* 'How's the prototype?'

'Spectacular. Sick how?'

'Boring story. Is it finished?'

Say no.

Fuming at his attempt at derailing the conversation, she breathed slow and deep. 'Maybe. Did you know he couldn't swim?'

Crap. 'No.' *Not at the time.* 'Are you staying?'

'Possibly.'

Dammit. This was getting too close for comfort. 'I think you could do with more time off,' he said. 'Take a holiday.'

Suspicion narrowed her glare. 'Is that right?'

'Sure. How about a nice sojourn round the Caribbean? All that sun, sea and sex would do you good. Loosen you up a little.'

She raised one delicate dark brow. 'Why, Finn, I didn't know you cared.'

'There's a lot you don't know about me.'

'Funny, I was just thinking the exact same thing.'

Now he remembered why he couldn't stand the woman. 'Anyway, I was saying. A holiday is just what you need.'

'Are you saying I don't look so good?'

'Well, now you come to mention it you *are* a little on the thin side.' True, most women would consider that a compliment, but Miss Scott wasn't like other women.

As predicted, she prickled like a porcupine. But at least she wasn't musing about funerals and swimming any more.

'Trading insults, Finn? I wouldn't advise it. You've buried yourself in so much dirt over the years I'll always come out on top.'

A growl ripped up his throat. 'Mmm… You on top. Now, *that* is something I would love to see,' he said, sending his voice into a silken lazy caress, frankly astonished at how much effort he was expending to keep this up. For the first time in history one of their sparring sessions was stealing great chunks of his sanity.

'Liar. Furthermore, I'm not one of your fans or bits of fluff, so do me a favour and keep those blues above neck level. If you're trying to intimidate me you'll have to do a better job than feigning interest and eying me up.'

'But it's so much fun watching you prickle.'

'Some of us have a deeper meaning in life than having fun, and fickle playboys don't bring out the best in me.'

'Oh, I'm not so sure about that.'

Fired up, she was a whole lot of beautiful. Which he supposed was why he'd always tumbled into the thrust and parry of verbal swords with her. Sparks truly did fly when he was duelling with Miss Scott.

Now she was breathing in short, aggravated bursts, her breasts pushing against her rumpled T, and his fingers itched to climb beneath the hem. She'd be *sooo* lusciously soft, one hundred per cent organic and berry-like delicious against his tongue as he sucked her nipple between his lips...

Heat scrambled up his legs, heading straight for his groin... Until she crossed her arms over her chest, jerking his attention to the red blotches that marred her delicate wrist.

'What are those marks?' Closing the gap, he leaned in for a better look. 'What *is* that?'

'That is a gift from your security detail, keeping the hordes at bay.'

Hordes at bay? 'Let me see.'

'No!' Tucking her hands tighter into the creases of her underarms, she regarded him as if he were ten kinds of crazy.

'Come on. Stop being a girl. It doesn't suit you.'

'You know, that's the first truth you've uttered since I got here.'

As he gently tugged her hand free his knuckles brushed over her soft breast. *Holy...* More heat raced south, pleasure and pain moving through him at full throttle.

Oh, man, the last thing he needed was his first hard-on in almost a year to be for this woman. It was an inconceivable prospect that was swiftly overtaken by the dark bruising marring her wrist, and his insides shook with anger as he remembered the sight and sensation of torn wrists, shredded skin, blood dripping from shackles.

'Finn?' she breathed. 'What are you...?'

With deliberate and infinite care he brushed the backs of his fingers down one side of her forearm and up the other. 'I...' *I'm sorry he hurt you. I'll make him pay. I swear it.*

'Finn?'

Tilting her head, she frowned. Cutely. The action softened the often harsh yet no less cataclysmic impact of her beauty.

Seraphina Scott wasn't pretty in the normal sense of the word. She was no delicate English rose. No, no. She was a wild flower. Tempestuous and striking. Made in technicolour. Hardy, tough. Weathering every storm, only to survive more beautiful than ever before.

And she was clearly waiting for him to expand. Trying to work him out.

Such a small thing, that softening. It made her appear vulnerable. From nowhere more words sped through his brain. *I'm sorry...I'm sorry. So very sorry I took Tom away from you. I would do anything. Anything to bring him back.*

How he wished he could tell everyone the truth. Let the world know what had truly gone down in Singapore. But with an ongoing investigation and a sense that he'd meet his adversary again one day it was impossible. Business hadn't been settled. Too many men roamed free. So if there was to be a next time he was going in alone.

As if she knew the direction of his thoughts, she shaped her lips for speech—no doubt to ask more questions he would never answer, couldn't even bear to hear. Tension throbbed like a living force, so heavy he could taste it, feel the weight of it pressing on his shoulders.

What was it going to take for him to get rid of her? He didn't want Serena near him. Hell, he felt dangerous at the best of times. Around her he felt positively deadly. The need to charge upstairs and throttle the security guy's neck roiled inside him, toxic and deadly, and surely he had enough blood on his hands.

Speaking of hands... For some reason he couldn't let hers go. She was trembling. It couldn't possibly be him. Finn required a large hit of G-force to feel moved.

Holding her wrist in the cradle of his palm, he reached up with his other hand to touch the wild mass of her hair. Hair the deepest darkest red, reminding him of ripe black cherries.

How long had he resisted the temptation of her? It felt like a thousand years.

Almost there and her eyes caught the movement, flared before she jerked backwards.

'Finn. Let go of me. Right now.'

Distantly he heard the words, the quiver in her command,

and knew they held no heat. Control slipped from his grasp and he fingered the stray lock tumbling over her shoulder.

Pure silk. Hot enough to singe. Fire burning on a dangerous scale.

Ignoring her sharp gasp, he corkscrewed the thick wave and tugged. Hard. Being rough. Too rough. But that was what she did to him. Severed his control. Fed his wildness. Even as the thought of hurting her fisted his heart.

'Fiiiinn...' she warned, as her chest rose and fell in rapid, mesmerising waves.

Familiarity rattled her. Always had. After the last time he'd touched her, however innocently, she'd avoided him for four years. Clever girl, she was.

Not once had he seen her embrace her father and he'd never noticed her with a lover. It couldn't possibly be through lack of interest. Whether they would admit it or not, every guy on every team wanted a piece of her, Jake Morgan in particular carried a huge crush. But they always kept their distance. Prewarned? he wondered. Or did none of them have the courage to take her on?

There was a story there. One he'd pay any price to discover. One he would never know.

And that, he realised, was his answer. Or at least he told himself it was.

The charm he'd been born with, the charismatic beauty he'd wielded like a golden gun since he'd been old enough to deduce the fact that it got him out of many a sticky situation, would be the one thing—the only thing—to drive her away. Back to London. Out of sight. Out of mind. Free from the claws of temptation.

It wasn't as if he could do any harm. Despite every word that fell from her delectable pout, she felt the same exquisite thrill of attraction he did. Hated it just as much as he did.

Decision made. It was bye-bye, Miss Seraphina Scott.

May the gods forgive him for what he was about to do.

He unleashed his desire and went in for the kill.

CHAPTER THREE

LIKE A RABBIT caught in the headlights, Serena's heart seized, and her eyes flared as the world's most beautiful man brushed the back of his knuckles up the curve of her jawline.

Weakness spread through her limbs and she started to shake as if she'd been injected with something deadly. And when he skimmed the super-sensitive skin beneath her ear and sank his fingers into the fall of her hair to anchor her head in place dark spots danced behind her eyes.

'Don't you dare,' she barked. Or at least she intended to. Bizarrely, it came out as more of a panting plea.

'You should know better than to challenge me, Miss Scott. Especially in that gorgeous husky voice of yours.'

'Honestly, Finn, will you stop that for just one minute?'

'What?'

'The lies.' She loathed them. Not only did they torment the girl beneath, desperate to believe him, they also whispered of a long-ago web of deceit, a dark betrayal that haunted her soul.

'I'm not lying, baby,' he murmured.

The crackle of energy sizzling between them turned sharper—a sense of anticipation much like the coiled silence before the boom of thunder.

Surely he wasn't going to...? He'd be crazy even to contemplate...

His body came up flush against hers—all hard lines,

latent strength and super-hot heat—sending shock waves straight through her. Then his free hand splayed over her waist, swept around the small of her back and tugged her closer still, until every inch of their bodies—her soft curves and his hard-muscled form—were fused together with need and sweat and fire.

Need? No, no, no. *Impossible.*

'*Wow*, you really do have a death wish, don't you? You're on a collision course for total bodily destruction here, Finn.' Bending her knee, she aimed it to jerk upwards into his groin. Or maybe from this angle she could hook her foot around his ankle and send him off balance...

Kiss.

His lips pressed against the corner of her mouth, then brushed across the seam of her lips.

Ohhh, not good—not good at all. Especially when he moaned low in his throat and started to...well, to nuzzle his way over her cheek, then flick the tip of her nose with his to coerce her head back. And whatever had taken over her body answered his every command.

A heated ache bloomed between her legs, and when he nibbled on her lips to prise them apart the electric touch of his tongue was like a shot of high-octane fuel surging through her.

Don't respond. Don't you dare kiss him back.

'No...' she breathed, hating him. Hating herself even more for wanting. Flailing...

Serena reached up to push him away but ended up grabbing fistfuls of his shirt, holding on for dear life, powerless to sever the warm, moist crush of his mouth against hers as he moved with a consummate and inexorable seductive ease to find the perfect slick fit for their mouths.

Oh, my life. His kiss was slow and lazy, not meant to enflame but to enrapture, and before she knew it she was whirling in the epicentre of the fiercest storm, bringing her own force of nature into play.

She shivered and arched into him. *Never* had she felt anything like it. That warm, damp place between her legs throbbed together with her heartbeat and she wriggled closer, pushing her breasts into his chest to relieve the heavy, needy ache.

Tender and fiercely intimate, he didn't take her will, he invited. He didn't invade her body, he lured. He didn't punish her for her internal struggle, he tempted and teased with an amorous touch.

The pure sensual pleasure of it all was enthralling, making her feel feminine in a way she'd never dreamed possible. A way no man had made her feel before.

He deepened the kiss—the languorous thrust of his tongue a velvet lash of tormenting pleasure. It poured through her veins, heated her bones and weakened her limbs. It blasted all thought from her head until her most basic sexual instincts screamed for him to be inside her. Instincts she'd never known she possessed...

There were reasons for that, of course. She—

Whether it was the rush of unwanted memories or the gentle touch of his hand deviating on a feral bent to roughly fist and yank at the hem of her T, she wasn't sure, but—*oh, God*—he might as well have dunked her in an ice bath.

Emotion was a burning ball at the base of her ribs—embarrassment, humiliation and a heart-rending vulnerability that brought tears to her eyes. *No! No tears.* But all of it, all at once, was so overpowering that her mind began to shrill.

Flattening her palms, she shoved at his chest. Finn instantly let go and took a large pace backwards, that awesome chest heaving as he held both hands in the air in a show of surrender.

Intelligent guy.

The walls of the hallway began to close in on her as she gulped hot air. 'What the blazes are you doing?'

Taut silence pulsated off every surface as Finn blinked

dazedly and scrubbed his palms down his face, playing the role of slightly rattled, wholly astonished, guiltless gent! He belonged on the stage—he really did.

He gave his head a good shake. 'Seeing if your lips taste as good as they look.'

'What?'

He must think her dense. A fool. She was so far removed from his usual entourage she might as well derive from another planet, and for months he'd poked and prodded at her blatant lack of femininity. Now he expected her to believe his impetuous come-on was legitimate?

He was messing with her and she knew it.

And how could she have forgotten Tom? The part this man had played in her brother's death?

Guilt climbed into her chest and sat behind her ribs like a heavy weight. It crushed her lungs, making her breath shallow, her voice high-pitched. 'Answer me, Finn! What was that about?'

His lips parting to speak, he faltered yet again.

Why did she feel as if he wanted to tell her something? Something vital. Something she desperately wanted to hear. Nothing but the truth.

Rightly or wrongly—more than the next race, more than his success or the victory of Team Scott Lansing—the promise of that truth was the only thing tempting her to hover in his orbit.

Hold on…

'Are you trying to get rid of me? Is that your game?'

Wow, it seemed the heights of her humiliation knew no bounds.

Finn blinked several times in rapid succession and with every flutter of those ridiculously gorgeous thick lashes his expression smoothed into unreadable impassivity, until once more she was looking at Lothario.

'Is it working?' he drawled.

'Yes!'

'Good,' he said, those legendary dimples winking at her. 'Then you'll be pleased to know the door is that way.'

With a swift finger towards said exit, he pushed open a panel to her left. One he strolled through before it closed behind him, leaving her standing there, jaw slack, twitching in temper. The nerve of the man!

Fury grounded her flight instinct.

He wanted rid of her? He could go to the devil! This was *her* family, *her* life, and she was staying put. Her team was in trouble because of him and he needed to pay his dues. Not forgetting the fact he was hiding something and she wanted to know *exactly* what. Maybe then she could start to repair her broken heart and let Tom go. Move on. Find some peace. Remember what it was like to enjoy life—although she often wondered if she ever had.

Two steps forward, she pushed at the panel of what appeared to be a secret doorway. If it hadn't budged an inch and then rebounded back with a slam she would have thought it locked. Was he leaning on the other side, trying to regulate his breathing like she was? *Don't be a gullible fool, Serena.* He'd be grinning like the feckless charmer he was, delighted that he'd got the better of her.

The second time she put all her weight behind the oak, pushed and stumbled into a room, tripping over her feet with as much elegance as a battering ram.

A zillion things hit her at once—mainly gratitude for the fact that her ungainly entrance was witnessed only by Finn's back as he swaggered towards the bed and the sheer extravagance of the room.

'Wow.'

Infinite shades of midnight blue, the decor was a pulse-revving epitome of dark sensuality and masculine drama, and about the only thing on this floating bordello that fitted the man himself. As if, after purchasing the mega-yacht, Finn had only stamped ownership on this one room.

'Did you run out of money before the renovations were

complete?' she asked, tongue in cheek, knowing full well he was one of the highest earning sportsmen in the world.

For a beat he paused at the side of the bed. 'Let's just say I decided the yacht didn't suit. She's on the market.'

'Now, that *is* a shame.' If he restored the rest of the yacht in the same vein it promised to be spectacular.

'Do you like my bedroom, Seraphina?'

His voice was a pleasured, suggestive moan as he flung himself atop a gargantuan carved bed covered in black silk sheets and propped his back against a huge mound of textured pillows.

'I love it,' she said, unable to hide her awe and trying her hardest to look anywhere but at him. 'Present company excluded.'

Black wood furniture lined walls of the deepest red, with the spaces in between splashed with priceless evocative art to create a picture of virile potency and sophisticated class. It was visually breathtaking. Until the intimacy of the dim lighting set her right back on edge.

Searching the darkened shadows behind her, she cleared her throat, 'Lights?' she said, and hoped she didn't sound as jittery as she felt.

Bending at the waist, he leaned sideways to press a button on the tall glass nightstand and the opaque ceiling flickered for one, two, three beats of her thundering heart before the night sky shone down upon the room, ablaze with a million twinkling stars.

The sheer magnificence pulled her eyes wide. 'Seriously?'

He plucked a large red apple from the colourful mound of ripe delicacies toppling from a crystal bowl, then straightened up and raised one of his heart-stopping smiles.

Just like that her unease drifted, melted like a chilled snowflake on a new spring breeze.

Moonlight frosted his body, from the open white linen draping his sides to the wide bronzed strip of naked torso in between, taking his powerful beauty from angelic to supernatural. Otherworldly. Dazzling, magical and utterly surreal.

And she forgot all about not looking at him, suddenly entranced.

He tucked one hand beneath his head, tossed the glistening red fruit up into the air with the other and his honed six-pack flexed and bunched—the sight bringing a mist of perspiration to her skin.

'So. Come back for more, Miss Scott?'

His sinful rasp shattered the spell he wove so effortlessly and she gave herself a good shake. The man was *lethal*.

'I have heard my mouth is highly addictive.'

Serena raised a brow and hoped she looked suitably unimpressed. She had no desire to stroke his ego or any other part of him ever again. 'Such a…tempting offer, Mr St George, but I think I'll pass. Your reputation has been highly exaggerated.'

Apple to his lips, he sank his teeth into the crisp flesh with a loud *crunch* and she dredged the taste of tart flesh from her memory banks, making her mouth water.

'Ah. Must have been the champagne, then.'

'What must have been the champagne?' she murmured, distracted by the rhythmic working of his lean jaw. It truly was *not* good form to be so sexy even when eating. 'The champagne, incidentally, that I did not drink.'

'The weakening of your knees,' he drawled, with a wicked satisfaction that rolled over her in hot waves before he let loose an irrepressible grin that seared her nerves.

One day… She thought. One day she was going to wipe that smirk off his face once and for all. The thought that today was as good a day as any made her let loose a smile of her very own.

Strangely, he froze mid-bite. As if her smile affected him just as much as his did her. The mere notion that he had the power to make her believe such a thing made her temper spike.

'Speaking of knees—I'm going to bring you down on yours, pretty boy.'

A curious tension drew the magnificent lines of his body taut, precisely as before, and she racked her brain to figure out the trigger. All she could think was that there was more to this man than met the eye.

In the next instant he relaxed. 'I do hope that's a promise, Seraphina. I'd be more than happy to oblige.'

Blowing out a pent-up breath, she deliberated over how long she could ride this roller coaster of emotion with Finn at the helm before she plunged to her doom.

Especially when he licked his lips hungrily and dropped his feral blue eyes to the seam of her jeans, to the zipper leading down to the tight curve of her femininity. From nowhere an image of Finn on his knees before her as she stood bathed in moonlight slammed into her mind's eye. *Oh, God.*

Ribbons of heat spun in her veins, moving through her blood in an erotic dance. Her skin was suddenly supersensitive, and her nipples chafed seductively against the soft fabric of her plain white bra. The shockingly carnal expression on his face made her wonder if he'd visualised the very same.

As if. He's just trying to distract you again and you're letting him!

She stiffened her spine and ordered her voice to sweet. 'Oh, I'm so glad. In that case, let me be the first to tell you the good news.'

Crossing one bare foot over the other, he leaned back with more of the insolence he'd doubtless been born with. 'Somehow I don't believe you mean *good* in the literal sense.'

'Oh, I don't know. We could learn a lot from each other, you and I.'

The true meaning of that statement lay between them, gathering momentum with every passing second. It would take time, of course. To get him to talk. To unearth his secrets. To make him crack. Thankfully she had all the time in the world.

Another flash of perfect teeth sinking into white flesh. Another lazy crunch. Another sexy swallow gliding down his throat. 'I doubt that.'

The lack of innuendo suffused her with pleasure and a heady sense of power. It seemed she was finally getting somewhere.

'Why don't you enlighten me, Miss Scott? Your excitement is palpable and I find I can barely stand the suspense.'

She deflected that sarcasm with a breezy flick of her hair off her shoulder. 'I would *love* to enlighten you, Mr St. George. Me and you? We're about to be stuck like glue.'

A shadow of trepidation passed over his face before he cocked an arrogant brow. 'And the punchline is…?'

Musing that the word *babysitter* didn't quite have the right ring to it, she let her impetuous mouth stretch the truth, not really giving a stuff.

'You're looking at your new boss.'

CHAPTER FOUR

FANS DESCENDED ON Monaco in their droves and celebrities flocked to the world's most glamorous sporting event of the year for the exhilarating rush of lethal speed and intoxicating danger. So it didn't bode well that Finn stood in the shade of the Scott Lansing garage, his temples thudding with a messy blend of sleep-deprivation and toxic emotional clatter.

He had to get it together. Get that little minx out of his head.

Hauling in air, he rolled his neck, searching for the equilibrium he needed, knowing full well the smallest of errors in these narrow streets were fatal. Overtaking almost impossible... And didn't that just make him smile? Feel infinitely better as a fuel injection of hazardous adrenaline shot through his bloodstream?

Monaco was hands down his favourite circuit in the world: the greatest challenge on the racing calendar. It never failed to feed his wildness and remind him that life was for living. A master at shutting off fear and anxiety, he was a man who existed in the moment. Life was too short.

Seize the day.

Finn closed his eyes, tried to block the memory those words always evoked. But of late, since he'd touched hell itself, his past refused to stay buried.

Thirteen years old and he'd watched his Glamma—the woman who'd been a second mother to him—die a slow, agonising death. *'Glamma, because I'm far too young and vivacious to be Gran,'* the award-winning actress would declare.

Even when she'd been sick and he'd sworn his heart was breaking—*'Carpe diem, Finn, seize the day,'* she'd say theatrically, with a glint in her eye that had never failed to make him smile. *'That's better. Always remember: frown and you frown alone, smile and the whole world smiles with you.'*

Yeah, he remembered. How could he possibly forget a legend who had been far too young and vibrant for her passage to the heavens. Then, when the cancer had seeped into the next generation and his mother's time had come—spreading more grief and heartache through his family, much like the stain of her disease, destroying her beauty, her vitality, her life—he'd vowed to live every day as if it were his last. And, considering the way Finn had handled her demise, he owed his mother nothing less.

His heart achingly heavy, he left the technical chatter of the engineers behind and stepped towards the slash of sunlight cutting across the tarmac, shoving the pain and guilt back down inside him.

Enthusiasts spilled over balconies and crammed rooftops as far as the eye could reach. The grandstands were chock-full, the area where the die-hard fans had camped from the night before roared with impatience, and huge TV screens placed for optimal viewing flickered to life. It was a scene that usually enthralled him, excited his blood. And it would. Any second now. It had to.

His attention veered to the starting grid, cluttered with pit crew and paddock girls flaunting their wares, and then muttered a curse when not one of them managed to catch his eye. No, no. The only woman who monopolised his thoughts was his ruby red-headed *boss*!

Talk about a simple meeting of mouths backfiring with stunning ferocity. Instead of pushing her away, he'd stoked her curiosity—and how the devil he'd managed to step away, not to devour her, he'd never know.

Good thing he was an expert at disposing of the opposite sex. He'd just have to try harder, wouldn't he? With a touch of St George luck, Serena would make herself scarce today.

He snorted in self-irritation. Now he was lying to himself. He might *need* her at the far ends of the earth but he *wanted* her here, didn't he? Why was that? She was sarcastic, she had a sharp, spiky temper, and she was beautiful but not *that* beautiful—he'd dated catwalk models, for God's sake. *Yeah, and found them dull as dishwater.* And on top of all that just looking at her made him feel guilty.

Self-castigation, he decided. Penitence dictating that he had to make himself suffer by hanging around with a woman who wanted him dead.

He rubbed at his temple and thrust the same hand through his damp hair. Where on earth was she? Some boss she was turning out to be—

He chuffed out a breath. Boss? Doubtful. Babysitter, more like. She had spunk—he'd give her that.

Suddenly the crowd erupted and in the nick of time he realised he'd stepped into the blazing sunlight. Up came his arm in the customary St George wave as the pandemonium reached fever pitch. On cue, he whipped out his legendary smile, even as the movement of his torso pulled his driver's suit to chafe against his scarred back and black despair churned in his stomach with a sickening revolt.

Keep it together, Finn.

'There you are. Playing to your adoring audience, I see.'

Whoa—instantaneous body meltdown. The woman held more firepower than the midday sun.

'How nice of you to turn up, Miss Scott,' he drawled, keeping his focus on the crowd for a few seconds longer. Let her think he was inflating his ego—the worse she thought of him the better—but Finn knew how far his fans had travelled, the huge expense. He'd spoken to hundreds of them over time after all.

'I would've been here sooner if I hadn't detoured to that

floating bordello of yours, looking for you. I much prefer today's security man, by the way. New shift?'

He shrugged. Made it indolent, couldn't-care-less. 'Probably.'

Alternatively Finn might have shown the other man the error of his ways the minute Miss Scott had stepped off his... What did she call it? Oh, yes—his *floating bordello*. Naturally Finn would have used his most amiable, charming voice. The one he used to express how tedious a situation had become, how boredom had set in. The very one which ensured that people made the terrible mistake of underestimating him. Shame, that.

If that *had* happened the man in question might have been escorted from the premises in a not so dignified manner, with a reference that not so subtly informed the world that he'd never work in the industry again. Together with the unequivocal, downright irrefutable notion that to meet Finn in a dark alley any time soon would be a very, *very* bad idea.

Would he tell her any of this highly amusing tale? God, no.

Why ruin a perfectly good reputation as a callous, no-good heartbreaker when it was security money couldn't buy. Women had more sense than to expect more than he could give, so there was no fear of broken hearts or letting anyone down. What you saw was what you got.

And Miss Scott was no exception. Not now. Not ever.

Rousing a nonchalance he really didn't feel, he glanced to where she stood beside him; hands stuffed into the back pockets of her skin-tight jeans, the action up-tilting her perky breasts, and his pulse thrashed against his cuffs.

Then his heart turned over, roaring to life as he checked out her white T-shirt, embellished with a woman clad in a slinky black catsuit and the words 'This Kitty Has Claws' stroking across her perfect C's.

How beautifully apt.

'Lucky kitty,' he drawled, stretching the word as if it had six syllables. 'Can I stroke it?'

A shiver rustled over her sweet body and his smile warmed, became bona fide, as she slicked her lips with moisture. 'If you need all ten fingers to drive I wouldn't advise it.'

'I love it when you get all mean and tough. It turns me on.' It was that survivor air about her. Did strange things to him.

'Forgive me if I don't take that as a compliment. Seems to me that anything with the necessary appendage flicks *your* switch.'

'You'd be amazed at how discerning my sexual palate is, Miss Scott.'

Very true, that. After a few disturbing front-page splashes in his misbegotten youth he'd vowed to take more care in his liaisons. Absolute honesty with women who read from the same manual. Short, sweet interludes. No emotions. No commitment. Ever.

The mere word *relationship* caused a grave distress to his respiratory rate.

Not only had he started to see himself as some kind of bad luck charm—a grim reaper for those he cared for—but he was also inherently selfish. Driving was his entire life. Women were simply the spice that flavoured it.

Existing in the moment wasn't exactly conducive to family ties when he travelled endlessly, partied hard, and there was every possibility there would be no tomorrow.

She snorted. 'Discerning? Yeah, right.' And she brought those incredible grey eyes his way, arching one brow derisively. 'Let's take this conversation in a safer and more honest direction, shall we? Where's your helmet and gloves?'

'Not sure. Be a good little girl and go get them for me, would you?' he drawled, his amusement now wholly legit.

She puckered those luscious lips at him and a layer of sweat dampened his nape.

'Don't push it, Finn. I promise you, you don't want to get on the wrong side of me today.'

He dipped his head closer to her ear and relished the way her breathing hitched. 'I would *love* to get on any side of you, Seraphina. Especially now I've tasted that delicious mouth of yours.'

Easing back, he licked his lips to taunt her with the memory. It certainly wasn't to try and remember her unique flavour—that tart strawberry bite sparking his taste buds to life. Incredible.

'In your dreams.'

'Always,' he said, knowing she wouldn't believe him. Odd that it made him feel safe enough to drop his guard, tell her the unvarnished truth—which was a danger in itself.

With an elaborate sigh she stormed into the shadows of the garage, her voice trailing off to a murmur as she spoke to the mechanics and engineers. *Yes, go—get as far away from me as you can.*

From the corner of his eye he noticed a news crew focusing on him with the ferocity of an eagle spotting its prey and his chest grew tight. *No chance.*

Feigning ignorance, he ducked his head and strode back into the shade. Where he ran smack-bang into a helmet.

'Here,' Serena said, slapping a pair of gloves in his other hand.

A shaft of shock rendered him speechless. She used to bring Tom his helmet and gloves. She used to murmur something too. At one time Finn had tried to eavesdrop, but he'd quickly decided he was being ridiculous and didn't care what she'd said.

Then she'd always run to meet her brother after the finish, whether he'd won or not. She'd run out and hug him warmly, affectionately, with admiration in her smile and trust in her heart.

Instead of the usual envy the memory evoked, he battled with another surge of guilt that she couldn't run to Tom any longer. Then called himself fifty kinds of fool for toying with the idea that she could run to him if she needed to. *As if.*

'Hey, are you with me?' She clicked her fingers in front of his face. 'You're phasing out, there. Something I should be worried about?'

Out came his signature smile. 'You worried about me, baby?'

'No. I'm worried about the multimillion-pound car you're likely to crash to lose the championship! Did you get some sleep?'

Strangely enough, the couple of hours he'd managed had been demon-free, with his new boss the star of the show. Which was typical of him—wanting something he could never have just to make the challenge more interesting. The win more gratifying. Because, let's face it, while he fed off the rush of success, it never seemed to be enough. He was always restless. Always wanting something elusive, out of reach.

So, no, he did not trust himself around her. 'I did catch a few hours, thank you. It's amazing what the presence of a sexy spitfire can achieve.'

Her delicate jaw dropped as she grimaced. 'You mean after I left you actually…?'

Finn shook his head in disbelief. She thought he was talking about someone else.

Why was it that she'd grown up surrounded by men and yet had no conception of her unique brand of sexuality? It was as if she lacked self-confidence. If so, he wished she'd start believing him. Wished he could show her what she did to him.

Too dangerous, Finn. Just get in the car, win the race, show her you're a fixed man and get her back off to London out of harm's way.

The pep talk didn't work a jot. And, come on, she might fancy the pants off him but it wasn't as if she would ever answer to this overwhelming burn of desire. One, she was an intelligent little thing and she had more sense. And, two, she hated his guts.

'After *you*—sexy spitfire that *you* are—left, I slept. Alone.'

Her mouth a pensive moue, she simply stared at him.

Finn watched the soft shimmer of daylight dance through the shadows to cast the lustre of her skin with a golden radiance, enriching the heavy swathe of her hair until the strands glittered with the brilliance of rubies. A shudder pinballed off every vertebra in his spine.

'Why do you do that?' she asked, more than a little frustrated.

'What?' Shudder?

'Say things you don't mean.'

'Who says I don't mean them?'

She gave a little huff. 'Past experience. You've always delighted in ensuring I know you see me as nothing more than a tomboy.'

'Tomboys can't be sexy?' She was the sexiest woman he'd ever laid eyes on. And that was before she wrapped that incredible body in leathers to straddle her motorbike or—*give him mercy*—put on a driver's suit. Then it was, *Hello, hard-on; bye-bye sanity.*

He had no right to slide his gaze over her body in a slow, seductive caress, trying to remember the sight.

The boots moulded to her calves shuffled uneasily. 'Stop it!'

'You don't like it.'

Statement. Fact.

'No. I don't.'

Why? Because the extraordinary chemistry bothered her? Or because she was experiencing it with the man who'd stolen her happiness?

While the reminder punched him in the heart, it didn't stop him from saying, 'So why don't you take the compliment for what it is, baby? The truth.'

Crossing her arms over her chest, she hiked her chin up. 'But I don't want practised compliments from your repertoire. They mean nothing to me. I merely want you to do your job.'

Knife to his gut. Fully deserved. For the first time in his life he rued his reputation.

The smooth skin of her brow nipped and he realised his emotions must be seeping through the cracks in his façade. He schooled his expression with ruthless speed as his guts twisted in anger. One false move with this woman and he'd be finished.

'Look, Finn....' She sighed softly. 'I know you want to win this race and you've held the title for four years, but positioned at the back...? It's too risky an endeavour for even *you* to try and take the lead. I don't think anyone has ever done it before.'

If that wasn't a red rag to a bull he didn't know what was. He was also *pretty* sure being careful wasn't the name of the game.

'So just try and get a decent finish and come back here with the car in one piece, okay?'

For a second he thought he saw fear blanch her flawless complexion. Fear for him. And something warm and heavenly unfurled in his guts. Until he realised she merely wanted the car back in one piece. *Idiot*.

'Yes, boss,' he said, with a cheeky salute as he sealed up the front of his suit.

'Good,' she said, and the word belied the cynicism in her eyes. 'Now, get your backside in that car and let's see some St George magic.'

Walk away. Finn. Walk away and stop playing with her like this. You cannot have her!

'You think I'm magic?'

'I think you display a certain amount of talent on the track, yes.'

'My talents—

'If what is about to come about of your mouth has any reference to bedroom antics I will knock your block off.'

Finn cocked a mocking brow. 'I wasn't about to say anything of the sort. My, my—haven't we got a dirty mind?'

'Liar,' she growled, long and low, like a little tigress, and he almost lost his footing as he backed out of the garage.

How did the woman do it? Make him feel alive for the first time in months. Make his smile feel mischievous and his body raw and sexual when no other woman could.

Narrowing her glare, she lifted one finger and shook it. 'I don't like that smile, Finn. I really don't. Whatever you're thinking, whatever stunt you're about to pull…'

The scorching rays hit his nape, the crowds chanted his name and he unloaded his charismatic arsenal and licked his lips. 'Trust me, baby.' Slanting her a wink that made her blink, he veered towards the Scott Lansing race car. 'Trust me.'

Finn was sure she muttered something like, *Not in this millennia*, and he smiled ruefully. If she had any sense she'd remember that.

Inhaling long and deep, he infused his mind with the addictive scents of hot rubber and potent fumes that stroked the air—as addictive and scintillating as the warm, delicious redhead he'd left back at the garage.

Within ten minutes he was packed tight behind the wheel, the circuit a dribble of glistening molasses ahead of him, pushing his foot to the floor until the groans and grunts of the powerful machine electrified his flesh. Oh, yeah, he was a predator, with a thirst for the high-octane side of life, the thrill of the chase. One goal—to win.

Pole position. Middle or back. Dangerous or not. Didn't matter to him.

This race was his.

Trust him. *Trust him?*

'What the blazes is he doing?' It was, quite literally, like waiting for the inevitable car crash.

One of the engineers whistled through his teeth. 'Look at that guy go. Phenomenal, isn't he?'

'Crazy, more like,' she muttered. Zero self-preservation. *Zero!*

More than once she heard the pit-lane channel go silent and probably wouldn't have thought anything of it—*if* she hadn't noticed him do that thing last night and this morning. Almost phasing out as some kind of darkness haunted his gaze. It was disturbing since he was renowned for his awesome ability to concentrate with such focus that nothing else existed but his car hugging the tarmac.

A battalion of bugs crawled up her spine and she glanced back at the shaded screen hanging in the garage.

'Grand Hotel Hairpin. Just ahead of him. Holy Toledo! It's a pile-up.'

Her heart careening into cardiac arrest, she held her breath, waiting for the iconic red Scott Lansing car to clear the haze of dust and debris. *Come on, come on. Stuff the car. Don't you dare kill yourself. I will never forgive you.*

Serena wondered at that. Decided it was because she hadn't managed to coax the truth about Tom's death out of him yet. Tom, who should be here. Racing in this race. Doing what he'd loved best.

A fist of sorrow gripped her heart. Too young. He'd been just too young to die. And despite everything Finn was too young to be chasing death too.

She had to swallow in order to speak. 'Where is Jake?' With a bit of luck *he* had more sense.

'Still holding fifth.'

A cackle of relieved laughter hit her eardrum as Finn's car flew past the devastation to take third place.

'I don't believe it,' she said, breathless and more than a bit dizzy.

'I do.' Her dad stood alongside her now, his attention fixed on the same screen. 'Whatever you said to him has obviously worked, Serena. What *did* you say?'

'That I was his new boss.'

Michael Scott's head whipped round with comical speed. *'What?'*

'Worked, hasn't it?' she said, knowing full well that her impulsive mouth had nothing to do with it.

Finn danced to his own tune, had his own agenda front and foremost. Moreover, just watching him race like this—with the ultimate skill and talent—made her even more certain there was more to his crashes and sporadic losses than met the eye. But for some reason today he was *mostly* focused.

'He's taking second place with one lap to go! It's gonna be tight, though.'

She snorted. 'He doesn't want to lose the Monaco title.' Then she squeezed her eyes shut as he almost rammed into the Nemesis Hart driver, swerved to avoid a crash and clipped his front wing off instead.

'Whoa—there goes the car coming back in one piece.'

Stomach turning over, she shoved her hands into her back pockets to watch the last minute on screen.

Heck's teeth, he was going to do it…

Admiration and awe prised their way through the hate locked in her chest. The man was *amazing*.

'Half a second. Unbelievable!' someone yelled.

A warm shower of relief rained down from her nape and her entire body went lax.

The crowd erupted with a tremendous roar and chanted his name: *'Fi-in Fi-in Fi-in.'* Every mechanic and engineer ran out into the scorching rays and Michael Scott—who hadn't hugged her since she was fourteen years old, when she'd been broken and torn and his face had been etched with fury and pain—turned round, picked her up and spun her around the floor.

She imagined it was how a ballerina felt—spinning, twirling, dancing on air. Her beauty delicate, feminine. Nothing like *her*.

Before she even had a chance to wrap her arms around his neck, to bask in this inconceivable show of affection, to actually *feel* his love, he abruptly let go and jogged into the pit lane.

Swaying on her feet, she swallowed hard—told herself for the millionth time in her life not to be upset. That she mustn't be angry with him for not wanting to be close to her. It was just the way he was. He only knew how to deal with boys.

'*Come on, Serena, get a grip, get busy, move on*,' he'd say. '*Boys don't cry.*'

Okay, then. Get busy. Move on.

Except alone now, with the dark shadows creeping over her skin like poison ivy, she felt…lost. Grappling with the annoying sense that she was forgetting something.

Oh.

This was the part where she ran out to Tom.

Cupping her hand, she covered her mouth, gritted her teeth and tensed her midriff to stop the sob threatening to rip past her throat. *No. No!*

She should never have come back here. Should have stayed away—

Footsteps bounded from the pit lane and she sucked great, humongous lungfuls of air through her nose, then blew out quick breaths. Over and over.

It was a good job too, because Finn strode into the shadows—and the intense magnetism he exuded was a tangible, vibrant combination of devil-may-care and decadent sin.

Blond hair now dark with sweat tumbled over his brow and he wore an indecipherable expression on his over-warm face, almost as if he knew exactly what she'd been thinking. *Impossible.*

Bolstering her reserves, she stood tall as he drew near and threw his arms wide.

'What did you think, baby?'

'I think that by the end of the season I'll be on a whole

lot of medication. Good God, you're a liability.' A very expensive, scorching hot, stunning liability.

'So you don't wanna hang around with me any more?' He clapped a hand over his left pec. 'I think my heart's broken.'

'Come on, Finn, you and I both know you don't have one. You take direction from another body part entirely.'

Standing there, smouldering with testosterone, he sneaked his tongue out to moisten his lips. When it came, his voice was a low groan. 'You think about my body parts?'

That was it. Later she'd have no idea how she could veer from abject misery to munching on the inside of her cheek to stifle a snort of laughter. He was incorrigible. She hated him. *Hated* him!

'I think about many of your body parts. Your neck, especially—the very one I'd like to wrap my hands around.'

She reminded herself that to be turned on by that cocksure smile was a gross dereliction of self-preservation.

'Did you need something?' she asked, thoroughly confused. 'You've left your fans wailing for your return.'

'No, I just wanted…' He lifted his hand and scratched the side of his jaw in an uneasy, somewhat boyish manner.

'What?' she murmured, distracted by a small scar she'd never noticed before—a thin white slash scoring his hairline. How on earth had he got that?

'I wanted you to say how awesome I am.'

'Don't be silly. You can barely fit your head through the open cockpit as it is. Keep dreaming.'

'Oh, don't worry. I will,' he drawled suggestively. And just like that she was transported back to his yacht, his kiss. Then came the heat, curling low in her abdomen, licking her insides, making her shiver.

Honestly, she was certifiable. Without a doubt.

Much as earlier, he began to back out of the garage, taking his dizzying pheromones with him, and within a nanosecond fury overtook her. For the playful banter. For the way she'd allowed him to affect her so utterly.

'By the way, I want to speak to you tonight,' she said sharply.

Before he hit the bright light his feet froze mid-step. 'Saying goodbye already?'

Tilting her head, Serena frowned. 'Now, why would I do that?'

'I won the race. I'll charm the sponsors at dinner. Disaster averted.'

That was why he was so focused on winning? To get rid of her? Surely not. His need to win overruled all else. Unless what he was hiding was of far more importance.

Her heart flapping like a bird's wings against a cage, she said, 'I'm not going anywhere, Finn. I promise you that.'

Gazes locked, they engaged in some sort of battle of wills—one she had no intention of losing. She was here to stay.

'Unfortunately, Miss Scott, I have a date this evening. With my good friend Black Jack. Unless you'd care to join us…?'

'*The Casino?* I wouldn't be seen dead there.'

And the smirk on his face told her he knew it!

'Then I guess you'll just have to catch me some other time, beautiful.'

Not if she could help it. The man had to get dressed on that den of iniquity, so she'd just have to corner him before he stepped foot on the harbour. There was no way on this earth she was going up to that swanky Casino, where the dress code pronounced that all women had to dress as if they were for sale. Not for love nor money. She didn't even own a dress, for heaven's sake.

Nope. She'd just have to catch him first.

CHAPTER FIVE

FINN DIDN'T WASTE any time calling in a favour and landing a suite at the most exclusive Casino in town—where all the glitz and glamour that made the city famous came together in a fairy-tale fantasyland of opulence and high-flyers—and ordering a tuxedo from one of the exclusive concessions in the marble and bronze foyer.

Strict dress code aside, at times he luxuriated in his debonair façade. Playing Casanova was generally more interesting than being himself. Also, as it turned out, his penthouse here had evolved into a necessity. Not only did he need somewhere to sleep with no lingering residue of the demons haunting him in the dead of night, but a gratifyingly quick sale had gone through that very afternoon. One of the members of a minor royal family reviving his Swiss bank account very nicely.

The fact he was Seraphina-free for the evening was also an added boon.

The plan was, he'd grab a couple of girls, lavish money on a few gaming tables, dance until the wee hours and then sleep. Great plan. The fact that he lacked enthusiasm…? Not so great.

Her fault. It's all her fault.

Had he actually stormed into the garage to check on her? According to his memory banks, yes, he had.

Since when had he left the hullabaloo of the roaring crowd for a woman? Never before in his life!

Do not panic—it's the guilt.

Knowing she missed her brother and veiled the ache with her beautiful bravado was killing him. The pain that lurked behind those incredible grey eyes was a fist to his gut. Her strength was formidable, but he couldn't help wondering what it cost her. Of late, holding his own façade in place came at an extortionate price, but the alternative fall out would be catastrophic. As soon as he opened the door to his emotional vault the contents of Pandora's box would be unleashed and all hell would break loose.

Now, sitting in the prestigious lounge known as the throbbing heart of the Casino, he palmed a tall glass of tequila and raised it to his lips, hopeful that the sharp kick and bite would burn the dull edges off his dark mood. For some reason the suave, elegant cut of his suit wasn't working tonight. He felt dangerous enough to burst out of his skin.

The sensation of black eyes staring into his soul reminded him of dark, agonising days and he downed the liquor—his first drink in a week—and it slid down his throat, trailing a blaze of fire to his gut.

Gradually the muted *whoosh* of spinning roulette wheels, the mumble of inane chatter and the evocative beat from a small band filtered through his mind.

The singer was a stunning blend of French beauty and passionate sultry vocals, and when he felt her eyes slither over him in blatant invitation the crystal in his fist cracked with a soft clink. What was he *doing* here? He'd sell his soul to be someone else for one day, one night—

Between one heartbeat and the next the hair on his nape tingled, shifting his pulse into gear.

Easing his totalled glass onto the low-slung mahogany table, he glanced covertly around the room—from the impressive plaster of Paris inlays and priceless art to each and every table in between. By the time he reached the archway leading to the main gambling hall every cell in his body was on red alert and his heart had roared to life.

It was the kind of stupefying feeling he'd used to get on the starting grid. The very one he'd lost what felt like aeons ago, leaving a dull imitation in its place.

Now the cause of that incredible sensation shoved heat through his veins as he caught a flash of ruby-red hair flowing across the foyer.

Within seconds he was on his feet. What *was* Miss Spitfire doing in here? Looking for him? She was a determined little thing.

In the main lobby he glanced left, towards the wide entryway—seeing the line of supercars curling around the fountain beyond—and then right, to fall beneath her spell as she disappeared around a darkened corner.

By the time he caught up she was facing a door, her hand in mid-air—

'You've come to the Casino to use the bathroom, Seraphina? Do you have a problem with the plumbing on your father's yacht?'

She froze, palm flat against the hardwood panel, and Finn watched her decadent long lashes flutter downwards to whisper over her satiny cheeks. No make-up, he mused, and her natural beauty was really quite breathtaking.

With a swift inhale she spun on her feet and then crossed her arms over her knee-length black coat. She arched one delicate brow. 'When a girl needs to go, a girl needs to go.'

'How right you are.' He needed to be rid of her just as badly. Because she was angry—no, she was furious—and he wanted to kiss that mulish line right off her lips.

'You could have told me you'd sold your bordello *before* I stormed the place looking for you.'

Ah.

'I would have if I'd known you were coming to visit, baby. You know how much I look forward to our little…assignations.' He felt a smile tug at his lips. Stretching wider as her gaze loitered over his attire and a shiver racked her svelte frame.

'Am I doing it for you tonight, Miss Scott?' he asked, his voice a decadent purr.

She grimaced as if she were in pain. 'If by "it" you mean making me regret the moment I ever laid eyes on you, then, yes, strangely enough you are.'

Aw, man, she was delicious. 'How do you feel about dinner?' It was a horrendous idea, but he suddenly had the urge to feed her. Fill out those over-slight curves.

'You mean *together*?'

'That's a bit forward, don't you think? But, yes, okay. I accept.'

Mouth agape, she slowly shook her head, clearly questioning his sanity. Oddly enough, that made two of them. 'Did you attend some school specialising in becoming the most annoying and arrogant person ever?'

'As a matter of fact—'

A tall blonde, dressed to the nines in a slinky red number, appeared from nowhere and motioned to the bathroom door. Finn stifled his irritation at her giving him the once-over and zeroed in on Serena as she clammed up, took a step back, and dipped her head until that glorious fall of hair veiled her face.

Unsure why it could be, but loathing the way she threw out distress signals, he curled his fingers around her upper arm and tugged her further along the hall to where the dim light imparted privacy.

Except every muscle in her arm tensed beneath his fingers and her gaze bounced off every surface until even *he* half expected someone to pounce.

'Hey, are you okay?'

'Peachy.'

She wrenched free and wrapped both arms across her chest. It was like watching someone erect guard rails.

Okay, so she didn't want to be alone with him. Yet she'd

been fine last night in his bedroom. What had she asked him for? Lights.

'You don't like the dark?' For some reason it made him think back to that odd ramble of Tom's—*'Protect her for me...she's been through enough...'*—and his fists tightened into hard balls of menace.

She bristled with an adorable blend of embarrassment and pique.

'Hey, so you don't like the dark? So what? Neither do I. When I was a kid I used to crawl into bed with my mum during power cuts, for Pete's sake. Some hard-ass Spider-Man I was.'

She blinked over and over, until the fine lines creasing her brow smoothed. 'Spider-Man, huh? Did you have the blue and red outfit too?'

'Sure I did. And the cool web-maker.'

Her small smile lit the corners of the hall. Finn wanted it stronger, brighter.

'Did you have a tutu or a Snow White dress? My baby sister had all that crap.'

She snorted. 'I doubt Snow White wielded a wrench, and I don't expect engine oil would wash out of a tutu very well.'

His every thought slammed to a halt.

Reared by men in a man's world. No mother—he knew from Michael Scott that Serena's mum had died giving birth to her. No sisters.

'Have there been *any* women in your life?'

She gave a blithe shrug but he didn't miss the scowl that pinched her mouth. 'Only my dad's playthings.'

'Ah. I get it.' The narcissistic variety. Or maybe weak, fawning versions Serena would have recoiled from. So naturally she'd kept with the boys, until, 'You feel uncomfortable around women.'

'No!' She kicked her chin up defensively.

Finn cocked one brow and a long sigh poured from her lips.

'I don't know what to say to them, that's all, okay? We have nothing in common.'

'You've never had any girlfriends *at all*?' The notion was so bizarre he couldn't wrap his head around it.

'Not really, no. Tom and I had long-distance schooling, and it was pretty rare to see girls hanging around the circuit.'

Finn kept his expression neutral, conscious that empathy wouldn't sit well with her. Yet all he could think of was his sister, surrounded by girlfriends, and she'd had their mother through her formative years. He dreaded to think what Serena's adolescence had been like. No shopping trips or coming-of-age chats, nor any of that female pampering stuff he'd used to roll his eyes at but which had made Eva fizz with excitement.

He was astonished that Serena had managed without a woman in her life. Had she been allowed to be a girl at all? And why exactly did that make anger contort his guts? They were nothing to one another; only hate coloured her world when she looked at him.

'So you have a sister?' she asked quietly, almost longingly, and his chest cramped with guilt. It didn't seem fair, somehow, that he still had Eva and Serena had no one.

'Yes, I do. Eva.'

Eva—who had suffered greatly from the demise of Libby St George. And what had he done? Turned his back on her, on both of them, and walked away to chase his dreams, his big break. Knowing what they'd go through because he'd seen it all before. He'd left Eva to cope, to watch their beautiful mother slowly fade away.

Finn had let them down. Badly. And, what was worse, he hadn't been the only one. His father, the great Nicky St George, eighties pop-star legend, had left to find solace in many a warm bed. Looking back, Finn still found it hard to believe he'd watched a good man—his childhood hero—break so irrevocably under the weight of heartache. And, while he felt bitterly angry towards his father to this day, he could hardly hate the man when he'd felt the same pain. When he'd let them down too.

Yet still his baby sister loved him. She was all goodness while he was inherently selfish.

Eva. His mind raced around its mental track. Eva would be perfect for Serena. A great introduction to the best kind of women…

Finn stomped on the brakes of his runaway thoughts.

It would be dangerous to take Serena to Eva. Eva might get the wrong idea. Serena might get the wrong idea. *He* might get the wrong idea. He was supposed to be getting rid of her, not fixing her and finding ways to keep her around! What was *wrong* with him?

'Through here.' He beckoned her towards another door. One he pushed wide and held as she warily followed him into one of the small lounges where the private games of the high-flyers were often held.

'Why do I half expect the Monte Carlo Symphony Orchestra to strike up any second?'

'It's the grandeur of the place. It's pretty spectacular.' Oppressive at times, but spectacular nonetheless.

'If you like that kind of thing,' she muttered, with a slick manoeuvre that brought her back flush against another wall.

Musing on why she'd cornered herself again, Finn lounged against the arm of an emerald antique sofa a few feet away and faced her. 'So, what do you fancy for dinner?'

She sniffed, the action wrinkling her little nose. 'I'd rather starve.'

'You've changed your tune pretty quick. Is it a habit of yours? It was only this afternoon you said, "I wouldn't be seen dead" in reference to this very establishment. What changed your mind?'

Pouting those luscious lips, she weighed him up from top to toe, her gaze burning holes in his ten-thousand-pound tux. He felt all but cauterised.

'First off, why don't you tell me why you're avoiding me?'

Because I can't tell you what you want to hear.

'Because every time I look at you I want to make love to that beautiful mouth of yours. It's addictive.' She was like a drug—the prime source of some very intense highs. 'But you don't want that, do you, Seraphina?' he asked, rich and smooth, with a sinful tone he couldn't quell even if he tried.

Up came her stubborn chin. 'No, I don't.'

'Then I would advise you to stay away. Because sooner or later we'll have another repeat of last night.'

It was only a matter of time. Whether she wanted to believe it or not.

From the way her pulse throbbed wildly at the base of her throat and a soft flush feathered her skin he knew she was thinking about their kiss. Was she still tasting him as he could her?

'I don't intend to make the same mistake twice. I know a car crash when I see one,' she said tartly. Then gave herself away by licking her raspberry pout.

She could taste him, all right. He'd also bet she wanted more and loathed herself for it.

Cursing inwardly, he allowed himself the luxury of drinking her in before he made his excuses and left.

Covered in a thin black trench coat, with a high, stiff collar and a straight no-nonsense hem just above the knee, she reminded him of a prissy professor. Though her perfectly sexy knees and her shapely bare calves smothered in luscious ivory skin ruined the imagery. As for her feet...

Finn clenched his jaw and breathed past the grin begging to be let loose.

Oh, man, did he want to see under that coat. More than his next breath.

'Do you like to gamble, Miss Scott? Try your chances with Lady Luck?'

'Not particularly. I'm not so sure I believe in luck.'

Her admission was a prelude to a charge in the air as secrets and lies swirled around them in an electrical storm.

'I'll make a deal with you,' he drawled. *Risky, Finn*—and didn't that just rouse his desire? He chose his next words very, *very* carefully. 'If you do something for me I may grant you one wish. As long as it's in my power to give.'

Up came her chin once more, her grey gaze narrow with scepticism as her need fought hand in hand with obvious discomfort. 'Deal.'

'Show me what you're wearing beneath that coat.'

'Wh...*what*?'

'You heard. Untie that sash, undo those buttons, pull that coat wide and show me.'

Chaotic emotion and energy writhed around inside him.

What he was doing he had no idea. All he knew was that common sense and control took a back seat when he was within five feet of her.

Closing her eyes, she took a deep breath, and the sultry swell of her breasts made heat, fast and furious, speed through his body.

Ah, hell, he should stop her.

Right now.

'A deal is a deal, Miss Scott. You don't strike me as the type to renege.'

She tapped her hands against the ruffle of material at her thigh and slowly, provocatively, tiptoed her fingers up to the knot of her sash.

Finn gritted his teeth as the ribbon-like belt sank to each side of her hips.

Every pop of every button was magnified, the sound echoing off the silk-covered walls, until she gripped the sides of the soft black fabric.

Then she heaved a bashful sigh, rolled her eyes, and pulled the lapels wide, giving him exactly what he was looking for.

'Happy now?' she snapped.

'Ecstatic.' Only Serena would storm into one of the most exclusive casinos in the world wearing a pair of frayed denims cut high on her toned thighs and another quirky

T-shirt—this one ocean blue, with two scuba divers and the words 'Keep Your Friends Close and Your Anemones Closer' riding across her taut stomach.

With no effort whatsoever, she lit up his dark, dark soul.

'What gave me away?' she asked, a hint of petulance smoking her tone.

He pointed his index south. 'Your feet.'

Her gaze followed the direction of his finger. 'What's wrong with my feet?' Her brow furrowed, her head shot back up, eyes slamming into his. 'And what's with that wicked gleam and that grin?'

'I've just never seen you in anything other than biker boots.'

'So?' she snarked. 'One of my dad's ex-lovers gave them to me, I think. This is the first time I've had them on.'

Light crept over marble-grey and Finn hurtled towards lucidity. The reason she wouldn't be seen dead here. The reason she'd shied away from the glamour puss outside the bathroom. Not only did she feel uncomfortable around women, she felt horridly out of place—and yet she'd come here to find him.

Beautiful *and* brave. He'd never wanted her more. And didn't that spell trouble?

'So I'll ask you again,' she groused. 'What's wrong with my feet?'

'Nothing, baby, they're cute.' The last thing he wanted to do was make her feel worse. She didn't have a clue.

'Cute?' she spat. 'Kittens are cute. I am *not* cute. And cut it out with the *baby*. It's driving me nuts!'

'Tell the truth—you love it. Every time I say it you careen into some kind of delightful fluster.'

The nuts part was that she *was* beginning to like it, and she didn't want to like anything he said to her.

'Don't be ridiculous,' she snapped. 'Now it's my turn. I want my wi…'

Her voice trailed off, eyes widening, as he pushed himself

off the sofa-arm and sauntered towards her. While he had every intention of playing fair, it wouldn't hurt to distract her, now, would it? If he tried to kiss her again she would either hit him or bolt. Either exit was fine with him.

When he was up close and personal she raised her head, and Finn caught sight of the wild flutter at the base of her throat.

'I bet you don't even realise you have the most beautiful, elegant décolletage.' He trailed one fingertip down the side of her neck. 'And this skin of yours is a perfectly gorgeous peach colour.' *Yeah, like peaches and cream, to go with that strawberries and cream voice.*

'St...stop saying stuff like that, Finn.'

No.

'Love the T,' he murmured as he brushed down between her breasts with the backs of his fingers, over the creased transfer of frothy waves in a blue ocean—'Keep Your Anemones Closer'. *Sorry, beautiful, not going to happen.*

Down, down he stroked—with fire unfurling at the tops of his thighs—and when he reached her navel—

He growled. Snatched his fingers away and slammed both hands against the wall on either side of her head.

'Wha...what's wrong?'

Finn closed his eyes. 'I need to look.'

'A...at what?'

'You know what. On your stomach.'

A tremble shook her voice. 'Only if you tell me what's wrong with my...my feet.'

Prising his eyes open, he focused on the perpetrators. 'Nothing is wrong. Nothing at all. They're pretty little... ballerina pumps. I think that's what they're called.'

'Do you know you pause when you lie?'

Great.

'Okay, okay. They're slippers.'

Her gorgeous face fell in horror and if she'd been any

other woman he suspected she would have burst into tears. Not Serena.

'They *are*?'

'Cute ones,' he said quickly. 'With little leopard spots on.'

Dismay vaulted into pique and she visibly vibrated before him. 'I refuse to feel stupid just because you know more about women's stuff than I do, considering how many you've had.'

He divined that any figure she could engineer would be highly exaggerated, but still… 'Agreed.' If she felt stupid she wouldn't let him take a peek at her belly button, now, would she?

'Fine. Go on, then. Get it over with. Take a look. But know this: I couldn't care less for your opinion.'

'Liar.' He brushed the pad of his thumb from the corner of his mouth across his bottom lip, eking out the suspense of the moment, then bent his knees and lowered himself into an elegant crouch.

Serena raised the fabric of her T-shirt with an innate feminine sensuality she wasn't even aware she possessed and vicious need clawed at his gut.

One look and he cursed softly.

All the will in the world couldn't have stopped him. Out sneaked his tongue and he licked the small loop and diamond-studded ball.

Cool was the silver against the tip of his tongue, and her soft flesh was a welcome splash of warmth as an aftertaste.

Holy…

She tasted of passion fruit and coconut and something else he couldn't quite catch, so he knew it would torment him.

That was it. He was a goner. He even felt his eyes roll into the back of his head. Wondered if hers were doing the same.

'You got any more?' he asked thickly, nuzzling her navel with the tip of his nose. All the while he was commanding his legs to stand up and back the *hell* away.

'M…more?' she said, or at least she tried to.

The way her midriff quivered he could tell her breathing was as bad as his.

'Piercings.'

'Piercings?'

What was she? A parrot?

'Yes!'

'No. No more…piercings.'

He moaned low in his throat. 'But something else, right?'

Silence. Only the staccato wisp of a desperate moan from her lips.

'Tell me,' he demanded.

So of course she said, 'No.'

'Oh, man, you're killing me, Serena.' Up he came, standing tall to press closer. To crush those gorgeous breasts against his chest.

When was the last time he'd felt like this? Like his old self but astoundingly better because his ever-present guard was low. Risky. *So* risky.

But when was the last time he'd thought about anything but Singapore? In one way it physically hurt to be near her, aware that he caused her pain. But in the next second he was a man again and there was heat. So much heat. Scorching his blood in a rush of need and pure want. Never had he felt anything like it.

Selfish as always, he wanted—no, *needed* one more taste.

'I warned you, baby. You should've left when you had the chance.'

Desperate to savour as much of her as he could, he dived into the heavy fall of her hair and closed the gap until they were nose-tip to nose-tip.

'This is crazy, but—do you *feel* this?' he asked, unable to hide the awe in his voice.

Fighting to keep her eyes open, she shook her head, rubbing his nose with her own. 'No…' she breathed on a hot little pant.

'Good. Me neither.'

Softly, languidly, he brushed his lips over her velvety pink flesh and the pounding of his heart jacked out of rhythm. Then the need that continually clawed at him grew steel-tipped talons and slashed through his gut, demanding he mark her, take her, glut himself on her.

And she was melting. There was no other word for it.

'I'm...' *Hard. So hard.* For the first time in almost a year. Thought obliterated, he crushed her body into the wall, then slanted his head and deepened his kiss. Like dynamite they ignited, and when she responded with a tentative stroke of her tongue his hands began to shake.

Her mouth was heaven—warm and wet, with the slip and slide of passionate lips—but, greedy as he was, he wanted more. A deeper connection. He longed for her to move, to touch him properly, covet his body with her small hands, be skin-to-skin. *Claim* him. Brand him as her own. Which was not only bizarre but hellishly scary.

Still the need went on. Because he wanted her to feel how hard he was for her, to know what she did to him, how sexy and desirable she was—

Whoosh! The door swung open with a bellow of male voices and they were flung apart as if electrocuted. It was comical in a way. Serena was visibly rattled and he doubted he looked much better. And since when had *that* ever happened?

She whipped the black fabric around her waist, veiling her body, and fumbled with the sash—her jerky movements made his heart thunder in a fiercely savage urge to protect.

'We leave *now*,' he commanded, livid that he'd placed her in this position.

They were halfway to the door when one of the men broke into laughter as he settled at a gaming table.

Serena crashed to a halt. Stared at the man's back. Paled to a ghostly white. And Finn's guts twisted, tying him into knots. 'Hey, baby?' he murmured. 'What's wrong?'

In response she bolted past one of the other guests like a

mare from the starting gate, almost knocking that man off his feet as she virtually ran out the door.

What the...?

By the time he caught up she was galloping down the hallway.

'Serena, stop. *Stop!*'

Edging his way to stand in front of her, before she trampled over half the Casino members, he slipped his finger under her chin and lifted it gently.

'Look at me. Speak to me. Do you know that guy?'

'No.' Hands trembling, she gripped the lapels of his jacket and leaned into him.

Finn could feel her warm breath through his shirt as she burrowed as if starved of affection, and he instinctively pulled her into the tight circle of his arms.

Holding her was like a chorus of pleasure and pain that struck at his guilt but sang a sweet note of solace, and he luxuriated in the feel of her.

'No!' She twisted and rolled her shoulders to wrench free. 'Get off me, Finn. Right now.'

Feet leaden, he took a step back, fists plunging to his sides.

Remorse and mortification darkened the grey hue of her eyes and he swallowed hard, knowing. It was Finn who was the issue here. She was ashamed of wanting him, crestfallen at her reaction to him, horrified she'd kissed him back at all.

Well, then... Considering the destruction he'd caused in his life, it was highly indicative and somewhat poignant that he'd never hated himself more.

CHAPTER SIX

She was hearing voices, seeing things. She *must* be. That laugh was dead and buried but still it crawled through her veins like venom.

Gorging on air, she calmed the violent crash of her heart before she completely lost her mind and tried to snuggle into Finn again. *Come on, Serena. Snuggle?* Being weak and needy was not a condition she'd ever aspired to.

Honestly, this night couldn't get any worse. Charging up here to confront him hadn't been the brightest idea, but she'd had an entirely different kind of tongue-lashing in mind.

Forget lethal weapon—the man was a nuclear bomb. And his kiss… *Holy moly.* There she'd been, quite content to pretend their last lip-lock had been an apparition. Why bother to remember when it couldn't possibly have been *that* shockingly good?

Except it *was* that shockingly good. And bad all at the same time.

Her reactions to him were ridiculously extreme. It was as if he flipped a two-way switch inside her—hate or lust. Which just made no sense. She'd kissed men she'd actually liked before and been slammed in a freezer, yet one touch from Lothario here and she burst into flames!

Sheer panic had her scrambling for perspective. Truthfully, she shouldn't feel so disgusted with herself, so humiliated for succumbing to him. Not when the entire female race swooned at those extraordinary cerulean eyes. Expired at that sinful, sensual mouth. And that was before he backed it up with a truckload of charismatic charm.

Serena was just one of many.

Ugh. The idea that she was turning into a woman like one of her dad's playthings made her feel physically sick.

And of course the dirty deed *had* to transpire with her wearing slippers, of all things—just her rotten luck. And Finn knew what they were. Of course he did. He'd probably tugged billions of the things off perfectly feminine feet.

How. Utterly. Mortifying.

At the risk of garnering attention, she whispered furiously, 'Don't you *ever* touch me again. Your hands are not welcome on me.' She was being unfair, she knew she was, but she despised herself for that momentary lapse.

'Noted,' he bit out, his jaw tight enough to crack, and she fancied his broad frame seethed with self-loathing.

Clearly she was losing it.

Serena edged around his broad frame, determined not to notice how he filled out his sinfully suave tuxedo to perfection. 'I have to go. I'll see you in the morning.'

She didn't slow her pace until she was free of the oppressive glitz and glamour, her feet step-step-stepping down the stone slabs of the wide front entrance.

'I'll walk you down to the harbour.'

Finn fell into place beside her, hands stuffed into his trouser pockets, and as if he sensed she was spooked he ground out, 'No arguments.'

It was the second time he'd brandished that arrogant, masculine tone like a swordsman in protective stance and it did something strange to her insides. Made her go all warm and gooey. Which naturally made her every self-defence instinct kick into gear. She wanted to tell him to get lost—preferably on Mars. But something stopped her.

It was that frigid, ominous laughter. Playing in her mind. An endless loop of pain and vulnerability. Vehement enough for her to say, 'Okay…' because in truth she felt infinitely safer with him beside her.

Down the cobbled streets they went, the only sound the *clickety-clack* of his highly polished shoes and the sensual whispers of couples strolling by hand in hand.

As always, the sight made her heart ache. Ache for something she'd never have. Relationship material she was *not*.

Suddenly cold, she wrapped her arms across her chest, and by the time the tang of seawater filled her lungs and the harbour was a glittering stretch before them she was waging an internal war against asking him to stay.

'Thanks for walking with me. I'll be fine from here.'

'Are you sure you'll be okay? Is there anything I can do? Anything you want, Serena?'

Cruel—she was being cruel. The last few months had turned her into a horrible, horrible person but she couldn't curb the truth.

'The only thing I want right now is Tom. He was more than my brother—he was my friend.' And she didn't want to be alone.

But you are alone, Serena, and you always will be. What doesn't kill you makes you stronger.

'I know,' he said, his voice deep and low, tainted with sombre darkness. 'Believe me, I know.'

It was a voice she'd never heard before. One that made her stop. Pause. Wonder at the torment engulfing his beautiful blue eyes.

'I would do anything to turn back the clock. Anything to change the words I said. If only I'd just told him no when he asked to come out with me. Countless times I've wished for just that.'

As if he'd hit her with a curveball, she swayed on her feet.

The way he'd phrased it, so simply, had brought it all down to choices. Tom's choice in asking to follow his hero. Finn's choice in allowing him to.

Strange to think how the twists of fate intertwined with free will.

Every day they lived a voyage of discovery, moved through life based on choices like forks in the road. They peered down all the options, considered, weighed the risks, finally made a choice—some good, some bad. Some affecting no one but themselves. The worst affecting those they loved. But all of them defining. Forging who they were.

She'd made hundreds of choices in her lifetime and had one major regret. A choice that had affected her dad's life, Tom's life too, until the day he'd died. One made when she'd been naïve about her place in the world, no more than a girl, but a disastrous choice even so.

'I would do anything to turn back the clock.'

Serena would too.

Instead she lived with the guilt, struggled with it, controlled it. Recognised it when she saw it in others. This time she saw it in Finn—such depth of emotion—her first glimpse in...forever.

First? No. She'd been struck with shards of his shattering façade since last night.

Glimpse? No. He looked *devastated*. Seething with a darkness she truly believed was pain.

'Finn?' Who *was* this man? Thawing the ice and hate she'd packed in her chest. 'Oh, Finn, you really liked him, didn't you?' He was grieving too.

Punching his fists deep into his trouser pockets, he cast his gaze over the moonlit ripple of the ocean. 'He was a good kid.'

Knowing this was her chance, she begged him, 'Tell me what happened that night. Your version. Please. My dad just keeps saying there was a storm and he fell overboard during the night, but when I checked there were no weather warnings, no reports.'

His brow etched in torment, he closed his eyes momentarily. 'It was…' His throat convulsed. 'Unexpected. There is nothing more to tell.'

His tone was as raw as an open wound and she ached for him, but— 'Why do I think there is?'

'Because you need to let go.' He shoved frustrated hands through his thick blond hair. 'Otherwise you'll find no peace, Serena. I promise you.'

A cool rush of sea air washed over her in a great wave and she crossed her arms over her chest, then curled her fingers around her upper arms and rubbed at the sudden prickle of gooseflesh.

'Peace? I don't know what that feels like. I never have.'

Finn stilled, watching her, predator-like. Then anger crept across his face, dark and deadly, and her pulse surged erratically at her wrist.

'Have you been hurt? In the past?' he asked, almost savagely.

It was as if his genetic make-up had been irrevocably altered and she could feel the ferocious fury of an animal growling through him. Not to harm—no, no. To protect.

She shouldn't like that. She really shouldn't.

'Serena?'

'I… Well…' She bit her top lip to stem the spill of her secrets.

Ridiculous idea. It had to be the way he visibly swelled beneath his suave attire as if to shield her. It made her heart soften and she couldn't afford that. Just the thought rebooted her self-preservation instincts and she dodged.

'To be honest, Finn, I'm not one for dwelling on the past.' She didn't want to remember being naïve and weak and broken. Didn't want Finn to suspect she was any of those things. She refused to be vulnerable to him. To any man ever again.

More importantly, she was over it. She'd made a life for herself. A good life. True, being initiated into the dark realms the world had to offer at fourteen years old was not conducive to relationships and all the messy complexities that came with them.

It was hard to trust, to let go. And, while she'd vowed her past wouldn't define her, or cripple her life with fear, any attempts she'd made at intimacy had been a dishearteningly dismal experience. She'd chosen a wonderfully sweet safe guy but she'd felt distanced somehow. Detached. Compounded by her blatant lack of femininity, no doubt. But she had her work, which she loved, and her team kept her from touching the very depths of loneliness. And if the tormented shadows still haunted her once in a while she fought them with all her might.

Feeling that infusion of bravado, she lifted her chin. 'Anyway, do I look like the kind of woman someone could easily mess with?' She hoped not. She'd spent years building her defences after all.

Finn slowly shook his head and his fierce scowl was tempered into a decadent curve of his lips as he murmured what sounded like, 'That's my girl.'

Their eyes caught…held…and Serena would have sworn she actually felt the odd dynamic of their relationship take a profound twist.

Before she knew it more words flooded over her tongue— a chaotic, unravelling rush she couldn't seem to stop.

'When I look at you I want to blame you, hate you.' And hadn't it been easier to blame Finn instead of just accepting it as a tragic accident from which no justice could be reaped? 'But on the back of those thoughts comes the guilt, the self-censure, because he asked *me* to go out with him that night and I wouldn't.'

She'd been horribly selfish, hating the social scene, knowing she didn't fit in, so she'd told him to go, to have fun.

'If I'd gone out with him he wouldn't have asked *you*.' Misery poured from her heart. 'I was such a coward.' Oh, God, could it have been her fault?

Finn surged forward, raised his arm and brushed a lock of hair from her brow so tenderly her heart throbbed.

'You can't take responsibility for someone else's actions, baby. He was old enough to make his own decisions.'

'Well, then I should've persuaded him to take professional swimming lessons—' Her voice cracked. 'Something. Anything.'

'Again, you can't make people do what they don't want to. You think he'd honestly want you to blame yourself like this?'

'No,' she whispered. Tom would go crazy if he saw her right now.

Crazy? She gave a little huff. If Tom knew she was being cruel to Finn he would go berserk. Finn had been his hero. He'd talked about him constantly. And hadn't *that* driven her insane too? Ensuring he was never far from her mind. Taunting her. Creating more anger. Powering more hate. But that wasn't Finn's fault. It was hers. Because she'd never understood her unruly all-consuming reactions to such a wild player. He was anything *but* safe.

'How did it happen?' she asked, suddenly weary. 'Were you there? All I want to know is that he didn't suffer.'

A muscle ticked in his jaw and he took a large step back, filching her heat. 'I was…asleep. It was the middle of the night.'

A black blend of torment and bone-wrenching guilt stole the colour from his beautiful face and from nowhere she wanted to throw her arms around him. He was hurting so badly. Like a wounded animal. It was like being tossed back in time, staring at her own reflection. She couldn't bear it.

Trembling, she reached for his hand, the despair and loneliness she'd suffered in the last months calling to her—reaching out for his, to share it. To comfort and be comforted. A craving she'd stifled for months.

All the torment. The guilt suffocating her. Suffocating him. When she'd thought he didn't care she'd wanted to punish him endlessly. Yet he'd buried it just as she had. And where was it getting them? Fate had dealt them a cruel card and unless they moved on all she could see lining the road ahead was endless misery.

Let it go...

Her fingers met his skin and as if she'd zapped him with three thousand volts he jolted backwards.

'I've already warned you once tonight, Serena,' he said roughly. 'You touch me right now and I'll lose it. Won't be able to stop myself from wanting more.'

The memory of him crouched before her, his hot gaze locked on her lower abdomen, his warm breath teasing over her flesh, sprang up in her mind's eye and heat drenched her body like a deluge of tropical rain.

'I...I don't understand you. Are you still trying to distract me or something? Because you're wasting your time, Finn, I'm not going anywhere.'

He rubbed at his temple as if she was giving him a migraine. 'I'm beginning to realise that.'

'Good. But I still can't fathom why you want more from me. I'm not—'

His turbulent gaze crashed into her. 'Not beautiful? Yes, you are. Sexy? More than anyone I've ever met.'

Yeah, right. 'I meant I'm not a woman. Not feminine—stuff like that.'

'Of course you are—'

'Er...hello? Slippers?' While *he* looked wicked and gorgeous in his devilish tux.

'In your own unique way.'

'No. I'm not.' *Was she?* 'Nor do I want to be.' Unveiling that secret part of her would only bring more vulnerabilities. Weakness.

Finn shook his head, his mouth shaping for speech. Then he seemed to think better of it. 'Listen; while the best place for you is far away from me, we have to work together, *bosslady*. At least until the end of the season.'

Was he saying he wasn't staying with the team? He must know her dad would want him to.

'I know that.' The strike of her conscience made her wince. 'About the boss thing…'

The ghost of a smile softened his sinful mouth. 'A slight exaggeration on your part, Miss Scott?'

'Could've been,' she posed lightly.

'You've got balls, Serena, I'll give you that.'

Their eyes locked once more and she held her breath. Wishing she could read him better. Hating her lack of experience. By the time he tore his eyes free she felt dizzy from the lack of oxygen.

'Regardless, we'll still be seeing a lot of each other, so I suggest we endeavour not to end up alone. Unless…'

'Unless?'

He shifted on his glossy feet. 'Unless you ever need…a friend.' He scrubbed his nape with the palm of his hand. A bit uneasy. A whole lot handsome. 'That's what you said, wasn't it? That you'd lost a friend too? So if you ever need one I'll be there.'

Oh, great. Now he was being all thoughtful. A little bit wonderful. The *last* thing she needed.

Friendship was a terrible idea. They clashed like titans. But she wasn't about to throw his offer in his face. She didn't have the heart. 'Okay. It's a deal.'

With a brief nod he turned to walk away.

'Finn?'

'Yeah?'

Am I truly beautiful to you? Did you mean it?

'Don't forget,' she said. 'You owe me a wish.'

Finn stripped his jacket from his body, yanked the black tie from his collar and slung them across the caliginous suite. Then he flopped atop the bed, face down, his insides raw and aching from being clawed to shreds.

Withholding the truth hammered at his conscience, making his temples pound until his vision blurred and he prayed for peaceful slumber. Not that he deserved it. The past was catching up with him, slowly but surely.

He'd been so close to telling her everything. Battling with a promise made, an investigation that could blow wide any day, and an insight that she'd been through her own version of hell.

What had happened to his brave little tigress? She'd cleverly derailed him and he'd never met anyone who'd managed that feat. Were they talking emotional or physical hurt, here? Though in reality maybe it was best he didn't know.

The imagery taunting his mind made him want to snarl and lash out—vicious, savage with the need for revenge. It made his guts ache with a peculiar primal need to take her in his arms and hold her to him, protect her. Kiss her tenderly, passionately, over and over—make her feel like a real woman.

How was he going to keep his hands off her if she took his offer of friendship?

Exhaustion pulsed through his bones and darkness called to him like an old friend, dragging him into the depths where only nightmares pulsed to life…

Singapore, September, eight months earlier

'Wakey-wakey, pretty boy.'

Derision leaked from the hoarse oriental twang as the sound of heavy boots clomping over concrete, cracking the grit and filth beneath inch-thick soles, penetrated the lethargic smaze in which his mind wandered.

Hair like the heart of a ruby…fire in its most dangerous form…

The twang grew louder. 'How are we feeling today?' But it was the jangle of a loaded key ring slapping against a military toned thigh that finally roused his head from its cushioned spot on the exposed brick wall.

His backside numb from sitting on the damp floor for hours on end, he conspicuously flexed the legs outstretched in front of him, knowing what was to come.

After all, he could set his watch by these guys—if he still had it. As it was, the rare platinum timepiece now graced one of the guard's thick, brawny wrists.

Four and a half million he'd been paid to wear that watch—to have his face plastered on every billboard from here to Timbuktu.

Easy money.

Exactly what these men wanted from him. He could have coped with that if it wasn't for the kid in the next cell. If that kid hadn't been in the wrong place at the wrong time and got dragged into this godforsaken mess.

He smacked his head off the pitted brick, wondering once again if they'd get out of here alive. Wherever 'here' was. Some place near the ocean, if the sporadic bites of salt water were anything to go by.

He craved a glance at the skyline. Light. Space. Or, better yet, an endless track to drive down, to escape from reality. As it was, he had too many hours to think—an overrated and highly dangerous pastime. If he wasn't imagining the peaceful waters of stunning grey eyes regrets suffocated him as they shadowed his mind like tormented souls.

The mistakes he'd made in his life. The hearts he'd broken in his youth. The way he'd abandoned his mother and Eva. What if he never had the chance to say sorry?

Chest so tight he could scarcely breathe, he stuffed the lot to the back of his mind, where all the other emotional garbage was, and let it fester. Concentrated on what he was capable of dealing with—Mr Happy in the khaki combats, who seemed to be snarling at him.

'There is something wrong with your tongue?'

Yeah, as a matter of fact there was. It hadn't tasted water for two days. But he'd guess Brutus, here, just wanted his answer.

How was he feeling? As if he'd had his insides scooped out and then shoved back in. With a blunt spoon.

'Great. Never felt better. Your hospitality is second to none.'

The you'll-pay-for-that smirk should have made him regret his smart mouth, but he had to keep their focus on *him*. *Always* on him.

'I am pleased to hear it.' The guard paused outside the kid's cell and Finn felt the familiar toxic churn of foreboding right in the pit of his empty stomach. 'And your friend?'

Already halfway up from his cosy spot on the floor, Finn almost lost his precarious stance. 'He's sick. Can't even walk. So leave him alone.' Then he smoothed the edge off his harsh tone and kicked up his lips, offering the legendary St George smile as he straightened to his full height. 'It's me you want, anyway. Isn't that right?'

Another smirk. Another churn of unease and sickening revolt in his stomach.

'Boring when they don't fight back.'

'There you go, then. Let me out of here.' He jerked his chin towards the kid. 'The view is depressing.' Or it would be for the kid pretty soon.

'Finn?' Tom croaked. 'Let me—'

'Shut up, kid.' Every muscle in his body protested as he coerced his legs forward as if two of his ribs *weren't* cracked and his shoulder *wasn't* dislocated. Piece of cake. 'I'm feeling cooped up in here.' His door swung wide. 'Give him some water, would you?'

The guard grinned, flashing a less than stellar set of teeth, eyes brimming with calculation. As if he knew something Finn didn't. As if the last four days had been foreplay to the main event.

Darkness seeped through the cracks in his mind and threatened to rise like some ugly menacing storm. 'You leave the kid alone—you hear me? Or no money.'

The laugh that spilled from those blood-red lips made his guts wrench tighter.

'Boss says the only thing I leave alone is your pretty face,' the guard said, and slapped said face with enough force to sting. 'Get moving.'

'Speaking of my generous host, I want to talk to him again.'

'Your wish is my command.'

Somehow he doubted that. Nevertheless, ten minutes later a big palm pushed on his shoulder—the dislocated one, thank you very much—and he fought the wince as he was slammed down into a black plastic chair in the corner of a room that looked like an interrogation hotspot out of a gritty cop show. But, nope, this was no TV set. Proof of which sat in the chair opposite, with a rickety steel-framed table separating them.

Face-to-face with his captor, it wasn't in Finn's nature to beat around the proverbial bush, so he kicked off today's festivities.

'Let's barter,' he managed to say through a throat that felt serrated with sticks. 'I'll trade you another five million if you let him go. *Now.*'

Eyes as black as his soul and sunk into a battered, rock-hewn face stared back at him. 'That's quite an offer, Mr St George. But I was thinking of a different kind of bartering altogether.'

'I'm getting tired of these games. What exactly is it you want?'

'Right now I want you to make a choice, racer-boy. The first of many.'

Behind him, the iron door ground open with a chilling squeal and a frigid bite swept through the room—so cold his bones turned to ice. The kid was behind him. He knew it.

'Forget choices. Make it another ten mill and let. Him. Go.'

'You don't like him being touched, do you, pretty boy?' he said silkily—in striking contrast to the sharp crack of knuckles that caromed around the room. 'So shall I play with him? Or will you?'

Finn's breath sawed in and out of his lungs. 'Twenty. That will be sixty million, transferred from my Swiss bank account within the hour. You can do what the hell you like with me. Deal?'

CHAPTER SEVEN

MONTREAL BASKED IN the warmth of a glorious dusk, the sky a canvas of fluffy spiralling ribbons tinged with orange and red, with only a blaze of yellow on the curve of the earth, where the sun kissed the horizon.

Its beauty failed miserably to improve her ugly mood.

'You'd better be in, Finn,' Serena muttered as she stormed across the endless blanket of tarmac towards his glossy black motor home.

Never mind the prescient darkness that had clung to her skin for two weeks since Monaco, like some kind of impending doom, Michael Scott—aka *dear old Dad*—had just pulled a number on her! As if the day hadn't been enough of a stress-fest.

The day? Who was she kidding? The last two weeks, working with Mr Death-Defyer, had been a roller coaster named persecution; emotions had dipped and dived all over the place, to stretch her patience endlessly. Was it any wonder she could hear the clang of looming disaster?

Still, she'd never forget this afternoon as long as she lived.

Another close shave as Finn scraped second place after going silent on the pit-lane channel for over two minutes. Heart in her throat, she'd snatched the headset from the chief engineer in the end. Not exactly the done thing, but she'd had to snap him out of it somehow.

He was getting worse. Darker. Harder. Taking unnecessary risks no other man would dare to chance. Why? She couldn't understand it. Unless... Unless Serena had made him worse. By storming into his life and throwing Tom's death in his face when he'd been trying to deal with the loss in his own way. Burying it. Just as she had.

It boggled the mind to think they had something in common.

God, she felt sick.

But had *he* been worried when he'd nearly obliterated himself? Heavens, no. While she'd popped migraine pills like chocolate drops he'd supplicated and beguiled the masses with his glib tongue and legendary rakish smile, standing atop the podium as if life was a fun park and darker emotions were aberrant to him. When she knew they were anything but!

Then—*then*—he'd swaggered into the Scott Lansing garage, again, and drawled in that sinfully rich, amused voice, 'What do you think, baby? Was I awesome?'

As if he *hadn't* just phased out while driving at over two hundred miles per hour!

Fist balled, she stomped up the metal steps and rapped on his door until her knuckles stung.

If she was an ace at burying pain and masking it with a brave face he was a pro—a grand virtuoso. But now Serena could see it. Feel his darkness more acutely.

Oftentimes behind the charming, irrepressible smile lurked a guilt-drenched agony she still couldn't bear.

Last night hadn't helped matters either. Bored—okay, plain nosey—she'd searched the internet for a peek of his sister and got a lot more than she'd bargained for. Not only was Eva Vitale the most beautiful woman she'd ever seen, but together with Finn she ran a huge charity for breast cancer in honour of their mother. Another death that must have crippled him.

By the time she'd trawled through all the articles and spotted the Silverstone driving day he held every year for sick and disabled children she'd cringed at all the heartless, dishonourable comments she'd perpetually tossed in his face.

The thought that she'd been so prejudiced against his type, his Casanova proclivities—enough to use him as an easy scapegoat for Tom's death—was making her seriously dislike herself.

The door opened on a soft swish to reveal the man himself, wearing a deep red polo shirt—*yum*—and a pair of washed-out stomach-curling jeans riding low on his lean hips.

As her gaze touched his bare toes that delicious drawl rumbled over her. 'Do I meet with your approval this evening, Miss Scott?'

Her heart thundered like a freight train through her chest and she crossed her arms over her breasts before it burst through her skin. 'You'll do.'

The ghost of a smile softened his sinful mouth—only to veer into a scowl as he searched her face. 'What's wrong? Has something happened?'

Yeah, I feel wretched.

This was a stupid, stupid idea, she thought for the millionth time. Fair enough doing practice laps and talking designs, but to come to his trailer? She was making their awkward truce personal and she knew it.

'Can I come in?'

His eyes said, *Do you have to?* His mouth said, 'Sure.'

Unconvinced, she battled with the urge to turn around and flee. But he'd offered, hadn't he? To be a friend if she needed one? And maybe, just maybe, he needed one too.

She was worried about him. Her conscience pleaded with her to help him before he well and truly did some harm. She just didn't know how. While she knew tons of men, she hadn't felt ready to spontaneously combust with any of them as she did with Finn. *So just ignore it, like you have for the last four years!*

Sucking in a courageous breath, Serena followed him into

the spanking new motor home—all sharp lines of glass and steel alongside huge cushy leather sofas.

'Nice place. Biggest and best on the lot. If I hadn't heard the endless man-muck around the pits—' she was *not* about to admit he was dubbed the world's greatest lover '—I would think your penchant for size compensated for some kind of deficiency.'

He flashed his sexy suggestive smile and her knees turned to hot rubber. 'Nothing lacking in that department, I promise you.'

'I'll take your word for it,' she muttered. Meaning it. Only to curse blue when her traitorous mind provided her with an image of the first time she'd ever seen him in the flesh, bar-boxer-shorts-naked, strolling into his bathroom. Where Serena had been... *Oh, God.*

A tingling flush crept up her neck until she felt impossibly hot. And the idea that she looked like some gauche ninny made her vibrate with pique.

'Uh-oh. I sense trouble.' Finn leaned against the slash of the kitchen bench, gripped the ledge on either side of his hips and crossed one ankle over the other. 'Okay, baby, spill it.'

Baby. *Baby.* She had to stop dissolving in a long, slow melt when he called her that!

'I'm...' Shifting on her feet, she eyed the door. South America was wonderful at this time of year. Maybe—

'Enraged? Incensed? Hopping mad? Splenetic? Thoroughly bent out of shape?'

'You swallowed a thesaurus, or something?'

'Nah, it's that school I went to. You know—the one that specialises in breeding the most arrogant and annoying people ever?' he said, flinging her words back at her.

'As you can see, I'm rolling around the floor laughing.'

He grinned.

She sighed. Glanced at the door again. Wondered why she felt hideously exposed. Sharing woes and asking for help wasn't weak or too feminine, was it? She didn't enjoy giving men the impression she was weak—it was like hand-delivering an invitation to be messed with.

Oh, to hell with it. 'My dad just decided not to launch the prototype at Silverstone.'

'Why not?'

A tinge of anger fired in his eyes. One that made her feel infinitely better. Even though her bad funk was technically *his* fault.

Because Finn here had officially earned the title 'too wild and problematic' to handle her multimillion-pound prototype. And she was angry. Noooo. She was upset. There—she'd admitted it, and miraculously the sky hadn't caved in.

'Doesn't matter the reason. His decision is final.'

Next year wasn't so far away. *It felt like forever.* It wasn't as if it would never happen. There was really no need for her to be so…devastated. 'Point is, he has a brunette over there, and I refuse to play nice when I feel—'

'Like someone peed in your biker boots?'

'Exactly.'

One side of his mouth kicked up ruefully before his focus drifted to the window, far into the distance, as if he'd virtually left the room.

Angst crawled through her stomach and Serena gnawed her top lip.

Yes, she was crushed, but she could easily have gone to a hotel. It was a convenient excuse and she knew it. Somehow she had to slide him back on track.

Letting go of a long, soft sigh, she sprinkled some candour on her remorse.

If she'd been courageous enough to look into her heart, to face her own fears, she would have accepted that culpability lay with fate. Otherwise she couldn't possibly have kissed Finn with everything she was. And, if she wanted to be brutally, painfully honest, blaming him had been a grand excuse to hate him even more. Since the moment she'd laid eyes on him he'd stirred a hornets' nest of inadequacies to sting her pride and spawn desires that defied logic. Reason.

Inadequacies she'd been slammed up against from when she was nine years old—ribbed for being 'too girly' to play—and had stolen a pair of blunt scissors to hack off her hair.

Desires she'd always had to force, coerce, to do her bidding. Determined her past would not define her.

Disaster.

Until Finn. Who had never failed to spark every female cell in her body to ignite. The sexual pull of his velvet gaze roving over her when he thought she wasn't looking jacked her pulse. Made her dream about the firm, sinful stroke of his hands moving over her skin and the hot drive of his tongue between her lips. Then came the heat, spearing through her veins like arrows of fire.

She didn't want her heart to thump when he was near or for weakness to spread through her limbs. He was still a Casanova. A prolific player.

He took a long, sensual pull of water from a tall glass bottle and she watched his smooth jaw work, his sexy throat convulse, and knew this was a stupid, stupid idea. *Tough.*

'So, can I stay here?'

'No!' he choked. A distressed noise followed by a splutter. A cough. A hard swallow and watering eyes. 'I don't do sleepovers.'

Her mouth going slack, she wasn't sure which to process first. The fact that he didn't do sleepovers with his women or the fact he thought she wanted to 'sleep' with him!

'I didn't ask you if you did. I asked you if I could hang out here while you go out and do your Lothario thing.' Okay, she was digging for info, but right now she didn't care. 'You know—borrow your place. Like friends do.'

Wincing inwardly, she hung on his reaction as she played the friend card, unsure if the tight knot in her stomach wanted him to pick it up or discard it.

'I was planning on staying in most of the night.'

'Oh.'

Come to think of it, of late there'd been no kiss-and-tell stories. No rumours of orgies or nightclub antics. Half of her gloried in the idea that he was abstaining from his playboy shenanigans and the other half hated the suspicion that he was becoming reclusive, withdrawing from the world even more.

For pity's sake, the man had her tearing herself apart!

Finn scrubbed a palm over the back of his neck. 'Fine. You can hang out here. For a little while.'

'I've never seen a "fine" such as yours right now, Finn.' At his quizzical expression, she elaborated. 'Like I'm sticking hot needles down your fingernails.'

His knuckles bleached white as they gripped the lip of the bench. 'Probably because that's what it feels like trying to keep my hands off you.'

A loaded pause sparked in the air. 'Seriously?'

'Oh, you're happy now?'

Maybe. It wasn't so bad resisting him if he felt the same. Maybe he hadn't been lying to her. Maybe he did find her beautiful after all.

Her heart smiled. 'I'll be even happier if you feed me and let me beat you on your games console.' *Friend stuff.*

He snorted. 'In your dreams, baby.'

She had the feeling that was exactly where he'd be tonight. In her dreams. Centre stage. Just as he had been last night. And every other night she could remember.

'You have until ten o'clock to triumph and prove your console supremacy, then I'm going out.'

'Oh.' That was *not* disappointment in her voice. Certainly not.

Finn cocked an arrogant brow and tilted his head, as if she'd presented him with a puzzle he couldn't quite figure out. 'I'll make you a deal.'

'I'm not keen on your deals. Last time I ended up—' *Ohh*, there it went. Stomach flipping over...

'Getting your belly button piercing licked?'

Hello, heatwave—blasting her from all angles as the incredible sensation of his hot mouth on her skin flicked over her on replay.

'It wasn't the most disgusting experience in the world.' *So you can do it again if you like.* No—no, he could *not*. It was a terrible idea. Crazy to think she was hurtling towards a lack of self-preservation as diabolical as his.

That legendary beautiful smile touched his lips and he raised one hand to scratch at his jawline. 'Deal is—if you beat me I'll take you with me.'

His grin said he was perfectly safe. That she didn't have a hope in hell of winning. Obviously he didn't want her going with him at all. Which naturally flipped every one of her excitable curiosity switches.

Poor guy. She almost felt sorry for him.

He'd been thrashed. By a girl.

Totally and utterly thrashed at supercars, tennis, football and loaded weapons—repeatedly. Then he'd fed her and fetched her soft drinks. Before she'd zonked out on the sofa in an alluring puddle of colour and vulnerability—the latter hitting him smack-bang in the solar plexus.

Seraphina Scott was extraordinary in every single way, and if he didn't give her a good shake pronto he was liable to kiss her awake like Sleeping Beauty. If he was any kind of prince material he would. As it was he'd lied to her repeatedly and lusted after her repeatedly.

Unfortunately some idiot had suggested he was friend material, and though it scared the crap out of him—because he wasn't the most reliable bloke on the planet, and his own sister could vouch for that—he fully intended to stick by his word. It was the least he could do after he'd caused her so much pain, despite the fact it was the equivalent of flinging himself onto the track lane mid-race.

The fact was, she fed his wildness. Unearthed all kinds of

feral, animalistic instincts until need was a constant claw that slashed his insides. Not just craving the heat of her sweet, supple body, but wanting to protect her at all cost, to touch that desolate tinge in her grey gaze.

She was a lonely soul right now.

It took one to know one. He'd been surrounded by people all his life, and yet soaked in a bone-deep loneliness he found impossible to shake.

Yeah, and impossible to understand too.

Easily bored, he relished variety. *Every day with Serena would be as unique as she was*, a little voice whispered. He told that little voice to shut up. It was being controlled by his libido and for once he wasn't listening.

Finn stared at her for a long moment, curling a strand of her hair around his finger. How could anyone even resist her? How long was it going to take before he snapped and crossed the bridge from friends to lovers? *An eternity*, his conscience told him, *because it's never going to happen. You're supposed to be keeping her safe, remember?*

'Hey, Sleeping Beauty.' He flipped his hand over to check his watch. 'It's nine-thirty and we have a date.'

With her sinuous stretch and a sultry writhe her T-shirt inched upwards until that sexy-as-hell diamond piercing winked at him.

Just like that an airlock cinched his chest. 'Come on, spitfire, get a shake on.' *Before I take that silver loop between my lips, flick it with my tongue and suck it into my mouth. Then I'll tear those jeans off and lick all the way down to your clit.*

Damn.

'Or maybe I'll just go by myself.' *Way better idea.*

'I'm coming, I'm coming,' she murmured, in that gorgeous, husky sleep-drenched voice.

He growled long and low. This was such a bad idea. What had possessed him to gamble with her? No one had ever beaten him. Ever. He should've known this minx would throw him for a loop—which only made him want her even more! *So cancel. Tell her something. Anything.*

The problem was he was already living one lie, and the thought of customising another pierced his guts as if they were twisted in barbed wire. Add in the suspicion that today's racing blip—courtesy of a flashback like no other—had totalled her aspirations of launching her prototype at Silverstone and he could never tolerate it.

'Where are we going?' She swung her legs off the leather couch, sat upright and shook out her hair until those spectacular ruby-red flames blazed down her back.

'Here,' he croaked, grabbing two caps from the marble bench and tossing one in her lap. 'Put this on.'

'Incognito?' Her grey eyes bolted to his, sparkled with excitement.

It was an effervescence that wasn't going to last long. Or was it? Continually she threw him, and this little jaunt might be just what she needed.

In a sudden burst of self-honesty he acknowledged that the temptation to take her had arrived shortly after the tickets. But the subject matter had made him pause. She was prudish at times, yet inquisitive at others—the delightful memory of her ear crushed against the bedroom door on his yacht came to mind—and he'd flirted with the idea that her past experiences were slim and less than stellar.

Meanwhile here he was, a veritable connoisseur in the erotic arts of passion and seduction, impervious to being knocked off his feet, suddenly disturbed—no, downright daunted—because this woman could easily take his legs from under him.

It took him five minutes to lock up, usher Serena round to the storage compound and heft the double doors wide.

Click went the automatic lights, flooding the space with fluorescence, blinding him momentarily as he waited for...

Her swift inhalation. A deep, rapturous moan. One that nearly brought him to his knees.

Did she *have* to be the hottest woman on the planet?

'*Ohhh*, yeah,' she breathed, her sultry voice loaded with salacious hunger for his latest toy. 'Your taste is impeccable, Finn. All that horsepower makes me twitchy. I think I'm about to have the ride of my life.'

Finn closed his eyes. He was doomed.

CHAPTER EIGHT

Serena was doomed.

Finn had driven her across the city behind the wheel of his high-spec, custom-made, invitation-only sports car, slamming her to the edge of the hot zone. Her hormones were frantic as she imagined him making love with the same intensity—with an inordinate skill and a passionate appreciation for the machine in his hands.

The way he smoothed the leather of the steering wheel with an amorous touch, curled his long fingers around the gearstick with a firm, sensual grip… She'd shuddered with pleasure just watching him.

Now, seated in a super-comfy armchair in a magnificent tent in the middle of Montreal, she was right back on edge. A thrumming mass of expectation.

From the outside the structure appeared like a giant theatrical dome, with multiple conical peaks that soared into the sky in a colourful array of blue and yellow stripes—reminiscent of Arabian nights. And inside the capacious space rivalled the outside's awe factor with a distinct flare of class and luxury. It was the type Serena liked—more avant-garde than ostentatious, cast by the heights of technology for performers to achieve mind-boggling feats. It was exciting and thrill seeking. Definitely her thing.

Something awesome was about to happen, and anticipation fired through her veins like gasoline sparking to ignite.

The dark-haired man sitting on the other side of Finn suddenly turned to face him. 'You're real familiar. Have we met before?'

Serena stifled a smile. She'd expected to lounge in some VIP suite, and being one of the masses was more scintillating than ever. Adding a kick of danger that they'd be discovered.

With the black caps pulled low on their foreheads and dressed in T-shirts and jeans—Finn in a yummy buttery black leather jacket, collar flipped high, and Serena in a dark blue hoodie—they created a perfect image of friends out for kicks.

Finn smiled, all charismatic charm, and held out his hand for an old-boy shake. 'I'm sure I would have remembered you if I had, sir. It's a pleasure.'

It struck her then. In many ways he was a showman himself. Although he blended seamless confidence and ease in any situation, she fancied he adapted to his surroundings, even altered his accent to fit. A veritable chameleon.

It was a talent she could only marvel at with no small amount of envy. Yet she couldn't quite figure out why he felt the need. Why not just be himself?

She could only presume, from the way he blocked his emotions, it was some kind of survival technique—and, let's face it, they'd both been reared on fame and fortune so she knew all about those. Except where she'd shunned it he'd danced beneath the limelight, albeit somewhat distanced by not being his true self. It was as if he preferred to be untouched by everyone around him. Now, *that* was something she definitely understood. Opening up wasn't easy. It invited all sorts of pain, disappointment and heartache.

But, more profoundly, what seriously blew her mind was the stranger who came into view when Finn ditched his façades. *That* man was the most fascinating of all.

It was the man who'd made her spaghetti in his kitchen—the one who'd tucked her unruly hair behind her ear, pouted when he'd lost at the video games, the one who seemed perfectly happy to hang out with 'normal' folk and swig cola.

As for the secretive girly smile on her face—that was down to the way he seemed more content. Not so restless and edgy. No dark pain in his eyes tonight. So any regret she'd harboured about going to him earlier in the evening had flown by the wayside.

'Hey!' the man next to him said. 'I know where I've seen you before. On the TV. You're that guy.'

Serena bit down on her lips and held her breath, curious to see if he'd protect his privacy, give them this one night. Craving the real him for a bit longer.

Finn raised his chin, his bewildered expression worthy of an Oscar-winning actor. 'Who?'

'The one who races them fast cars.'

Frowning, Finn turned to face her, his voice thick and deep enough to carry a perfect American drawl. 'Hey, baby, do I look like that race-car driver?'

Suddenly slap-happy, as if she'd had one too many beers, Serena glanced past Finn to the stranger. 'That British guy?' she asked incredulously.

With a dubious flush, the other man shrugged. 'He could be.'

'No way.' Shaking her head, she leaned back against the pad of her chair. 'He's weird-looking. And his eyes...' She deliberately pulled a shudder up her spine.

Finn cocked one dark blond brow, excused himself graciously, then twisted his mighty fine torso and leaned into her.

'What's wrong with his eyes?'

'They're weird. Cerulean blue and yet sometimes...' She left him dangling for a few blissful seconds in an effort to get him back for all the times he'd toyed with her.

'Sometimes...?' he demanded.

'They change colour. Gleam in a feral kind of way. Hypnotic.'

'Hypnotic?' he murmured silkily, his skin flushed beneath the shadowy peak of his cap. 'Maybe it depends what he's looking at.'

Their gazes caught, held in timeless suspension, and the pull tugged at the base of her abdomen until warmth flooded her knickers.

A groan ripped from his throat as if he knew. Could smell the scent of her arousal.

'And...' She smothered her lips with moisture. 'He has this serious animalistic vibe going on. He *growls*.'

Sculpted in black leather, his broad shoulders rose and fell as the tempo of his breathing escalated. 'Do you like it?'

'I love it.' She'd been lured, ensnared, and now she wanted to be caught—

No. *No!* God, what was going on with her? She had to cut this out. Think *friends*.

The hand that lay on his muscular thigh fisted and he pulled back an inch or three. 'Do you know what Seraphina means, Miss Scott?'

She gave a little shake of her head and he elaborated.

'The fiery one.'

Right now that made perfect sense.

'So be careful that you don't get set ablaze. You don't want to get burned, do you, Seraphina?'

'You *burn* women?' she whispered, sounding more intrigued than appalled—and how ridiculous was that? Of course the man burned women. He had a much-publicised trail of ashes in his wake to prove it.

'Badly,' he murmured, his voice tinged with regret. 'Hence my rules.'

Throat swollen, she had to squeeze out the words. 'What rules are they, Finn?'

'No commitment. No emotional ties. Just pleasure beyond your wildest imagination.'

'That sounds...'

'*Good*. It's good, baby. For as long as it lasts. A few hours at the most. Then there's nothing but emptiness. So believe me when I say keep safe and don't be lured by your inner fire. Especially when it ignites for me.'

A ten-bell siren blared through her head, silenced her desire. He was only being brutally honest. No flippant innuendo from this man. No play on words. No clever retort. She liked the real Finn St George, she realised. Very much. He was an arrogant, seductive, sexy blend of bad-boy meets boy-next-door.

Keep safe. Good advice. Not that commitment interested her. Emotional ties made her blood run cold. She'd just lost one man she'd loved, and being obsessed with a player who rapped on death's door with alarming frequency wasn't her idea of a rollicking good time.

Still, what if Finn was the only man she'd ever want sexually? Was she crazy to want to experience such pleasure once in her life? She knew the game, the rote, had been a spectator all her life. She could play by the rules, couldn't she?

Serena fancied he could see the internal battle warring inside her, because he raised his hand and swept a strand of hair from her brow with a shiver-inducing graze.

'Trust me, beautiful. It's a bad idea.'

The main lights dimmed and what remained was a black canvas ceiling dotted with tiny pricks of light. It was like sitting beneath a million twinkling stars. So romantic that yearning pulled at her soul.

Finn eased back into his own chair, leaving her oddly bereft. Until the music struck an almighty beat and she felt the punch of power deep in the pit of her stomach. Then the full instrumental peeled from the band, the sound caroming around the vast expanse to infuse the atmosphere with what she could only describe as a seriously evocative sensual bent.

'Oh, my life.'

The thought slammed into her psyche within seconds. Finn hadn't intended bringing her here at all. So who…?

As if he could hear her mental meanderings, he murmured, 'I was coming by myself. This is a new cabaret-style show directed by a friend of mine and he sent some tickets over last night. He knows I like to blend occasionally, and they often debut in Montreal. I've no idea what to expect.'

She was pretty sure he had a better idea than she did.

'All I know is that it's strictly over eighteens and it explores human sexuality.'

Okay-dokey, then. Right up her street. *Not.*

The risqué undertone of the music was a prelude to a stage lifting from beneath the floor, bringing the performers into view, still as statues. Until the Moulin-Rouge-type beat peaked with an almighty crescendo…

The cushioned pad beneath her bottom quaked, sending a vibration straight to her core, making the hair on her arms stand on end.

And then the artists came to life.

Heat that had nothing to do with the amount of bodies packed in one space and all to do with the hedonistic bent of the performance shot through her bloodstream, growing ever hotter when the stage became a writhing mass of mind-boggling feats of flexibility and synchronicity.

Bodies were bending, stroking, touching. Hands glissaded over painted flesh, the vivid colours of their skin alive with sensuous beauty.

Hanging from the dollies above the plinth were three massive chandeliers from which acrobats were suspended, and they too began to move in a series of gyrations, spinning and twisting as they swung from one bar to another in a dizzying spectacle.

Oh. And they were all half naked. Half naked and—

She sucked in a sharp breath and Finn leaned over.

'You okay?'

'Mmm…' It came out like a groan, because where Finn had made her hot and bothered seconds before the show, now she was burning up. *The fiery one.*

'You want to leave?'

'Absolutely—' She had to take another breath as one of the female performers wrapped her legs around her partner, locked groins tight and bent backwards to the floor, as if he were sliding inside her, as if...

'Okay, let's go.'

'—not. No, I'm not leaving. I'm staying right here. A tornado whipping through the room wouldn't move me as much as this. It's... They...they're *beautiful*.'

Dancing, whirling, bending—the women were incredible acrobats, so much femininity and strength all rolled into one stunning blend.

'So strong,' she whispered in awe.

'They have to be. Strong-willed to train so gruellingly. Strong-minded to hold their positions, trust in their abilities. Believe in their talent. But elegant and graceful at the same time.'

Yes, and all the while remaining strong of heart, body and soul. No shame, only dazzling radiance.

Still staring at the stage, her mind spun. 'What are you getting at, Finn?'

'Maybe I'm just pointing out that being a woman doesn't render you weak, and being strong or unique doesn't make you less feminine.'

She didn't see all women as weak. Did she? Then again, she'd never known many women. Only her dad's bits of fluff, and they all seemed desperate somehow. Serena had watched them, thinking how bizarre they all were, flitting to and fro, trying to make her dad happy, in the idiotic assumption he would keep them. Desperate. Weak. But wholly feminine. Had she subconsciously knitted the two together?

Finn had told her she was feminine. His words, *'Of course you are... In your own unique way...'* came back to her. She'd taken them as a kind of insult, but at the same time had longed for him to mean it. Despite or perhaps because of the shoe-slipper debacle.

Finn saw far more than what met the eye. Behind the celebrity persona he had a depth of intensity and an intelligence that astounded and intrigued her.

'People underestimate you, Finn,' she murmured, and the show continued all around them, just as the world still spun, ignorant of the seismic shift inside of her.

Seismic since she suspected that he was not only right but that her issues ran far deeper. Too deep for her to delve into that gorge right now.

'Always a bad idea,' he said, with an arrogance that made her smile.

With her gaze glued to the sinuous, serpentine movements on stage, she could feel him staring at her.

'It's enthralling, don't you think?'

'Absolutely mesmerising,' he said, still watching her.

'Provocative,' she whispered.

'A unique kind of sensuality.'

Her heart did a trapeze artist flip in her chest. In Monaco he'd said similar words to her.

Unable to resist a moment longer, she turned to look at him.

Face flushed, he licked his lips, as if his mouth was over-dry.

'Finn…?' she breathed. 'Aren't you going to watch?'

'I am watching, baby. The only thing worth looking at.'

Whoosh. Her heart did another flip. Three somersaults and a free fall. And just like that she struggled to breathe.

Before she knew it her eyes had closed and she leaned forward, needing his mouth on hers so badly her entire body ached—and that was *nothing* compared to the flood of moisture low in her pelvis, the incessant clench demanding satisfaction.

French vocals drifted on the air—a sultry line that enhanced the suggestive notes pluming around them:

Would you like to sleep with me tonight?

Another Serena might have asked—a braver version, one who was confident enough to know she could satisfy a man like him, one who knew she'd feel no regrets in the morning. The real Serena couldn't guarantee any of that.

His warm breath trickled over her lips, yet intuition told her he wouldn't close the ever-so-small gap—a virtual Grand Canyon, considering the past that lay between them and all the reasons for them to rebuff this weird and wonderful attraction and simply walk away.

Just the thought that he might take the decision from her kicked her doubts to the kerb and she prised her eyes wide.

His eyes were as dark as midnight, glittering like the stars above, and from nowhere she found the strength to move in, close that gap, lick over his full bottom lip and then bite down to tease with a gentle tug.

Lust...

Finn growled.

Heat...

'Back off, Serena.'

More. Another lick. Another soft suck. Another tender bite. He returned it with sharp yet gentle teeth, then kissed away the sting, causing her to shiver and the deep ache in her body to spike.

'You really want me to take you right here?' he rasped.

That stopped her.

Visibly shaken, her hand trembled as she brushed the hair from her sticky nape and leaned back in her seat. Her sensitive breasts chafed against the cotton of her plain bra and she had to stifle a whimper.

Who knew how long she sat there, her lower body contracting around thin air, while a surge of mortification because she couldn't control her own body inched her anger levels up the charts?

Intermission hit and, unknowing what to say, what to do, feeling seven kinds of stupid that she couldn't make light of the fact that she was teetering on the edge of an orgasm or handle it in some practised feminine way, she launched to her feet.

'I'm going to the Ladies'.'
And she shot through the crowd at a fast clip.
She had to cool off and there was only one way to do it. As far away from Finn St George as she could possibly get.

CHAPTER NINE

'Don't get a fright,' Finn murmured, taking a tentative step closer to where she stood in the dark corridor that led to the plush offices at the rear of the tent. How she'd found her way around here he wasn't sure, but for the six minutes it had taken to find her he'd never felt so ill in his life.

Seemingly ignorant of the shadows enveloping her, Serena faced the wall, her head bent forward, brow kissing the evocative red plaster, as her supple body shook violently.

His heart hammering, his insides writhing in a chaotic mess, Finn braced his hands on either side of her head, then buried his face in her neck and inhaled a sweet burst of summer fruits—a scent that pacified, a taste that he'd come to associate with her. One he would never forget. One he wanted to lap right up.

He nuzzled up to her ear. 'Let me take the edge off, baby.'

He shouldn't have brought her here. She was burning. He'd never seen anything like it. Or felt anything like it. He was going insane with lust. Yet he had no intention of taking his pleasure from her. For once in his life he was going to be unselfish. Give instead of take. Douse her fire well and good.

For a second he thought she'd refuse, and despite knowing it was probably for the best he felt his guts twist tight. And then she turned and, *bam*, her mouth was on his, and she was twining her arms around his neck and thrusting into his mouth.

Just like that his largesse slipped a gear. *Aw, man*, this was not good. This was going to be harder than he'd thought. Much, *much* harder if the erection that strained against his zipper was anything to go by.

Grateful that she'd found her way round to this section of the tent, Finn picked her up, wrapped her legs round his waist and carried her straight into his friend Zane's office, thanking fate that he'd passed the man only moments ago and orchestrated thirty minutes of privacy.

He kicked the door shut behind them and braced her against it, his lips never leaving her mouth as he rolled his hips against her heat to create the friction she needed.

His little tigress moaned and purred around his lips, thrust her hands into his hair and held on while he took her on the ride of her life.

'Finn, Finn, Finn...'

'It's okay, baby. It's okay. I'll get you over.'

'I don't like this. I've never felt like this before. It's never been this way before.'

The words poured out on a rush but he got the general gist. Sex didn't usually flip her switch. Bastard that he was, he revelled in that.

'This doesn't feel normal,' she whimpered.

'I know, beautiful.' *Nowhere near normal.*

Which was the entire problem. He was *feeling* things. Desperation, need, a want like no other. A bone-deep fervour to protect, to satisfy her every craving, her every wish, to make her come over and over until her cries of ecstasy filled his mouth. To give her the world and the stars beyond. Too much. It was all just too damn much.

Holding her up with one hand, he smoothed around her small waist, then un-popped the button of her jeans. Her piercing teased and tormented his fingers and he growled as his flesh turned to granite. *Keep it together...keep it together. What are you? A virgin?*

He wanted *in*, and the angle was all wrong, so with a light squeeze of her deliciously pert rear he loosened his hold and splayed his hand beneath the T-shirt on her back to keep her close. The touch of her fevered skin was like an electrical charge up his arm.

What he wouldn't do to have a good, *long* look at the body that had featured so prominently in his dreams. To claw at her clothes and tear her panties off with his teeth.

Serena shimmied to the floor, snatching kisses as if she never wanted to leave his mouth, and burrowed under his polo shirt, making him sweat.

Okay, then. She wasn't the patient type. Which was dangerous with a capital D because *he* was—it was the only way to stay in control.

'Slow—slow down, baby.'

She had to slow down. Before he buried himself in her dewy heat and lost himself inside her.

'Oh, God, this is so good,' she moaned.

'You knew I would be.'

'Arrogant man.'

With great pains he managed to focus on her luscious mouth and devour her, trying his hardest to focus as he slowly but surely eased the waistband of her jeans down her hips and encountered some lacy girly version of boxer shorts.

Oh, man, he was a goner. 'I have to look.'

'Now, where have I heard that before?' she panted.

Finn pulled back and ripped her hoodie and her T-shirt over her head; his temples were pounding, his blood was pounding, his erection was pounding. Everything was pounding.

Her jeans were rucked around mid-thigh, her biker boots sculpted her calves and those subtle curves were making his vision swim. Then he was seeing red… *Red?* Bra and panties. Closet girl, that was what she was.

'Red,' he growled.

His first thought was, *She's perfect*. His second thought was, *Oh, hell, she's perfect*.

Lamplight spilled over the room and he could just make out the lustrous tone of her ivory skin dusted with freckles. He wanted to lie her down and count them all, give them names and kiss every one. He wanted to crush her to him and hold on tight. And from nowhere came the senseless idea that he could be a one-woman-forever man, that she could trust him always.

With defcon speed he ruthlessly shut the notion down. He was *never* taking the risk of hurting her. He'd already done too much of that already and she didn't know half of it.

'Stop staring at me!'

'No chance.' He was looking and she was going to learn to like it, to know how seriously sexy she was.

He cursed blue to get his point across. Lots of the F-word and *gorgeous*es and *sexy*s flying out of his mouth at two hundred miles per hour.

Then he kissed her hard, to back up every word with a truckload of ardour just in case she wasn't getting the point. And with each thrust of his tongue and every swivel of his hips desire mounted, until her rapture created a cloud of erotic fervour and her rich arousal plumed in the air.

Oh, man, he wanted to bite her, mark her, brand her like the animal he was inside.

Hand splayed, he rubbed his palm over her piercing and sank it beneath her shorts, delving to touch her hot heat.

A tortured moan filled the air. His. Hers. Theirs.

She was slick and swollen with want, and when her hips bucked, moisture trickled down his finger.

'Serena…' he groaned, tormenting her with a good dose of exquisite friction.

Gingerly he peeled one shoulder strap down her upper arm, and when her perfect C's popped free the room spun as if he was on a whirly top. They were like works of art. Firm but soft. Each underswell lush and round and topped with a dusky rose nipple.

'You're so beautiful, Serena.'

Taste—he simply *had* to taste her.

Finn cupped her breast and trailed his mouth down her neck. The anticipation of reaching her tight nipple thrummed through his blood, and when he flicked his tongue over the taut peak and simultaneously pushed one finger deep inside of her, a keening cry ripped from her throat.

This was agonising. He wanted her. All of her.

Hot little pants escaped her mouth and the sight of her teeth buried in her bottom lip sent another jolt through him. When he closed his lips over her puckered flesh and sucked, the scent of her arousal filled his nostrils, making him hard enough to penetrate steel.

As if she'd lost the ability to hold her head high, Serena tipped it back to smack the wall. 'Oh. My. Life. Finn…!'

He sank his finger deeper inside her body, this time a little harder, and felt her tight walls close in, grab onto him.

He had a big problem here—a huge problem. And if he wasn't careful he would explode in his hipsters. She was so tight.

'Been a long time baby?'

'Mmm-hmm.'

She was petite to start with, and the way he was sized he would snap her in two. *Not an issue. You're not going there.* It still didn't stop him from imagining the sensation, the hedonistic pleasure, of spreading her across Zane's desk and licking her from head to foot before he plunged deep inside her slick channel.

Her hips pivoted in time to his rhythm and she grabbed his shoulders and arched her back, seeking deeper penetration.

'More?' He pushed a second finger to join the first and she spasmed around him, saying his name over and over with soft, heated, anguished cries of ecstasy.

Keep it together. Don't lose it. Don't you dare.

With one last light squeeze of her breast Finn skimmed up and over her collarbone to rub her bottom lip, back and forth. Then he pushed his index finger inside her hot moist mouth at the same time as he thrust his two fingers deep and thumbed her sweet spot to tease out her pleasure.

Plunge and stroke, here and there, until she writhed and swirled her tongue around his finger. *Holy...* And when he touched her nipple with a nice long lave of his tongue...

She *broke*, splintered, shattered, coming long and hard, spasm after spasm racking her body. The walls of her femininity closed in, squeezing his fingers as she flew apart at the seams, clamping violently in a stunning erotic symphony.

Sweat trickled down his spine, making the tight, scarred skin of his back itch. *Hold it together. Hold it.*

As she tumbled from the heights of bliss, rolling in wonder and passion and exhilaration, Finn leaned his forehead against hers, jaw locked, his total focus on willing the erection bursting out of the top of his jeans to chill out. Willing his body not to come just from watching her orgasm.

He needed air. *Now.* He was shaking from head to foot and his teeth were clamped so tight he nearly cracked a molar.

'Finn?' she breathed.

'Give me a minute.' He squeezed his eyes shut.

Her small hand slipped off his shoulder, smoothed down his chest, and didn't stop until she cupped his erection through his jeans.

He hissed out a choice curse. 'Careful, beautiful.' He placed his hand over hers to lift it to his mouth and kiss her palm. 'This can't happen between us, Serena. For starters, I haven't got a condom.' He sounded a hoarse, desperate man. Very true, that.

'It's already started, Finn.' Back down she went, fingering his jeans. 'I'm safe. You're clean, right?' She began to rip his belt buckle free.

Once more he tugged her hand away, knowing he'd never make it a third time.

'Serena, I've never had sex without a condom in my life.'

This could *not* happen. He needed a condom. It would be too close. Too intimate. Too everything.

Without a barrier he'd lose it. Lose himself. Inside her. He would mark her. Brand her. Have real trouble letting her go.

'We're stopping before we go too far.' *There. That should do it.* He sounded forceful and arrogant and domineering. And just so he could cut off the screenplay in his head he hitched up her bra strap and veiled her gorgeous breasts.

'Don't you *want* to sleep with me, Finn? Be inside me?'

He groaned long and low, never having wanted anything more in his entire life. Right now an endless reel played in his head. She was so utterly perfect for him. But he was *not* the man for her.

In another life he would think he'd finally found The One. If he'd been a different man. If he'd made different choices and hadn't caused so much pain. Pain he knew he'd eventually cause her again. He was too selfish. Unreliable.

He was also taking too long to answer, because she'd tugged her jeans into place and wriggled back into her T. All the while trying to school an expression made up of dejection and embarrassment.

'I don't do it for you, do I?'

Finn cupped her face and kissed her softly on the mouth. 'One look and you do it for me, beautiful. You always have. But, like I told you before, it's a bad idea. You'll wake up in the morning and hate me even more. Regret every minute. Feel only emptiness. It's a stone-cold feeling, Serena, I promise you.'

She stared into his eyes. 'So what was that? Friends with benefits?'

'Sure—why not? You needed me.'

'You need *me* too.' She dipped her head to where he was straining against denim and licked her lips in bashful invitation. 'At least let me…?'

Finn reared back, creating some space. *Hell, no.* If she

knelt before him, took him into her mouth, he would never get the picture out of his head.

'I won't take pleasure from you. That was for you, just this once. Never to be repeated.'

If they reached this point again he'd be powerless to stop.

The only reason he had this encounter under control was because they were in Zane's office, with no condoms, flanked by secrets and lies.

Here she was, beginning to trust him, and she couldn't. It was insane. She was forgiving him, tumbling into his arms under the influence of deceit, and he could not sink into her body, look into her eyes as he came inside her, without her knowing the full truth.

'There are many things I'm not proud of in my life. If I take from you, if I use you, it will be one too many. Do you want a friend, Serena? Or a one-night stand that leaves you frozen? We can't have both.'

For long moments she stared at her feet, drew patterns with the toe of her boot.

Then she glanced up and gave him a small, indecipherable smile. 'Then I guess...a friend.'

Finn swallowed. Hard. 'Good. Friends it is.'

Satisfied he'd taken the hard edge off his need, he grabbed her hand. 'Come hither, Miss Scott, the night is young.'

Halfway out the door she crashed to a halt, and Finn followed her line of sight to their entwined fingers, dangling between them.

Well, what do you know? He hadn't even realised. 'What's up, baby? You never held hands with someone before?'

Brow nipped, she gave a little shake of her head. 'No.'

Finn shrugged, made it easy. 'Me neither.' And before she could make more of it he hauled her out of the room. 'Now, let's get out of here. Don't know about you, but I'm starving.'

For a woman he could never have.

CHAPTER TEN

'WHAT'S GOING ON?' Serena tucked her bike helmet under one arm, shook the damp kinks out of her hair with the splayed fingers of her free hand and closed in on the small crowd gathered at the pits. 'What's the SL1 doing down here?'

One glance at her big beauty, squatting on the Silverstone circuit, looking every inch the sleek, glorious feline she was, and Serena felt her heart swell up with pride.

It wasn't until the silence stretched that she realised several pairs of peepers were soaking in the sight of her going all goo-goo—over a *car*, for heaven's sake. *Sometimes you're such a girl, Serena.*

Tearing her eyes away, she glanced up at Finn and thought, *Oh, great, here we go again.*

The early-morning sun picked out the bronze and golden tones of his hair and his deep cerulean eyes twinkled knowingly.

'Good morning, Little Miss Designer, how nice of you to roll out of bed to join us.'

His voice was deep and devastating, richly amused and lathered in sin. Then his delicious fresh scent whispered on the breeze to douse her body with scads of heat.

'While you've been getting your beauty sleep I've driven fifty laps in your pride and joy.'

Tensing, she felt the hard lip of her helmet dig into her

hip. 'I don't understand.' The only reason he would practise in her racer was if her dad had changed his mind—

Her stomach began to fizz—which was absurd. Serena knew the kind of miracle *that* would take, and she didn't think Finn had demolished every car on the fleet. Yet.

Saying that, she'd rarely seen those dark clouds of guilt overshadowing him during the two weeks since Montreal. And the thought that she'd succeeded in finagling his attention long enough for him to move on made her soul smile.

Finn swiftly dispersed the group with an arrogant jerk of his head and leaned against the car's lustrous patina. Then he crossed his arms over a delicious cerise polo shirt and ran his tongue over his supremely sensual mouth.

A mouth she shouldn't be staring at, hungering for. The problem was, her new BF had taken her to the heights of ecstasy, and every time she looked his way every blissful, shattering moment came back on a scalding rush.

Car, Serena. Focus.

'So what did you think? Of my car?' A sudden swoop of nervy fireflies initiated a frenzy behind her ribs.

'She's much like the woman who designed her. A fiery bolt of lightning.'

Okay, then. A few happiness bugs decided to join the midriff party. 'She handles well?'

'Unbe-frickin-lievebly. She pulls more G's than a space shuttle. Her curves are divine and she worships the tarmac. She's a dream, Serena. You've done an amazing job.'

The world vanished behind her eyelids as she tried to calm the internal flurry and take a breath. All the hard work, the late nights, the testing and retesting over and over, and *still* she waited for her dad to tell her she'd done well. But the admiration and respect in Finn's gaze, from a man who'd driven the greatest cars in the world, was even better.

Oh, who was she kidding? It was awesome. She felt like flying. Having a real girly moment and jumping and whooping. Which was just silly.

'Good. I'm glad.'

Finn leaned towards her and Serena was lured by his sheer magnetism. She drew forward until his husky breath tickled her ear.

'You can squeal if you want to, baby, I won't tell anyone.'

She jerked backwards. 'Don't be ridiculous.'

That fever-pitch-inducing smile widened and one solitary indentation kissed his cheek. Despicable, infuriating, *gorgeous* man.

'So how did this happen, anyway? My dad said—'

'We had it out last night. Talked long enough for him to see sense.'

From nowhere a great thick lump swelled in her throat.

Oh, honestly, he had to stop doing stuff like this. Because every time he did, another teeny slice of her heart tore free and vaulted into his hand. Serena couldn't recall the last time someone had pushed for what *she* wanted. Even Tom had tended to side with their dad.

'You'll soon learn,' he began, his voice teasing and darkly sensual, 'that it's always best to leave business down to the men, Serena.'

The blissful feeling vanished. 'You only say that stuff to pee me off.'

A devilish glint entered his eyes...

'When I tell you my condition you'll be even more so.'

'I don't like that look.' A little bit shrewd. A whole lot devious.

'You have to attend the Silverstone Ball tonight. That's the deal.'

There it went. In point five of a second. '*It*' being her stomach, hitting ground level with a sickening thud.

'No way. You know that's not my scene.'

Black-tie extravaganza to kick off the weekend of racing with VIP clientele and the usual coterie, sipping champagne, dressed up to the nines in...? No.

Just no!

'Hold up there, handsome. Your *condition*? What do you need *me* there for?'

Never mind the dresses and the shoes and the dancing and the mind-numbing chit-chat, if he thought she was suffering that soiree only to watch him portray Lothario he had another think coming!

'Your car needs to be unveiled and it's the perfect venue. You *have* to be there. This is your big moment. You need to revel in it, enjoy it. Come on, Serena, I dare you.'

'Ooh. Low, Finn, real low.' The beast knew exactly how to get a rise out of her.

Huffing out a breath, she stared unseeingly at her car while a war raged inside her. As far as big moments went this was pretty huge.

She chose her words carefully. 'On my own?'

If he was taking a woman she wanted to know so she could prepare herself. It was crucifying, waiting for him to choose a new starlet.

True, she'd been batting away the sneaking suspicion that he'd already done so for days. What with the odd phone calls he refused to answer in front of her. The ones that made his jaw set to granite as his gaze locked on the screen before he glanced at her with something close to remorse.

If not a woman, who else?

Then again, she doubted he'd had the time to wield his charm elsewhere. More often than not they were together. Which brought on a whole new set of problems. Because while she liked having him as a friend—a pretty cool friend, as it turned out, who'd sneaked her into the premiere of the latest action flick last night—it was getting harder and harder to keep her hands off him.

All in all, since Montreal her sanity was slowly being fed through a shredder.

'You'll hardly be on your own, Serena. The entire team is going and you'll be walking in there with me.' He gave her a wink that made her feel dizzy. 'I get first dance.'

Oh. Well, then. Those fireflies started doing an Irish jig. He was taking *her*, not some flashy starlet. He was going to dance with *her*, not the latest paddock beauty. As friends, of course. Unless he'd changed his mind…

Suddenly *her* mind made the oddest leap, to a vision of her biker leathers, and a groan ripped from her chest. 'And what exactly would I *wear*?'

He chuckled at that. Actually laughed.

'What's funny?'

'And she says she's not a woman.'

Serena threw him a few daggers, wholly unamused.

'Don't worry, okay?' A smile seeped through his voice. 'We'll find something.'

'*We?* Are you worried I'll turn up in T-shirt and jeans and embarrass you?'

Fully expecting some wisecrack, she was unprepared for the way he reached up and tenderly brushed a lock of damp hair from her brow. Only to melt when he stroked down her cheek with the side of his index finger.

'Listen to me. I would dance all night with you wearing a driver's suit—I wouldn't change you for the world. But what I *don't* want is for you to feel uncomfortable or out of place. Why don't you think of it as an adventure? If you have the time of your life, that's great. If you don't, nothing lost. At least you'll have tried. For you. And you'll have given the SL1 the launch she deserves. Come on, it'll be fun.'

The only thing she heard were his words *I wouldn't change you for the world*. And she knew he meant every single one.

'Know what I tell every rookie when he faces the fast lane? Fear is a choice. Don't choose it, Serena.'

In some sort of Finn-induced trance, she murmured, 'Okay.'

She could do this. Launch her car. Dance with Finn. Keep it friendly.

If he still wanted that. She wasn't so sure any more. In

truth she had no idea why they were still fighting it. *Stone-cold morning-after, full of regrets about being one of many.*

'Good.' He delved into his pocket and whipped out his mobile. 'I'll go make some calls and we'll head back to the Country Club. Within two hours you'll have half a boutique in your suite.'

Another wink as he backed towards the garage and her insides went gooey.

'Trust me, baby.'

Trust him.

Why did he always say that? Because he wanted her to trust him so badly? Or was he transmitting some kind of subconscious warning that she shouldn't? The problem was, his warnings were now falling on deaf ears.

Especially since his predicted 'stone-cold emptiness' had evolved regardless. Wherever they went, whatever they did, when the time came to part, stone-cold was exactly what she felt—right down to her bones.

Until her sheets twisted with hot longing and her mind saw an evocative cabaret with her and Finn centre stage. Her only thought: *I want that man. I always have and I'm going to have him.*

To hell with it all.

It was becoming harder and harder to control that voice, to silence the woman inside.

Serena ambled across the tarmac towards the perimeter, enticed by the serenity of lush green meadows—an endless landscape of possibilities. She struggled to remember if she'd ever seen her life that way. As an adventure. Always the pragmatist, she'd never been a dreamer.

There was Finn, with his rich and wondrous, albeit debauched past, but at least he'd lived life to the full. While she'd been fighting that voice, the woman she was inside, since she was thirteen years old, having just rolled onto her stomach in bed, only to wince as the sensitive mounds of flesh on her chest crushed against the mattress. Then a few days later the stomach pain had come, to signal an even bigger humiliation—how to buy panty liners surrounded by men. And that had been nothing on the hormonal avalanche making her feel confused, wishing more than ever that she had a mum of her own. She'd been lost—like a stranger in her own skin. Trapped in someone else's body.

Looking back, it was all so clear to her now. Raised a tomboy, she'd hastened to repress her nature. Yet slowly, secretly, she'd begun harbouring fantasies of more. Dreaming. Easily beguiled by a man who'd lured her with lies and deceit, making the temptation to be all things feminine a compulsion she couldn't resist.

Tipping her face skyward, she let the sun warm her face and breathed through the hurt in her heart. The sinister backlash would stay with her always.

Ever since Finn had made her realise she saw women as weak the idea had rubbed her raw, like a scratch to her psyche.

The naked truth? She was petrified of being a woman. It led her to make bad choices. To walk headlong into betrayal. Pain. Weakness. It led her to lack-lustre sexual encounters as her body fought her will.

So here she was. Twenty-six years old. Still trapped.

Until Finn touched her and she threatened to burst out of her own skin.

Serena knew it was foolhardy but she wanted a good long look at the woman beneath. The person she'd stifled and ignored. And she trusted him.

Fear is a choice.

So hours later, when rails upon rails of dresses in every shape and hue lined her rooms, she duelled with the bouts of anxiety and doubt and managed to conquer each and every one.

For years she'd vowed that her past would not define her. Yet it had. All along. Well, no more.

A strong woman would pursue what she desired. If Finn

was prowling for some female company to take to his bed tonight Serena wanted to be it.

They could still be friends afterwards. She'd just have to prove it to him.

'I'm in the cocktail bar. Come for me?'

Finn strolled into the bar of the swanky Country Club and made a quick sweep of the softly lit circular lounge.

Designed in a sinuous art nouveau style, the architecture was a showcase for curvy lines where no shadows could lurk and deep furniture made from exotic woods, lending a warmth that pervaded his bones. A warmth that grew hotter as his eyes snagged on his prey, her back facing him, perched on a high stool at a central island bar made of iridescent glass.

Whoosh. His blood surged through his veins, drowning out a soft croon.

For one, two, three beats he stared. Because something was different and he certainty had faltered. Then she leaned towards the barman as if she hung on his every word…tipped her head back with infectious laughter and graced him with her exquisite profile.

'Holy…'

Confidence. She was incandescent with it.

His heart cramped, stopped and started again, as if he were crashed out on a gurney in need of some chest paddle action.

Commanding his feet to move, he ordered himself to be calm—not to pick her up, twirl her around the floor, tell her she looked every inch the stunning beauty she was. Not to kiss her hard on the mouth before taking her upstairs to slake this crazy lust and devour her gorgeous body for days.

Instead he scoured his mind for an appropriate Finn St George comment that would do the job whilst ensuring they slept between separate sheets—because his control was as treacherous as an oil slick.

This thing, this friendship between them, was taking on a dangerous bent, and losing the precarious hold on his sanity wouldn't be pretty.

The dilemma being, he couldn't disengage himself from her heavenly pull.

When the moon rose so too did his demons, and there he lay, tormented, although adamant that his endless procrastinating would cease with the rising sun. Then she appeared, all fire and dazzle, with her snarky wit and her beautiful smile, dragging him from the darkness into the light more magnificently than any sunrise could ever do. Leaving him torn asunder once more, frustrated and infuriated with the ugly little corner he'd found himself in.

Keeping her in the dark had been an easy enough decision to make after Singapore, when he'd still been able to taste the metallic tang of blood and they hadn't been face-to-face. All black and white, his reasoning had been crystal clear. Protect her at all costs. No harm done.

But as one day had overtaken another *simple* had accelerated to *beyond complicated*.

Now Finn was loath to tamper with her contentment, to substitute the happiness in her eyes with hate and betrayal. At the same time he was selfish enough to want her to look at him that way a while longer. As if he was a good man. As if he *hadn't* led her brother to his death. As if his day of reckoning *wasn't* hurtling towards him.

Before he even reached her side she stilled. Curled her fingers around the beaded purse on the glass bar-top. Closed her eyes and just…breathed.

Honest to God, what they did to each other defied logic. It was a car bomb waiting to detonate if he didn't defuse it somehow.

Gripping the back rail of her stool, he became enraptured by her fiery river of hair—the way the sides were loosely pinned back to create a cascade of soft, decadent curls down her back.

Thought fled and he dipped his head to kiss her bare shoulder. But he slammed on the brakes in the nick of time, making do with a long, deep inhale. In place of her usual fruity undertones there was an evocative note of something dark and distinctly passionate, reminiscent of her arousal.

His body quaked as that scent registered in his brain like a Class A narcotic and he growled in her ear, 'Looking good, baby.'

A slight tremble passed over her before she swivelled on her bottom and slipped off the stool. Then he got a really good look, and his heart started doing that palpitation thing again. *Wow*, she was filling out. That over-thin look of Monaco was being replaced with subtle curves.

Her pewter dress was snug, held up by one heavily beaded shoulder strap which trailed down the side of a boned bodice, cupping her breasts, moving down to a small bustle at her hip. Her skirts were frothily layered, plunging to the floor in swathes of a lighter toned silver, the hue turning darker by degrees to charcoal and finally edged in ebony. It was a sexy version of rock-chick princess, with Serena lending it her own unique kick.

He was left with the ludicrous urge to lift the froth and take a peek at her feet.

A small smile teased her lips. 'Don't tell me. You need to look.'

Finn shrugged, feeling oddly boyish. He'd never been obsessed with a woman, and the hunch that obsession was definitely the evil he was up against made him recoil, take a step back.

Serena, however, took that as an invitation to show off, and she slowly, seductively, inched her skirts up her calves, then lifted her dainty little foot and flexed her ankle this way and that.

The diamond-studded sandals twinkled in the light, sending prisms of colour to dance across the walnut floor.

'You're very pleased with yourself, there, Miss Scott.'

Smoky sultry make-up enhanced the colour of her grey gaze as she sparkled up at him. Lips glossed, pink and full taunted him as she spoke in a rush. 'I am. No boots, no slippers, and I can actually walk. Who knew wedge sandals actually existed?'

The way she was looking at him—confident, serene, enchanting...

Dammit. How was he going to get through this night? Need was a ferocious claw in his gut, slicing deeper with every second.

'You look sensational, baby.'

'Why, thank you, Finn. But do you know what's really scary?'

'What?'

Her brow nipped, as if she were controlling her emotions. 'I think I do too.'

'That's my girl.' His voice cracked under pressure. 'Let's get this show on the road. The helicopter awaits.' He held out his arm and shut down every possessive instinct in his body. 'Shall we go to the ball, Miss Scott?'

She slipped under the crook of his arm, pressed her breast in tight to his side and his pulse shot through the roof.

'Why, yes, I believe we shall, Mr St George. I have a feeling this is going to be a night to remember.'

Finn tried to swallow around a lifetime of regrets. 'Curiously enough, so do I.'

CHAPTER ELEVEN

'Congratulations, Serena, she's a beauty.'

'Thanks!' she said for the hundredth time as she cut through the swathe of racing drivers, TV pundits and VIP celebrities littering the champagne reception.

Despite her stomach doing a really good impression of a cocktail shaker, she'd slipped free of Finn's arm an hour earlier. Half of her was adamant not to appear clingy and her other half was determined to venture out on her own. An endeavour that had whipped her into a whirlwind of team chit-chat, photos and promo for the SL1 until she felt high as a proverbial kite.

It couldn't possibly be the champagne. Truthfully, she thought it was a disgusting blend of wince-worthy tartness and bubbles exploding up her nose. She'd do anything for a beer.

Spotting a familiar face in a bunch of footballers, she pulled up alongside her dad, waited for a lull and then tugged at his sleeve. 'Have you seen Finn anywhere? We're supposed to be heading into the marquee for dinner.'

'Not lately. Good God, you look stunning, sweetheart. I had to pick my jaw up off the floor when you walked in.'

'That makes two of us.' Jake Morgan sidled up to join them, his chocolate gaze liquid with warmth. 'You look fantastic, Serena.'

'Oh, stop, now you're making me blush.' She gave a small

smile to soften the brush-off—she still wasn't used to compliments. She kept expecting someone to shout *Impostor! Fraud!* Even if she felt…well, beautiful for the first time in her life. All giddy and girly.

And if that aroused an anxious tremble in her stomach she ignored it. There'd be no dark shadows tonight.

She took a deep, fortifying breath and switched gears. 'I can't wait to see my baby whizz around Silverstone tomorrow.'

'She'll win for sure,' someone said.

'Too right she will.' *As long as Finn kept his mind on the game.*

'Can I get you a drink before we head over?' Jake asked.

Inwardly cringing at the thought that she'd end up with another glass of fizz, she said, 'Actually, Jake, I'll come with you.'

The bar was the traditional mahogany type: deep and framed with brass rails. Serena gripped the cold metal as they deliberated over the mirrored wall of various optics.

'What does gin taste like?' she mused.

'Not sure, but it used to put my mother in a crying jag.'

Serena snorted a laugh, turned round. 'Really?'

And *that* was when she caught a glimpse of dirty blond hair in the mirror's reflection and twisted to see Finn laughing in that charming, charismatic way of his.

'You pick, Jake. I'll be back in a tick.'

Off she went, diving through the throng and popping out at the 'Finn cluster' planted at the top of some stone steps leading to the vast lawn—a lush green blanket saturated with an array of iconic racing cars from past to present, as well as supercars, helicopters and yachts in a huge luxury showcase.

As if Finn sensed her behind him he reached round, grabbed for her hand, then pulled her into the fray and introduced her with practised ease and a pulse-thrumming smile. A smile she tried to emulate as he assaulted her senses, rubbing his thumb over the ball of her hand, making her bones liquefy and then leaning in until his dark scent fired heat through her veins.

'You enjoying yourself?'

'Yeah, I am. Surprise!' she said, only to cringe at the quiver in her voice, musing that she might be a league too deep with this man who effortlessly consumed her. 'Are you coming in for dinner? We're being seated any minute.'

'We?'

'Jake is at the bar, ordering drinks. He's waiting for me.'

Finn glanced towards that very spot, staring with an enigmatic hardness that turned pensive. Then he squeezed her hand until she flinched. *What the—?*

Jerkily he released her. 'Sorry, beautiful.'

If she didn't know better she would think he'd shocked himself.

'Sure, I'll follow. You go ahead,' he said, with an austere jerk of his head and a dark note to his drawl that she couldn't grasp.

As it was, they were halfway through their appetizers when he finally deigned to join the highly sophisticated mix, whipping out all the weapons in his loaded arsenal to schmooze his tardiness away.

And while every man and woman fell beneath his spell Serena stared at those tight shoulders, filling out his suave custom-made tux, and fought with disquiet. He appeared ruffled. As if he'd been thrusting his fingers through his hair. Or someone else had. *Stop. Just stop. You're being ridiculous.*

Soon, she told herself. As soon as the first band came on he would come for her to dance. Although the anticipation was a killer. Especially when she could feel his eyes burning into her flesh when he thought she wasn't looking.

What he failed to grasp was that her every sense was attuned to his high frequency. Every word from his lips dusted over her skin like the petals of the wild orchids that trailed from the crystal centrepiece, and every deep, sinful chuckle tightened the flesh between her legs. The waiting, waiting, slowly drove her insane, until at one point his gaze was so intense a tornado whipping through the room couldn't have stopped her meeting it across the table.

Finn placed his palm on his chest, as if his heart ached, and, *oh*, her own thumped in response. But then he pulled his phone from the breast pocket and she realised it must have been on vibrate. *Idiot.*

Her stomach hit the velvet seat with a disheartened thump even as she tensed with the chill of suspense.

Much as he had on another few occasions, he stared at the screen, then glanced back up, his demeanour fierce, indecipherable, his jaw locked tight, something dark and portentous swirling in his eyes.

Guilt. Another woman. It had to be.

Throat thick, she had to swallow hard. 'Aren't you going to answer it?'

It was the same question she'd previously voiced, and for the first time she *wanted* him to say no. Not to spoil the moment. Their night.

Except this time he stood. 'Yes. I've been waiting for a call. It's…important.'

'Is that right?' She sounded snarky, but right now she couldn't care.

One of the black-and-white-garbed waiters lowered a gold-trimmed plate in front of her and the sweet aroma of salmon and asparagus hit her stomach like battery acid even as she told herself she could be leaping to conclusions. But why act so guilty if it was innocent? Either way, she had no right to be upset, no claim on him whatsoever. *Exactly.* She was not furiously jealous. Absolutely not. That would mean she was far more emotionally involved with him than good sense allowed.

'I'll be back in a while.'

Mutely she nodded. Forty minutes later she was still calling herself fifty kinds of fool. He'd left. He must have. And while an orchestra of pain and hurt struck a beat inside—

directed at herself for believing she had a shot with him—she refused to let him take her pride from her tonight.

The bolt of fortitude was like taking a match to gasoline, and fury hit her in an explosion of fire. Once again she'd set herself up for a fall. But she wasn't going down. Not this time.

'Serena? The band is striking up. Would you do me the honour?'

Glancing up to Jake's handsome face, she felt her throat pulse, raw and scratchy. Was she seriously going to sit here all night like a fool, waiting for a man who might never come back? Was she really that desperate?

'Sure, Jake,' she said, ignoring the forlorn thump behind her breast telling her that this felt very, very wrong. 'That'd be great.'

It was like being confronted with his nemesis. The antithesis of everything he was.

Guts writhing in a chaotic mess, Finn leaned against the wall at the rear of the dimly lit ballroom, thinking how poignant it was to be enveloped by shadows—everything Serena feared—as he watched Jake Morgan enfold her hand and beckon her to the dance floor.

His body jerked on a visceral instinct to go over there, stop the other man from taking her in his arms. But, dammit, he could be honourable for once in his life. Step aside. Let the guy make his move. It was a thought he'd battled with all night. Would have surrendered to if it weren't for the undesirable, inexplicable, violent primal instincts that demanded he protect her. Possess her. Take her. Make her his.

But Finn knew the fall out from such selfishness. It had chased his career, fed off the high-octane rush of success, abandoned his mother when she'd needed him, left Eva to the heart-wrenching fate of watching her die. It had cost this woman her brother. So this, he assured himself, was an argument he would win. He wanted her to be happy.

One of the country's top bands struck out with a Rat-Pack number and when Serena offered Jake a small smile and moved into his embrace, white-hot lightning shot up his forearms, tearing through muscle. He had to shake his fists loose. What was wrong with him? He had to get a grip.

Jake was a good guy. Reliable. Honourable. Chances were *he* could remember the names of every woman he'd slept with.

Jake was trustworthy. What was more he hadn't just ended a call to the Chief of the Singapore Police, who'd discovered a new lead and was about to make an arrest.

Insides shaking, he blanked his mind. *Back away, Finn. Back the hell away.*

She could have a relationship with this guy. Finn knew nothing about those apart from the fact that the mere word spawned ramifications that were bad for his respiratory rate.

Across the room Jake fitted his hand to Serena's dainty waist, tugged her close, whispered in her ear, and Finn felt the first fissure *crack* in his sanity. His every possessive, protective instinct kicked and clawed with steel-tipped talons, tearing his insides to shreds, until he was back in that cell, fists balled, ready to protect what was his. And had it worked? No!

The dark licked around the edges of his life.

'Finn?'

Sweat trickled down his spine, making the skin on his back itch as violence poured through his veins. He'd been a stranger to brutality before Singapore and now, like then, it coated his tongue with vile bitterness.

Pain shot up his temples.

'Finn? You okay, my man?'

Michael Scott.

'Gotta go,' Finn said. 'Something's come up. Can you tell Serena…?'

Any response was lost as he shoved through the double doors, commanding his body to stay in control before darkness engulfed him and his demons wreaked havoc on his soul.

Serena waltzed across the marble foyer of the Country Club as if her squished feet *weren't* throbbing and her legs *didn't* feel as if they'd been chewed by a Doberman.

Heart weary, her only thought a hot bath and some sleep, she rode the elevator to the top floor, then slipped through the yawning metal doors—and stumbled to a halt.

A maid shuffled on her feet outside Finn's suite, biting on a torn fingernail.

Unease coiled through Serena's midriff. 'Is there a problem?'

The brunette jerked upright, wide-eyed. 'I...I'm sorry, Miss Scott, I heard a crash as I was passing so I knocked to check everything was all right.' She gave a tremulous smile. 'He isn't answering. You're with Mr St George, yes?'

Serena frowned, then realised the maid must have seen her in his suite earlier, put two and two together and came up with six.

A crash? Oh, God. What if he was hurt? Had had some kind of accident?

Chin up, she lied through her teeth. 'Yes, we're together. Don't worry—I'm sure everything is fine. But, while you're here, I've lost my room card. Could you switch me in, please?'

Antsy, suddenly slapped with the suspicion that he could be having sex in there—which would seriously be one humiliation too many—Serena tap-tap-tapped one diamanté toe on the floor.

As soon as the maid dipped into a curtsey and turned to walk away Serena slipped into the room. A room filled with dark shadows. She blinked rapidly to adjust her vision and when the scene crystallised, she sucked in air at the sight before her. One surely from her nightmares.

Trashed. His room was completely and utterly trashed.

Clothes were strewn all over the floor, as if his luggage had been overturned from the stand. A floor lamp was lying drunkenly on one side and the bed was stripped; dark silver satin pouring over the sides. The notion that he'd just had frenzied sex all over them crushed her heart.

It wasn't until she spotted the man himself, hands braced on the curved walnut bar, head bowed, white dress shirt damp and clinging to his back, that a portentous sensation crept up her arms. This didn't look like a seduction scene. It looked like—

'Oh, my God, Finn, has your room been ransacked? You have to call Security!'

Spotting the phone on the bedside table, she dashed over to call Reception.

'You know,' he said easily, 'that would be a very good idea. Perhaps they could take me away and lock me up.'

Reaching for the phone, her hand froze in mid-air. '*You* did this?'

She took his silence as a yes and shivered right down to her toes.

The atmosphere had turned thick with danger. She could virtually *feel* his darkness, blacker than ever before. And the urge to turn, to leave, was so strong she had to push her feet to the floor until they rooted—she would *never* be frightened of this man.

'But why?'

'Get out, Serena. Now. Before I break.'

Break? What was he talking about?

He swiped a bottle of tequila from the marble bar-top and poured the liquid into a crystal tumbler.

'Finn?' she said, panicking as he raised the glass to his lips and took a long swallow. 'What are you doing? You're driving tomorrow!'

'Nagging, Miss Scott? Now, that is a typical female trait.

One unbelievably hot dress and you're halfway there already.'

'You were the one who dressed me up! Only to disappear on a booty call and leave me there.'

A humourless laugh broke past his lips. 'A booty call? Is that what you thought?'

'What else was I supposed to think?'

With a severe kind of control, completely at odds with the state of the room, he turned to face her and air hit the back of her throat. His beautiful blue eyes were black with guilt, devastation and fury. So much fury it poured off him in waves. Great tidal waves of anguish.

'Hold up there, Lothario. What are you angry with *me* for?'

Slam went the glass to the marble and liquid sloshed over the crystal rim. 'No booty call. But it didn't take *you* long to fall into the arms of another man, did it?'

Serena flinched at the scathing lash of his tongue, the cut biting deep.

She'd messed up. Royally.

Raising one arm, Finn pointed due west and emotion gushed on a voice thick and unsteady. 'Do you have *any* idea how hard that was for me? To see his arms around you, holding you close? To walk away thinking you were better off with him?!'

Words blasted from him like bullets—*bang, bang*—until she rocked where she stood. Then she cursed for thinking the worst of him.

'I'm sorry. I waited and he asked me to dance. That's all we did—dance. I...' Her heart was beating so hard and loud she could barely think. But never mind her pride. She owed him this much. 'I only want you, Finn.'

Serena held her breath, waited. She didn't think it was possible for him to look even more tortured, but he did.

'You have to leave.' He stabbed his fingers through his

damp hair, then pawed down his face. 'Please, Serena, just go. I don't know how long I can hold on.'

Realisation hit and her entire world narrowed to this point. This man. 'So don't. Let go.'

Though her insides trembled, she commanded her feet to move deeper into the shadows and reached up to grip the zipper hook at the side of her dress. Slowly she tugged downward.

Fists clenching, he shook his head. 'Stop. Just stop. I'm on the edge here, Serena, and I can't control myself with you. I don't think you'll like that.'

As if he'd tossed her into a bramble bush, her skin prickled all over with the flash replay of violent hands gripping her throat, twisting her wrists, pinning her down—

No. *No!* This man was Finn. Granted, she'd never seen him so dark before, and it made her wonder if she was missing something, but still… 'I can handle it. I can handle you. I'm stronger than that, Finn.' Clearly he lacked faith in himself but she trusted him. Completely. Utterly.

She dragged the single beaded shoulder strap down her arm and teased the satin past her plunge bra to her waist.

His throat convulsed. 'Don't you dare, Serena. Don't you *dare*.'

She hurled his words from the yacht in Monaco so long ago back at him, amazed at how far they'd come, how far they'd travelled. 'Oh, Finn, you should know better than to challenge me. Especially in that gorgeous husky voice of yours.'

Shimmying, she eased the rucked material past her hips and the pewter satin rustled to the floor to pool at her feet. Leaving her standing in a black plunge bra, tiny lace panties and studded heels. Now, if she could just breathe she might get through this.

With his shirt agape, she could see his chest heave and the way he looked at her—with such heat. Such fierce desire and molten need.

A look so hot she melted beneath his gaze, pooling like gasoline, brandishing her earthy colours. Raw, elemental and utterly flammable.

'Serena,' he growled. 'I'm hanging on by a thread here, baby girl.'

'You know what, Finn? I love it when you call me that.' To think this man could have any women in the world and yet wanted her intimately, with such desperation, made her feel invincible. Confident. Beautiful. A real woman for the first time in her life.

He pointed at the door. 'You've got three seconds to run. Three.'

Up came her chin as she walked towards him with a sway in her hips she'd never before possessed, and then she pressed her hand to his hot flesh, felt the rapid thump of his heart beneath her palm.

'Two,' he bit out. Sweat glimmered on his skin and his broad shoulders quaked as he fought the immense power of his body. 'I can't promise I won't hurt you.'

'I *know* you won't.'

No more waiting. Avoiding. If this signalled the end of them, the end of their friendship, so be it. She didn't want another friend. She wanted a lover—the only man she'd ever truly desired.

'The fight is over, Finn.'

'One,' he said fiercely. 'You're making the biggest mistake of your life here, baby.'

'Then so be it.'

Snap.

CHAPTER TWELVE

Fast and frenzied, as if he were lost beneath an unseen power, entranced by a dark, feral spell, Finn simultaneously crashed his mouth over hers, gripped the front fastening of her bra and tore it wide.

'Skin,' he commanded around her mouth as he tugged the straps down her arms and tossed the black scrap across the room. 'I want nothing between us.'

'Whatever you want.' Her voice was as shaky as the rest of her and for a second her inner voice whispered that she was mad. Totally out of her league. With no idea of how to give such an intensely passionate man what he needed.

Following her instincts, she placed her hands on his honed chest, then swept them up and over his shoulders, taking his shirt with her until it bunched and locked around his thick upper arms.

Finn shucked it off the rest of the way and grappled with the fastening at the front of his waist.

She'd never seen him like this. Ever. No practised seduction. He was uncoordinated. Lost. And to think she was the inducement made her blood surge with elation and fear and an excitement so intense she ached with it.

A sharp hiss whistled through his teeth as he fought with his tuxedo trousers and she simultaneously pushed his hands away and broke their lip-lock. 'Let me do it.'

Not easy when he sank his hands into the fall of her hair,

tilted his head and crushed his lips over hers, banishing every thought from her brain. He ravished her with a kiss that was desperate and messy but she loved it. Loved the way he thrust his tongue into her mouth and groaned with need and contentment. A sound of soul-wrenching solace.

Now she was the one who fumbled with the rotten button. Heavens, he was bursting past the satin waistband, and when she thumbed the velvet head of his erection and encountered slick moisture her knees refashioned themselves into rubber.

A deep groan rumbled up his chest and he simply...tore the trousers off, buttons pinging, material shredding—the sounds of patience evaporating in the sultry air.

Then his long, thick length was in her hand and she couldn't even close her fingers around it. *Oh, my life.* She stroked up and down his erection as best she could and a sharp tug at the base of her abdomen made her insides clench. It felt as if she was contracting around thin air.

'Finn,' she whimpered. 'I need you inside me so bad.'

With an agonised moan, he jerked from her grasp. 'Soon. We need to slow this down or it will be over before it's even started.'

A sob of frustrated need broke from her throat. 'Finn, *please.*'

'That's it. Say my name. Tell me you want this. Want me.'

'I do. I do.' A wave of dizziness hit her and when she realised she wasn't breathing she gasped in air.

He nuzzled deliciously across her jaw, scraped her neck with his teeth, and somehow she knew exactly what he wanted.

'Go ahead—do it,' she demanded, frantic for his mark, and he sucked on her skin until her eyes rolled into the back of her head. She had to clutch his wide shoulders to stop dissolving in a puddle at his feet.

Beneath her palms she felt his tight muscles relax, as if he was slowly relinquishing the image of someone else and staking his claim on her. Branding her. And she loved it. Loved his sublime body too. From the lean ridges of his washboard abs to his sculpted arms—arms that made her feel gloriously safe, protected, coveted. Girly needs, but she was too far gone to care. She was tired of fighting them, weary of the constant struggle to stay strong. She only wanted him to hold her tight. For just a little while.

'You're so beautiful, Serena.'

Wherever his lips touched his urgent breath left heat—all the way down to her breast, where his hand cupped, where his thumb brushed over her tight nipple.

Her flesh ached for more, puckering when he took it into his mouth to swirl it and tongue it and suck it in a way she felt deep inside her pelvis.

She started to cry out but his mouth came right back, covered hers again, his fierce kiss silencing her until she surrendered to the sheer bliss of it all.

Finn splayed his hand over her stomach, rubbed her piercing with his palm, and his erection jerked against her bare thigh. Oh, that definitely did it for him. She wondered, then, what he'd think of the base of her spine...

'As divine as these panties are,' he said hoarsely, wrapping his fingers around the lace, 'you're even more so.' And he tore them clean off.

'*Ohh*, my life.'

Then he cupped her intimately, possessively, wickedly. 'Wet...*sooo* unbelievably wet and hot.'

The deep rasp of his voice, the seductive touch of his fingers against her slick and swollen folds, made her move to create the friction she craved, and within seconds her knees gave out.

'I've got you, baby.' Curving his arm around her waist to hold her upright, he thrust a finger inside her.

'Finn... Finn.' Needing his lips back on hers, his taste on her tongue, she pushed into his mouth with a boldness she'd never before dared, mimicking what he was doing with his hand as she rode his finger to completion.

The vibrations gathered force like a flock of birds sprouting wings and flying up into the sky, taking her with them far up and away as her body flew apart at the seams.

Flailing, she clutched his tight shoulders—shoulders that shifted in a delicious pattern as he gently tumbled her atop the bed.

Shivering, tingling with aftershocks, she writhed on the cool satin as he crawled over her.

'*Aw, man*, you are so incredibly, amazingly perfect. You drive me crazy, Serena. From the first moment I saw you I wanted you in my hands.'

Those very hands were shaking, but no more than hers, as he stroked up her waist and teased her ripe nipples in an unrelenting current of pleasure.

'You...you did?' Arching her back, she silently pleaded, then opened her legs wide to coax him into settling between her thighs.

He did too. Lowering his delicious weight until she could feel his hardness where she wanted him most.

'Oh, yeah. And know what else?'

'What?'

'I wanted to know how you would taste. Not only here...' He laved her nipple and gently sucked the peak into his mouth, stoking the internal fires he'd just doused. Then he shifted further down, gave the silver loop a quick lick. 'And here...' Another shift. 'But especially...here.'

Before she even knew what he was about he was at the juncture of her thighs and taking a long, leisurely cat-like lick up her still swollen folds, which still beat a tattoo of lingering pleasure. She couldn't possibly...

Serena bucked off the bed. Okay, this was really new to her, and she wasn't so sure, and it was a raw, open feeling.

'Finn?' she breathed, with vulnerability lacing her voice, making it almost inaudible.

'You taste so good, baby. I'll never get enough of you.'

Oh. His words were intoxicating, making her feel giddy,

making her heart soar. Which was just silly—she knew full well she needed to keep her heart out of this.

'Trust me. Relax. You'll love it.' He trailed lush, moist kisses across her inner thighs and she could feel his hot breath dusting her flesh. 'Heaven. I'm in sweet, delicious heaven. I love how good you taste. I knew you would.'

Gently, he sucked her clit into his mouth, pushed his tongue inside her, and every rational thought evaporated as he devoured her body and mind.

Within seconds she was writhing, fisting the trillion-count sheets. 'Finn! I can't take much more.'

'I want you mindless. Desperate. Needing me as much as I need you.' His gasped words were threaded with a hint of delicious agony. 'Able to take all of me.'

'Finn, please. I'm going out of my mind here. I'll do anything. Just give it to me, for heaven's sake—'

With a primitive sound that rumbled from his chest he crawled back up her body, prowling like a starved animal, his eyes dark as midnight, his body shaking with the strain of holding back.

'Anything?'

'Anything,' she said, softly panting, her gaze fastened on his delectable mouth.

'Beg me for it.'

Time stilled together with her heartbeat.

Power play. Control, she realised. Dominance. Her effect on him scared him. Made him feel out of control. And he wanted it back.

Yet how many times had *she* felt that way? Vulnerable, desperate to regain command of her life after the attack.

With no hesitation she reached up, cupped his gorgeous face, brought his mouth down to hers and kissed and begged and pleaded, told him exactly what she wanted him to do, using every uncouth word she could think of, until his eyes sparked electric blue and the arms that braced either side of her were shaking. And then—*thank you, God*—he thrust inside her in one powerful lunge, filling her huge and hard, covering her body with his, his possession so total she ceased breathing.

'Bliss. Sheer…bliss.'

Her lashes fluttered downward as his solid flesh pulsed inside her, making her feel exquisitely stretched. He felt *shockingly* good.

Pausing, perhaps as stunned as she was, he held still, his lips against the throbbing vein in her neck where he inhaled deeply.

A sharp arrow of unease burst through the rapture. 'Finn…?'

'Shhh, baby. I'm listening to your heartbeat, deep and hard and true. I'm soaking in your scent, rich with your arousal for *me*. Knowing…'

'Knowing?' she whispered.

'This is the closest I'll ever get to heaven.'

Oh. Her heart filled to bursting for him.

Serena sank her fingers into his damp hair and held him tightly to her. All the while fighting a punch of panic. This shouldn't be so intimate.

A chord of vulnerability sang to her heart and she squeezed her eyes shut. She didn't understand any of this. Not her body's reaction to him nor the emotions swirling inside her.

Finn finally raised his head and began to move tentatively. 'Look at me,' he ordered.

Serena opened her eyes to see him braced above her, his expression dark and fierce, so intense she trembled beneath him. Then, with their gazes locked, he began to move faster, pumping long and deep and hard, sweeping her up in a vortex of sensation so strong, so powerful, she cried out once more.

Finn captured her mouth with his—his tongue a tormenting lash of pleasure—and sank one of his hands under her bottom, lifting her, the better to meet his powerful thrusts, and grinding against her.

'Oh, *yessss*,' she moaned, raising her legs and wrapping

them around his lean hips. Her head tossed back and forth on the comforter as she fought to hold back the waves that threatened to crash over her. Almost sobbing with the fierceness of her need.

'Look at me,' he ordered again, louder this time. Heightening the sharpness of her desire. As if he didn't want her to forget who was inside her, dominating her, loving her body with his.

As if Serena could ever forget. Impossible.

She hastened to focus on his flushed face, where a thin sheen of sweat glistened on his forehead. His breath was hot and fast on her cheek; his erection throbbed inside her...then he suddenly crashed to a halt.

After a quick pause, in which he possessively gripped her waist, he pulled back. 'I want you with me when I fall. I don't want to be alone. Come with me.'

She tried, she really tried to push a *yes* past her lips, but at that moment he pushed so deep inside her that she felt him in every cell of her body and nothing came out but a high-pitched moan as she surrendered, let herself be dragged towards a climax the likes of which she'd never known.

'Finn...' she said brokenly, panicked that she wouldn't survive—that she'd die from pleasure, break after having him and losing him, shatter beneath his searing intensity.

'I know...I know.' He smoothed her damp hair back from her face. 'I'm here, baby, right here. Not going anywhere.'

She began to ride the shuddering crest. All-powerful, potent, almost violent as it ripped its way through her.

'That's it. Come for me.' He caught her small frantic cries with his mouth, tangled his tongue with hers as he upped the pace and pushed her higher than ever before.

'Finn!'

Climax was a blinding white-hot rush and she broke from his mouth as convulsions racked her body, making her spine arch violently.

Finn gave a final lunge, his dark-as-midnight eyes locked on hers, and at that moment she'd swear he touched her soul.

He stiffened, then came on a silent shudder that went on and on and on...

'*Yessss...*' she breathed, riveted on his gorgeous face, ravaged with pleasure, as he poured himself into her, giving her it all, and she'd never felt so strong, so powerful in all her life. She was a woman who'd just shattered this man. This beautiful, wonderful, amazing man.

A man who gave a convulsive thrust before he collapsed on top of her with a low sound of feral ecstasy. Then he wrapped her in his arms as if he never wanted to let go and nuzzled her neck, pressed a lingering kiss to the sensitive skin beneath her ear.

Serena stroked his damp hair from his brow and revelled in the feel of his body—heavy, slick and replete against hers.

Voice gruff, he murmured against her neck, 'You okay, beautiful?' with such tenderness that her chest ached.

'More than okay. That was...outrageously good.'

'Unbelievable.' He lifted his head, caught her gaze. 'Incredible.'

As if unable to stop himself he dipped his head to kiss her again—a kiss so sweet and tender that a lump pulsed in her throat and all she could think was that she didn't want to leave. She wanted to lie here forever and ever. With him.

Gently, he rolled onto his back, taking her with him, his hardness still locked inside her body, holding her tight as though fearful she would vanish into thin air.

'You'll stay here. All night. I can't let you go yet.'

'I'll stay.' Serena buried her face in his neck, tasting the musky scent of their passion and the remnants of his dark cologne. Desperately trying not to overanalyse his every touch, his every word.

He didn't do sleepovers. He'd told her that before. So maybe she was different from all the others—special enough to hold his attention. *Careful, Serena, you know better than that.* '*Yet*' implied that he would let her go come morning.

Fighting the hollow emptiness in her stomach, she snuggled closer, until they clung to one another as though braced for a turbulent storm.

For now she'd just enjoy him. Take what she could. Nothing would stop her. Not even the sound of her heart cracking wide open.

Selfish. He was so selfish craving the entire night with her. No doubt he would go to hell for it. So what was new? At least he'd have tasted heaven on the way.

Self-loathing gnarled and twisted in his guts like thorny branches as the tight skin on his lower back nipped, reminding him of what lay between them. And although it was wrong to hide, he was grateful for the shadows. The only light came courtesy of the thin slice of moon shining eerily through the leaded windows, ensuring he languished in the grim certainty that his world would come crashing down with the dawn—and if this was all he had of her he was taking it. Taking it all.

Spooned into the delicate delineation of her back, with her soft skin whispering over his chest, he toyed with a lock of her ruby-red hair; corkscrewing a silken strand and watching it bounce like a loaded spring.

Aw, man, he had it bad. Knew she could steal his heart as it lay vulnerable outside his chest.

Something close to panic clutched his throat and he felt driven to lighten the mood, to lift the portentous silence, fall back on the charm that never failed to smother his emotions.

'I do find you in the most delicious compromising positions, Miss Scott,' he said, his voice a decadent purr as he kissed the graceful slope of her shoulder.

She groaned. 'Don't remind me.'

'You never did tell me why you broke into my trailer through the bathroom window four years ago.'

'I...I didn't know it was your trailer! It was identical to ours. It was pitch-black, I was tired, I'd just come back from London and my key wouldn't work.'

He trailed one fingertip down her upper arm and a quiver took hold of her svelte body, ruining the indignant tone she was aiming for. He smiled mischievously.

'Yeah, whatever. You just wanted to see me in the shower.'

'I didn't even know you!'

'Hey, no need for panty-twisting. On the scale of women trying to get my attention it veered towards the tame side. It was quite the introduction. I was the perfect gentleman too—caught you before you went splat on the floor.'

'*Gentleman*? You said my boots were the sexiest things you'd ever seen and if I wanted your body I had to leave them on!'

'Ohh, yeah! Go get them and I'll prove how serious I was.'

He'd been deadly serious—until he'd locked onto that stunning gaze of hers and his world had tipped upside down. Then his only thought had been how quickly he could shove her back out through the window and transport her to another planet. Which didn't quite explain why, at this moment, she was gloriously naked in his bed.

She coughed out an incredulous laugh. 'You're insatiable.'

'Only for you,' he said. Meaning it. She'd ruined him. No other woman in the world seemed real any more—just mere cheap imitations that might as well not exist.

Crap, he was in big trouble here. And when she canted her head and peeked up at him, brow nipped, gauging his sincerity, his stomach hollowed out.

This was getting too deep. He knew it. She knew it. He could tell by the way she turned away, scissored her legs out of the silk sheets and moved to perch on the edge of the bed.

'I should go. Let you get some sleep. You have to race in the morning and...'

And he didn't care, he realised. He would rather she stayed. Which was scarier still.

'Serena—'

That was when he saw it, in the ivory glow of the moon shimmering over her back. Artwork, moving across the base of her spine.

'Aw, baby' he growled. 'That is one hot splay of ink.'

Her spine flexed as she stiffened for a beat, then she murmured, 'Thought you might like it.'

With one touch her body softened and he traced the design with the tip of his finger, skimmed the garland of tiny pink and purple flowers outlined in black, curling into a circle to form the traditional peace symbol and then swooping outward in an elegant trail to each side of her back. But it was the small butterflies at either side, fluttering at her hip bones as if poised to fly from their captivity, that cinched his chest.

'It's beautiful, Serena.'

Intuition told him there was more to this than met the eye, but before he could pry she said, 'Finn…?' with such vulnerability that he was powerless to do anything but nuzzle closer and worship the ink with lush, moist kisses, smoothing his hands over every inch of skin he could reach, caressing her, loving her.

Until she tumbled into his arms and he made love to a woman for the very first time. Took them both soaring to the euphoric heights of nirvana, where life as he knew it ceased to exist.

When reality knocked at the temporal door of his mind Finn was half sprawled over her, one leg flung over her thighs, one arm tucked around her waist, his head cushioned on her soft breasts. Even in slumber she cradled him close, her affectionate fingers toying with and stroking his hair.

Longing nearly shattered him.

It was like coming home. An indefinable precious feeling of utter peace he wanted to wake to every morning. She felt perfect in his arms. All soft, warm woman. *His* woman.

He wasn't letting her go. He was *never* letting her go. He—

He froze. Something foreign slammed into his chest as reality hit and his life skewed dangerously.

No. No, she could never be his, he told himself, fighting the crush of what felt suspiciously like panic. Fear. He had no choice but to let her go. Watch her walk away, powerless, as her endearing affection hardened to hate.

This was what he'd been afraid of all along, he realised. Losing himself. Relinquishing his hold on the reins of his life, allowing his emotions to rule until he wanted it all. Needed a woman he could never have.

Gingerly he eased back and cool air slapped his sweat-drenched body with lucidity.

It was all for the best, right? Yes. Absolutely. He'd only cause her pain in the end, with his uncanny knack of hurting people. Eventually he'd let her down as he had Eva. He didn't trust himself not to.

Yeah, he shouldn't forget the notion that he was some kind of bad luck charm for those he cared for. Had he been able to save his mother? Tom? No. Well he'd be damned if he took Serena down too.

Curling up on her side, Serena snuggled into the pillow, subconsciously reached for him. His heart kicked with the demand to pull her into his arms. Hold her tight. Adore her. Never let her go…

Finn launched off the bed, stumbled to the bathroom and with a quick flick of his wrist at the controls turned the shower spray to fast, hard and mind-numbingly cold.

There he stood, hands braced on the sandstone tiles, head bowed, while the water pounded his scalp and shoulders and he commanded his heart to stop beating for her. He shoved common sense down his throat until he nigh on choked on it, oblivious to time or place… Until bright light slashed through the room and a sharp, pained cry rent the air—

'Oh, my God, Finn! Your back. Baby, your back.'

Slam went his heart against the wall of his chest and he cursed inwardly. How could he have forgotten even for a moment? *Idiot*. This was what she did to him—banished thought until he operated like a loose cannon. Out of control. He hadn't wanted her seeing him like this, finding out this way.

Drenching his lungs with fortifying air, he commanded his heart to calm and relished the sanity that rained over him, bringing with it relief. So much relief it punctured his nape and made his head tip back until he stared at the whitewash on the ceiling.

It was over.

Now she'd loathe him. Just as he deserved. Hate him. Run. Far, far away from him. Before he hurt her, ruined her life beyond repair.

Slowly, inexorably, he allowed the cold to bleed into his veins, into his soul, until he was frozen to his emotional core. Braced for the highway to hell.

CHAPTER THIRTEEN

SCARS. SCARS ALL over his back. And she was shaking from head to foot, going all female crazy on him, her heart a searing fireball, acidic tears splashing the backs of her eyes—which was the wake-up call she needed to give herself a good shake. Careening into an emotional abyss wouldn't help anyone here, least of all him. But—*oh, God*—she could virtually feel his pain, as if the sensations of brutality had been exhumed from the Stygian depths of her memories. And her heart ached. *Ached* for him.

Serena snatched a thick warm towel from the rail, shut the water off and stepped behind the curved glass screen, striving to avert her gaze and failing miserably.

'You've been beaten,' she breathed, her throat clotted with anger and grief, because although time had endeavoured to heal him he'd been whipped and burned and— *Oh, my God*... 'When, Finn? When? How? Why?'

How could she not have known? Why hadn't he told her?

His torso swelled on a deep inhalation before his shoulders hardened to steel and he turned with excruciating slowness. Dark blond hair plastered his brow, falling into glacier-blue eyes as cold as the frigid droplets that clung to his naked skin.

A shiver shook her spine. Never had she seen him cold. Wouldn't have thought it possible from the man who beguiled the masses with his stunning smile and charismatic charm. It was the equivalent of dunking her in the Arctic.

'Singapore.'

One word, delivered in a voice so cool and sharp she knew it was just the tip of an iceberg.

'S...Singapore?' The floor tilted and her arm shot out to brace her weight; her palm slipped on a cool trickle of condensation as her brain was flooded with implications.

'Yes,' he said, devoid of emotion as he snagged the towel from her hand and wrapped it around his lean hips.

Singapore.

'Tell me...this has nothing to do with Tom,' she said, her voice barely audible as her mind whirled faster than the room. 'Tell me there's no connection. Because that would mean—'

Oh, no. Please, no.

'I've lied to you all along,' he admitted. Detached. Hateful.

Serena closed her eyes. 'I...I trusted you.'

She waited for the hot, pungent wash of anger and anguish to weave hotly through her veins, but all she kept envisaging were those barbaric scars marring his golden skin and all she felt was numb.

'No, you didn't, Serena. And if you were starting to it was against your better judgement, I'm sure.'

He was right, of course. She hadn't trusted him at all in the beginning. Amazing what the onslaught of sexual attraction could achieve. Gradually blinding her until a thick, dense veil of molten desire shrouded her eyes to what she'd suspected all along.

The truth she'd been waiting for all these months.

The truth this man had told her didn't exist.

Damn him. And damn her cursed heart too. How could she have been so naïve?

'I want the truth, Finn. And don't you dare lie to me again.'

'Put something on,' he ordered.

That chilly tone simultaneously made her shiver and feel bemused. Why was he being this way? So closed off. Aloof. Poles apart from the adoring, affectionate man she'd given her body to—as if he simply didn't care any more. The snaking suspicion that he never truly had coiled in her chest, constricting her lungs until her breath hissed past her throat.

No, wait. She would not think the worst of him again—not until she'd heard him out. There could be a perfectly good explanation for all this. Right? *Oh, God.*

'Here.'

He unhooked a white robe from the back of the door and she shoved her arms into the soft cotton, then tied the sash and nipped the lapels at her throat.

With an austere jerk of his head he motioned her towards the lounge area, where two cushy emerald-green armchairs sat at angles on either side of the marble fireplace. 'Have a seat. I just need a minute to dress.'

'I'd rather stand,' she said, altogether too jittery, needing the succulent warmth of the honey-coloured carpet brushing the soles of her feet to ground her somehow.

Every second was an endless stretch as her brain worked overtime. Then he reappeared, wearing a black T-shirt, low-slung jeans and a hardened façade that made her stomach tighten in response.

Just who *was* this man?

No daredevil swagger this night.

Gait stiff, body taut, he braced his forearm on the marble mantel and stared into the lifeless grate.

'We were taken from a private club in Singapore after our drinks were drugged. Out cold for about twelve hours. We woke up in an old wartime holding cell near the port.'

'You were...' *Breathe, Serena, breathe.* 'Taken? Like, for ransom?'

'Thirty million was the starting bid.'

Down she went, collapsing onto the nearest chair, while her thoughts tripped over one another. But when his meaning hit and collided with the imagery of his horrific scars the juxtaposition struck like a bolt of lightning and she began to shake. All over.

'Was...was Tom beaten like that?'

The hand at his hip balled into a tight fist and his legs flexed as he forced himself into the ground. For a split second she allowed herself the fantasy that he wanted to come to her, hold her.

'No,' he said, as black and hard as the mound of coal he was fixated on. 'He didn't suffer in that way.' Glancing up, he met her eyes, and for the first time she saw a frisson of emotion warm those ice-blue depths—sincerity. 'That's the absolute truth. So don't even picture it in your head. Didn't happen. Promise me you will remember that.'

She frowned, unsure what to believe. 'I don't understand. How come he wasn't touched when you were? It doesn't make sense.'

He held still, willing her to trust him—at least in this. It was important to him, she realised.

'Let's just say they had far more interest in me.'

What? Even that failed to compute. Why would criminals be partial to Finn—?

Air hit the back of her throat, where a great lump began to swell, and she bit down on her lips.

Panic flitted across his face. 'Hey, Serena, are you listening to me? Did you hear what I said?'

She swallowed thickly. 'You *made* them more interested in you.' He had an astonishing flair for it after all. 'You took the brunt of it, didn't you?' she asked, a little bit shocked, a whole lot awed.

Yet he merely hitched one shoulder in blatant insouciance as if it were nothing. *Nothing?* What? Did he think he'd deserved it, or something?

Switzerland... Sick...

'You were beaten so brutally that you spent months recovering in Switzerland, didn't you?' *In hiding.* 'And that is why you didn't come to Tom's funeral.' While she'd cursed and berated him, blind to it all.

'Yes,' he admitted.

Curse her throbbing heart, because the thought of him being alone, broken and torn, all that time in such pain...

His cerulean-blue eyes darkened dangerously as they narrowed on her face. 'Do not look at me with pity, Serena. I took your brother into that club. A club I knew was notorious. He *trusted* me.' Anger spewed from him, driven by the self-loathing that contorted his face. 'I led him into that hellhole and don't you forget it!'

Slapped with his fury, she rocked where she sat. Then she prompted her lungs to function properly as she sieved and scrutinised his way of thinking, only to recall their conversation on a harbour many moons ago.

'You didn't lead him, Finn. It was his choice. *His* choice. Back at Monaco you told me I wasn't responsible for the decisions he made. That I shouldn't feel guilt because he wouldn't want that. Are you going to tell me you lied about that too?'

Please don't. Because I'm already confused, wondering what has been real, and I'm afraid that every word from your mouth has been a lie.

'No, but—' His brow crunched for a beat. 'This is different.' Pushing off the mantel, he swung away and began to pace. 'I came out alive. He didn't.'

Now, *that* was a fact she couldn't dispute. To think that all this time she'd never known, had been kept in the dark—

'My God, Finn, did he even drown at all? What happened to him?'

Flinging himself down onto the opposite chair, he let the clasped ball of his white-knuckled hands dangle in the space between his open legs and met her gaze.

'Long story short: it was a get-rich-quick scheme run by some highly intelligent brains who had a perverted opinion of hospitality.'

He grimaced, as if the memories tasted vile on his tongue, and her heart thrashed for him.

'After about four days the bartering began, and on the fifth day they brought Tom in. Threatened him. Gave me the choice to do him over or they would.' A mirthless huff burst past his lips. 'The kid always looked at me like I was some kind of hero and there I was, inclined to knock him unconscious rather than allow the guards to maul him.'

The space behind her ribs inflated with his pain and her stomach gave a sickening twist. Because it was sick. Twisted. Perverted. 'Oh, Finn.' What a decision to have to make. It must have been torture for him—for them both.

'They knew fine and well he was my weakness, and I couldn't stand the lack of control.' With a rueful shake of his head he glanced towards the wide double doors leading to the balcony, where the strokes of dawn painted the sky in amber and gold. As if he searched for peace and beauty in the midst of such horror. 'To wrench some of it back I threw more money in the pot, and within two hours sixty million had been transferred from my Swiss bank account into one on the Cayman Islands.'

Self-derision twisted his full lips and her back crushed the downy cushions as she braced herself.

'It was a long shot, so I wasn't particularly surprised when two days later we were moved to an abandoned liner off the coast. I knew then we weren't getting out of there alive.' He jabbed his fingers through his hair. 'Tom was getting weak, losing his will. I got desperate. Bribed one of the guards to get him out. He could only take one of us for risk of getting caught. I didn't bother telling Tom. Didn't want him objecting to leaving me behind. He was an honourable kid.'

His voice cracked and the fissure streaked through her heart.

'Courageous too. You'd have been proud of him, Serena.'

Her trembling fingers slapped over her mouth to capture the sob that gathered force in her chest and burned the base of her throat. After all they'd been through together she was *not* going to break in front of Finn. She was not going to be weak.

'Next night, as planned, the guard smuggled him out. Whether he was anxious to get back before his absence was noticed or whether there was a struggle, I don't know, but he decided to drop him close to the port...'

His devastating gaze locked on hers, filled with pain, such heart-wrenching pain, that she sank her blunt nails into her palms, trying to stay motionless...

'So he could swim the half-mile to the shore.'

'Oh, no,' she breathed.

'Serena, I didn't know—or I would've warned the guard. I didn't know he could barely swim and I sent him to his death.'

The walls of her chest clamped vice-like as she shook with the effort not to crack. She had to stay strong for both of them. It was all so tragic. So heartbreakingly unfair.

Swallowing thickly, she prayed her voice wouldn't rupture. 'You couldn't have known unless he'd told you. He was really embarrassed about it.'

He'd been petrified of deep water too, but there was no way she was telling Finn that; he had enough to carry on his conscience. *Oh, Tom, I'm so sorry I wasn't there for you.*

Back she went, hurtling towards the emotional precipice, her eyes pooling with moisture. God, how did she make them stop? Averting her face, she blinked rapidly as her defences began to splinter.

Apparently she wasn't the only one, because in a flash Finn was striding across the floor and plunging to his knees in front of her. *Her* Finn.

Moving in between her legs, he brushed a lock of hair from her temple in a tender graze and pressed his lips to her cheek. 'I'm sorry. I'm sorry. So sorry I took him from you.'

The sound of his voice, so broken and desolate, slapped some strength into her spine and she cupped his face with a firm, warm touch and hardened her voice.

'You didn't take him from me. *They* took him from me. It was not your fault.'

'How can you say that? I am the sole reason he is gone. They wanted my money, Serena.'

'No. If that were true they would have taken just you. They saw an opportunity and they took it. Don't you see? You were both in the wrong place at the wrong time.'

His jaw tight enough to crack a filling, he frowned deeply. 'I sent him out there.'

'You were trying to save his life. It was a tragedy borne from their actions, not yours.'

A sense of *déjà vu* flirted with her mind. How many times had someone said that to *her* after the attack? Yet had she ever truly believed them? No. Since Finn had come into her world she'd realised her life was built on shaky foundations and she'd never truly moved on.

She didn't want that for him. To be trapped in some kind of stasis, haunted by the past.

She swept his damp hair back from his brow and his eyelids grew heavy. 'This is going to ruin you, Finn. This guilt that is driving you. I want it to stop. Tom wouldn't want this.'

Finn's frustration ignited and he jerked from her grasp, bolted to his feet and veered away from her. 'That's your emotions talking after sharing a bed with a born seducer. Sooner or later it will pass and you'll blame me—hate me as you should.'

'I'll never hate you, Finn. Ever. Nor will I blame you. You need to accept that.'

For an infinitesimal moment he simply stared at her. His expression was pinched with pain, but it was the intense flare in his cerulean eyes that lifted her spirits. Hope was reflected there…faith that slowly diminished as if the lights were going out in his soul.

'Serena, don't you see what you're doing? You're allowing good sex to drive your emotions and cloud your judgement. Already you've forgotten that I've lied to you for months.'

Unwilling even to consider how easily incredible sex could be downgraded to 'good' within hours—she wasn't ready for that reality just yet—she felt a burst of unease fire through her stomach. Nothing had been forgotten. But some sixth sense beat an ominous warning that his answers would never suffice. Only hurt. Badly.

Ignoring the tumultuous roil inside her, she lifted her chin. 'First off, don't speak to me like I'm some female and I don't know my own mind. I promise you it's not misted by desire up there. But maybe now is a good time to tell me why. Why you lied to me. Why, almost a year later, I would still be in the dark if I hadn't walked in on you tonight.'

The more she considered it, the more bewildered she became. And, if she were honest, there was a good dose of humiliation in there at her naïvety too. Once again she'd fallen into the hands of deceit, and the fact that those hands belonged to Finn was a bitter pill to swallow.

Finn flung the double doors wide, inviting the bite of British morning air to swirl around her ankles. Then he braced his hands on the overhead frame and looked out onto the green acreage surrounding the Country Club, the golden wash of dawn warming his pale complexion.

'Fact is Tom's drowning ruffled the rogue guard and he tipped off the Singapore police to my whereabouts.'

It wasn't difficult to comprehend the acrid tinge to his dark voice—Tom's death had likely saved Finn from a worse fate and *that* was anathema to him.

'The brains behind the operation disappeared—the ransom too, through laundering. There have been a few leads but it's slow going. We didn't want you in any danger, getting caught up in the ongoing investigation. I suggested you were told the same story as everyone else. Your dad agreed. He didn't want you hurting any more than you already were.'

'Wow, tough love must have gone by the wayside that day.' Then again, Michael Scott couldn't handle her at the best of times. Showing his love didn't come naturally or easily.

'Plus,' he began warily, his arms plunging to his sides, 'I kind of promised Tom I would look out for you. Make sure you didn't go looking for blood.'

The rush of anger drained away as quickly as it had come, leaving a numb sensation bleeding into every inch of her. Yeah, that was exactly what Tom would have done. But that wasn't the reason she crossed her arms over her chest to calm the dark storm brewing behind her ribs.

'Would this promise to look out for me be the reason you offered to be my friend weeks ago?' *Say no. Say no.*

Keeping his gaze averted, he shoved his hands into deep denim pockets. 'You could say that, yes.'

Whack. His words punched her midriff, making her flinch. 'That's very...*noble* of you, Finn.' Was that really her voice? That cracked melody of sarcasm and bitterness? A portrayal of a heart betrayed.

There she'd been, blissfully ignorant, revelling in the idea that he wanted to spend time with her. God, she'd even luxuriated in the way his guilt had eased, making him more content—had rejoiced in the sanguine expectation that *she* was the reason for it. And all the while he'd been keeping a promise. While she could grasp his need to, as far as she was concerned as soon as their friendship had developed into more they'd gone way beyond that. Why not just tell her before they slept together? It felt like dishonesty.

'You know what really gets to me?' she said, pleading with her strength not to abandon her now. 'Every day you omitted to tell me the truth, and every night I came closer to...' *To falling for you.* 'To trusting you. To sharing your bed. How could you do that, Finn? Lie with me...' *Make love to me with such intensity.* 'While keeping something so huge, so important to me a secret?' *Give me a good reason, please.*

When he finally turned to face her, one corner of his

mouth lifted ruefully. 'I've never pretended to be a saint, Serena. The sinner in me simply couldn't resist you.'

Their eyes caught…held…and she told herself she was misreading the fierce fervour in his gaze. That all along she'd imagined the emotional pull. If he'd felt more for her he would have had the decency to tell her the truth well before he'd taken her body. *What had you been secretly hoping for, Serena? That he was falling like you were? You're a fool.*

'I warned you, baby. That you were making the biggest mistake of your life.'

Yes, he had. *'So be it,'* she'd said, and here she was.

The cyclone of torment in her chest picked up pace and the strain of keeping her head high wrought a deep throb in the muscle of her nape.

It was a foolish heart and a fledgling female pride that spoke. 'Tell me something, Finn. Is every woman your *baby* too?' *Please say no.* In truth, she wished the words right back. Didn't want to hear she'd meant nothing to him. A silly, stupid girly part of her wanted to keep hoping she'd been different from all the others. Special in some way. As unique as he'd frequently told her.

A muscle ticked in his jaw and his brow pinched for one, two, three beats of her thundering heart. Then he hitched one broad shoulder in insouciance.

'Naturally.'

And just like that her stomach hollowed and she felt emptier than she ever had before.

'Naturally,' she repeated, with all the blasé indifference she could muster as she fought the anguished throb of her body.

Lashes weighted, she allowed them to fall until he disappeared.

Serena Scott—one of many. Like all the nameless faces that had wandered through his life. Her father's too. A woman she'd sworn she'd never become.

Anger hit her like an explosion of fire. At him, yes, but

equally at herself. For opening up once again. Being susceptible, vulnerable to a man.

Why did unlocking your heart, daring to dream, have to hurt so much? Have to end in crushing heartbreak and pain? There she'd been, lying blissfully in his arms, believing every word from his lips. Sure he was coming to feel more for her, that she was enough to hold his attention. Teasing her mind's eye with more blissful nights, more exciting wonderful days. A future.

Enough.

On a long sigh she opened her eyes. Literally and figuratively.

Thank God she'd discovered the truth before she'd fallen in love with him. It was petrifying to think how close she'd come to doing just that.

'Serena?'

That deep voice, now perturbed, laced with concern, brought her attention back to where he stood.

Ah. Worried he'd hurt her, was he? Well, admittedly she'd love to rail and scream at him, but the little pride she had left was too precious. When she walked out of this suite it would be with her head high and dignity roiling inside her.

In fairness, he'd never pretended to be honourable with regards to women, and he'd warned her over and over. It was hardly his fault she'd strived to be a player, convinced she knew the rules, adamant that she'd come out unscathed. Instead she'd believed every expertly practised word. Misread every artful amorous touch.

How could she have been so naïve? Again! Lesson learned.

Moreover, right now the man teetered on the edge of a black abyss and she refused to be the one to push him over— she'd vacationed in hell before, and the view wasn't pretty.

Fear. Flashbacks. Nightmares. Menace surrounding you, burrowing into your soul. It didn't take a genius to figure out his erratic behaviour on and off the track in the last few months now either. Even his own survival was anathema to him. He wished he'd died too. Or more likely instead of Tom.

Come to think of it—dread curdled with her pique, making her stomach churn violently—it was entirely plausible that he was suffering from some kind of survivor's guilt. She'd read about that somewhere—probably a pamphlet in some clinic. And if that were true he needed help.

Somewhat reluctant to bathe in those beautiful eyes, she met them regardless. 'Forget about you and me. We both knew it was just sex and now it's over.' His throat convulsed but she was determined not to read anything into it. Bad enough that she'd imagined he flinched. 'I'll never be ashes in your wake, Finn. You know me better than that.'

'Good. That's good.' Relief soothed his taut features and he padded out onto the balcony and gripped the iron railing—white knuckles stark over black.

Why could she still feel his pain as if it was a living, breathing entity inside her, melding with her own? As if they were bonded somehow? Heavens, it *hurt*.

Serena glanced at the door leading to her suite and escape beckoned like an old friend. Her feet itched to run until she was too exhausted to feel anything. 'I should go,' she said abruptly. 'We both need some sleep.' If she felt battered and bruised from riding an emotional roller coaster he had to feel just as bad.

Which was likely why she couldn't move. Found herself ensnared in a vicious primal pull. Honestly, it was like turning her back on a wounded animal. She couldn't do it. Despite everything, she couldn't leave without trying one last time.

The problem was no matter what she said no words were going to convince him he wasn't to blame.

Frustration ate at her.

Leaving her angry aching heart indoors, she followed him onto the balcony. A crazy notion stirred up a hornets' nest inside her even as she winced at the risk, at how he'd react, and wondered if she could even manage it without shattering.

Easy, she came up behind him. 'Don't get a fright,' she said softly, echoing his sentiment from the cabaret at Montreal. A night from her dreams... With deft speed she slammed the door on her reminiscing. *Focus.*

His honed frame tensed.

'Finn, it's okay.' She laid her hands on his back, as gentle and calming as if he were a skittish colt. She smoothed them around his waist, wrapped her arms about him and pressed her cheek to the soft, freshly laundered fabric of his T-shirt.

'Serena,' he choked out, muscles flexing as his grip tightened on the rail.

After a *'Shh...'* that ripped her soul, his shoulders dropped and he began to ease.

'Let me?' she asked, tiptoeing her fingers beneath the hem of his T and tentatively inching the material upwards before she pulled back.

One look at the deep white criss-cross lines that marred the centre of his back, the puckered skin between his shoulder blades, and her chest ached viciously. Tears pooled, brimmed once more, and this time she let them fall. Unable to stop the rain. Surely she owed Tom nothing less.

Boys don't cry, Serena.

Well, this *girl* did.

Silent tears seared her swollen throat—for him, for Tom—as she leaned forward and tenderly kissed his back once, twice, before she rubbed her cheek against him gingerly, affectionately.

'Thank you,' she whispered, her voice as raw as her heart. 'Thank you for making his last days bearable. For protecting him for me. For trying to save his life.'

'Serena...' he breathed, almost longingly, as his big body trembled.

'Please don't let his death be for nothing. You have your entire life ahead of you. He'd want you to live it.'

Torso convulsing, he hung his head.

Enough. No more. It was all over now.

Serena let the fabric fall and trailed her fingers down his sides in goodbye. Then she turned and walked away with her head held high. Ready to fight another day.

CHAPTER FOURTEEN

THE SILVERSTONE CIRCUIT was an almighty roar and the chant of Finn's name from his fiercest homeland supporters rang in his ears as he stepped off the winner's podium with a farewell wave and shot through the crowd. He hadn't seen Serena since dawn, and the perpetual torment from his heart and conscience had him hurtling towards insanity.

He had to see her. Check she was okay. In truth he'd swear he could feel her pain, and his arms ached to hold her—hell, his entire body ached for her. Had done since the moment she'd vanished from his suite. Since she'd ripped his heart out by pleading with him to live his life. The way she'd touched him so affectionately, forgivingly, would stay with him always.

It had taken every ounce of strength he possessed to keep his hands fisted on the iron rail, not to turn around and reach for her. But no matter how hard he tried he couldn't believe for one second that she could forgive him. He was convinced the only reason she hadn't looked at him with hate in her eyes was because of the incredible night they'd shared. Or maybe he'd taken Tom's place in her world. A rebounding kind of need.

Eventually, when she realised that, she'd walk away—and he'd be in so deep it would kill him. He'd lose her. Just as he lost everyone he cared for. It was inevitable.

So, while it had torn him apart to sever their connection, he knew it was for the best. For both of them.

In and out of the Scott Lansing garage he went—his guts twisting at the barren space—before he jogged round to the back of the pits, where a myriad of luxurious motor homes were parked.

Smooth tarmac gave way to the crunch of gravel beneath his boots and dark shadows crawled eerily over the dirt, up over the high-gloss black paintwork of the fleet, as if thick, ominous clouds slowly usurped the sun. He shuddered…

Then crashed to a halt.

There stood Michael Scott, at the bottom of the steps to Finn's motor home, wearing an expression that weakened his knees.

Skin clammy, he clutched at his chest, felt the thrash of his heart against his palm. 'Wha…what's happened?' *No, please God no. Please let her be okay.*

'What you've got to understand about Serena, my boy, is that when her emotions get too big for her she runs. Always has, since she was a little girl.' Regret deepened his voice. 'Don't suppose it helped that she never had a mother in her life. I take it you told her everything?'

Finn tried to swallow as relief and heartache vied for space behind his ribs. She'd left him. 'Yes. Everything.' Then he remembered the phone call he'd taken before the race. 'The police in Singapore have just made an arrest.'

The older man took one step forward and laid a heavy hand on Finn's shoulder. 'Good. Now we'll get some justice. I know you tried to do right by my son.'

Finn locked on to Mick's sincere gaze, desperate to believe him.

'Serena must know it too, considering all your body parts are intact. Time to move on, Finn. Let it go.'

Maybe he nodded; he was too numb to be sure.

'Can't guarantee she'll come back in a hurry. Last time,

after the funeral, she was away months. She's not going to London. I know that much. But she did leave you this.'

Michael passed him a white envelope, with Finn's name a messy scrawl across the front, then patted his shoulder and sidestepped to walk past.

'By the way, she watched the race—asked me to say you were awesome out there and that you'll know what she means.'

A ghost of a smile touched his lips. Finally the woman uttered the words he'd tried to tease out of her for months. *Aw, man*, was it any wonder he adored her?

'Yeah, I do. Thanks, Mick.'

Bones weighted with dread, he plonked down on the top rung of his steps and thumbed the sticky flap of the envelope. Patience wasn't his strong suit and after two seconds he tore it apart, until her letter was in his hands.

On a long exhale he unfolded the crisp sheet and stared for a long moment, watching a fine drizzle dust the page.

Despite the chaotic churning of emotions inside him, her messy handwriting brought another smile to his lips. He missed her already.

Dear Finn,
I've never been one for goodbyes, but in the last few weeks you've helped me say another kind of goodbye—to Tom, so I could lay him to rest. Despite how our friendship came about you've been a friend to me in many ways, shown me much about my life, and I'd like to return the favour. So I'm calling in the wish you owe me.

Now, I know what you're thinking: my logic is a bit backward—how can my favour be your wish? But hear me out, okay?

It dawned on me earlier, when I left, that it doesn't matter if you never believe my word or believe in my forgiveness. What truly matters is that you learn to forgive yourself. Otherwise, and trust me when I say this, you'll never truly move on. Which is why I'm about to tell you something very few people know and I'm asking you to keep it close to your chest.

Long story short, as you would say, my first naïve crush was with one of Tom's friends. One who quickly turned hostile. And for a long time I blamed myself for what happened afterwards.

I should probably explain that I was young, with no women around, and not really sure how to handle boys. I figured I'd rather be one of them, and that was fine until I came to that awkward age where they began to treat me differently. Anyway, I was fourteen, and let's just say I liked this much older boy—or should I say man? He was Tom's age: nineteen.

He weaved his web, spun his lies, told me anything and everything—'I want you, Serena, I love you. Come meet me, Serena, I won't hurt you'—until I fell for him. I started to dress up—girly stuff—flirted a little, sneaked out with him, but I wasn't prepared for what came back at me.

Turns out 'no' didn't mean no with him.

The first time he tried to force me I managed to get away, and he persuaded me not to tell Tom or he would hurt him. Foolish, I know, but I think it's easy to believe anything at that age. Spider-Man comes to mind...

Anyway, he began to follow me, watch me from the shadows, and I was frightened for a long time. Then one night, during a huge party downstairs, he came up to my bedroom. He'd been drinking. He overpowered me. I was beaten up pretty bad, among other things, and I'm sure he would've gone all the way if Tom hadn't come in.

There was a huge fight and Tom got seriously

hurt—we thought he'd never drive again—but he pulled through. Of course he blamed himself for not reading the signs sooner, so you see I'm not surprised he asked you to watch out for me. He became very protective.

I saw a counsellor for many months and she tried to help me past it. In many ways she did. She made me accept that I didn't ask for it. I didn't deserve to be beaten. She certainly helped me to stand tall, but in reality I never truly moved on. I didn't completely let go of the blame. Of the thought that if I'd been braver, stronger, told someone sooner, Tom's health and career wouldn't have hung in the balance for so long.

I didn't let go of the idea that my behaviour was at fault. Because if I had I wouldn't have suppressed the woman I am inside.

You've shown me that, Finn. Helped me see so many things. But watching you struggle this morning I realised I'm still searching for peace.

Choices.

I'm choosing to let go, Finn. To forgive myself. I wish you would too.

At the bottom of this note is the number of the counsellor I saw, and my wish is that you go and see her, even if it's just the once. She can help you if you'll let her. It's strange, but I used to resent my dad for sending me—just thought he was palming me off on someone else. But I can see now. He was too close to the situation. Too emotionally involved. Which is why I think you need to speak to someone who isn't personally connected, you know?

You're a survivor. We both are. Let's make the most of this life we have. If not for us, for Tom.

Well, that's it, I guess. Take care of yourself and try not to crash my car, okay? Look after her. She

may be a fiery bolt of lightning with a tough outer shell but underneath...she's still just a girl.
Serena.

The paper fluttered to the dirt as Finn leaned his elbows on his knees and pressed the heels of his hands to his eyes. Moisture smothered his palms as his shoulders shook in the suffocating silence.

Underneath...she's still just a girl.

Idiot. He was such an idiot. He hadn't just hurt her; he'd caused more damage than he'd ever dreamed possible.

Was it any wonder she'd stifled her femininity? And what had he done? Given her confidence, told her she was unique in every way, encouraged her to open up to him. And in the next breath, fuelled by his own fears, he'd insinuated that she was just another good-time girl who meant nothing to him, expecting her to take it like the tough cookie she was—and succeeded in stripping her raw. Forgetting for one moment that *underneath she's still just a girl*. One who'd been tampered with when she'd been merely fourteen years old.

Against all the odds, no matter what life threw at her, she came out fighting.

'You have no idea how proud I am of you,' he murmured, to no one but himself, wishing she was here and he could hold her. 'How brave and beautiful and strong and amazing you are to me.'

Finn rubbed his eyes, then clawed down his face.

Why did he keep hurting people? He knew not to let his emotions engage. Knew he was like a loose cannon, made bad choices. He'd left Eva to suffer, sent Tom to his death. Now he'd hurt Serena too.

What was more she'd been betrayed barely out of adolescence and now Finn had done it a second time. She'd never trust him again—not in a million years.

Any last vestige of hope died in his soul as she disappeared with his heart.

He needed more than some shrink. He needed a miracle. One perfectly beautiful little miracle.

Every cell in his body screamed for him to go and find her, make it all better somehow. But what would he say? *I'm sorry* didn't sound anywhere near what she deserved. And that was all he had to offer. Apart from more hurt in the long run. He was messed up and he knew it. He also knew he was far better off alone.

He just had to hope she found the peace and happiness she deserved.

As for him, he had a wish to take care of.

He owed his girl nothing less.

CHAPTER FIFTEEN

Five weeks and two days later...

THE MONZA POST-RACE party was the epitome of Italian style and elegance, held in the vast courtyard of a lavish hotel. But the midnight sky, twinkling with diamanté brilliance, acted as the perfect ceiling and only served to remind Serena of a magnificent tent in Montreal.

Champagne spurted from a towering ice sculpture like an ivory waterfall, to pool and froth at the base. But the bubbly effervescence only struck a chord of the Silverstone Ball.

Closing her eyes momentarily, she breathed in the sweet calming scent of the wisteria draping the balconies overhead and turned to her dad. 'I have no idea how you talked me into this. I've only been back a few hours. I could be in my PJs, eating nachos and watching a movie right now.'

Instead she was a nausea-inducing swarm of anticipation in killer heels, trying to perfect a smile that said she was having a ball. All the while wondering if he would come, who he would bring, what she would say to him. So much for the blasé *oh-hi-how-are-you?* she'd been hoping for at tomorrow's meeting.

'Yes, well, frankly I was getting sick and tired of the "I *vhant* to be alone" Greta Garbo routine. I'll only let you hide for so long, Serena.'

'I wasn't trying to hide,' she hissed.

'Whatever you say, sweetheart.'

Serena sighed. She'd just wanted their first hello to be on equal ground, and she refused to think less of herself for that. Not after she'd spent weeks trying to get over the man she'd purged her soul for. Writing that letter had taken her back, splintered her defences, but the thought of him hurting, being in so much pain, had somehow outweighed her survival instincts. And if the tabloids were to be believed he was back on top form, oozing charisma with that legendary smile of his, so it was worth it to see him happy. Moving on.

True, seeing him with another woman had been…hard, but she'd needed that push to move on. Now she was just… peachy.

Which didn't really explain why the sight of her dad smiling devilishly at some curvy blonde sparked her off. 'I don't get this "variety is the spice of life" business. What exactly is so wonderful about variety when they all look the same? There's something cold about it. About them.'

She couldn't understand the appeal. Not compared to the hours of scorching bliss she'd experienced in Finn's arms— all the more intense for the way she'd felt, she was sure.

'That's the point. It doesn't mean anything. It's safe.'

'That's like going on a ghost train with your eyes shut. Going through the motions—'

'With none of the emotions. Exactly. For me, it's because I'll always love your mother. She was The One for me. All the others since were just flash and no substance. Safe. A way to ease the loneliness, I guess.'

Serena frowned up at him as the floor did a funny little tilt. When she'd been a little girl she'd often asked about her mum. He'd tried to talk about her, but as she'd got older she'd thought his struggle and avoidance meant he hadn't truly loved her. But clearly he'd loved her intensely.

A pang of bittersweet happiness eased the ache in her chest. To think it had been *her mother* who'd had the power to win his heart. It explained so much about him. She almost asked him for more, but this wasn't the time or the place. Instead she murmured, 'Never thought of it that way.'

Safe. Untouched. That suited Finn to perfection too, didn't it? The showman who wore his charming façade to veil the tortured man beneath. But, unlike her mum, Serena hadn't been enough to win his heart.

'Don't suppose you're thinking about Finn right now?'

'I'm doing nothing of the sort,' she said, casting him a dour look before she did something stupid like burst into tears. When she was supposed to be peachy!

His graphite eyes twinkled knowingly before his handsome face took on a contemplative look etched with remorse.

'I doubt I've given you much decent advice in your life. I was ill-equipped to deal with two young kids—especially you. That's something I'll always be sorry for, Serena. But when I lost her I had to…'

Her voice as raw as her throat, Serena quietly finished for him. 'Get up. Get busy. Move on.' For all their sakes.

He gave her a rueful smile. 'But let me tell you this. If you're anything like me, or all the Scotts before you, you'll get one shot at true happiness. If you think Finn's The One don't let him go without a fight.'

Serena bit her bottom lip to stop it trembling. 'I'm not interested.' It didn't matter how much she hurt, how much she wanted, she was never opening up again. 'Anyway, he's already moved on.'

'You sure about that? Because the man who came to see me yesterday, asking for some time off so he could go gallivanting to find…' he made inverted comma actions with his fingers '…"his girl" didn't look like he'd moved on to me.'

A paralysing ball of hope bounced in her chest and she swiftly batted it away. No more foolish daydreaming. 'He has "girls" on every continent. He's moved on, I'm telling you.'

'Positive? Because that same guy, who's just walked through the archway, clapped eyes on you and looks like he's been hit with a semi-truck, is on his way over.'

'Oh, my life.' She wasn't ready—nowhere near ready.

'So you might want to get rid of that deer-in-the-headlights look and bear in mind another of Garbo's sayings.'

Huh? 'Which is?'

'Anyone who has a continuous smile on his face conceals a toughness that is almost frightening.'

'And why should that affect me?'

'No smile tonight. I get the feeling the shackles are off. I hope you're ready for this sweetheart.'

Right now the only thing she was ready for was to launch herself over the twelve-foot stone wall encircling the courtyard. She would have done if she hadn't been wandering around Europe aimlessly for the last month, only to find herself in some café in Paris, nursing a lacklustre cappuccino and the realisation that it didn't matter how far she ran, her aching heart still lay inside her chest and the memories lingered. Peace was nowhere to be found and solitude just made the emptiness deeper. She had to face him. Prove to herself she was over him.

'How far?' Appalled by her serious case of the jitters, she nailed her feet to the paved slabs. *'How far?'*

An unholy glee lit up her father's graphite eyes. 'Thirty feet and closing.'

She stifled the urge to smooth her riotous mane, insanely grateful that she'd developed a fetish for dresses, and silently chanted an endless loop of, *He will not affect me. I am completely over him. He will not affect—*

'Good evening, Miss Seraphina Scott.'

Ohh, this was not good. 'This' being the hellish swarm of fireflies lighting up her midriff in a mad, wild rush at the mere sound of his rich, sinful drawl.

More than a little woozy, she focused on turning gracefully, determined not to fall at his feet. She took a deep breath, raised her chin, then pivoted on her entirely too adventurous heels…

And went up in flames.

Doomed. She was totally and utterly doomed.

Dressed in a sharp black custom-fit suit and a thin silk tie, as if he'd just stepped off a movie set, Finn St George struck a stunning pose of insolent flair. All potent masculinity and devilish panache.

Confident as ever. A little arrogant. A whole lot bold.

Pure joy lapped at her senses—she'd missed him so much.

All that deliberately unkempt dirty blond hair was now long enough to curl over the collar of his crisp white shirt and that face... *Oh, my life*, he was so amazingly beautiful.

No depraved gleam in those cerulean blues tonight. Fantastical as the idea was, she fancied those eyes were darkly intense, savagely focused on her—a hunter stalking the ultimate prey. After weeks of living a dull, aching existence her body came alive, as if it recognised its mate, and her heart fluttered, trying to break free from the confines of her chest—

Serena slammed the cage shut and stamped on the brakes of her speeding thoughts. She would *not* misread those practised looks or his artful words. Not ever again.

He made her vulnerable to him with a click of his übertalented fingers, but demons would dance with angels before he stole more of her heart or her pride. So she dug out the biggest smile in *her* arsenal and directed her voice to super-sweet.

'Hey, Lothario, miss me?'

He wanted her now. *Now!* Fiercely. Possessively. Permanently.

When Mick Scott had texted him twenty minutes ago—*Guess whose girl is here?*—Finn hadn't trusted his luck but had tossed some clothes on nonetheless.

Now if he could just get over the shattering bodily impact of his first sight of her in weeks maybe he could think straight. As it was he had claws digging into his guts, demanding he haul her into his arms, delve into those fiery locks and slash his mouth over hers. But he reckoned since he'd messed up so catastrophically that winning her heart was going to require some finesse.

Mick eased by, patted Finn's shoulder and murmured, 'Try not to mess it up this time.'

Finn swallowed. Hard. Then told himself to forget about his boss and focus on his future. His entire life wrapped in a sensational electric-blue sheath. If she'd have him. Forgive him. Let him love her. Because that was all he had—his love.

This was it. The greatest risk of all. Because nothing came close to the potent charge of adrenaline that barrelled through his system when he was within ten feet of her. Fifty championships wouldn't even come close.

Had he missed her?

'I certainly have, Miss Scott. In fact I can easily say I've been miserable since the moment you left.'

He'd been plunged back into another hellhole, this one definitely of his own making, and he was determined to rectify that, no matter how long it took.

Granted, his admission hadn't worked the way he'd hoped—not if the stunned flash of incredulity in her sparkling grey gaze was anything to go by. Even the two feet separating them was a hot whirlpool that snap, crackled and popped with her pique.

Aw, man, maybe he was playing this all wrong. But the truth was he was nervous. *Him*. The man who flirted with death and had practically invented the word *reckless*.

'Yeah, okay, which is why you've already moved on and couldn't even spare me a phone call.'

Finn shoved his hands into his trouser pockets in case he lost his tenuous grip and just kissed the living daylights out of her. 'I wanted to give you some time to figure out how you feel. It hasn't been easy for me, Serena. It's been bloody agonising. You have no idea how many times I drove to the airport—'

'Going on holiday, were you?'

If his guts weren't writhing in a chaotic mess he would smile. That sassy mouth drove him crazy. Always had. And clearly she'd re-erected those barriers of hers. Well, he'd just have to pull them down all over again. He was fighting to win, and Finn St George always won.

'Dance with me?' He held out his hand. 'Give me your first dance—the one we didn't share back at Silverstone. Please?'

The truth was he just wanted to hold her. If he could make her remember what they were like together maybe she'd give him a chance.

She took so long to make her decision—her flawless brow nipped as she scrutinised his face—that Finn was headed for an aneurysm by the time her dubious voice, said, 'Okay. One dance.'

Before she changed her mind he grabbed her hand and practically dragged her across the courtyard—weaving around tables to a space right at the back of the dance floor, dimly lit, semi-private and leading to the gardens beyond.

Then he wrapped his hands around her dainty waist and hauled her into the tight circle of his arms to sway to an Italian love ballad. *Perfect.* She felt amazing, and when her deliciously evocative scent wrapped around his senses the ice in his veins started to melt.

'Finn,' she squeaked. 'I can hardly breathe.'

'Breathing is highly overrated. Do you really need to?' This was bliss for him and, selfish as it was, he was taking what he could while he could. *To hell with that. You're gonna win her back—she isn't leaving you again.*

'Yes, I do. I...'

She softened against him, twined her arms around his neck, and that glorious frisson of pleasure and pain jolted his heart.

When he pulled her closer still, crushing her soft breasts to his chest, a moan slipped past her lips—the kind she made when she was naked and sprawled all over him. Blood rushed to his head, making him simultaneously dizzy and hard. Not to mention astoundingly possessive—which he figured must be the reason he put his big fat foot in it.

'Have you been...seeing anyone?'

The spark of her ire crackled in the air and she stiffened in his arms.

Seriously? Could he be making a worse job of this? Where was his famed charm and charisma? Gone. Obliterated. By a five-foot-four spectacular bundle of fire.

'You've got some nerve,' she whispered furiously. 'Spouting rubbish about missing me, accusing me of seeing someone else, holding me as if you're petrified I'm going to vanish into thin air when you couldn't even last three weeks!'

Reluctantly he pulled back a touch. 'Three weeks before what?'

'Quenching your carnal appetites,' she hissed.

Finn just shook his head. 'You've lost me, beautiful.'

'Does Hungary ring any bells? Your much publicised photographs with some flashy starlet were all over the front page, so don't give me any bull crap.'

He couldn't help it. He grinned for the first time in aeons. 'You're jealous, baby.' *Aw, man,* he was definitely in with a chance. She had to feel something for him. *Had* to.

Her gorgeous face got madder still. 'I am not jealous at all. I don't give a flying fig who you dance the horizontal tango with—and don't you *dare* call me baby.'

Damn. What had possessed him to suggest she was one of many? A woman who'd witnessed her own father go through women like rice puffs.

'I never touched that actress, beautiful. It just so happens that was the only gig I went to and the woman couldn't take the hint so I left. There's been no one since you. In fact, you're the only woman I've slept with in well over a year.'

Those impossibly long sooty lashes fluttered over and over.

'Oh...'

And when she softened once more victory was a balmy rush, blooming out all over his skin.

Needing her taste in his mouth, he stole a lush, moist kiss from her lips. 'What's more I've never called anyone baby but you, Serena. And I never will. Because you're mine.' Another kiss. Then another. 'All mine. Unique in every single way—'

Suddenly she wrenched from his hold, took a step back.

'You've never called anyone baby but me, Finn? So you either lied to me then or you're lying now. Either way, I'm not interested. I...I can't do this again with you.'

The pain darkening her grey gaze punched him in the heart.

'I don't know if I can trust anything you say. I don't even know if your touch is real.'

The blood drained to his toes and a cold sweat chased it. 'You can. I'll prove it to you—

'Look, I just flew in a few hours ago and I could do with some sleep. I'll see you tomorrow, okay?'

Before he could say a word she darted off, swerving around the other couples on the dance floor.

Finn scrubbed a hand over his face. Okay. Maybe he should give her more time. The problem was, he couldn't abide her thinking she meant nothing to him. He was beginning to realise he'd made another huge mistake in not going after her sooner. But he'd been broken and he'd wanted to be whole. For her.

Oh, to hell with it.

Finn caught her up halfway to the exit, mid-throng.

'Oh, no you don't,' he said, swerving to block her path. She looked up, all flushed cheeks and wide eyes. Yet he couldn't decide if she was astonished that he'd chased her or that he was garnering them an audience.

'I'll follow you to the far ends of the earth, Serena.'

As for the onlookers—if he had to unveil the real Finn

St George to the world, show them the vulnerable man beneath to win her back, so be it.

'You're not getting away from me this time. I let you run once because I was scared, but I won't make the same mistake twice. I've made too many mistakes with you and I'll be damned if I make another.'

Finn would swear he could have heard a pin drop.

Until she breathed, 'Scared?'

'Terrified. But I'm not any more. I love you. You hear that, baby? I. Love. You.' Then, in front of hundreds of guests, he cupped her astounded face in his palms and kissed her with everything he was. With all the love in his heart and the need roiling inside him. Until neither of them could breathe and her shock gave way to desire. To the incredible bond he could feel pulling at his soul.

'Tell me you feel this,' he whispered over her lips.

'I…I feel this.'

'This has never been a lie, beautiful.'

Now came the hard part, he acknowledged. Convincing her that he meant every single word.

Dazed and disorientated, Serena suddenly found herself being lowered to her feet beneath a secluded pergola in gardens enchanted by moonlight. The wolf whistles and the roar of the crowd still rang in her ears and her lips were swollen from the wild crush of his ardour…

'Did you really just do that?' He'd kissed her in front of everyone. She was sure he had. Then he'd carried her out of there. He must have.

Sucking in air, she inhaled the minty scent of dew-drenched leaves as Finn took a step back, his eyes dark with desire, gleaming with intent.

Heat skittered through her veins. She felt hunted, and it was the most sensational, awesome, stupendous feeling in the world. If only her pesky inner voice would cease whispering doubt because she'd been seduced by his charm before.

'Finn? You do realise that come tomorrow morning the whole world will know you've just told me…' She still wasn't sure she'd heard him right. Or perhaps the truth of it was she couldn't bear to hope. To dream.

'That I love you? Good. It's about time. Then everyone will know that you're off limits.'

His voice was thick and possessive and dominating and it made her shiver. 'And you too!'

'That's the point, Serena.' Tenderly, he stroked his knuckles down her cheek. 'Because until you start believing that I'm yours and you're mine we're going nowhere. Until you believe that you're the only woman in the world for me there'll always be doubt. I've lost your trust, and I need to win it back before it's too late and I lose you forever.'

The impact of his words, his touch, his closeness, was earth-shattering. 'Just be honest with me, Finn. That's all I want.'

'And that's what you're going to get. Always.' His chest swelled as he inhaled deeply. 'I let you believe our friendship had been because of a promise I made to Tom, but that was just an excuse I gave myself to be with you. To spend time with you. Truth is, I've always wanted you, Serena. Since the first moment I saw you. And when I was in that cell thoughts of you kept me going. Looking back, if you hadn't come to Monaco and burst into my life again I would be dead right now. Because I was headed that way. I thought it should've been me. Not Tom. I wished I'd died instead. Until you.'

He cupped one side of her face and she nuzzled into his touch. Insanely grateful that he was still here.

'And that made me feel guilty, because suddenly I wanted to live and I thought I didn't deserve it. Then I was falling for you, and I wanted your love and I knew I'd never have it. You asked me a question that morning: why I'd waited and waited to tell you the truth, all the while digging myself into a deeper hole, until it was too late.'

She gave him a little nod.

'I was scared. Scared out of my mind. Of losing any chance I'd ever have with you. Try telling the woman you love that you were responsible for her brother's death.'

Her defences splintered as her heart swelled and beat so hard she feared it would burst from her chest. He loved her. He really loved her.

'Oh, Finn, why didn't you just tell me that? Why make out that I meant nothing to you? You hurt me.'

'I know, and I'm sorry. But I was messed up. Just wanted to push you away. Didn't believe for one second you could forgive me, let alone feel the same. The guilt and pain was crippling me, Serena. It wasn't until I read your letter. Oh, baby, your letter.' He wrapped one hand around her nape and gently kissed her forehead. 'I'm so sorry you went through that. But the more I read it the more I realised that for you to trust me with your past you had to genuinely believe Tom's death wasn't my fault. It gave me hope you had feelings for me too. And when I thought about what you went through... I've never met anyone like you. You're so beautiful and brave and strong. You make me want to fight. Be a survivor. For *you*.'

She could barely speak past the enormous lump in her throat. 'I was so worried about you. Once I realised you had some kind of survivor's guilt I thought, *I'm going to lose him too.* I would've done anything to prove that I didn't blame you.'

He frowned pensively and brushed his thumb across his bottom lip in that boyish way he did sometimes. Uneasy. As if he wanted to ask her something.

Serena laid her hands on his chest, felt his heart pound beneath her palm. 'Finn?' God, she wished she was better at this man-woman thing.

He seemed to think better of it and said, 'I owed my girl a wish, so I went to meet this shrink.'

Serena smiled up at him. She knew she was beaming but she was so proud of him.

'We do this thing…the shrink and me…where I have to come up with worse outcomes. She said it was really difficult, except I had an answer in a nanosecond.'

'What did you say?'

'*You* could have been there too. *You* could've been taken from me too.'

'Oh, Finn.'

'So I've started being grateful for that, you know?'

That was it. Moisture flooded her eyes.

'Aw, baby, I'm sorry. I keep making you cry.' Leaning down, he kissed away her tears, dusting his lips over her cheeks.

'Anything makes me cry these days. It's not natural!'

'Don't tell me. Boys don't cry, right? *Wrong.* I cried on and off for days when my mum died. Couldn't understand the injustice of it all. She was the most loving, self-sacrificing woman you'd ever meet. The good people always die.'

'That's not true. *You* didn't die, Finn, and every day I'm grateful for it.'

'You are?' he asked, with that pensive stare she couldn't quite grasp. There was something oddly endearingly vulnerable about him.

'Every day,' she assured him.

'Let it go, you said. Make a choice. Forgive myself. And I am. I'm trying. But the fact is it isn't only Tom I have regrets over. I've carried guilt for years over abandoning Eva when my mother was diagnosed. I was so selfish. Only thinking about the next race. But when I look back, the truth was I couldn't take watching her die. Seeing pain and heartbreak tear through my family again. I went to see Eva a couple weeks back, to say sorry. She doesn't blame me, Serena, not one bit. She said I had to let it go, that life was too short.'

'I like her already.'

'You'll love her. Her and Dante. They've just had a baby boy and he's amazing, and when I watched the three of them—a perfect little family—all I could think of was you and how I wanted that with you. How I could easily give up everything—the racing, the risks—to have that with you. Only you.'

She gripped the lapels of his jacket in order to stay upright. 'You want me and you to…have a family? A home? Like…together?'

He gave a somewhat sheepish shrug. 'Well, yeah, a family would be nice—but only if you want to. I'll be happy just to make you mine. Okay, you look horrified. It's too soon. I'm jumping the gun—'

'No. No. You're not. I've just never thought that far ahead before. What was the point of hoping for something I'd never have? Guess I didn't think I was wife material.'

That, she realised, had been the problem all along. Her insecurities. If she was honest she'd never been able to wrap her head around Finn wanting her. So it had been easy to think his every word and every touch was a lie. To avoid the pain of disillusionment. Heartache. So she'd run before she'd got too deep. Though in reality it had been too late. She'd already fallen.

And now—now she could have it all. And she felt like dancing and skipping and whooping and being really girly.

She bounced on her toes. 'What does a wife do, anyway?'

'She designs spectacular cars and wears biker boots and funky T-shirts. At least *my* wife will. I love you just the way you are, baby girl. You're The One for me.'

Ohh, here came the tears again. 'I am?'

'Sure you are.' He speared his fingers into her hair, rubbed the tip of her nose with his. 'I won't lie to you. I'm still scared of something happening to you. Of giving you my heart without ever holding yours in return. But if you give me a chance to prove my love, to prove that we could be good together, that I won't let you down, I can win it. I can win your heart. Just give me a chance.'

That shadowed gaze was back and she gasped, realising how intensely vulnerable he felt. 'Oh, Finn, I'm sorry. I'm such an idiot. You don't have to win it. It's yours. I'm madly, insanely in love with you.'

His head jerked so fast she reckoned he'd have whiplash in the morning. '*What?* That's impossible.'

'I promise you it is completely, utterly, absolutely possible.' She sank her fingers into the hair at his nape and pulled him down for a kiss. 'I literally fell for you when I tumbled in your window all those years ago. But you were a virtual carbon copy of my dad and I knew the rote. A boatload of broken hearts and weakened women in your wake. I hated you for making me vulnerable to that. But deep down I've always wanted you. Me all awkward and tomboyish, you all confident and sinfully beautiful—and, as it turns out, wild and honourable, with the ability to be completely and utterly selfless.'

'Hell, Serena, you scare the crap out of me when you say stuff like that. Then again, you always have.' He nuzzled into her neck. Breathed her in. 'Are you sure you…love me?'

'One billion per cent sure. Only you can make me feel like a woman. Only you can make me feel amazing. I love who I am with you. You're everything to me. I'm not saying it's going to be easy—life never is. We have millions of choices to make and sometimes we'll trip and fall and make mistakes. But we'll get through it all. We'll make it work. Together.'

Lifting his head, he ensnared her with a fierce, ardent gaze. 'You were designed especially for me—you know that? All my life I've taken risks on the track, but never with my heart. I never wanted to get close to anyone just to lose them. I didn't want to be touched—' He took her hand and laid it over his heart. 'In here. But you do more than touch me, Serena. You *own* me.'

Trust and love, hope and joy filled the warm air between them and she jumped into his arms. 'I'm yours. Take me home. Now. Please.'

With a sexy smile that made her insides gooey, he coaxed

her legs around his waist. 'That would be my place,' he said, with a hint of delicious possessiveness that promised a night to remember.

'That's what I said. I've never known what home felt like. What it was. I've been searching for it for years. Peace. Perfect blissful peace. I've finally found it, and it's in your arms.'

Finn tightened his hold and began to walk her into a future she couldn't wait to begin.

'And that's where you'll always be. Forever.'

* * * * *

THE PRINCESS AND THE REBEL BILLIONAIRE

SOPHIE PEMBROKE

To Rachael Stewart, Andrea Bolter and Jessica Gilmore – my perfect matches!

I've loved working with all of you on this series. Thank you for making it so much fun!

CHAPTER ONE

PRINCESS ISABELLA OF AUGUSTA turned her back on the huge, glass-fronted villa, eschewed the view from the decked terrace out over the beautiful Lake Geneva towards the Alps, and glared at her assistant, Gianna, instead.

'This is a bad idea.' Unthinkably bad. This was breaking rules that had been drummed into Isabella before she could even walk.

Gianna tossed her highlighted caramel hair over her shoulder. 'I don't have bad ideas.'

That was a blatant lie, as Isabella had met some of Gianna's ex-boyfriends when she'd brought them to the palace.

'You told me you were taking me to see Sofia.' Isabella's cousin, Sofia, would never dream of doing something so risky and ridiculous as this. Sofia followed The Rules.

Of course, The Rules had led to Sofia marrying the love of her life and living in the lap of luxury in Lake Geneva with her husband and three adorable children, while also running her charity foundation for injured donkeys. The Rules hadn't been quite so kind to Isabella, but they had at least kept her safe and out of trouble.

This plan, she sensed, was a *lot* of trouble. Especially if her parents found out.

'This is better than another visit to Sofia,' Gianna said persuasively. 'This is a whole week of freedom, Your Highness. One week where you can be Bella for a change.'

'I'm always Bella with Sofia,' Isabella pointed out mulishly. She pushed away any thoughts of the one other person outside the royal family who'd been close enough to call her Bella, for a time. It would only make her miserable.

'*Sofia* thought it was a brilliant idea,' Gianna countered.

Isabella paused, blinked, and regrouped. 'Sofia *knows* about this plan?'

'Of course! Who do you think is covering for you if the King and Queen start asking any questions?'

It wouldn't be her parents, Their Royal Majesties King Leonardo and Queen Gabriela of Augusta, who'd be asking the questions, though, Isabella knew. It would be their private secretaries, or another member of household staff. Someone like Ferdinand, her father's right-hand man, whose job depended on all the royal children and cousins following The Rules.

His previous right-hand man had been fired after the last time Isabella thought there was a chance to break them. She'd been wrong, of course.

Just as Gianna was wrong now.

Isabella shook her head. 'Someone will find out.'

'They won't.' Pulling a folder from her laptop bag, Gianna spread out the papers on the high-gloss table in the middle of the terrace. She motioned for the Princess to take a seat and, dubiously, she did.

'Look.' Gianna pushed the top page towards her, and

Isabella took in the stylised M of the logo, and the words 'discretion guaranteed' underneath. 'This isn't your usual dating agency, Your Highness. M only works with the rich and famous, and it offers them something they can't find anywhere else.'

'A villa on Lake Geneva?' Isabella said, knowing she was being facetious.

Gianna rolled her eyes, probably hoping her employer wasn't looking. '*Privacy*. They offer you one week with your perfect match in an ultra-exclusive, completely private and secluded location—they even arrange security, at a discreet distance.'

They were, Isabella had to admit, very much secluded. While the shores of Lake Geneva boasted many small towns and villages—as well as the city of Geneva itself—on both the Swiss and French sides of the border, it was large enough that villas, like the one Gianna had driven her to from the small private airfield where they'd landed, were miles away from any other signs of human habitation. Their nearest neighbour, as far as Isabella could see, was across the lake—far enough away that she could only make out the winking of sunlight on the windows of the building.

As for the rest of it...

'How could this agency possibly know my perfect match? Some sort of algorithm, I suppose, based on my star sign or my photograph?'

'No, not at all,' Gianna said patiently. 'You fill in an incredibly detailed personality test—'

'Which I didn't do,' Isabella pointed out.

'I did it for you.'

'Doesn't that rather defeat the point?'

Gianna gave her a long, steady look. 'Your Highness, I've been part of the palace since I was a child. I was your friend long before I was on your staff. I've seen you grow up, stifled by the court and their rules. I've seen *you*, all these years. Seen you cry. Seen you laugh. Seen you—'

She broke off there, but Isabella knew, instinctively, what her friend would have said. *Love.*

Gianna had been there the last time Isabella broke The Rules. She knew exactly what that had done to her.

If she wanted her to risk it again...there had to be a good reason.

'The point is, I know you,' Gianna went on. 'I know your hopes and your dreams, your loves and your hates. And I was willing to be honest about them on the form, which I know you wouldn't have been. You'd have been thinking about what the palace expected from you, what your parents wanted, what The Rules said. Anything except how you actually felt or what *you* wanted.'

'You're right,' Isabella admitted softly. 'I would have done that.' She pulled the brochure from M closer. 'It says here there's a video interview required, too? I didn't do one of those.'

'Yes, you did.' Gianna smiled wickedly. 'Remember that Internet chat you did with that website? The one for young women, seeking their place in the world?'

Isabella frowned. She didn't do many interviews or royal events these days, if she could possibly avoid it. But Gianna had been insistent about doing that particular one...

'The one with that woman? The pretty one, from America? Morgan? No, Madison. Madison Morgan, right?' She'd liked that interview. Madison Morgan had asked her all sorts of interesting questions—much better than the usual stuff she got asked in interviews like that. As the third child of the King and Queen of Augusta she was a princess, but she'd never rule the country—that was down to her brother, Leo, named for their father. She'd never had any real role beyond doing what she was told. So all anyone really asked her was who had designed her dress, and which parties she'd be attending. The answer to the first was usually, 'Ask Gianna,' and the second, 'None if I can possibly avoid it.'

Morgan had asked her things about her*self*. Who she was, who she wanted to be. What mattered to her most. What her ideal date looked like... *How did I not see it?*

In fact, there *had* been a couple of moments that had struck her as odd during the interview—questions that didn't quite make sense, comments she didn't understand. At the time, Isabella had put it down to cultural differences, or her being out of practice at interviews, or even the language barrier. Her English was fluent, and she was usually good at picking up idioms, but still, it wasn't her native tongue and that could cause problems sometimes. And there hadn't been anything to set alarm bells ringing—besides, Gianna had been there the whole time.

Of course, she had. Because she'd set this whole thing up.

'Why, Gianna?' Isabella asked now. 'Why did you do this?'

'Why did I risk my career and my future to find you a week of freedom and bliss with a man who might be your perfect match?' Gianna smiled, softly. 'Because you deserve it, Bella.'

How long since her best friend had last called her by that nickname? Too long. They'd become employer and employee, not friends, the moment Isabella reached adulthood.

Gianna took her hand. 'I've seen you, fake smiling through every date your family has arranged with a "suitable suitor". Every boring Augustian duke or lord, even the ones twenty years older than you. I've seen you miserable and lonely, because not everyone gets as lucky as Sofia did, and finds their perfect match in the palace. I've seen you trying to find a moment to just be you, away from the bodyguards or the cameras or the men who want to marry into the royal family. I've seen you withering away in that palace ever since Nathanial—'

'Don't.' Isabella shook her head violently. 'Not…just, don't.'

'Okay. Okay.' Gianna ran her fingers soothingly over the Princess's arm. 'But you were miserable, Your Highness. And I saw something I could do about that…so I did it.'

'Do you really think this will change anything?' Isabella met her friend's gaze with her own, and found nothing but compassion there. 'One week with some guy? It's not like he's going to magically turn out to be a mysterious aristocrat or something. He won't be someone my parents would let me marry—I've already met every single guy they consider suitable. So it can't ever be more than this—just one week with someone I *might* be… compatible with.'

She felt a slight heat rise in her cheeks as she said the words. She hadn't been *compatible* with anyone for a very long time. Just once, in fact. With Na— No. She wasn't even going to think his name.

Did Gianna really think that a week with a man some agency thought was her perfect match would fix everything that was wrong with Isabella?

'Maybe it won't change *everything*,' Gianna admitted. 'But it might help. At worst, it's a week of fun and freedom—no bodyguards, except Tessa from your staff, and the small security team the agency sent to guard the perimeter, and they'll all be at the cabin on the edge of the estate. No royal obligations, no expectations. Just a guy that you might like…and the chance to have some fun, if you want it.'

'I'm not looking for that, either,' Isabella said flatly. How could she? *That* was definitely against The Rules.

Gianna sighed. 'Bella, this isn't some sort of hook-up agency I went to here. It's M. The premier, most expensive and exclusive dating agency in the business. Whoever they've sent to meet you, he's not here for sex. He's here to get to know you.'

The knot in Isabella's stomach started to loosen, just a little. 'You're sure?' Maybe she could come out of this having made a friend. A friend would be nice. A lover would be…trouble. Lots of trouble.

'Sure.' Gianna glanced over Isabella's shoulder, then gave her a mischievous grin. 'But looking at your Perfect Match, you might want to consider just a *little* romance this week.'

Isabella's heart thudded in her chest as she realised she *wanted* that. She wanted to find someone to talk with, relax with, laugh with, even love with, in a way she'd hadn't in so long. In a way she'd stopped hoping for.

But what was the point, if it was only for one week?

She shook her head. 'No, Gianna. A friend is one thing. Anything else is—'

'Against The Rules,' her friend finished for her, rolling her eyes.

'Yes.' But it wasn't just The Rules, Isabella realised. It was the risk. To her reputation, her family…her heart. She'd risked it all for love once before. It wasn't a mistake she intended to make again.

Gianna was still staring blatantly at the glass-fronted villa where Isabella's perfect match was waiting. If she wanted this week away from reality, Isabella knew she had to turn now. Had to see what sort of person M had decided was right for her. Had to open up her mind and her heart to the possibility of a friendship beyond The Rules.

Sucking in a deep breath, Isabella turned slowly to face the villa on the lake, and stared up through the glass to the man standing, one hand on his hip, the other holding a phone to his ear, looking down at them from what had to be the bedroom.

Was he really so tall, or was it just because she was looking up at him? Either way, the glass and the distance between them couldn't hide his admirable figure—the breadth of his shoulders, the muscles showing through the tight T-shirt he wore, or the long legs with their thick thighs… His black hair was cropped short, his skin as tanned and warm as her own Mediterranean complexion.

He was, she had to admit, the best-looking man she'd ever been set up on a date with. But then, the bar for that had never been particularly high.

Most of all, though, he looked like trouble.

He looked down, and her breath caught in her chest as his gaze met hers.

Maybe Madison knows what she's doing, she thought as the funny feeling in her chest moved lower, turning warmer. Maybe this guy wasn't her perfect match, but she couldn't deny the heat she felt at the idea of a week alone with him.

She pushed it aside. A new friend, that was what she was looking for here.

Even if that new friend looked like sin and risk and everything she'd spent every moment since Nathanial avoiding. She couldn't imagine what M thought they'd have in common, but she supposed there must be something. As Gianna said, they'd been matched on their personalities, first and foremost.

'So, you're going in?' Gianna asked, a giggle in her voice.

Isabella swallowed. 'Well, I've come this far.' She'd already left all but one of her security staff at the airport, lied to her parents about where she was, and apparently dragged Sofia in on the deception. 'What's one week?'

One small risk—a week away, getting to know a new friend. After that, she'd go back to The Rules. She'd be Princess Isabella again, and everything that entailed.

But first, she'd have this one week of freedom.

With him.

Matteo Rossi stared out over Lake Geneva through the huge panes of glass that spanned the whole front of the villa. It was quite the view, he had to admit that. The lake glistening in the late-afternoon sun, the snow-peaked mountains in the distance, even in June. And it was definitely in the middle of nowhere—which he was pretty sure his management team had insisted on. Nowhere for him to get into trouble, and wasn't that the whole point of this week?

'So, it's nice?' his manager, Gabe, asked on the other end of the phone line, probably happily ensconced in his office in Rome, preparing for the next race. A race where Matteo pointedly *wasn't* driving, even though his broken leg had healed perfectly well already. 'Madison promised it would be nice.'

Ah, yes, the famous Madison Morgan. Former child actress and now the owner of the M dating agency, the latest strategy Gabe and the others had hit on to slow him down, and the reason he was now stuck in Switzerland and not on the racetrack where he belonged.

'It's fine,' Matteo said dismissively. He'd stayed in some of the finest hotels in the world, from Abu Dhabi to Las Vegas and home to Rome. This villa was just a building, impressive though it was.

'And is *she* there yet?' There was a knowing lilt in Gabe's voice, a teasing note. Because Gabe wasn't talking about Madison, of course.

He was talking about Matteo's Perfect Match.

Matteo rolled his eyes just thinking the words.

'No, she's not here yet.' But then he looked down at the terrace outside the villa and saw two women talking. One—with caramel hair and a skirt suit—was obviously talking a mile a minute, if the way her hands were waving around was anything to go by. She was pretty, Matteo conceded. But his attention was already held by the other woman, the one with her back to him.

Dark curls tumbled down her back, loose and wild, falling almost to where her waist nipped in before curving out over generous hips. From what he could tell from behind, she had her arms folded in front of her, one hip tilted out as she stood, as if she was listening to what her companion had to say but didn't really believe it.

Her. He felt the word run through his body more than he consciously thought it, but he knew in an instant it was true. If she wasn't the woman Madison had picked for his perfect match, then the woman was doing her job wrong.

Suddenly, the idea of this week in exile wasn't looking quite so bad.

Except, no. Because whichever woman was here to meet him, she'd be expecting something he couldn't give. The M agency didn't do booty calls; his perfect match was expecting true love. Commitment. Forever.

Matteo had far too many adventures in his future to even *think* about settling down with someone. Which meant he couldn't give the woman the wrong idea.

Still, they'd been matched on personality, so hopefully

hanging out with her for a week wouldn't be too bad. They could blow this place and go explore the region. There had to be *some* interesting things to do around here, and, if she was his perfect match, she'd be up for an adventure.

Just as long as he made it clear she couldn't expect anything more.

'Are you looking forward to meeting her?' Gabe asked. Was it just guilt keeping his manager on the line so long? He'd sent Matteo here, away from his team, away from racing. They'd told him it was for his own good—a treat, even. But Matteo knew the truth.

This was a last-ditch attempt to repair his reputation— and his sponsorship deals. Apparently some of his most recent adventures had cut a bit too close to the line. Were they hoping that the lure of true love would tame him? Stop him chasing after the next adventure, taking bigger risk after bigger risk?

If they were, they were going to be disappointed.

'I guess,' he replied. After all, he wanted to save those sponsorship deals, too. Not to mention his career. He'd already made more money than he could spend in a lifetime, on and off the track. But if he didn't have racing, his dream career, what would he do?

Whose dream career? The whispered question in the back of his mind surprised him.

See, this was what happened when he slowed down. He started thinking. And unless he was thinking about speed and angles and winning, what was the point? As a rule, Matteo getting all introspective wasn't good for anybody. He acted, that was who he was. Who he'd always been.

Only since Giovanni died.

That voice. Matteo shook it away and turned his attention back to the women by the lake instead. Women, he understood. The thoughts that came to him late at night, or when he wasn't distracted by something fun...those he didn't *want* to understand.

But as he looked down, he realised the woman with the dark hair, his possible perfect match, had turned around to face him. Even through the glass, and over the distance between them, he felt it the moment her gaze met his. A feeling that hit his chest and spread through his body. And he wasn't entirely sure he understood that, either.

It was just her curves, he told himself. The way her folded arms highlighted her perfect breasts, the narrowness of her waist and the arch of her hips. Or her mouth, full and luscious. A purely physical reaction to a beautiful woman, nothing more. Of course, it was.

'It's just one week, Matteo,' Gabe was saying, when he finally tuned back into the phone conversation. 'Just... stay out of trouble this week. Finish healing.'

'My leg—'

'I know, I know. The doctors said it was fine, but they also said not to push it too far, too soon. And that's basically your motto in life, so...just take the week. When you get back, we'll come up with the next stage of the plan to get you back out on the racetrack. But, Matteo?'

There was something in his manager's voice that made him nervous. 'Yeah?'

'If you *did* happen to come out of this week happy, in love and ready to settle down with the love of your life... I don't think any of your sponsors would be disappointed.'

Because as much as they wanted the maverick, risky moves that won races, they needed him to appear a good role model for the younger fans, responsible enough that people trusted the things he was selling, however tangentially.

How do they expect me to be a champion and *a boring, stay-at-home guy, all at the same time?* The adrenaline was in his blood. The need to live life to the fullest, to chase every dream, tackle every challenge, beat every odd—on the track and off.

Except, the last time he'd gone adventuring, the odds had beaten him. Calling Gabe from the hospital to admit that he'd broken his leg while cliff diving, two weeks before the Dutch Grand Prix, had not been his finest moment.

Everyone wanted him to slow down—just not when he was behind the wheel.

Matteo sighed. 'Message received.' He hung up.

Down below, the terrace was empty—and he heard the electric buzz of the front door closing and locking behind whoever had just keyed in the confidential code. A code only he and the woman who was supposed to be his perfect match had.

No sign of the other woman outside, either, so he couldn't know exactly who was waiting for him downstairs—he just hoped he was right in his guess.

He didn't believe for a moment that some agency could find him his dream woman based on a questionnaire— one he'd been forced to fill in while still in the hospital— or a brief video interview, which he'd done with his leg in plaster, propped up on Gabe's coffee table.

But if the right woman was waiting downstairs—if she really was a match for his restless, reckless spirit— they might at least have found a way to stop him thinking too much. And Matteo would take that as good enough for now.

CHAPTER TWO

IT WASN'T UNTIL the door swung shut behind her, the alarm beeped, and the sound of Gianna's car driving away down that long, private driveway faded, that Isabella realised this could be a massive mistake.

She was alone in a house in the middle of nowhere with a man she'd never met. Sure, Gianna said there were security personnel in the cabin down the driveway—including Isabella's own long-term security woman, Tessa, apparently—towards the perimeter of the grounds, but what if she was wrong? What if this was a set-up? What if Gianna had been blackmailed into bringing her here? What if…?

No. Gianna never would—not for anything. One betrayal didn't mean Isabella had to keep looking for another one around every corner, and, besides, she was a very minor royal of a very minor Mediterranean country. Nobody would go to this much trouble to set her up, would they?

Isabella forced herself to breathe slowly, mindfully, as she took in her surroundings. Modern, sparse furnishings—the opposite of the palace at Augusta with all its heavy wood and dark antiques. Bright white walls, and comfortable-looking sofas loaded with cushions and blankets in various textures and shades of white, both looking out over Lake Geneva. She supposed the interior designer who furnished the place hadn't wanted anything to distract from that incredible view, through that all-glass wall out to the water.

She felt calmer already. This villa might not be like anywhere she'd stayed before—her family tended towards the traditional, even when travelling—but there was something about it. Something peaceful.

Hopeful, even.

This place gave her hope that she might be able to take this week to regroup, to find herself again after so long feeling adrift in her royal world.

Following The Rules was all well and good, and after everything with Nathanial she understood better than ever why it was important. But still, she couldn't help feeling hemmed in sometimes. As if she were pushing against tightly woven walls of cloth holding her in, stopping her from stretching, from reaching out for something more.

Maybe here, in peace and solitude, she could figure out what that something more was.

Except she wasn't alone, was she?

She heard a tread on the stairs behind her and knew it must be him. Her perfect match, if such a thing really existed.

She hoped he wasn't dreaming of too much from this week. A fairy-tale ending with a princess, for instance. Because however nice he was, that wasn't in her power to give. Friendship was all she had to offer.

Pasting on a smile, Isabella turned away from the lake to face him.

Gosh, he was even better looking up close. That cropped black hair, curling tightly against his skull. Those bright green eyes. And that body...tall, lean but obviously muscled; she'd been able to tell that even from a distance. Up close it was almost overwhelming, the sheer physicality of him.

He was staring at her, too. Good. At least she didn't have to worry about being accused of ogling. She wondered what he saw. Did he know who she was? Probably not, unless Madison had told him; she wasn't exactly highly visible outside Augusta, most of the time, and the palace had been keeping an even tighter rein than normal over her publicity since the incident five years ago.

Isabella frowned. Should she know who *he* was? He looked faintly familiar, in some way, but she couldn't put her finger on it. And it wasn't as if she were particularly well up on the rich, famous and notable of Europe—or the world—either. Since her father mostly just involved her brother Leo in international business, the only men she really got to meet were potential suitors. Especially since Nate.

And none of her suitors had *ever* looked like this man.

'Hi,' he said, finally, a wide, open smile spreading across his face. 'I'm Matteo. Matteo Rossi.'

Even the name rang a bell, but she still couldn't tell from where.

She moved forward to meet him as he descended the last few steps, and held out her hand. 'Isabella.' And then, because there was no point trying to hide these things, she continued, 'Princess Isabella of Augusta.'

Matteo's eyebrows shot up and, instead of shaking her hand as he'd clearly been about to, he twisted it and brought it to his lips. 'Should I bow?' he murmured as he kissed the backs of her fingers.

He should, really, she supposed. But the warmth that spread through her from the touch of his lips on her skin was more than an adequate substitute.

'It's probably going to get a little awkward if you have

to go around the house bowing to me all week,' she said, after pretending to consider it for a moment. 'I think we can let it go, just this once. Under the circumstances.'

Matteo straightened up and stepped back, but kept a hold of her hand, a wicked smile dancing over his lips. 'Good to know, Your Highness.'

'Isabella, please.' Maybe she didn't want to be a princess this week. Not with this man.

Maybe she wanted to be something more than just royal. Human, perhaps.

'Ah, but I'm only a humble racing-car driver, Your Highness,' he teased. 'Are you sure it would be appropriate?'

'*That's* where I've seen you before!' Isabella snapped her fingers as it came to her. Humble racing-car driver her foot. Even *she* knew that he'd made the rich list last year, his billions earned from racing and sponsorship deals ratcheting him up the rankings. 'Matteo Rossi. I watched you race in Barcelona last year. You won, of course.'

That had been a treat for her. A rare trip out of Augusta with Leo and his wife. A chance to escape the stifling air of the palace, just for a few days. She hadn't seen much of Barcelona, but watching the cars racing around the track she'd envied them their freedom. Until her sister-in-law, Princess Serena, had pointed out that they only ever went in circles, and only where someone else pointed them.

Isabella had wondered if maybe *nobody* had the kind of freedom she dreamed of sometimes, late at night, with the windows open. But looking at the man in front of her now…he didn't seem hemmed in by anybody.

She would bet he could go anywhere, any time, with anybody, whenever he chose.

And he was here in Lake Geneva with her.

A nervous excitement jolted through her at the realisation. Maybe she could learn a little freedom from this man. And she had a feeling she would enjoy the lesson.

A princess. Madison Morgan thought his dream woman was a freaking *princess*?

Matteo hadn't exactly spent time memorising the names and faces of European nobility, but he was still surprised he hadn't recognised her. Hell, she'd recognised *him*, and he was nobody, really.

Well, he was the world champion, but what did that really mean to people who didn't follow the sport? What did it mean to *royalty*?

He was still holding her hand. He should stop that.

He'd been so relieved when he'd walked down the stairs to find the curvaceous, dark-haired woman standing with her back to him again, looking out over the lake. The idea that she might have left before he found out if that instant connection he'd felt when their gazes had met meant something had been unbearable to him.

Now, he wasn't sure what any of it meant. The Princess seemed…cautious. Guarded, perhaps. There was something in her eyes, even when she was joking about him bowing, that told him this was not a woman who let people in. Which was okay by him, since he didn't particularly want or need anyone getting close to him, either.

But a princess. He was pretty sure she'd never climbed Machu Picchu or been bungee jumping or travelled across America in a convertible, as he'd done over the past few years. From her tone when she talked about watching him race in Barcelona, he suspected that was the most excitement she'd had in years. Just *watching* someone else have fun.

That was what royals did, wasn't it? They hid away

in their palaces and watched over other people actually living their lives.

Which begged the question, what was a princess doing signing up to an exclusive dating service? Let alone spending a week in a secluded location with a strange man, like him. She couldn't really believe *he* could be her perfect match, could she? And if she did, he needed to disabuse her of that idea pretty quick.

More than ever, he was glad he'd already resolved that this week would be about friendship and fun, rather than romance or anything more. He liked a risk as much as the next guy, but he *definitely* wasn't Prince Charming material.

Somewhere behind him, something pinged. And then it did it again.

'Is that…some sort of security alarm?' Isabella asked, her eyebrows furrowed.

Matteo listened to the ping. 'I think it's an oven timer, actually.'

Even a place as designer and minimalist as this villa on the lake had to have a kitchen, right? And it sounded as if someone had planned dinner for them.

'Come on, Princess. Let's go investigate.'

Downstairs had seemed completely open plan—with sitting areas and a dining table and a well-stocked bar with stools, all looking out towards the incredible view. But first appearances could be deceiving, Matteo realised. Behind the white stone staircase that ran from the centre of the room up to the first floor was a hidden corridor—one that led to a state-of-the-art kitchen, and a pinging oven timer.

With a little trial and error, Matteo found the right button to stop it pinging, turned down the oven temperature and opened the door. There were oven gloves hanging right next to it, and he used them to lift out a steaming dish of lasagne. His mouth watered at the sight. This was *proper* food.

Normally, when he was training, he watched his diet carefully to keep himself at peak fitness. Everything made a difference on the track and, besides, he was usually training for something else as well—like the Machu Picchu hike, or the Paris marathon, or a cross-Channel swim.

While he'd been in recovery with his broken leg, he'd kept up the habits—keen to show the team that he was ready to get back out there the moment it was healed. But since he'd been sidelined anyway, sent to Lake Geneva to keep him out of trouble…surely a little lasagne wouldn't hurt.

He turned and placed the dish on a waiting trivet on the marble counter, and found two plates already set out with fresh salad, complete with gleaming red tomatoes, and the gloss of oil and balsamic vinegar. A marble bowl filled with crusty bread sat beside it. Matteo touched it; still warm.

'That door must lead to the housekeeper's quarters,' he guessed, nodding towards a slim white door, almost camouflaged between the kitchen cabinets. '"Discreet household staff included,"' he quoted from M's literature.

'It looks delicious.' Isabella's eyes had lit up at the sight of the food. He supposed having actual staff would just be commonplace for her, growing up in a palace. But for him, even since he'd reached the heights of his career and grown more or less accustomed to having staff and help around for the day-to-day essentials of life, it still felt like an incredible luxury.

If Giovanni could see me now. On holiday with a princess, with staff *to do all the cooking and cleaning.*

His brother wouldn't believe it. Not even in his wildest dreams. Not after their childhood in Rome, both taking on their share of the household tasks while their mother worked two jobs to keep a roof over their heads.

But Giovanni couldn't see him, and neither could his mother. Or if, as Matteo sometimes let himself hope, they could look down from above and watch him, they couldn't tell him what they thought of his lifestyle—his success, his billions in the bank, his fame.

Sometimes, he wished they could, so he could hear their advice. Other times, he thought it was just as well they couldn't. He could only imagine the bickering.

'There was a table out on the balcony upstairs,' he said impulsively as he dished up the lasagne onto the waiting plates. 'Why don't we take it up there to eat?'

Isabella nodded and, between them, they loaded up a couple of trays with the food and cutlery, as well as the carafe of wine and the glasses that had been laid out for them. Negotiating the stairs slowly, Matteo made a joke about not dropping anything on these stone floors and was gratified when Isabella laughed.

He wasn't sure what he'd expected when she'd said the word 'princess', but this pasta-loving beauty wasn't exactly it.

He heard her falter behind him, though, as he reached the bedroom. Placing his tray down on the table on the balcony, he turned back to find her staring at the bed.

'There's another bedroom next door,' he told her, quickly realising the cause of her alarm. 'I thought I could use that one, if you wanted to be in here? I think the staff have already brought up our bags.'

Her gaze flickered from the bed to the solitary suitcase beside it—her suitcase, he assumed, since he'd already put his next door. Who knew how the staff had managed that without them noticing.

The view was just as good from both rooms, he'd decided, and the balcony here stretched between the two rooms anyway, accessible from either one of the glass doors that were in place in lieu of windows or walls, over the lake.

'Oh, okay. Great.' Her stretched smile didn't look quite natural, though. Matteo tried to look reassuring as he reached over to take the wine and glasses from her.

Of course, she still thought this week was about romance and love—and sex. Whereas he'd already known that true love wasn't on the cards for him, even before the discovery that she was a princess. They were worlds apart in so many ways—but she'd come here under a false assumption. That he was looking for love.

He needed to set that straight.

Pouring a glass of wine for them both, Matteo waited for Isabella to take her seat at the small balcony table before sitting down himself. His mother had instilled *some* manners in him, at least.

Then he waited until she'd taken a large mouthful of lasagne—so she'd have time to think about her answer—then asked his question.

'So, what's a princess doing using an elite dating site? Don't you have to marry a prince or something?'

The food—delicious as it was—turned to ashes in her mouth at Matteo's question.

Don't you have to marry a prince?

He'd put his finger straight on the biggest problem with this whole set-up. She wasn't free to fall in love with whoever M decided her perfect match was. And she needed to tell him that.

'Not necessarily a prince,' she said, with a small, one-shoulder shrug. 'But a lord or a duke, yeah. Preferably Augustian, to make my father *really* happy.'

'Are there many Augustian lords and dukes your age?'

'I think my cousin married the last of them.' She didn't begrudge Sofia her happiness—or her husband. But it did narrow the acceptable dating pool quite considerably.

'Ah. So that's why you're here?' Matteo grinned. 'Because I think you already know I'm not a duke or a lord.'

No. He was a *racing-car driver,* of all things. Isabella could just imagine her brother's face if he knew where she was right now, who she was with. Leo sometimes seemed even more hidebound and determined to follow The Rules—or, at least, make Isabella follow them—than the King and Queen were.

For a man who was supposed to be her perfect match, it was hard to think of anyone less suitable. From what she knew of his reputation—which was mostly stuff she'd heard whispered in the crowd in Barcelona last year—he was a risk-taker, a daredevil. A Lothario on the racing circuit.

The absolute opposite to the stuffed-shirt lords her parents had been setting her up on dates with for the last five years.

But if he realised she wasn't really his perfect match, he didn't seem too disappointed.

Isabella reached for a piece of bread and dipped it in the waiting oil and vinegar. Her mother, if she were here, would have looked despairingly at Isabella's hips. But she wasn't here—nobody was, except Matteo—so it was safe to be a little bit rebellious, right? *Ooh, look at you, eating bread. You rebel.*

And having dinner with a racing-car driver. That probably counted more.

'I'm here because my assistant, Gianna, lied to me,' she said casually, as if things like this happened to her all the time.

Matteo sat back in his seat, eyebrows high, his arms folded across his chest. 'She told you that you were meeting a prince?'

'She told me I was going to visit my cousin for the week, like I often do at this time of year. That's what she told the palace, and my parents, too. Nobody knows I'm here except for Gianna, my cousin Sofia, Tessa—the longest serving and most trusted member of my security team, Madison Morgan—and you.' It felt dangerous, giving up that secret. Information that could hurt her, if Matteo chose to share it with the papers, or via the internet.

But it felt good, too. Freeing.

What was that quote? Publish and be damned. But she didn't think that Matteo would suddenly jump on social media and reveal her whereabouts. After all, discretion was guaranteed by the M dating agency, and she couldn't imagine Madison Morgan would be very happy with him—or give him another chance to find his one true love—if he broke that rule.

Which brought her back to her original problem. Matteo was there to find his perfect match. That was who he was expecting to meet when he walked into the villa. And instead he got her—a princess who couldn't fall in love with him even if she wanted to, and had now admitted she was only there because she was tricked into it.

She must be quite a disappointment to him.

It was probably a good job she was used to being a disappointment to people.

'I'm sorry,' she said. 'You came here to find your perfect match, and it's only the first night and I've already ruined that for you.' She got to her feet. 'This wasn't fair.

Let me call Madison and explain, and I'm sure she'll refund you, or find you an *actual* perfect match for your next date.'

Matteo laughed, and Isabella paused half out of her chair, unsure what was funny about the situation.

'I'm not laughing at you,' he said after a moment, obviously sensing her discomfort. She was a princess. She really wasn't used to people laughing at her—well, apart from her older siblings, of course. Leo and Rosa could always find *something* hilarious about her words or actions—when they weren't being horrified.

He motioned for her to sit back down, and she did so cautiously. But there was still lasagne and bread left—she assumed the meal had been planned towards his cultural heritage, and wondered whether tomorrow might bring an Augustian speciality, or even a Swiss one—and she hated to leave good food uneaten.

'So why *are* you laughing?' she asked, reaching for another piece of the delicious, still-warm bread.

'Because this whole situation is hilarious.' Matteo leaned across the table, closer to her than anyone who wasn't an employee or a blood relative had been in a very long time. Then, swiping the last piece of bread from the bowl, he said, 'You see, I didn't choose to come here either.'

Isabella blinked. 'You...didn't?' He was already sitting back in his chair, smirking at her as he chewed his prize, but she could still feel his breath against her cheek as he spoke.

What was it about this man that affected her so? Was it just that it had been such a long time since she'd found a man attractive at all? Now, sitting across the table from Matteo Rossi, with all that lean, long muscle and that smirk… Isabella admitted to herself that it had *definitely* been too long.

Not that she could really do anything about that, unless she wanted to marry one of the stuffed shirts Leo kept setting her up with.

Back to the point. 'So, why are you here?'

This was supposed to be their perfect date, their chance to find true love—without the usual scrutiny of the press or the public. But if *neither* of them had chosen to be there at all, where did that leave them?

'Same reason as you, more or less.' With a shrug, Matteo reached over for the carafe of red wine and topped up her glass. 'My management team thought it was a good idea.'

'Why?' Isabella thought she understood why Gianna believed it was a good idea for her to be there—a chance to kick back, relax, have the freedom to be herself, and maybe even have some fun. But surely Matteo had all those things available to him in the real world, in a way that the Princess of Augusta really didn't.

'To keep me out of trouble.' One eyebrow arched up above Matteo's bright green eyes. 'Although we might be able to find just a *little* bit of trouble here this week, don't you think?'

And from the heat that pulsed through her body at his words, Isabella had to agree.

This man could be an awful lot of trouble.

CHAPTER THREE

Her eyes darkened at his words; he could see it, clear as day in the fading evening light.

But he couldn't do anything about it.

She's a princess, Matteo. It was his mother's voice in his head, even after all these years. *Have some respect.*

Yeah, he was pretty sure Gabe and the sponsors wouldn't have sent him here if they'd known who his perfect match was. They'd be too afraid of his causing an international incident or something.

Matteo wasn't entirely sure it wasn't a possibility himself.

He looked away, turning his attention back to the bread in his hand as if it were the most fascinating thing on the balcony, and added, 'I mean, if you're my perfect match, you must like a little adventure, right? There have to be places to explore around here…'

He trailed off as he saw her eyes widen in horror. Yeah, his first instincts hadn't been wrong. The Princess wasn't a risk-taker.

'Or we could hang out here at the villa, get to know one another,' he finished with a sigh.

Isabella visibly relaxed, her eyes lighting up. 'That sounds nice. It's not often I get the opportunity to make a new friend.'

He couldn't help but return her smile. It might not be the week he'd plan for himself, but he got the impression that the Princess needed to be gentled along in this. By the end of the week, he was sure he'd manage to talk her into *some* small adventure.

'So if you were tricked into coming here, what made you stay?' Matteo asked, curious.

Isabella looked up and met his gaze with her own, direct, brown one. And just as it had when she'd looked up at him in the window of the villa earlier, his chest tightened.

For a moment, he was almost certain she was going to say, *You.*

She didn't, and he tried not to feel disappointed at that.

'At the palace my life is rather…let's say tightly controlled.'

'You mean boring?' he guessed.

That raised half a smile from her. 'Amongst other things. And I decided that a week away from that—a week to relax and be myself, not just Princess Isabella—might be good for me. Plus,' she added, with an impish grin that lit up her whole face, 'I was pretty sure from the moment I saw you that the last thing you'd be was boring. And that was before I even realised you were a racing star!'

No, Matteo had never been accused of being boring. At least, not since Giovanni died, and he started living his life for both of them.

'So, you're looking for someone to help you relax and have a bit of fun for a change, then, rather than your true love?' That worked out nicely for him, even if her idea of adventure didn't match his.

'I guess I am.' Isabella sounded almost surprised at her own words, as if she hadn't really factored him into her plans, despite what she'd said about him not being boring. 'What about you? What are you looking for out of this week, if it's not your perfect match?'

What *was* he looking for?

'Well, like I said, my management team are just hoping to keep me out of trouble.'

Isabella raised her eyebrows at that. 'Seems kind of an extreme way of doing it—going through all the rigmarole of setting you up with the M agency. It's not exactly cheap, either, from what I understand.'

'One hundred grand deposit,' Matteo agreed with a wince. Even now that amount was a tiny drop in his investment and savings accounts, he still couldn't help but imagine his mother's horror at the casual way he spent it. 'But at least most of it goes to charity.' He'd donated his chunk to the cancer charity he'd supported ever since they'd helped Giovanni through those last weeks and days. That way, something good was coming out of his side-lining, he'd reasoned.

Isabella gave a low whistle, which seemed kind of out of keeping for a princess. But then, he was coming to suspect that she wasn't just any princess. 'You must have *really* got in a lot of trouble for them to go that far. What did you do?'

'Broke my leg cliff diving,' he admitted, and she winced.

'Ouch. It's better now?'

'Yeah. Docs all say it should be as good as new.' Even if it still ached a little, most days. He was doing his strengthening exercises, and he sure as hell wouldn't let it affect his driving. That was what mattered. 'But I was out of commission for a while. Couldn't race, couldn't work out, couldn't do anything much.'

He'd hated that—the inaction—more than anything.

That was still one of the concerns he had about this week. If she expected him to sit around doing nothing...he'd end up abseiling down from the roof out of sheer boredom.

'It wasn't just the broken leg, though,' he admitted. 'I guess the team—and Gabe, my manager, in particular—were fed up with my antics in general.' In fact, he knew they were, because those were the exact words Gabe had used at the team intervention. He'd been lying there in his hospital bed, lucky to be alive, and Gabe had been ranting about 'your antics putting everything at risk'.

He'd apologised later, although Matteo hadn't needed him to. He knew what fear and love sounded like together, and Gabe had been like an older brother to him since he'd lost his own.

'You're a bit of a daredevil, huh?' Isabella asked.

Matteo shrugged. 'You could say that. I like adventures.' It sounded easy, when he said it like that. The truth was more complicated, of course, but wasn't it always? And in his experience, girls didn't want to hear the truth. They wanted the story, the fairy tale of the wild and reckless racing-car driver. Even if behaving that way on the track would only get people killed. Matteo was always responsible behind the wheel, even if no one watching would ever see that.

And that was the problem. The public—and the sponsors—only saw him speeding around corners at work, then taking risks in his private life. His reputation was established—and it wasn't the sort of reputation that got him respect.

'And now you're stuck here with me for a week, in a luxury villa with excellent food.' Isabella polished off the last of the wine in her glass and glanced over at the desserts still sitting on the tray.

'Pudding?' Matteo suggested and she nodded enthusiastically. The Princess liked her food. Matteo made a mental note in case that came in useful some time.

He got the feeling he was going to get to know a lot about the Princess this week. And he found himself strangely thrilled at the idea.

Maybe *she* was his next adventure after all.

Isabella had expected to struggle to sleep in a strange place, but the bed in the villa was so comfortable, and the food, wine and company over dinner had been so pleasant, that she found herself sleeping in the next morning.

By the time she woke, the sun was already high above the lake, streaming through the gauzy curtains that covered the floor-to-ceiling windows—and she could hear the sound of coffee cups on the balcony.

Coffee. That sounded like something worth getting up for.

Dragging herself out of bed, she wrapped her dressing gown around her, blushing as she realised what Gianna considered appropriate nightwear for a princess on holiday wasn't exactly modest. Her pale pink silk pyjama shorts and matching camisole were barely covered by the thin, short white broderie wrap.

She paused for a second by the glass doors to the balcony. Maybe she should shower and dress before heading out. But the coffee smelled so good...

'If you don't get out here quick, I'm going to eat all the pastries,' Matteo called from outside. 'I'm starving.'

Well, that made the decision for her. There was no way she was missing out on pastries.

Matteo was already sitting at the table they'd shared the night before—at some point in the night, it must have been cleared and reset, as it was now laden with pastries and steaming hot coffee. Isabella looked around and spotted a small staircase she'd missed the previous night, leading down to where she imagined the kitchen door must be at the side of the house. Whoever their house fairies were, sent to take care of them this week, they were certainly discreet and silent.

Taking a breath, Isabella stepped forward, her princess smile in place, and took her seat opposite him. 'Good morning.'

His eyes widened as he looked up and clocked her nightwear, but he didn't say anything, which she appreciated. And he poured her coffee, which she appreciated even more.

'Have you been up long?' She took the cup and lifted it to her lips, breathing in the bitter scent and taking one cautious, hot sip.

Matteo shrugged. 'A little while. Went for an early morning run by the lake, then came back for a shower. When I came out, I found breakfast ready.'

'You still run on holiday?' Exercise for Isabella was limited to yoga classes with Gianna, and walks around the palace estates.

'It's a habit,' he replied. 'Plus I'm still strengthening my leg. The physio gave me exercises, but now it's more about rebuilding my stamina.'

'I wouldn't have thought that driving was a particularly fitness-focused sport.' Although given the way his muscles showed through his thin white T-shirt—dampened in places from the water dripping from his tight black curls—she wasn't really surprised to learn that he took his physical fitness seriously.

'I hear that a lot.' Matteo leant back in his chair, one foot propped up on his other knee, his arm sprawled across the railing on the edge of the balcony. Just looking at him made her cheeks feel warm at her suggestion.

Of course he was in peak physical condition. 'Actually, fitness is really important in racing.'

At least he didn't seem annoyed by her comment. 'How come?'

'Well, first off there's the strength needed for controlling the car at high speeds.' Matteo ticked that point off on his finger before raising another one. 'There's the heat to contend with in there, too. But most of all, it's our hearts.'

'Your heart?'

'A race can be two hours long,' Matteo explained. 'And our hearts are pumping at way above normal levels for that whole time—like we're exercising hard for a sustained period. The G-forces over a two-hour race are immense—you feel like your head weighs ten times what it normally does.'

'I hadn't thought about any of that,' Isabella admitted.

'No reason you should,' he replied, with a shrug. 'For me, the biggest thing is my brain.'

'Yeah?' She also hadn't really thought of racing as a particularly cerebral activity either, but she figured it probably wasn't a good idea to mention that.

'Racing needs split-second reactions, it needs me to be able to think ahead, to calculate risks and take them quickly. If my body is tired, my brain gets tired too and my concentration starts to lapse. I can't afford that in a race; it could cost me too much.'

Not just the winner's flag, Isabella realised. If Matteo lost focus out of the racetrack, if he wasn't up to the rigours of a two-hour race, it could cost him—or someone else—their life. She shivered, even though the morning was warm.

He seemed to sense her discomfort with the topic and moved on.

'So, what do you have planned for today?' Matteo

topped up her almost empty cup of coffee and she took it gratefully, sipping the hot liquid carefully while she considered her answer.

Planned? She didn't have anything planned. There was no Gianna standing there with her schedule for the day, reminding her of appearances she'd reluctantly agreed to make, or letters she needed to write. No member of the royal household summoning her for another awful, awkward date with a man she didn't want to marry. No rules keeping her from escaping into the city and exploring alone. No security guard trailing after her, even—although she suspected that if she tried to pass the gatehouse where the security staff were staying, she'd soon pick one up.

The point was, there was nothing she was *supposed* to be doing today. Which meant she could choose for herself.

What a luxury.

And a pity she had no idea what to do with it.

'I saw a well-stocked bookcase inside,' she said eventually. 'Maybe I'll read.'

'Sounds good,' Matteo replied, not really sounding as if he meant it.

She supposed that was a little antisocial, considering she was supposed to be getting to know her companion better. 'There were some board games too, I think?'

A wide smile spread across Matteo's face. 'Now, that sounds more like it. But I warn you—I'm very competitive.'

'Why am I not surprised?' Isabella asked, grinning in return.

By later that afternoon, Matteo was regretting almost everything about this week.

Well, that wasn't strictly true. Mostly, he was just regretting his personal promise to himself to keep his hands off the Princess.

From the moment she'd appeared that morning, dressed in those indecently short pyjamas and a wrap that was basically see-through, he'd been struggling to keep his eyes—and his libido—where they belonged.

He'd thought that playing board games would help. After all, he associated them with being a kid, playing with his brother. They were inherently unsexy, and she'd even put real clothes on to play them. It was the perfect 'new friend' activity, right?

Except it turned out that Princess Isabella had a competitive streak to rival his own, and the wicked smile that flashed across her lips every time she was winning sent heat flashing through his body.

And that wasn't the only problem.

Isabella reached past him for the dice, her warm skin pressing against his arm as she moved. The dark curls of her hair hung over her face, and he could smell roses when he breathed in.

He tensed, waiting for her to retreat again—but when she did, the softness of her breasts brushed against his shoulder, forcing him to swallow hard.

This was unbearable.

Because M knew what it was doing. The agency, or Madison Morgan herself, had picked his perfect woman—at least in one way. Isabella was beautiful, curvaceous, oozing an unconscious sex appeal that was driving him insane.

He had a whole week alone with the most beautiful woman he'd ever seen in real life, and he was going to spend it playing Monopoly.

This was why he needed to get out of the villa and *do* something. Sitting around only let him think and feel and imagine, and that wasn't good for either of them right now.

As soon as she'd passed go and collected her money, Matteo grabbed for the dice and rolled them. Isabella moved his piece for him, since it was on her side of the board, and gleefully shouted, 'Rent!'

Thank God. Handing over the remains of his pretend savings, he sprang to his feet. 'Then that's me out. You win. Uh... I need to go for a run.'

Her forehead creased adorably. *Not adorably. Just normally. Like any normal woman.*

'Didn't you already go for one this morning?'

Yes. Yes, he had. 'Gotta catch up on training, right?'

'Sure,' she replied, not sounding convinced. 'Um, I'll see you for dinner, then?'

'Definitely.'

Because even he wasn't as unchivalrous as to leave his only companion all alone for dinner. Nothing to do with the almost orgasmic look that crossed her face whenever she was eating the food here.

He was almost *certain* she wanted him too, not that she'd been obvious about it. It was the little things, the ones he only saw because he was looking for them. The way her eyes darkened when she smiled at him, the way she bit into her lower lip and looked away when he smiled back. The heat that seemed to sizzle between them, whenever they got too close...

In the end, he didn't bother changing into his running gear, and just walked straight out along the path that meandered down towards the edge of the lake and around it. He needed to think, not run, this time.

Identify the problem, Matteo. This was no different from a problem with a car, or a bend of the track he couldn't quite hit right. No different from any of the challenges in his life he'd overcome to get where he was now.

He'd taken trips and risks other people didn't even dream of. He'd trekked Machu Picchu, done solo skydives, skied mountains others just sat and looked at. He'd come from nothing and made his billions. He risked his money as easily as his life, and he *always* came out on top, whatever the concerns of his management team.

He beat the odds, every time.

And he wasn't going to be thrown off his game by a princess who was too scared to leave the house.

Maybe the problem wasn't that she was beautiful. He'd met many beautiful women in his life, and had plenty of them in his bed, come to that. But none of them had ever filled his mind the way Isabella had over the last day—to the point where even an innocent game of Monopoly had led to him imagining making love to her on top of the damned board.

Was it the princess thing? No. He'd never had any particular interest in royalty, and his money and his fame had put him in plenty of aristocratic company before now without problems. Royalty were just one more type of celebrity really, weren't they? And he had enough celebrity of his own.

Except…there was one aspect of the princess thing that made a difference.

The untouchable part.

Matteo groaned aloud as he realised, scaring a bird in a nearby tree into flapping off in a hurry. Lowering himself to sit on a flat rock by the water's edge, he looked out over the huge expanse of Lake Geneva towards the distant mountains and thought his way through to the heart of the problem.

He'd promised himself, even before he'd met her, that

he'd keep this week light. That he'd focus on friendship. Because the woman he'd be spending the week with was looking for her perfect match, and he wasn't offering true love to *anyone*. He was there under false pretences, and it would be wrong to lead her on.

Except, of course, by making Isabella forbidden fruit, he only wanted her more. And the fact that she was a princess, that the royal family would never allow her to date him, let alone marry him, well...

Matteo had never done well with being told what he could and couldn't do. Even by himself.

So. He'd identified the problem. Now he just needed to figure out what to do about it. Because nothing had changed—

Wait.

Yes, it had.

He'd been assuming that Isabella was here looking for her Prince Charming. But she wasn't. She'd been manipulated into coming, just as he had.

She wasn't looking for love from him.

Matteo smiled to himself, as Lake Geneva shone in the June sunshine.

Because that opened up all sorts of possibilities.

Isabella was nowhere to be seen when he finally returned to the villa, so Matteo headed to his room and showered and changed for dinner. As he towelled off his hair, he heard movement on the balcony—but by the time he'd dressed and went to investigate, whoever had been out there had gone.

Their discreet housekeeping staff had left them another feast, though. Obviously they'd observed their preference for eating on the balcony and brought dinner straight to them this evening. Tonight's dinner, when he peeped under the silver cloche keeping it warm, appeared to be some sort of fish dish with rice that smelled amazing.

'Is it time for dinner?' Isabella appeared in her doorway. The jeans and T-shirt she'd worn during the day had been replaced by a bright red sundress, and the matching lipstick she wore made Matteo all the happier he'd figured out his issues during his walk.

She did appear subdued, though, and dinner passed relatively quietly, without any of the chatter they'd enjoyed at breakfast, or the night before.

Her eyes lit up as he unveiled the tiramisu waiting for them on the nearby trolley, though, and Matteo decided it was time the address the elephant in the room.

Except Isabella got there first.

'I think we need to talk,' she said as he reached for the serving spoon for the tiramisu.

'I agree,' he replied.

He heard her take a deep breath, as if steeling herself for something unpleasant. He added an extra spoonful of pudding into her bowl, just in case.

'The thing is...we're stuck here all week, right? Together. And since playing board games clearly isn't your cup of tea, neither of us are *actually* looking for true love, and we're both supposed to be staying out of trouble...what do you suggest we spend this week doing?' she asked.

Matteo handed her the over-full bowl of dessert and sat back in his chair, trying not to smile. She'd given him the perfect opening.

'Well, I see it as an opportunity.' He hadn't, until he'd spent the day trying to keep his hands off her. Now, it was all he could think of.

'An opportunity?' She took a spoonful of tiramisu and

slipped it between her lips, her eyes fluttering shut with pleasure as she tasted it. 'Mmm, you have got to try this.'

It wasn't the pudding he wanted to try, though. It was her. He wanted to taste her lips, and the cream still lingering there. He wanted to kiss every inch of her curves. He wanted to learn all the other things he could do to coax that satisfied, pleasured moan from her mouth.

And after a day of fighting it, he was done.

'I will,' he said, swallowing. 'And yes, an opportunity. After all, we still have everything M promised, right? A week of seclusion. The freedom to do whatever we want, without anyone watching. And we were chosen to spend the time together because we're supposed to be perfectly matched. Compatible, if you like.'

What was the point of trying to resist a temptation that had been so perfectly selected to tempt him? If she didn't expect true love from him...what was stopping them?

Her eyes were open now, wide and wondering—so wide he could almost read the thoughts passing behind them. Maybe she hadn't been thinking them before, but now he could tell that her thoughts echoed his own. She was seeing the possibilities, too.

Matteo couldn't be the only one feeling the chemistry between them. That kind of sensation only happened when it went both ways, in his experience. And M had got one thing right, at least—the chemistry between them was like nothing he'd ever felt before.

He wanted to know where that would lead. Where it could take them. And from the look in Isabella's eyes, she did too.

She wasn't saying anything, though. And he didn't want to rush her.

She was thinking about it. That was enough for tonight.

Leaning closer, over the table, Matteo dropped his

voice to a low purr—the one an ex-girlfriend had told him sounded like his engine warming up. 'I'm not a prince, Isabella. And I've got no interest in being one, either. After this week, we'll both go our own ways, right? Back to the lives we live in our own worlds. But until then… why not make the most of the freedom we've been given this week? Live a little dangerously.'

Reaching out, he swept way the morsel of cream that clung to her full lips, then sucked his finger into his own mouth to taste it, hearing her breath hitch at his movements.

'I… I don't know.' He could feel her holding herself back. Was that just her royal upbringing, or something else? Was it just because he wasn't a prince? Because the attraction between them definitely wasn't all in his imagination. He could see it in her glassy eyes, pupils blown. In the way she swallowed and her tongue darted out to wet her bottom lip and, *God*, he wanted to kiss her.

But he wouldn't. Not until she told him herself that she wanted that too.

'Think about it,' he murmured. 'And I'll see you in the morning.'

Then he turned and headed for his lonely bedroom, knowing he wasn't going to be thinking about anything but her tonight.

CHAPTER FOUR

Isabella did not have a second restful night.

She left the dinner dishes on the balcony and retreated to the calm, cool bedroom to follow her usual bedtime routine, just as she had the night before. A bath, with the lavender oil she always travelled with, followed by her skincare regime—the one her mother said would keep her looking 'acceptable' for longer. Then, wrapped up in her pale pink silk pyjamas, she curled up on the bed with her book.

She barely read a page.

In fact, she'd gone through her whole routine on autopilot.

Think about it, Matteo had said. It seemed as though she'd be doing nothing but.

He'd barely touched her—just removed a blob of cream from her lips. A mother or nanny might have done the same, brusquely or absently. But when *he* did it…

His fingertip brushing against her lip had sent sparks firing through her body—sparks she hadn't been sure she was capable of even feeling, any more. That slight pressure had been enough for her to imagine his touch everywhere else—over every inch of her body.

There was no ambiguity in what he'd been suggesting. In fact, she was almost surprised neither of them had mentioned it before. Gianna had hinted at it, of course, but Isabella...

Isabella had suggested they play board games.

She groaned at the memory. How out of touch was she with men and romance that this idea hadn't occurred to her?

Except that was a lie, and Isabella tried hard not to lie—even to herself.

She *had* thought about it, from the moment she'd seen Matteo standing above her on the balcony and known he was supposed to be her perfect match. She'd thought about it every time he stood close enough for her to feel the heat of his skin or smell his cologne. Every time she'd brushed past him to retrieve the dice when they were playing. Every time he'd smiled at her or watched her enjoy dessert. She'd just been too scared of what that meant to even consider doing anything about the thought.

Now, snuggled down on the cool, crisp sheets, Isabella stopped trying to ignore the possibility, and let herself think about it properly.

One week. No rules, no prying eyes, no consequences.

For this one week she could cut loose. And if she wanted, she could take Matteo as a lover—bring him to her bed and let him worship her body, and explore his in return. He'd made it clear that was how he'd choose to spend this week, rather than playing Monopoly.

She supposed that was a fairly common thing for him. She was sure his daredevil attitude to life continued into his romantic entanglements, too. She hadn't followed his career particularly closely, but even she'd seen enough clips on the Internet or in papers to know that he never dated the same woman twice, but always had a beauty on his arm whenever he wanted one. Picking up a woman for a week of debauchery and seduction was probably par for the course in his downtime.

But for her...

She hadn't been with a man since Nate, and even that had been a lie. She wasn't a virgin, but she definitely wasn't experienced, either. And honestly, since Nate she hadn't really been interested in anyone all. She knew there were plenty of stories on Augustian social media about her love life, but they were all fabrications.

Her heart had been broken, and her faith in people severely dented, by her first foray into love. It was one of the reasons she'd been so unsure about the whole idea of her 'perfect match' in the first place.

Except that wasn't what she was here for, and it wasn't what Matteo was offering, either.

He was offering a week of giving in to the chemistry between them. A week of pleasure, she was sure. A week of fun, strings-free.

And she wanted it. She had to admit that much to herself.

But was she brave enough to take it? Even knowing what had happened last time she'd let go in such a way?

She wasn't sure. And by the time she fell asleep that night she still hadn't decided.

Her dreams were filled with unfamiliar images—and feelings. The water of Lake Geneva, lapping around her. The scent of the flowers that grew in the pots on the balcony, mingled with the more familiar lavender of her pillows, and a spicy, new scent that she knew was Matteo himself.

Skin on skin, slick with water and want. That was all she remembered when she awoke, unsatisfied and frustrated, from a night of dreams.

And now she had to face him again.

Great.

Isabella took her time washing and dressing, trying to scrub the dreams from her body in case Matteo could see them on her, somehow. Or smell them, perhaps, the way she dreamt she could still smell him in the air around her.

But eventually she had to admit to herself that she was just postponing the inevitable. She had the whole rest of the week here in this glorious villa, beside this beautiful lake, with Matteo. Not making the most of it would be a terrible waste.

Throwing open the doors to the shared balcony that joined their bedrooms, Isabella let the morning air rush in, and felt her own breath rush out.

Once again, Matteo was already sitting at the table on the balcony. There were shadows under his eyes that suggested his sleep might have been as disturbed as her own. But he looked up as she appeared, and a slow smile spread across his face at the sight of her, making him look instantly younger. More free.

Was he remembering that moment last night, too? The one when he'd been close enough for her to kiss, if she'd moved her head just ever so slightly? Was he thinking about the suggestion he'd made to her?

The smirk on his face suggested he probably was.

'Good morning,' he said, his voice low and warm. 'Sleep well?'

She took her seat. 'Like a baby.' It wasn't a lie. Babies were notoriously bad sleepers, weren't they?

'Me too.' The smirk hadn't gone anywhere. 'So, how are we going to spend our second day in secluded paradise? Chess? Poker?'

He was teasing her now, but she didn't rise to it. Instead, she looked out over the lake, the balcony suddenly claustrophobic, despite all the fresh air. This villa was huge, and she knew that if she asked for space Matteo would give it to her. He wasn't the kind of man to press where he wasn't wanted, she could tell that already from the way he'd backed off last night after the merest suggestion of more.

The problem was, she wasn't at all sure she wanted him to keep backing off. But she wasn't certain enough to let him in, either.

She wanted him; she wasn't lying to herself about that any more. But it was *so* against The Rules. And beyond anything she'd let herself want for so long—ever since Nate. The desire she felt for Matteo…it was overwhelming, and terrifying.

And it felt amazing, all the same.

She stared out over the water and the mountains in the distance. The June air was warm and welcoming, but the breeze from the water kept things fresh in the shady trees that surrounded the villa.

She didn't want to be trapped inside today—otherwise, this villa was no better than the palace in Augusta that she'd escaped from.

Maybe she wasn't ready to take the risk of letting Matteo in quite yet. But perhaps she could take the tiny risk of letting herself out. Just a little bit.

One small first step towards where she was almost ready to admit she really wanted to go.

To bed, with Matteo.

Isabella placed her empty coffee cup down on her saucer. 'I'm going for a walk, down by the lake,' she said, before she could change her mind. That would give her time and space to keep figuring out what she wanted from this week. Time away from the allure of Matteo's smile, or those green eyes that pulled her in whenever she caught them.

Matteo grinned. 'Great! I'll come with you.'

* * *

There was a narrow path, leading away from the villa in the opposite direction from the easier one he'd taken for yesterday's walk, down the slope of the ground to the water's edge. Matteo hopped down it easily, hands in his pockets, then looked back to find Isabella picking her way along the uneven ground more cautiously.

'Need a hand?' He stretched out his arm to offer his assistance, but Isabella shook her head.

'I'm fine.'

That was a lie if ever he'd heard one. Oh, not with the path—he was sure she was more than capable of making her way down that alone.

But Princess Isabella of Augusta was not fine.

Perhaps it was just being away from the palace and out on her own for what, he imagined, had to be the first time in a long time. But he suspected it had more to do with the ideas he'd put in her head over dinner the night before.

She was a princess, not a casual hook-up in his usual fashion, he knew that. But still…they needed to find a way to entertain themselves this week, right? And since his usual methods of adrenaline-seeking were off the table, Matteo could only think of one good one.

Not to mention the fact that the more time he spent with her, the more inevitable them falling into bed together seemed. So why put it off? Why not enjoy the hell out of it while they had the time? Now he'd made the decision, Matteo was done denying what he wanted.

But back to the Princess.

After he'd retreated to his room the night before, Matteo had done a little internet research. Only natural, really, he figured. After all, she knew who *he* was, and was presumably familiar with his reputation. It was only fair that he use the tools at his disposal to put them on an equal footing. Thank goodness for high class Wi-Fi in such a remote spot.

Augusta, he'd learned, was a tiny little country—one of those ones squeezed between the bigger, more familiar European powers. Still, its monarchy had its fans—especially the next generation. Matteo was secure enough in his own masculinity to admit that Isabella's older brother, Leo, the Crown Prince, was handsome, built, and probably the subject of teenage Augustian girl fantasies, despite the fact he'd got married a few years before. Her sister, too, was married off, as were all the cousins and second cousins—at least, the ones over twenty-one.

Isabella, at twenty-eight, was already gaining articles about her being 'on the shelf', which seemed kind of ridiculous to Matteo, who was already five years older than that and had no intention of marrying any time soon. But it was different for royals, he supposed.

There'd been a short mention of a boyfriend in one of the articles from a few years ago, but nothing much more. And he'd avoided most of the gossipy pieces; he knew from his own experience how inaccurate they could be.

'Okay?' he asked as Isabella reached the bottom of the path.

'Fine,' she said again.

He wished she'd stop saying that.

Because the thing was, Matteo had only known the Princess for less than forty-eight hours, and he already knew it was a lie. She was beautiful, witty, bright and fun to be around—and he thought that was more to do with her natural personality than her royal training. She didn't ask the 'have you travelled far?' or 'what do you do?' questions he'd been asked on being presented to other members of other royal families. She didn't keep up that screen of polite reserve, of smiling because she was supposed to smile, or listening because she was supposed to listen, not because she was happy or interested.

And yet...she was definitely holding back. He could sense it in the straightness of her back, the way she paused too long before answering his questions. The way uncertainty would flash behind her eyes whenever he got too close.

He'd seen that before—in other women, and in friends, too.

Someone had hurt her. Someone she loved.

Not that it was any of his business, he knew.

And yet...part of him wanted it to be.

She's just one more challenge, that's all, he told himself. And she wasn't even on Giovanni's list. He needed to let it go.

'Which way do you want to go?' he asked as they reached the edge of the water. The path, a little more established here, stretched out in both directions, surrounding this corner of Lake Geneva. To the right, it joined up with the path he thought he'd taken yesterday.

Matteo's geography was a little rusty, but he seemed to remember that the lake was *huge*, almost like an ocean between the countries of Switzerland and France. Driving in from the private airfield where he'd landed, he'd passed dozens of small lakeside towns and resorts, before disappearing into the trees that surrounded the villa he and Isabella were staying in.

Maybe he'd persuade Isabella to go explore some of them with him one day, once she trusted him a little more.

'That way.' She pointed to the left, seemingly randomly, but as they broke out of the tree cover Matteo decided it was a good choice, all the same. Up ahead was a small jetty, seemingly attached to their villa, since there were no other residences in sight. A speedboat, painted in white and blue, was moored up beside it practically calling his name; he would have to take that out on the water this week. Maybe he could even convince Isabella to join him in that adventure, if she wouldn't risk the towns...

There was also, he realised somewhat belatedly, another, much easier path down from this side of the villa. Oh, well; coming down the forest path had been an adventure. And wasn't that what he was known for?

'It's beautiful here, isn't it?' Isabella said.

He looked at her. The June sun beat down on her dark curls, making them shine so brightly they were almost white where the light hit. Her face was tilted up towards the sky, soaking in the warmth, her arms loose at her sides and her white cotton sundress dancing around her calves in the slight breeze.

She was beautiful. Never mind the damn lake.

Again, he felt that tug of lust down low in his belly, the one he'd been vaguely conscious of since the moment he first saw her, standing with her back to him on the terrace. 'It's gorgeous,' he replied, a beat too late.

Isabella turned to him and smiled. 'I'll race you to the jetty.'

And before he could even process her words, she was already running, racing towards the slatted wooden platform that jutted out over the water.

He could have caught her easily, if he'd started moving immediately. But instead he took a moment to watch her run, her hair flowing in the wind, her curved calves flashing under her thin white skirt.

Then he caught her.

In a few long strides, he reached her side and, as they approached the jetty, wrapped an arm around her waist to catch her, pulling her body tight against his as she laughed and he grinned against the warmth of her hair.

It was a game, a moment of lightness and fun...and then it changed.

Like a cloud passing over the sun, Matteo felt all the playfulness of the moment disappear in a shadow of an instant.

Her curves pressed against the planes of his body, soft and yielding in his arms, and for a second he almost forgot there was clothing between them at all. Her hair smelled of roses and sunshine, and it overwhelmed his senses. He heard her breath hitch in her throat and realised that he'd stopped breathing altogether.

He'd known she was beautiful. But like this, pressed against him as if the only place she belonged was in his arms...she was so much more.

She was magnificent.

He should let go. That would be the gentlemanly thing to do. But how could he when this felt so right?

'Matteo...' She twisted her head to look up at him, her tongue darting out to moisten her full lower lip in a way that made him groan with want. He was so instantly, painfully hard, pressed against her, she had to know exactly how he felt. What he wanted. How he needed her.

He'd expected to see uncertainty in her eyes. But when he met her gaze with his own he found only a reflection of his own want.

Lust surged through him as he hauled her up until his mouth met hers. He kissed her the way he'd wanted to since he first saw that lush mouth of hers—deep and hard and as if there were nothing more in the world but the two of them.

And she kissed him back, matching his passion as she turned in his arms, raking her hands up into his hair to hold him closer. God, how had he thought this siren reserved and shy? Instead, she was everything he needed to remind him he was still alive, still had adventures to find, places to explore.

Like her entire naked body. Preferably now. They'd been promised seclusion, right? He hadn't seen another villa for miles before he reached theirs. No one would see if he stripped her dress from her and made love to her here on the sun-warmed wood, right? And even if they did... Matteo was past caring.

But Isabella was not, it seemed.

As he reached for the straps holding her dress up and slowly pushed them down her arms, she wrenched her mouth away from his at last. Her eyes were still wild, her hair curling in all directions where he'd been running his hands through it. And her mouth—those gorgeous plump lips—was swollen from his kiss.

Matteo started to drop his hands from her body, but she grabbed them before he could, holding them between them, crushed against her breasts. His fingers itched to reach out and stroke the line of her neck, down past her collarbone and under the white cotton of her dress. But he made himself wait and listen.

This, he assumed, was where she told him all the reasons this was a bad idea, reminded him that she was a *princess*, so could never think of acting on the obvious attraction between them. He tried to prepare himself for the inevitable, even though his body was clearly still far more optimistic than his mind.

And then the Princess said, 'Race you to a bed.'

CHAPTER FIVE

Isabella dropped his hands, turned and started to run.

She had no real hope of being able to outrun Matteo—not that she really wanted to, for long. But if she acted fast enough, perhaps she could outrun the voice in her head reminding her of all the reasons that this was a terrible idea.

She didn't care. Not right now. And maybe that would come back to bite her later, but she'd deal with that then.

This was her week of freedom. Her week to be Isabella, not the Princess. Her week to find her own happiness, her own pleasure.

And from just one kiss, she already knew that Matteo Rossi could give her a hell of a lot more pleasure than anyone else in her life ever had.

Her blood pounded in her ears as she raced up the path towards the house—the simple, straight one, not the one through the trees they'd come down. She wasn't wasting any time getting back to the villa now she'd made her decision.

No, she hadn't decided. More…followed her instincts, for once.

From the moment Matteo had caught her, the instant she'd felt his body against hers, she'd known she was done fighting the attraction between them. Because if she left this villa at the end of the week without sampling everything he was offering, she knew that she'd regret it for the rest of her life.

She could hear Matteo's thudding footsteps on the path behind her, slow and steady, as she approached the villa. He was pacing himself, of course. He didn't want to beat her, and he wanted to save his energy for what would happen when he *did* catch her.

Isabella allowed herself a small, secret smile at the thought. God, she couldn't wait for him to catch her.

She risked a glance back over her shoulder and found him almost right behind her. Her heart was racing—was it because of the running, or the pursuit? Or because it knew what was coming next...

Finally, finally she reached her destination.

Grabbing the handle of the large, sliding glass door that opened up the whole ground floor to the outside world, she yanked it open and tripped inside. Matteo's arm was around her waist in an instant, keeping her upright, keeping her close.

'Caught you,' he murmured into her ear, and she shivered in delight.

'I don't see a bed yet,' she whispered.

In response, Matteo swept her up into his arms and strode purposefully towards the stairs. 'We can fix that.'

Isabella laughed. 'You don't need to carry me!'

'I'm not risking you running away again.'

But she wouldn't, she knew. Maybe she *had* made a decision, after all.

One to make the most of every moment of freedom she had this week. One to put aside her fears and The Rules and her trust issues and go with her feelings instead. Her body, even.

Gianna had given her this week, and now Isabella was giving herself *this*.

She wasn't going to let herself back away again. Not for anything.

They'd barely made it up the first step, though, when a sharp, ringing sound rang out through the villa.

Matteo froze, mid step.

'Alarm?' Isabella asked.

'Phone,' Matteo corrected her.

The noise repeated. And repeated.

'Right. Of course.' She knew what a phone sounded like. It was just that in her world, a noise like that was more likely to be a fox setting off one of the proximity alarms at the palace, or a sightseer getting a little too enthusiastic about their visit and pushing through an alarmed barrier to a room that was out of bounds. 'Leave it.' It was the reckless kind of thing she did this week—ignoring phone calls and alarms.

The phone was still ringing. And Matteo was still holding her, motionless on the stairs, obviously at war within himself.

Finally, he sighed and put her down. 'It could be the security team,' he said, far too reasonably for her liking. 'If we don't answer, someone will come up here and interrupt us anyway. And I'd rather take the call fully clothed than deal with a burly security guard bursting in when I'm buried deep inside you.'

His voice dropped on the last part of his sentence, and Isabella felt it resonate through her body until she was throbbing with the need to feel him there, not just talking about it.

But instead, Matteo swept across the room, picked up the receiver and barked, 'Yes?'

As she watched, his demeanour softened a little even

as his shoulders slumped in resignation. 'Madison. Hi. Yes, we both made it here okay.' He looked up and caught Isabella's gaze with his own, apology in his eyes. Then he chuckled at something the dating-agency owner had said, and he looked away. 'Getting you to check up on me, are they? Sure, sure, you always check in on day two. Well, you can tell my management team that I am staying out of trouble. The Princess and I have been for a lovely walk through the woods this morning, and around the lake to the jetty.'

Isabella smiled. The truth, if not the whole truth.

She could see the strain on Matteo's face as he tried to remain polite, to convince Madison—and presumably, by association, his team—that he was behaving. Not that she imagined they'd be complaining too much about his seducing her—or the other way around, if she was honest. After all, why send him on a dream date if they didn't want him to, well, find a little relaxation that way?

Still, this conversation was going on far too long for her liking. Isabella smiled. She had just the way to fix that.

If he'd honestly believed that this was just a courtesy call from Madison Morgan to check that they'd settled in okay, Matteo would have hung up in an instant. But he knew his team, his management. He knew Gabe.

He'd been ignoring his phone ever since Isabella had arrived, and that would have Gabe worried. So he'd found another way to check up on him. His manager had always been a little overprotective of the talent.

No, that wasn't fair. Gabe had always been overprotective of *him*. And if he'd set Madison up to make this call and Matteo didn't answer…well, those security guards would be bursting in again any moment. And he *really* didn't like being interrupted.

'Everything has been perfect,' he reassured Madison. *Everything apart from the timing of this phone call.* Because now Isabella had an excuse to overthink, to start listing all the reasons this was a bad idea. And that would lead to her changing her mind.

He could almost see the thoughts passing over her face as the occurred to her. She took a step back up the stairs, getting ready to run.

The attraction between them was undeniable, but even he had to admit the logistics weren't great. If he'd *actually* been looking for his one true love, he'd have been pretty pissed off. But as it was, this worked perfectly for him. Although he knew his team had been hoping this week might lead to a stable girlfriend for him, one who might take over responsibility for keeping his feet on the ground and the whole of him out of hospital for a while, that wasn't what Matteo wanted.

He just wanted Isabella, naked, under him, on top of him, and anywhere else she wanted, for the rest of this week. And Madison Morgan, matchmaker extraordinaire, was going to ruin that for him. The irony was actually painful.

But then, something changed, somewhere inside Isabella's mind. He'd probably never know exactly what, but he didn't really care.

A wicked smile flickered across her lips. And then, her eyes wide, she reached up and untied one of the bows at her shoulders that held up her dress.

Half of the white fabric of the bodice fell, sliding over the curve of her breast to hang under it, revealing the intricate, gossamer-thin lace of her strapless bra.

Matteo swallowed, his whole body tense with need.

God, he wanted to drop the phone, race over there and take that perfect peak in his mouth.

But he also wanted to see what Isabella did next.

He didn't have long to wait. Slowly, deliberately, she reached up and untied the other bow.

The white sundress slipped away from her skin, hanging around her hips, leaving her torso covered only by that see-through bra.

On the other end of the line, Madison was saying something about the boat at the jetty, but he wasn't listening. He was picturing his hands, his mouth, his body on those perfect curves. His gaze followed the gorgeous, undulating line of her, curving down over her shoulder, swelling over her breasts, dipping in for that narrow waist before flaring out again at her hips, where that damned sundress still hung, caught on the sheer generosity of her body.

'Right,' he said to Madison, with no idea what he was agreeing with.

Isabella smirked, as if she knew exactly how distracted he was. Maybe she did. Her eyes were almost black, and even at this distance he could tell she was breathing harder than her actions warranted.

She's turned on by this too. Thank God.

How had he thought, even for a moment, that this princess was buttoned up and boring?

'Yeah, of course,' he said, even though the words were meaningless. Matteo didn't take his eyes from Isabella for a moment.

And as he watched, she put her hands to her hips, and pushed the white cotton over them.

The dress fell to the floor, and Matteo gripped onto the edge of the telephone table hard, just in case he suddenly passed out from wanting her. It didn't seem completely impossible right now.

Had he ever been this hard, this desperate for a woman before? He didn't think so.

And he'd barely even touched her, kissed her.

God, he wanted to do so much more.

He let his gaze roam from her perfectly painted toes—her sandals abandoned by the door, he supposed—all the way up those long, shapely calves and thighs. He skirted past her wispy lace panties—because he knew there was no way he could keep control of himself if he lingered too long there—and continued along the curve of her waist, over her breasts, up to her face and met her gaze with his own.

The desire he saw there echoed the one throbbing through his body, and he knew he couldn't wait any longer. However exquisite the feeling of drawing out this pleasure had been, now he needed to act, not watch.

Isabella reached behind her back, unfastened her bra, and let it fall to the ground. Her magnificent breasts bobbed in front of him, and Matteo swore he was starting to see stars.

'Madison, I have to go.' He dropped the phone back onto its receiver and raced towards the stairs.

Definitely time to act.

Isabella laughed as she darted up the stairs before he could reach her, heading straight for her bedroom. A striptease for a man she barely knew hadn't exactly been on her to-do list for the week, but she *had* decided to go with her instincts for once...

And seeing the lust in Matteo's gaze as he'd watched her, she was glad she had. She'd felt powerful, in control of her own future for once—at least, her immediate future. The one that ended with her and Matteo in her bed. Taking control in such a way had calmed her re-emerging nerves about that part, too.

She careened around the corner into her bedroom, squealing as he caught her at last, wrapping an arm around her waist and hauling her to him, just as he'd done down by the lake.

'That was cruel,' he rasped against her ear, the desperation clear in his voice.

'I think the word you're looking for is "inspired",' she corrected him.

'That too.' He pressed a kiss to the patch of skin where her neck met her shoulders and she squirmed in his arms as pleasure fired through her nerves. 'You like that?'

'Mmm,' she agreed.

'Good.' Lifting her roughly, he dropped her down onto the bed from a just high enough height that she bounced. 'Let's find out what else you like.'

She'd thought that stripping for Matteo would be a treat for him. She hadn't anticipated how much it would turn her on, too.

She didn't do things like this—not least because, as a protected Princess of Augusta, she'd never had the chance.

Now she *had* that chance, just for the week. And she was going to take it.

Isabella moaned as Matteo kissed his way down her throat, over her collarbone, and further down, towards her breasts. With an appreciative noise from the back of his throat, he closed his mouth over her nipple, running his tongue around the sensitive nub until she writhed underneath him. God, that mouth wasn't only made for talking. She could feel him smiling against her skin before he released her with a pop, and moved across to give the other nipple the same treatment.

His hands weren't still either. As his mouth worked on her breasts, his hands brushed up and down her sides, caressing the curve of her hip. Then suddenly, they slipped underneath her, gripping her and pressing her against him.

Oh, she could feel him. He'd been keeping his weight off her, but now... She might be stripped down to her panties, but he was still fully clothed—and still, she could feel the hard length of him pressed against her bare skin, even through his jeans. Could imagine the size and the feel of him in her hand. In her mouth. Inside her...

It had been so, so long. And she'd spent too long thinking that the mistakes that came out of her last venture into lovemaking were her fault, that they meant she wasn't destined to have this in her life.

Yet here she was.

Matteo pressed one last kiss to her nipple then looked up, his green eyes bright as he met her gaze.

'You okay?' he asked.

'I will be.'

He smiled at that. 'Tell me what you need.'

You, inside me. The thought was instant, but saying the words was another matter. She bit her lip and watched his eyes darken.

'I need the words,' he said, sounding as though just talking was taking all of his self-control right now.

Maybe it was.

And yet, she knew if she said, *No, I can't, let's stop,* he would. Nate would have cajoled her, told her to stay with him a little longer and she'd change her mind.

Matteo would back off the second she said the words.

Maybe that was one of the reasons that, this time, she didn't want to.

'I want you to make love to me.' It came out a little faster, a little more desperate than she'd intended, but Matteo didn't seem to mind. Quite the opposite, in fact.

With a noise in the back of his throat that was almost a growl, he lowered his head and kissed her again, deeper and deeper. Which was wonderful, but wasn't getting him any more naked, so Isabella set about rectifying that instead, her fingers making quick work of the buttons of his shirt before she stripped it from his shoulders.

She let herself be distracted, for a moment, by all that lovely hard muscle and tanned skin, brushed with a dusting of dark hair. Closing her eyes, she ran her hands over the planes and dips of him, just as he'd done to her, memorising his body by touch alone.

But she couldn't allow herself to be *too* distracted. Opening her eyes again to find Matteo watching her, she held his gaze as she reached determinedly down to unfasten his jeans.

He helped her push his jeans and boxers down over those long, muscled legs, then stripped away her panties too, and suddenly there was nothing between them at all. Well, nothing that mattered right now.

She swallowed, as her gaze roamed down the length of him. It really had been a long time…but now she was here, she was almost dizzy with the need for him.

'Condom?' she asked breathily, as a reminder to herself that she hadn't completely lost her mind.

Matteo reached across to the small table beside the bed and pulled a strip of them from the drawer. Excellent.

'You're sure?' he asked again as he ripped open the packet.

'Very.' She took the condom from him and reached out to roll it securely in place. She wasn't taking any chances.

His breathing ragged, Matteo reached for her again, and Isabella went willingly into his arms, ready to embrace her freedom.

Making love to a princess, Matteo had decided, was probably the same as making love to any other woman.

But making love to Isabella? That was something new. Something special. Something totally unexpected—and a little unsettling. He'd thought this would be something else to tick off his list of adventures, another risk to take, even.

So why did it feel like something else?

The way she'd affected him since the moment he saw her should have been his first clue. He'd never wanted a woman the way he'd wanted Isabella. Wanted to touch her, to feel her in his arms, to smell her hair and taste her skin, to get as close to her as it was possible for two people to be.

And now that he was…he couldn't remember why he'd ever wanted to be anywhere else.

Holding himself up on his elbows, he let her guide him inside her, taking things at her pace, not his. Slowly, slowly he filled her, giving her time to adjust to him before he moved any more, watching her face carefully for every reaction.

Isabella's eyes were closed, her face clear and smooth, and for a brief, horrible moment it occurred to Matteo that she might not have done this before. That, as a princess, she might have been kept pure and chaste and…oh, God, what if he was her first?

Then her eyes flashed open and she gave him that wicked grin he'd seem when she was beating him at Monopoly. 'What are you waiting for, superstar? *Move.*'

And he did.

What had started slow and sweet and careful soon became more frantic, more desperate as they moved together, in perfect synchronicity. Isabella's hands clutched at his back, pulling her to him, driving him deeper with every thrust. Matteo had a feeling this would be over in an embarrassingly short space of time...but at least they had the rest of the week to make up for it.

Tugging her round, he flipped them so he was on his back, letting her ride him to her own pleasure. Long, loose dark curls hung down over her breasts as she moved, more languidly than he'd be capable of right now. Her chin tilted up, that aristocratic neck long and elegant, she bit down on her plump lower lip and Matteo thought he might be done for. Reaching up, he brushed the hair away from her breasts to cup them with his hands, and ran his fingers across her nipples, making her shiver above him.

Good. He needed to know this was affecting her the same way it was him.

'Isabella.' Her name came out as more of a moan than he'd intended, but it worked. Her eyes fluttered open and she looked down at him, her hips not losing their sanity-depriving rhythm for a moment.

The lust he saw in her eyes was the same one he felt coursing through his blood. And that was all it took for his baser instincts to take over.

Grabbing tight hold of her hips, he thrust up into her, gratified when she upped the speed of her own movements to match him. Not losing pace for a moment, he shifted one hand towards her core, teasing her with his fingers and driving her further and further to where he needed her to go.

And just when he thought he might lose his mind, she

gasped and tightened around him, again and again as she cried out, her hips stuttering to a stop as he thrust once, twice, three times more...and felt his world explode.

'Oh, God.' Isabella slumped against his chest, sweaty and sated and salty sweet under his kisses. 'That was a good idea.'

'Glad you agree,' Matteo murmured against her skin. Although, 'good idea' weren't exactly the words he'd have chosen.

Transcendental, perhaps. Life-changing. Magical.

He blinked, and forced the thoughts away. It was just sex, same as any other sex he'd had with many other women. Sure, he was more attracted to Isabella than any of the other women he'd met lately—maybe ever. But that was just chemistry. Physical lust didn't mean anything more than an incredible time between the sheets.

And he was just lucky he got to experience that for a week, before going back to the real world.

Isabella rolled away from him, leaving his skin cooling in the breeze from the open window as she lay beside him on the huge bed. Last night, lying in his own bed next door, he'd felt frustrated, adrift and alone. Before that, he'd felt unsettled and aroused and distracted by being around her.

Now, he only felt sated, relaxed and as if there was nowhere in the world he'd rather be.

He blinked at the thought. When had he last felt that way?

Speeding around the racetrack, it was a familiar feeling—especially as he cornered the last turn before the flag. But outside a racing car? That feeling was a lot harder to find.

On the top of a mountain, perhaps, looking out at the blue sky and great depths below. The second when he jumped from a plane, in the moments before he opened his parachute. Or when he sprang away from that cliff-side and dived towards the water—before he broke his leg, of course.

But those highs only ever lasted until he reached solid ground again. Until the race was over, the adrenaline gone.

Until now.

He'd travelled the world on one adventure after another, taking bigger and better risks, beating the odds—chasing the adrenaline high that reminded him he was alive, when so many others weren't. He'd taken chances that terrified the people around him so much that they'd sent him here, a last-ditch attempt to keep him safe and out of trouble.

And here, in Isabella's bed, he'd found that same peace he hunted for, that same high.

He just had a feeling it also came with a whole different sort of trouble.

Shifting onto his side, he watched Isabella's chest rise and fall as her breath slowly returned to normal.

'What are you thinking?' The question was out of his mouth before he had a chance to think whether he really wanted to know the answer. Because the odds of Princess Isabella of Augusta feeling the same as him right now seemed slim.

They both knew what this week was about, and it wasn't about transcendental feelings of satisfaction with the world. It wasn't about him finding a way to get his adrenaline high that didn't involve breaking any bones or taking any risks. Although he knew his team wouldn't mind if that was the case...

This wasn't a permanent solution. This was one week, that was all. Princess Isabella wasn't about to turn to him and tell him he'd so rocked her world that she loved him and wanted to make him her prince.

Which was good, because he didn't want that either.

Still, he couldn't help but smile when she turned her face towards his and said, 'Do you think there's any more food downstairs? I'm starving.'

CHAPTER SIX

Isabella hadn't been lying when she told Matteo she was hungry. But as he laughed and pulled on his jeans to go and raid the kitchen for her, she had to admit she hadn't been telling the whole truth, either.

She'd been thinking about taking chances. And how good it felt to take a risk for a change.

How buttoned up had her life been? Oh, maybe it wouldn't have been obvious to the casual onlooker. To someone who only knew her through her publicity photos or the palace's social media channels, she must seem the ultimate carefree princess. Never having to worry about the things that consumed so many other people's lives—like having a roof over their heads or enough money for food or keeping their family healthy and well. She'd always had a home at the palace—not to mention the 'summer house', a mansion in the hills of Augusta where the court could decamp in the hot weather—and royal property she could use throughout the country. She'd never had to prepare her own food, although since she'd been an adult her rooms had their own kitchen where she *could* cook, if she chose. Meals—no, banquets—had been the norm in the palace. The best doctors in the land—in Europe, the world—had been at their beck and call when required.

Isabella wasn't playing poor little rich girl. She knew how lucky she was.

It had just taken until now to realise what freedom truly felt like.

'I'm starting to think the staff here might be psychic.' Matteo pushed the door open with his knee, grinning as he appeared with a heavily laden tray. 'That, or we were a lot louder than I'd thought.'

Isabella pulled herself up to rest against the padded headboard, the sheets falling away from her body and leaving her bare from the waist up. 'What did they leave us?'

Matteo didn't answer immediately, apparently too busy admiring the view as his gaze roamed over her torso. Isabella didn't reach for the sheet to cover herself.

Yesterday, I would have done.

Yesterday, she'd have been embarrassed at the idea of someone listening to her having sex, and providing snacks ready for afters. Yesterday, she'd have blushed at the blatant ogling Matteo was indulging in.

Today...today she felt like a different person. Had done since that moment by the lake when she made her decision to embrace the possibilities of this week.

And she wasn't done embracing yet.

'I'm getting hungrier, here,' she teased, and Matteo gave her a shameless grin before setting the tray down on the bed and perching beside it.

'We've got coffee, cookies, some sort of gooey cake... plenty of sugar to keep our energy levels up.'

'Good.' She smiled up at him—her best princess smile. 'I think you're going to need it.'

Later, quite a lot later, when the cake was demolished to crumbs, the dregs of the coffee were cold, and Isabella's muscles were relaxed to the point of melting into the mattress, Matteo turned on his side and propped his head up on one hand.

'What changed your mind?' he asked as he studied her.

Isabella tried not to shift uncomfortably under his gaze. After all, the man had touched, tasted and loved every inch of her body over the course of the last handful of hours. Maybe longer; the sun looked a lot lower in the sky than she'd have thought...

'Changed my mind about what?'

'About me.' He raised his eyebrows. 'I mean, last night I definitely got "this is not behaviour befitting a princess" vibes from you. But today...' He left it hanging, their mutual nakedness doing all the talking for him.

'Maybe I just decided that I deserved a week off from being a princess.'

'And is that something you do often?'

'Never.' Except that was a lie, and here, beside him in her bed, Isabella found that she didn't *want* to lie to Matteo. Not even to preserve her reputation, or the monarchy of Augusta's reputation, come to that. 'Once,' she amended.

Curiosity flared behind Matteo's green eyes. 'Tell me? I mean, if you want to. Since you're just being Isabella this week, not a princess.'

'And this is something normal people do? Talk about their romantic disasters?' She wouldn't know. Her family had told her to lock it away inside her, pretend it never happened. Deny everything if Nate ever tried again to make another story out of it—although she suspected that Leo had paid him enough to make it worth his while to pretend it hadn't happened, either, after the initial flurry of press.

'This is something that normal people do,' Matteo confirmed. 'Well, some of them, anyway.'

'Not you?'

'I don't have romantic disasters.'

'Just cliff-diving ones.'

'Just those,' Matteo confirmed, with a grin.

'Although...that's not what the gossip magazines say.' Isabella shifted closer, her hands under her head as she curled towards him. 'They're forever talking about which heart you've broken now.'

Matteo rolled his eyes. 'You shouldn't pay any attention to them. They'll say anything to get people to buy a copy.'

'I don't know,' Isabella teased. 'There are a lot of photos of you...'

He reached over to brush his hand over her waist, almost light enough to tickle, before pulling her closer. 'Is this the part where I tell you none of them meant anything before you?'

It was her turn to roll her eyes, now. 'If this was a normal M dating agency week of passion, or whatever they call it, probably. But I think we both know neither of us are here for *that*. So the truth will do just fine instead, thank you very much.'

Matteo loosened his hold on her side, and flopped onto his back. 'The *truth*? No one ever seems to care about that.'

'I do.' Because she knew she couldn't trust herself to interpret the world without it. People lied, all the time, and she wasn't sophisticated enough in the way of life outside the palace to even tell when it was happening.

'Fine. I like women—I like their company, and, well, I like sex.'

'I noticed,' Isabella said, with a smirk.

She didn't add, 'So do I.' Because she hadn't known that she did, not like this. Not until today.

And that was a discovery she was still adjusting to.

'But I'm always upfront with women about what I can

offer,' Matteo went on, oblivious to her omission. 'I'm not in the market for a serious relationship, or anything more than a few nights of fun. I've got too many other things to do.'

'Like go cliff diving.'

'And win world championships.'

Isabella stretched out her legs under the thin sheets, feeling her well-used muscles protest at still being expected to move. 'But you've done both of those things now,' she pointed out. 'What else is on your list?'

There was a pause she didn't expect after her question. Not one that felt as though Matteo was trying to think of something to say, or remember what daring plans he had next. More as though he was trying to decide whether to share it with her.

She wondered how outrageous it had to be, for that.

Finally, he moved to sit up against the headboard, and reached for his phone, swiping across the screen a few times before handing it to her.

She'd expected a website or a booking email or something—perhaps for deep-sea diving in the Red Sea, or a trek into the Himalayas. Instead, she found herself looking at a photo of a handwritten list.

He had an actual list.

Except…she frowned at the carefully printed words at the top of the page in the photo.

Giovanni Rossi's Bucket List

This wasn't Matteo's list. Even though she could see that he'd carefully crossed out plenty of items on it—including cliff diving. And becoming the racing world champion.

'I don't understand,' she said, handing back the phone.

Matteo took it from her, glanced at the screen with an indecipherable look on his face, then placed it back on the table beside him. He looked...lost, somehow. She hadn't expected that from him, especially after the self-assuredness he'd shown in bed.

On impulse, she nestled closer, until he wrapped one arm around her shoulder as she rested her head on his firm chest.

'My brother,' he said, eventually. 'Giovanni. He was three years older than me.'

Isabella heard the *was* and knew that nothing that followed was going to be good.

'He was the daredevil, when we were kids,' Matteo went on, a fond smile on his face. 'Always the one getting into scrapes or trying the impossible just to prove that he could.'

He fell silent, and Isabella could feel the weight of that silence in the air around them.

'What happened to him?' she asked, when she couldn't bear it any longer.

She'd braced herself for a car accident, or some other sort of dangerous, reckless end. Which was why Matteo's reply made her gasp at the tragedy of it all.

'He was diagnosed with terminal cancer when I was sixteen.' His words were flat, emotionless, but Isabella could tell that was through practice. He said it the same way she said Nate's name, these days, and it had taken her years to perfect that emptiness between the syllables. *Nath-an-ial. Ter-min-al.* They sounded the same in her head.

'I'm so sorry, Matteo.' Isabella pressed a soft kiss to his skin and wished there were more she could do. But grief was grief, wasn't it? Whatever the cause, it was personal, and permanent.

He shrugged, and she felt the shift of his muscles under her cheek. 'It was a lot of years ago, now. Seventeen, almost.'

'Still. He was your brother.' Nathanial had been her world, and he didn't even have the good grace to be *dead*.

'Yeah.' Matteo slumped a little lower against the headboard, pulling her closer until her whole body half covered his. 'After he got sick…he made this list. All the things he'd wanted to do in his life but was never going to get the chance. I… I helped him. Because I think, even then, I thought he was going to get better. I thought it would give him something to look forward to, once the treatment was over. But instead…' She felt him swallow and wrapped her arm a little tighter around him. 'He died. And I was just left with this list. So I promised myself—promised him, really—that I'd do every single damn thing on it. Everything he didn't have time to do. Everything that was taken from him. And I am. I have.'

Become world champion. The list item floated in front of her mind's eye. Had Matteo based his whole career on his brother's dying wish list?

She couldn't ask that. She'd only known the man a couple of days, however much some algorithm somewhere said she was his perfect match.

But she could hear the grief in his voice—still there, not diminished at all by every challenge he crossed off his brother's bucket list. Unresolved.

'So what's next?' she asked instead. 'What's left on the list?' Because as far as she could tell, almost everything had been crossed off.

'Well, even Giovanni didn't envision making love to a princess,' Matteo joked, although there wasn't any real humour in his voice. 'So… I guess I'm pretty much done.

Becoming world champion...that was his big dream, and I did it. And went cliff diving to celebrate.'

Isabella half smiled at that. 'I guess that means you'll have to start writing your own list now, then, huh?'

'I guess it does.' There was a hint of amazement, disbelief even, in his tone. But it was gone before she could even be totally sure it was there at all, as he twisted them around so she was underneath him again, and all she could think about was how right his body felt against hers. As if they were two parts of the same whole.

'But the list can wait?' she guessed as he pressed her further into the mattress, his arousal obvious against her belly.

'The list can *definitely* wait,' he agreed, before kissing her.

She hadn't answered his question.

Matteo didn't realise it until he awoke to the early morning light filtering through the gauzy curtains that barely covered the glass front of the villa. In fairness, he'd been far more preoccupied with all the things she *had* been telling him—*more, now, again*—to focus on the conversation she'd sidestepped.

But lying there in the pale June dawn, with Isabella's body curled against his, he realised, and he wondered.

How had she persuaded him to tell all his secrets about Giovanni, about the list, about why he did the things he did, and still managed to evade telling him *anything* about herself? In fact, beyond the small detail of her being a princess, he wasn't sure he'd found out anything personal about her at all.

Was that part of being royal? The ability to ask polite questions and listen to the answers without ever giving anything in return? He didn't know. Isabella was the first royal he'd ever spent real time with, beyond the polite niceties, and he had a suspicion that she wasn't exactly typical.

He looked down at her, sleeping in his arms, and considered what he *did* know about her.

She wasn't looking for true love.

She hadn't been enamoured of any of the suitable prospective husbands Augusta had thrown up.

She hadn't come here through her own choice.

She wanted a break from being a princess—and she'd done that only once before…

What had happened then? Matteo was willing to place money that someone had hurt her. Someone had made her this way—cautious and careful. And if she was letting that go this week, with him… Matteo wasn't sure he could bear to see her go back to her buttoned-up ways afterwards.

Ever since he'd admitted that the chemistry between them was unavoidable, he'd hoped. He'd flirted and he'd hinted and he'd hoped—but he hadn't really expected. He'd figured a week of frustration and an inappropriate royal crush was probably punishment from the universe for something—maybe the broken leg, maybe the hearts he knew he'd broken, even when he'd been trying not to.

But he hadn't imagined this. Hadn't dreamt for a moment that their second full day together would lead to a race to the jetty and that kiss…not to mention everything that came after.

His position hadn't changed; he was the same man who'd seen a curvaceous brunette on the terrace below and hoped.

But Isabella…she'd become someone new overnight. Consciously, intentionally. She'd made a decision to be Just Isabella, rather than the Princess—but Matteo knew without her having to say the words that it wasn't a permanent change. This week was a holiday from being herself. Except, having seen how free and alive she seemed... Didn't she deserve to be that way all the time?

He wondered if he could convince her. If he could show her, in the days they had left together, that she could be whoever she wanted to be—not just in Lake Geneva, but in Augusta, too.

To do that, he suspected he'd need to get her to open up and tell him the story of the last time she tossed aside her crown for a while. And perhaps that was something she needed to work up to.

So he'd start small instead. See if he could show the Princess that taking risks could be fun, sometimes. Even *outside* the bedroom.

Isabella stirred in his arms, and Matteo smiled to himself as he bent to kiss the top of her head, settling more comfortably down beside her. He wouldn't sleep any more, he knew, not now he had adventures to plan. But she was going to need her rest.

She wanted a week off from being a princess? Well, then... Matteo was going to give her the best week's holiday she could imagine.

And maybe by the end of it, she wouldn't want to stop.

'So, what are we going to do today?' Isabella asked, some time later that morning, as they shared coffee and a late breakfast on the balcony outside their rooms.

Matteo raised his eyebrows in what he'd been told was an expressive manner, and she rolled her eyes.

'Is your plan to spend the *whole* week here in bed?' It wasn't, of course. But he couldn't quite tell if she was actually disapproving of that idea, or just felt some princessy need to pretend she was.

'Would that be such a terrible plan?'

When she smiled, her dimples popped into existence, and it made Matteo smile back, every time. They didn't show up, he'd noticed, in her official Princess Isabella smile, the one she'd given him that first night they'd met—the smile she was displaying in every single photo of her that seemed to be in the public domain, at least the ones that he'd been able to find online.

The dimples only appeared when she was truly smiling with happiness or amusement. Matteo had started counting the number of times he got to see them, and the total was already gratifyingly high.

'Maybe not *terrible*, exactly,' she said, her voice a soft purr. 'But I figure we might need a small break. Sometimes.'

Matteo sighed dramatically. 'Oh, I suppose you're right.'

She tossed a small piece of bread at him, then giggled and ducked when he tried to throw one back.

'Actually, I had thought we might go on a small adventure today,' he said, once the mini food fight had died down.

Across the table, Isabella stilled with what he knew instinctively was apprehension. Fear, even. Fear that felt more than just a general nervousness of the unknown, somehow.

'What sort of an adventure?' Her tone was cautious. Matteo supposed he didn't blame her. After all, he *was* famous for choosing the more extreme sort of adventures.

'I'm not going to force you to go skydiving or anything,' he said to reassure her. She didn't look particularly reassured. 'I thought we might take the boat out on the lake.'

She blinked. 'Boat?'

'The one that was tied up by the jetty. We saw it yesterday?'

Her cheeks turned pink. 'Oh, yes. Of course.'

'You did *see* the boat, right, Isabella?' he teased. 'I mean, you weren't so distracted by something that you failed to even notice the big boat tied up right next to you?' Okay, so it was quite a small boat in reality, but the point still held. She'd been so focused on his kisses, his touch, she'd lost all track of her surroundings.

The thought made his body start to tighten, and he was reconsidering the whole boat-trip idea when she tossed another piece of bread at him—this time, covered in jam.

'I saw the boat,' she said shortly, and he was fairly sure it was a lie. 'But do you really think we should take it out? I mean, I don't know anything about boats. Would we need to take one of the security team with us?'

'It's a fairly basic boat; I've driven them before. And there are life jackets here somewhere, I'm sure. We'll be fine. We won't even go too far from the villa, if you don't want to.' It was the smallest step he could think of for her to take, after she'd already taken the much bigger one of allowing him into her bed.

But it could be the first step to a new mindset for her. One where she didn't always automatically say no to things, until she was compelled to change her mind by events—or, in their case, sheer physical chemistry.

She looked down at her hands, suddenly the reserved, unsure Princess she'd been on arrival again—rather than the mischievous Isabella who tossed bread at him and made him come completely undone in bed. He watched as she came to a decision, lifted her chin and, with a determination he didn't really feel the suggestion warranted, said, 'Okay, then. We'll go out on the lake.'

Matteo smiled to himself. Stage one of his plan was complete.

CHAPTER SEVEN

Isabella was not at all sure that this was a good idea.

On the face of it, a short trip out on a boat on a lake, still miles away from anywhere, wasn't exactly a dangerous threat. But she was compiling a mental list of reasons this could be a disaster anyway.

1) They could capsize and drown, despite their life jackets.
2) Some paparazzi on a boat might find them and take photos through those ridiculous long lenses they had, and then her parents would know she wasn't with Sofia and it would be like Nathanial all over again.
3)...

Okay, that was all she had for now. But surely they were reason enough not to risk it?

She sat, tucked up in her life jacket, at the far end of the small boat from where Matteo was starting the engine. Despite the life jacket he wore—at her insistence—she could still enjoy the sight of his arm muscles as he worked to untie them from the jetty, the thick muscles of his thighs as he braced himself against the movement of the boat. She swallowed as she watched a bead of sweat work its way down his neck in the bright June sunlight...

Right.

3) They might not be able to keep their hands off each other, even on a damn boat, and then they'd take their life jackets off and cause the boat to capsize and then they'd definitely drown. Probably while paparazzi took photos of her naked, and it would be even worse than everything with Nathanial had been.

'You're catastrophising,' Matteo said mildly as the boat chugged away from the jetty.

Isabella blinked. 'I'm what?'

'You're thinking about all the things that could possibly go wrong out here on the water.'

'No, I'm...' He gave her a look, and she sighed. 'Fine, I'm catastrophising. But that's what keeps me safe—thinking about all the things that could go wrong *before* they happen.'

It was a lesson her father and mother had drilled into her after Nate. That she was not somebody who could just take chances, or jump at opportunities and see where they led, or—and this one was said with a certain amount of disgusted disbelief—*follow her heart*.

She was a Princess of Augusta, and with that privilege came expectations, amongst them the always unstated rule that she would not cause any sort of scandal to fall upon the royal house.

Well, unstated until that horrible week after Nate had left, at which point it was stated quite firmly and repeatedly, as if she had somehow missed it in the undercurrents of her upbringing.

She hadn't, of course. She'd just believed that love

trumped duty somehow. She'd believed in happy endings, and in everything working out for the best.

She knew better than that now.

She knew better than to be on this boat. To be in Lake Geneva at all. To be spending the week in the bed of a *most* unsuitable man.

But she was doing those things anyway, even though she knew what her parents, her brother would say.

You're making the same mistakes all over again.

Except Matteo wasn't Nate, and they weren't in Augusta, where her every move was tracked and recorded and reported. There was a privacy agreement in place with the M agency; she'd checked.

They were alone in this part of the lake; the sun was shining down and it was a beautiful day. She should relax and enjoy it.

Except she couldn't.

Matteo settled himself opposite her in the small boat, where he could watch her *and* where they were going, which she appreciated.

'Can you trust *me* to keep you safe?' he asked softly. 'Just for today?'

On the face of it, it was a ridiculous question. He was a risk-taking daredevil, known for his chequered history with women and famous for driving too fast around racetracks. He was the *last* person anyone should trust to keep them safe, right?

But once again, Isabella's heart spoke louder than her head. 'Yes,' she said gently. 'I trust you.'

Matteo smiled, as warm as the June sun. 'Good. Then sit back and enjoy the trip.'

The lake was surprisingly peaceful, once she'd stopped catastrophising. Isabella leaned back against the edge of the boat and tipped her chin so the sun streamed down on her face as the air brushed past her, raising the ends of her shorter curls around her shoulders.

'You are very distracting up there, you know,' Matteo said, and when she looked up, he was watching her intently.

'If you try and seduce me here we'll capsize the boat.' That wasn't catastrophising. That was physics. She knew how...vigorous their lovemaking could get.

'More's the pity.' Shutting off the small engine, he let the boat drift a little on the water. 'Well, if seduction is off the table, how about lunch?'

Isabella sat up with interest. 'We have lunch?'

'Of course, we have lunch.' Matteo grinned. 'I found it ready for us in the kitchen before we left, all packed up in a cool bag.'

'The invisible servants really do know their stuff.' Had they heard them talking about going out on the boat, or just guessed when Matteo went searching for life jackets? Either way, they were as good at anticipating their needs as any of the staff at the royal palace. Leo or her father would probably want to steal them if they knew about their existence.

Which they wouldn't. Because once this week was over, Isabella would never speak of it again, and she and Matteo would be the only people in the world who ever knew it happened.

She'd never speak to Matteo again either, probably. Certainly never make love to him again.

'Hey.' Matteo frowned as he paused in pulling out the food from the bag. 'What just happened? You look like the sun just disappeared.'

Isabella forced a smile, shaking her head to rid it of the thoughts. They wouldn't go. 'It's nothing,' she said, when it was clear that her smile wasn't enough to convince him. 'I was just thinking about what happens after this week is over.'

He stilled for a moment, then placed the container of strawberries he was holding on the seat between them that was serving as a table.

'You mean between us? Or for you?'

'Both, I suppose.'

'Well, I expect that depends on you, really, doesn't it?' he said, his tone careful.

He really was from a different world if he believed that. 'Not exactly.'

'Because of the princess thing?'

Her whole life reduced to a 'princess thing'.

'Because there are expectations placed on me.'

'Stay out of trouble and marry a duke? Isn't that about the size of it?' He made it sound like nothing. 'Because the thing is, Isabella, I kind of had the feeling that princesses were people too. Real flesh and blood people, who felt things and wanted things and deserved to live their lives the way they wanted.'

She could feel his words in her veins, filling her body with the hope of them. Reaching across the seat between them, he ran his fingers up her hand, before circling her wrist with them, the pads of his fingertips resting on her pulse point, feeling the beat of her heart as it thrummed through her.

'See?' he whispered. 'Not just a princess.'

Isabella pulled her hand away. 'Maybe not. But I *am* a Princess of Augusta, and that means something. Maybe not to you, but to my family, my country. And to me.'

How had this conversation got so deep, so fast? She wanted to go back to tossing jammy bread at him or sinking her body down on top of his.

They should have just stayed in bed today after all. This whole thing was much easier to navigate between the sheets than out of them.

He sat back, studying her so keenly that she had to force herself not to fidget under his gaze. 'Wouldn't your family just want you to be happy?'

She almost laughed, the idea was so absurd. 'Have you *met* many kings and queens?'

'A few,' he replied, with a shrug. 'But I'll admit I never had time to discuss their daughters' sex lives with them.'

That did make her laugh, despite herself. How did he do that? Always lighten the moment, just when she was getting down?

'So what would the obedient Princess of Augusta do next?' he asked.

That one was easy. 'She'd go home to the palace and continue life as always. Public engagements, charity events, hospital visits, that sort of thing.' When she couldn't get out of them.

'And blind dates with aristocrats you already know you don't want to marry.'

'That, too.' But in some ways, Isabella had come to realise, that was better than the alternative. Because at least when she went into something knowing it wasn't for ever, that it wasn't even what she wanted, her heart couldn't be broken at the end of it. Not this time.

'Okay.' He leant forward, his forearms resting on those muscled thighs as he held her gaze. 'And what does *Isabella* want to happen next?'

Something else. She had no idea what, but there had to be more than just that, didn't there?

Except last time she'd tried to reach for it, her whole world had almost come crashing down.

'The same thing,' she said coldly. 'I *am* the Princess, after all.'

'Of course.' His eyes were sad. 'And I don't suppose the Princess would be allowed to socialise with a reckless, common-born racing-car driver, either.'

'I don't suppose she would.' Isabella ignored the sharp, short pain in her chest at the thought.

Matteo turned away, his attention apparently back on steering the boat again, even though they weren't moving. 'Then it's just as well we agreed at the outset that this was just for the week. We can have all the fun we want together, then go back to our real lives as if it never happened.'

'Just as well,' she echoed, and wondered how to convince herself that she wasn't lying.

Their boat trip hadn't exactly given him the information he'd hoped for from Isabella, but Matteo had to admit it had crystallised exactly where they both stood in their current situations.

They'd agreed that first night that this could only be for the week, and it wasn't as if he was even looking to change that. But the idea of Isabella being stuck in a life that was so obviously suffocating her…that unsettled him. A lot.

Still, she was a princess. Maybe that royal status—and the money, prestige and luxury that went with it—was more important to her than happiness, or freedom. It would be for a lot of people, he knew. Money might not buy happiness, but it could buy a hell of a lot of other things, as he'd discovered as his career had progressed, and the prize pots and sponsorship deals got bigger.

Matteo wouldn't judge. Well, he wouldn't judge *much*. But he might feel a little bit of pity.

They'd separated and gone to their own rooms after their outing on the lake, both intuiting the need for a break from the unrelenting closeness of the past day or two. But it was already Thursday, and Matteo knew that their time together was limited; he didn't want to waste any more of it. Four days down and three more to go...

He knew he should just relax and enjoy Isabella's company while he had it. But somehow, that wasn't enough. He needed...what, exactly? To help her? To change her?

Or just to know that he'd had an impact on her life. That this week had meant something to her.

Because he was starting to feel as if seven days with Princess Isabella of Augusta might have more of an impact on his life than he'd ever imagined it could.

At the end of it, he'd walk away with a smile and a kiss and a thank you, the way he did with all of his love affairs. And he was perfectly happy with that plan.

He just didn't try to fool himself any more that forgetting Isabella would be as easy as forgetting any of the women who had come before her.

M knew what it was doing, after all. The dating agency had found him someone who, in another world, could have been his perfect match. He'd thought that meant someone like him—someone to take adventures and risks with, because she had the same adventurer's spirit as him.

Instead, they'd given him someone who needed him. Someone who he could ease out of her comfort zone, even while she calmed him. Not to the point of being a different person—he was still hankering for his next adventure. But when he was with her...it was as if she soothed his restless edges. As if he could rest for a while, between risks.

Being needed reminded him of his brother. Being

soothed reminded him of his mother. The two people he'd loved most in the world, both of them gone, now.

And Isabella…she could be…

No.

He didn't want that kind of love again—not when he knew how easily it could be taken from him, the way his brother and his mother had been. And he didn't want the obligations love forced on him, either. He'd seen it with other drivers on his team, and in races. They fell in love, they got married, started families even—and that was when they lost their edge. Because taking risks for themselves was easy; taking risks for people they loved was another game entirely. One that not many were made to play.

He needed those restless, reckless edges of his. He couldn't let Isabella smooth them down too much, whatever Gabe and the others hoped.

Even if he had wanted to follow up on this dream date matching, once the week was over, it wasn't what Isabella wanted either. She wanted to go back to a life he could never be a part of. Her stifling, royal life.

So really, there was no point thinking about what happened after this week until it was over. There'd be another adventure waiting for him and he'd take it, as he always did. Giovanni's list might be finished, but there were more adventures that his brother had never even dreamed of. Not to mention a racing career to get back to. He still had two lives to live, to make the most of, for Giovanni's sake.

All the same, when he heard movement out on the balcony that linked his bedroom to Isabella's, he couldn't help but head straight for the door.

Three days.

He couldn't afford to waste any of them.

'When do you think they put this out here?' Isabella didn't turn around as she asked the question, her back still towards him. Apparently she was as attuned to his movements as he was to hers.

He turned his gaze from the way her curls were swept over one bare shoulder, above a thin, strapless sundress that clung to her curves down over her hips, then flared out to swirl around her legs to mid-calf. On the table in the centre of the balcony was another feast, ready for their evening meal. How had the servants got that there without him noticing? Okay, he'd been preoccupied with his thoughts of Isabella, but still...

'The staff here are starting to get a little creepy now.' He took his seat, grinning up at her as she laughed.

'Well, as long as they keep the food coming.'

'True.' She sat down opposite him, the evening sunlight sinking into her midnight hair, the most beautiful woman he'd ever seen in real life—and the most unattainable.

Yeah, there was no way he was going to be forgetting Isabella of Augusta any time soon.

Which meant he had to make sure she didn't forget him, either.

They'd do this on the terms they'd agreed—one week, then it never happened. But while the rest of the world might never know about their week, he needed to be sure that *Isabella* would keep it with her. Maybe even let it loosen her up a bit.

It was the one thing he *could* give her. A parting gift, say.

They ate their meal in companionable silence, their only conversation comments on the food, or the wine. But under their sparse words, Matteo could feel all the things they weren't saying.

Would they really make it the whole week without any of them coming out? He doubted it.

'I was thinking about tomorrow,' he said as Isabella finished off her chocolate dessert.

He loved watching her eat, loved the secret smile as her mouth curved around her dessert spoon and she savoured the taste. He knew now that she looked the same way when she wrapped her mouth around him, and he knew also that he'd never forget that. The image of her sinking down to her knees in front of him, hands on his thighs as she eyed him up, was burnt into his memory for ever. Thankfully.

She swallowed her dessert, and he swallowed his thoughts.

'What about tomorrow?' she asked.

'How would you feel about another little adventure?' *Before you go back to locking yourself up in that palace again.*

She froze, just for a moment, her eyes darting to one side as she formed her response. 'An adventure? What sort of an adventure?'

He was pushing her, faster than she wanted to go. But they had so little time left...

'I thought we could slip away from here, take my car out to the nearest town, have a look around?' How could they come all the way to Lake Geneva and not see anything more than a villa and the water and the views? 'You know I'm not one for sitting around, doing nothing. And as you so rightly pointed out, we can't spend *all* week in bed. So we need to find some other things to do. Right?'

Isabella wasn't looking so sure, however.

'What about our security detail?' That wasn't a no. He'd take it.

He flashed her his most wicked grin. '*Cara*, I'm a

racing-car driver. If you think I can't lose two guys in a big black car on these roads, you really haven't been paying attention.'

Isabella clamped her sun hat to her head with one hand and grabbed hold of the car seat beneath her with the other. Oh, how on earth had he got her to agree to this?

Actually, she admitted to herself, she knew *exactly* how. He'd fed her the remains of his chocolate pudding, then moved the table aside to kiss her—first her mouth, then her neck, then down to her breasts, pulling the elasticated top of her strapless dress to her waist, effortlessly. Just as she'd imagined him doing when she'd put it on that evening.

And then he'd pulled the whole thing down her body, nudging her to lift her hips from the chair so he could drag the fabric down her legs, slow enough to drive her crazy as he followed it with his kisses…

Isabella blushed at the memory, but she had to admit it *had* been convincing. She'd agreed to today's day trip easily, breathlessly, by the time he was done. She'd let him make love to her out there on the balcony, in full view of anyone who cared to be looking—which she hoped was nobody, but you never really knew with those long lenses, did you? Plus there was the mysterious villa staff, and the security team—

The security team Matteo had effectively out-driven and lost ten minutes ago, with a driving manoeuvre she'd never seen anyone pull on an actual road before. She was fairly sure it would have got him disqualified on a racetrack, too.

'Where did you learn to drive like that?' she asked as they took another corner at speed. The road they were on now followed the line of Lake Geneva, past more villas and wooded areas. Hopefully the security team were still circling the lake in the opposite direction, unaware of Matteo's clever double-back.

'I took a police driving course,' Matteo said, driving with one hand on the wheel, the other on her thigh. 'Made friends with one of the instructors, and even got to go out with the *polizia* a couple of times.'

'Of course, you did.' Because there was excitement, risk there that he couldn't find in everyday life. That was what Matteo Rossi lived for, right?

And now she was living it with him—ditching her security team, heading out to some town she'd never heard of with a man she'd only known a few days… God, she'd been here before when she was young and stupid, and she'd sworn she'd never do anything like this again.

But then Matteo had stripped her naked on the balcony and made love to her on a blanket until she'd seen metaphorical stars as well as the ones in the sky above her. And suddenly she couldn't say no to him.

It really was a good thing that they only had a week together. Any longer and who knew what he'd talk her into? Selling the Crown Jewels of Augusta on eBay to finance a cave-diving trip, or something, probably.

One week of taking risks with Matteo. She had to admit, it wasn't what she'd expected from her early summer break.

Her phone buzzed in the pocket of her sundress, and she pulled it out, not surprised to see Gianna's number on the screen.

'Tell them you're fine and you'll be back later tonight,' Matteo said as she stared at the ringing phone. 'It's easy.'

Biting her lip, Isabella pressed answer.

'Your Highness? Oh, thank goodness. Is everything okay? The security team at the villa—'

'Everything is fine, Gianna,' she interrupted, keeping her voice as calm as possible, and hoping Gianna couldn't tell how far over the speed limit Matteo had been going. He'd slowed down a little now they were away from the villa, enough that she could just about hear Gianna over the rushing air racing over the convertible. 'You can tell the security team not to worry. We'll be back tonight.'

'Are you sure?' Despite the wind, Isabella could still hear the worry in her friend's voice.

She looked over at Matteo behind the wheel, sunglasses in place, smiling as he drove through the Swiss countryside.

'Yes,' she said. 'I'm sure.'

Because it might only be for a week, but she wasn't ready to start saying 'no' to Matteo Rossi just yet.

Isabella lost track of how long they'd been driving, focused instead on Matteo's hand on her thigh, and the secret smile on his face under his sunglasses. Was this how normal women felt? Out for a drive with their...no, she wasn't sure there *was* a word for what she and Matteo were. Lovers, she supposed, was closest. But somehow it didn't feel right. It wasn't...enough, somehow. Which was ridiculous, given that she'd known him all of four and a half days and they'd spent most of that time in bed.

She focused on his driving instead. She'd never taken lessons, or a test, or even sat behind the wheel of a car. She was always in the back, being driven places, never driving there. Never choosing her destination or even her direction herself.

She wasn't now, either, she reminded herself. She had no idea where they were even going. She just hoped that Matteo did.

'There it is,' he said eventually, and Isabella forced

herself to pay attention to her surroundings again, rather than just her thoughts. Here she was, in this most beautiful of locations, and she was—

'Wow!' She interrupted her own thoughts as she finally took in where they were headed.

There, jutting out over the water of Lake Geneva, was a castle—a proper, fairy-tale castle.

'I thought it might be rather old hat to you, living in a palace like you do,' Matteo said, with a grin.

She smiled back. 'Not one like this, though.'

The palace at Augusta was very grand, filled with tapestries and red brocade and family portraits and all the other things royals seemed to need to prove their place in the world. But the truth was the original palace had burnt almost to the ground in the late nineteenth century, and the rebuilt version, while beautiful, didn't have the history of a place like this. Or the magic.

'What's it called?' she asked, still wondering at the sight.

'Château de Chillon,' Matteo replied. 'Chillon Castle.'

Fat round turrets climbed towards the bright blue sky, joined by boxier square ones, many of them topped by flags that fluttered in the light summer breeze. She could imagine Rapunzel sitting at the top of one of them, her hair hanging out of the window just waiting for a prince to scamper up it and set her free.

'Do you want to go inside?' Matteo asked.

'Can we?' She felt her eyes widen. Only strictly arranged visits were allowed at the castle in Augusta, and Isabella had spent the last few years carefully avoiding any of them.

Matteo just smiled.

It turned out that tourists were welcome at the Château de Chillon, and nobody seemed to notice that one of the tourists was actually a visiting member of another royal family. Isabella kept her sunglasses on to hide her face, but, honestly, she didn't think anyone was looking at her anyway. The castle was full of enough treasures to draw attention away. From the open courtyards to the friezes painted on the walls—not to mention the views out over the lake and the mountains, or towards the vineyards.

'Besides,' Matteo murmured in her ear as they took in one of the displays of armour, 'who would honestly expect a real princess to be walking around with the rest of the tourists?'

After they'd toured the rooms of the castle that were open to them, they climbed to the top of the keep in the centre of the castle and took in the view all around them. Standing close behind her, Matteo whispered information about what they were looking at into her ear as he turned her to face different directions.

'And that, down there, is where I'm taking you tomorrow,' he said finally.

Isabella squinted to see where he was pointing. 'The Château café?'

Matteo shook his head. 'The town of Montreux.'

CHAPTER EIGHT

MATTEO WAS STILL grinning to himself as he showered the day off him and changed into loose trousers and a shirt for dinner on the balcony that evening. The trip to Château du Chillon had been a success, and Isabella had already all but agreed to another outing tomorrow.

'I'd never have seen this, if I hadn't met you,' she'd whispered to him, as they'd stood atop the keep tower, looking out over water and mountains and towns and fields. 'Thank you.'

He'd known then that he couldn't stop yet.

As much as he wanted to take Isabella to bed and keep her there for the rest of their stay at the villa, there was a certain joy in exploring their surroundings with her too. His favourite part was watching Isabella get to pretend to be a normal, ordinary person, rather than a princess. The pleasure she took from fading into the background and watching others—even when they were just sitting in the café together sipping coffee—was palpable.

I gave that to her. She'll remember that.

It was something, at least.

And, he thought as he headed out to meet her on the balcony, he was almost certain that their day trips into tourist life wouldn't be the only things she remembered.

She'd remember the nights they had together, too—the same way he would.

Those nights were seared into his memory for ever, he knew that already.

'What's on the menu tonight?' Matteo's blood warmed at the sight of Isabella in another one of her sundresses. This one, he noted, tied around the neck, covering her high to her throat and down to her ankles. While it showed off her beautiful shoulders, it was definitely more modest than many of the others she'd worn.

Then she turned to get to what had become, over the past few days, her chair, and he saw that the whole back was missing, the fabric draping down over the swell of her bottom, so low that he was pretty sure there was no way she was wearing anything at all under the dress.

God, he hoped not. Even if he wasn't entirely sure how to get through dinner without knowing for sure.

Isabella lifted the metal cloche covering their plates and revealed a chicken dish with a creamy mushroom and leek sauce, plus a side dish of potatoes, and licked her lips in anticipation. Matteo's body tightened at the sight. He wanted her to look at him that way, and soon.

'I've been looking forward to this all day, haven't you?' she said. 'I'm starving. Not that the sandwich in the Château café wasn't lovely too...'

How were they still talking about food? When she looked like that and he hadn't touched her for *hours*.

Had he totally regressed to being a teenager, unable to think about anything but sex? Apparently so.

Then she looked up and met his gaze, and he watched her pupils widen further. Was she having the same thoughts that he was? It looked likely. And yet, decorum dictated that they eat dinner before anything else.

Matteo hated decorum. But despite all his efforts, Isabella was still ruled by it.

That, or she was just tormenting him for fun.

Dinner was an excruciatingly pleasurable torture. Every mouthful she took made him want to kiss her more. Each time she reached for her wine glass that damn dress shifted around what he was now certain were her bare breasts, and he ached to touch her.

Isabella kept up a light conversation about the château and the sights they'd enjoyed that day, seemingly unaware of his distraction, until she'd finished the last mouthful of her lemon mousse.

Then she smiled at him, warm and wicked, and he knew that every moment of the meal had been intentional.

'What shall we do with the rest of our evening, I wonder?' she said, her voice too innocent to be real. 'It's been such a lovely day, and we only have such a limited time here, it seems a shame to waste the later hours. We could walk by the lake, perhaps, or in the gardens. Or maybe there's another board game around here somewhere we could play...'

She started to stand, and Matteo's hand shot out to circle her wrist with firm fingers. 'Or I could take you to bed right now and see how loudly I can make you scream using only my tongue.'

Her pulse kicked up a gear under his fingertips, and he knew they weren't going to be playing Monopoly again any time soon.

'Or we could do that.' Isabella's eyes were nearly black as she slid into his lap, warm and wanting.

Matteo slid his hands up under the fabric of her skirt, palms against the smooth skin of her thighs. 'Was this whole meal just a plan to torture me?'

'Well, I was genuinely hungry.' She kissed his neck, and he shivered with need. 'But honestly? Yes.'

'Why?'

She shrugged, and everything moved under her dress in a way that made his everything stand even more firmly to attention. Any moment now, he was going to untie that tiny ribbon bow that held the dress up and let it fall away completely. Then he'd know for sure what was under it.

God, he hoped it was nothing but Isabella's bare skin.

'Because…you were in charge today,' she said. 'You drove, decided where we went, how long we stayed. And I loved our day out, I really did—and I wouldn't have had the courage to take us there myself, even if I *could* drive. But…'

'You wanted to be in charge of something too,' he guessed. 'In control.'

'I suppose so.' She shrugged again and he nearly lost his mind. 'Silly, really.'

'Not at all.' How often did a princess get to decide anything about her life? Not nearly often enough, was Matteo's guess. 'So, do you want to choose our activities for the rest of the week?'

She tilted her head a little as she studied him, and he realised he could look right down the side of her dress. *Definitely* no bra.

He'd let her decide everything if she'd just let him confirm the 'no underwear' part of his hypothesis.

'No,' she said finally. 'Not all of them. Just some of them.'

'That sounds fair.' He swallowed. 'So, do you want to play Monopoly, or…?'

Isabella reached up behind her neck and unfastened the bow that had been driving him crazy for the last hour. Then she stood up, let the dress fall to the floor of the balcony, and stalked naked back into her bedroom.

'We're definitely going with your plan for this evening,' she called back over one bare shoulder. 'What are you waiting for?'

Matteo hurried to his feet and after her.

They only had two more days, after all. He didn't want to waste a moment.

At the palace in Augusta, a week could feel like a year if there wasn't anything interesting going on—or, as often happened, if she was avoiding getting caught up in official royal engagements where her only purpose was to smile and stay quiet. Here on Lake Geneva, Isabella's week with Matteo seemed to have passed in a flash.

Which wasn't to say they hadn't made the most of their time together. Quite apart from the hours spent exploring each other's bodies, or whispering thoughts and histories to each other in the dark, Matteo had taken her on the sort of everyday adventures she'd never been allowed to have before.

He hadn't pushed her too far, ever, but just slipping away from their security detail—who'd been surprisingly sanguine about it after the first time, so she suspected Gianna had had a word and told them to let them go—felt like a rebellion. Putting on a floppy straw hat and wandering incognito around the resort town of Montreux, eating lunch in a side-street café where no one knew who she was, or even who Matteo was, had felt liberating. Swimming in the waters of Lake Geneva, with Matteo's arms around her as he stole wet kisses, had been something entirely new.

And then there were the nights.

After Nate, she'd never really expected to feel such

passion again—or to trust it if she did. But with Matteo, everything seemed so natural. Whatever her body needed, he was always there to give it to her. And she felt no embarrassment in needing to learn what he liked, what he wanted, what made him moan and flip them over and thrust into her until they both fell over the edge of pleasure together.

Being with Matteo had felt nothing like her time with Nate. Nothing like anything she'd ever experienced before.

And now, too soon, it was time to say goodbye to it and head back to the real world.

They'd elected to spend their last day together at the villa—mostly in bed, which was fine by Isabella. The morning had been a haze of pleasure and the occasional pastry and coffee, when they needed to build up their energy reserves again. They'd managed a small walk down to the water's edge and along the path after lunch, but the temptation to touch and kiss and more had been too great, and it wasn't long before they were back in bed.

Maybe they were just reassuring each other that they were still there. For now. Isabella wasn't sure. She was trying to ignore the fact that, after tomorrow, she'd be on her own again.

'What are you thinking about?' Matteo murmured against her shoulder.

She twisted under the light sheets until she could rest her cheek against his chest. 'Tomorrow, I guess.'

Matteo was silent for a moment. 'Back to the real world, huh? You going to miss me?' He grinned as he said it, and she knew it was just a joke, a request from his perfectly healthy ego.

'I'll miss *this*.' She pressed a kiss to his skin, then lifted her face to kiss his lips, too. 'This week…it's like

I've been a different person. It's strange to think I have to say goodbye to her tomorrow morning.'

And to you.

'You've been able to be Isabella. Not just the Princess.'

'Yeah.' And now she wasn't sure she wanted to go back to being the Princess at all. But what choice did she have? It was who she was. Who her family expected her to be.

She'd always known that her place in the family, the love of the King, Queen and all their subjects, were contingent on following The Rules. Ever since she'd heard the whispered stories about her Aunt Josephine, and her banishment from the palace after she fell in love with the man who looked after her horses—old gossip by the time it had reached ten-year-old Isabella's ears, but still shocking. Aunt Josephine had refused to give him up, and that was why Isabella had never met her.

Everything that had happened with Nate had only reinforced the lesson and confirmed to her that nothing had changed. Augusta was still as rule-bound, stuffy and unforgiving as always.

Beside her, Matteo shifted, lying flat beside her on his side so he could meet her gaze. 'You told me that you'd taken time off from being a princess once before. But you never told me what happened.'

'No, I didn't.' And that had been intentional. She'd distracted him, got him to tell her his secrets instead. He'd shared about his brother's death, his bucket list, everything.

And she'd kept her secrets close, locked inside, as always.

'No one can ever know, Isabella.' Her father's words. And, always remembering Aunt Josephine, she'd lived by them.

'Will you tell me now?' Matteo asked.

Isabella bit her lip as she considered. Matteo wouldn't spill her secrets—if he was going to, he had far juicier stuff to share now after their week together. Plus, there was that non-disclosure agreement he must have signed before coming to Lake Geneva in the first place.

Besides, she knew in her heart that Matteo wouldn't betray her that way.

Except I thought the same thing about Nate, too.

Was that why she didn't want to tell him? No, she admitted to herself. It wasn't fear that was stopping her telling him the truth. It was shame, or at least embarrassment. That she'd ever been that naive, trusting girl.

That, in some ways, she still was.

'If you don't want to—' Matteo started, but she cut him off.

'No. I mean, yes, I don't. But not because of you. Because of me. Because it's just so…stupid.'

This wasn't like the secrets he'd shared with her. Nothing so tragic as a dead brother, or as noble as fulfilling his lost dreams. This was just…humiliating.

'Okay.' Matteo looked confused. She didn't really blame him.

With a sigh, she sat up, drawing the sheets up to cover her bare breasts. 'I'll tell you. But bring me some of those chocolates first, okay?' She was going to need something sweet to counteract the bitterness of the memory.

He flashed her an indulgent smile, then retrieved the box of truffles from the table in the corner, placing them on the bed between them as he settled back down next to her.

Isabella took one and stuffed it in her mouth as she figured out how best to begin.

'I've never told this story to anyone,' she said. 'The

only people who know are the ones who lived it with me. So if I don't tell it well, that's why. Okay?'

'Okay.' Matteo wrapped an arm around her shoulders, pulling her closer. 'And if you want to stop, if you decide you don't want me to know, that's fine too, okay? I won't push.'

Another difference between him and Nate. Nate had *always* pushed. He'd had to, hadn't he? It was his job.

'When I was twenty-two, I met a guy.' God, how many tragic stories started that way? Too many, Isabella was sure. 'Nathanial was Augustan and from a decent enough family to be invited to an event at the palace, but not aristocracy, so not a suitable courtship partner for me in the eyes of my family. But I thought I was in love, of course. At his urging, I'd throw off my princess persona and escape the castle to be with him. He was my first love, my first everything really. Being with him was the first time since puberty that I felt like myself, like Isabella, not just a princess.'

'So, what went wrong?' Matteo asked. 'Your parents found out?'

'They did,' Isabella admitted. 'But not until it showed up in the papers. It turned out that Nate was an aspiring reporter, and he'd used his flirtation with me to get photos, quotes about my family, insider gossip from the palace, everything. He sold it to the *Augustan Times* in return for a job there.'

Matteo swore. 'Bella, I'm… That's awful. I'm so sorry.'

'It was a long time ago. Five years—no, nearly six since it started.' And in that whole time she'd kept her distance from everyone, kept herself safe behind the title of Princess, using it as a barrier. Until this week.

'What happened next?'

'Isn't that enough?' She flashed him a grin, but she could see from his eyes that he knew the aftermath mattered almost as much as the event itself. She sighed and went on. 'The palace put out a statement denying most of it—saying he was a desperate young man who had made up these quotes and stories to find fame. But there were photos of us together, and too many of the stories rang true with other gossip, so I don't think anyone believed it. It was easy enough to see what had really happened. I'd been a fool.'

Matteo shook his head. 'You were taken advantage of. You were in love.'

'I'm not even sure I was, now. Not really. Love...you think you know what it is when it happens for the first time, don't you? But now, I'm not sure I'd recognise it if it jumped up and down throwing heart confetti at me. I just... I don't know how anyone trusts anyone else that much. Not without a non-disclosure agreement, anyway.' She laughed at her joke, but he didn't.

'Isabella.' His bright green eyes were serious. 'You know I wouldn't tell anyone about all we've shared here this week, non-disclosure agreement or not.'

'I do.' She couldn't have explained how she knew she could trust him, but there was no doubt inside her that she did. She'd trusted him with her body all week. She could trust him with her secrets, too.

'Anyway, my parents—and my older brother, Leo— were all horrified at the peril I'd placed the palace in. Those are their exact words, incidentally.' She almost smiled at the memory, except to this day the sight of the King and Queen and the Crown Prince of Augusta all staring at her in disapproving disbelief was still the thing that gave her the most nightmares. 'They couldn't believe I hadn't seen what was happening. In fact... I wondered if they actually thought I'd done it on purpose, as some sort of rebellion.'

'Did you ever ask them that?'

Isabella shook her head. 'No. We…after all the initial lectures and lessons about how to guard my royal privacy—or, more pertinently, theirs—we never talked about it again. His name is never mentioned in the palace, neither is that whole period of my life. It's as if it never happened.' As if she'd never been anyone but Princess Isabella at all. Just as Aunt Josephine had been written out of the family history.

Matteo was silent for a long moment, his lips pressed against her hair. She could almost hear him thinking.

'Do you think…this week…?' he said, finally. 'Has it given you anything?'

She didn't have to think about the answer. 'It's given me everything.'

The chance to be herself, for once, not her title. The ability to explore all the things she'd never thought she'd have again. To take a few risks, to live a little.

But most of all, it had enabled her to trust her own judgement again. To believe that Isabella was a person worth being, princess or not.

She couldn't put all that emotion into words, though. Not without ugly crying, and ruining their last, perfect night together. So instead, she reached up and wound a hand around the back of Matteo's neck, pulling his mouth to hers, putting all of her feelings into her kisses instead.

And as he responded she knew that this was the perfect way to spend their final hours together. Lost in each other, bodies so close they were almost the same person, without any more secrets between them. Just enjoying this space out of time, where they could be themselves.

This is perfect, Isabella thought as Matteo made love

to her, the intensity of their coupling somehow so much more than the other nights they'd spent together.

So close, as her body tightened and her release swelled within her, and Matteo began to move faster as she fought to match his pace.

So perfect, as her orgasm crashed over her, and every muscle in her body seemed to tense then relax, drifting away on a contented cloud of daydreams.

In fact, everything was perfect, until Matteo jumped up and swore, loudly and proficiently.

'What is it?' she asked, forcing her trembling body to sit up.

He met her gaze with grave eyes. 'The condom broke.'

CHAPTER NINE

THE NEXT MORNING—the last morning—Matteo sat on the balcony with his morning coffee and watched Isabella leave.

Except in reality she'd already left him, hours ago. The moment the damn condom broke, she'd shot out of his bed and his life.

He'd tried to talk to her, of course. Offered to find the nearest all-night chemist that might provide a morning-after pill or something, but she'd refused to listen. Told him she'd handle it herself.

Which he expected meant she'd be asking one of her royal advisors to handle it, since he couldn't exactly see her walking into a pharmacy herself to do it.

But after all the walls they'd broken down between them over the past week, it frustrated the hell out of him that this had put them all back up again.

She hadn't even joined him for breakfast that morning—which meant she hadn't eaten anything at all. Behaviour so unlike the Isabella he'd come to know this week, he'd really started to worry.

She had come to say goodbye, though. He supposed that much politeness at least was bred into princesses.

'My assistant will be here with my car any moment,' she'd said, lingering in the doorway to the balcony. 'I'm going to go and wait downstairs. So... I guess this is goodbye.'

'I'll take your bag down for you,' he'd offered, but she'd shaken her head.

'Even princesses can carry a bag, Matteo.' It had been a joke, he supposed, but he hadn't laughed.

Because that was what she was again, wasn't it? Princess Isabella, a world away from him.

And because of a stupid piece of latex, he hadn't even been able to enjoy their last night together.

'It's too much, Matteo,' she'd whispered through the door, after she'd shut it on him. *'Too much risk. This whole week... It's too much.'*

She wasn't wrong. He'd spent a sleepless night trying to deal with just how much it all was. And how saying goodbye suddenly seemed so much bigger than it had in his head, now he really had to do it.

He wasn't a fool. He hadn't expected this week to end with hearts and flowers and a royal wedding, even before she'd told him about her experiences with the idiot reporter. And he hadn't wanted it to, either.

Matteo Rossi wasn't the settling-down type, and he definitely wasn't anybody's idea of a prince.

But the idea of never seeing Isabella again—never touching her, never kissing her, never making love to her again—that made his whole chest ache in a way he hadn't anticipated when he'd stood on this balcony a week ago and looked down to see her standing on the terrace.

Maybe M knew what it was doing after all. Because he'd never met a woman so perfect for him.

If only she weren't the most impossible person for him to love, all at the same time.

This was for the best. He had to remember that. He needed to live his own life, a life he couldn't live if he was worrying about her—or even if he knew she was somewhere, worrying about him. Love, like the love he'd felt for his mother and brother, came with limits, and it came with loss and pain.

He didn't have space for any of those things in the life he was living for himself, and for Giovanni.

A car pulled around the corner of the driveway, out from the trees that shielded the villa from the passing roads, and halted beside the terrace. Tinted windows, probably bullet-proof glass, and high wheels that put the driver and passengers above many of the other cars on the road.

A carriage fit for a princess—a modern-day one, anyway. Even if Augusta seemed to be stuck in the past when it came to the rules it expected its princesses to follow.

The honey-blonde woman Isabella had been arguing with the day he first saw her—Gianna, his memory filled in—stepped out from the back seat and hurried across to the terrace. Just like that first day, he was too far away to make out their conversation, but the concern on Gianna's face was evident even at a distance. What did she see in Isabella's face that made her look like that?

He wished he knew. That he could see. That he could take the Princess in his arms and kiss her better.

Was Isabella feeling as torn up as he was right now? Or was she just telling her friend about last night's accident and begging her to help make it go away.

His child…

No. That was stupid. It was one broken condom; the chances of Isabella being pregnant were low, surely?

Just imagining it was another way to hold onto her, beyond the end of this week. And that wasn't something he could do; they'd both been clear enough about that from the start. Nothing had changed in either of their worlds outside this place.

Even if he felt like a different person inside, all of a sudden.

Down on the terrace, Gianna put her arm around Isabella and led her towards the car, carrying her case in her other hand. Matteo watched intently from the balcony. Would she turn around? Would she wave goodbye? Did he even want her to? He wasn't sure.

Isabella reached the car door, and he braced himself for her disappearing behind those tinted windows, and the prison of her position as Princess. But, at the last minute, she paused and looked back up at him.

He drank in that last glimpse of her. That creamy skin, the dark curls that bounced past her shoulders. The curves he'd held close. The lips he'd kissed.

She raised her hand, a last royal wave. He huffed a laugh he knew she'd never hear and blew her a kiss instead.

And then, with the closing of a door and the purr of an engine, Princess Isabella of Augusta drove out of his life for good.

'Are you really sure you're okay?' Gianna asked as the car door shut behind her, and the driver started the engine again. 'I thought you were having fun! When you texted, you said it was good, that he was nice.'

Her head was buzzing with all the things she'd never said to him. With the memory of that awful moment last night. With the fear and the risk that had sent her running from his arms.

'I'm fine,' Isabella lied. 'Really.'

Gianna clearly didn't believe her. She reached across the seat between them and took the Princess's hand in her own. 'If he did something, said something, you need to tell me now, Your Highness. He signed a non-disclosure agreement, so we can sue him to high heaven if he tries to sell his story, but if there's anything more—'

Isabella sobbed a laugh. 'No! No, honestly, Gianna. It's nothing like that. He was…he was wonderful.'

And she'd run out on him, too afraid to face the risks she'd been taking.

No birth control was one hundred per cent effective, she knew that. There was always the risk of pregnancy, from the moment she'd decided to take him to bed.

She'd told herself that it was Matteo making her take more risks—ditching the security detail, swimming in the lake, pretending to be a normal tourist—but she'd taken the biggest one all by herself. She'd let him into her bed, into her body.

Even *that* wasn't the biggest risk she'd taken this week, even if the magnitude of what she'd done was only now crashing down on her as she drove away.

She'd let him into her *heart*.

And now she wasn't entirely sure how to get him back out again. If that was even possible.

Was this how Aunt Josephine felt?

Gianna's expression had gone from concerned to horrified. 'I should never have sent you. Oh, Your Highness, I'm so sorry! It was meant to be fun, a chance for you to relax…'

'It was all those things,' Isabella sobbed. 'Honestly, I'm glad you set it up.' Even if now she couldn't stop crying.

'Isabella, what *happened*?' Gianna asked, desperately, and Isabella knew her friend had to be worried because she'd used her name, not her title.

'I don't know,' Isabella replied. There were still tears

dripping down her face; she could feel them plopping off her chin and nose and into her lap. God, she was a mess. 'I don't know.'

I'm very afraid I might have started to fall in love. And I might be pregnant. And both of these things are impossible, and no one can ever know.

Matteo hadn't wanted a perfect-match love affair any more than she had at the start of the week, and she had no reason to believe his feelings on that had changed. They were from two different worlds, and they both wanted to stay in them. Love was off the table.

She should ask Gianna to take them by a pharmacy, or to call the royal family doctor, or something. She needed to do something about that burst condom.

This wasn't just an ill-advised affair. This wasn't an immature fling gone wrong. It wasn't some photos and embarrassing quotes in the paper.

A princess, pregnant out of wedlock? A single-mother princess?

Augusta was a conservative country, and its monarchs were the most conservative of all. Her parents might never get over the shock. They'd forgiven her once, for being young and stupid. They'd blamed her naivety, given her the benefit of the doubt and helped her cover it up. Hammered home The Rules to make sure she couldn't make the same mistake twice.

But she wasn't so young now, and she didn't feel stupid, or as if her time with Matteo was a mistake. Would they forgive her again? Or would this be one transgression too far?

She should make sure she didn't put them in the position of having to decide.

She should.

But instead, she hugged herself and cried. For the life

she'd had a glimpse of, the possibilities she'd walked away from, and the future she knew could never be hers.

He wasn't back on the team.

Matteo had left Lake Geneva for Rome, ready to throw himself back into his normal life, only to discover that his normal life wasn't ready for him yet.

'That leg needs another few weeks of physio,' Gabe told him on his return. 'Doctor's orders—don't blame me.'

He did, of course. He blamed everybody there for messing with his career, his head, his future.

For showing him something he couldn't have. Something he'd never even imagined he might want, until now.

So now he was sitting in Gabe's office—feet on the desk, of course—figuring out his next move.

'You do realise you don't have to be here, don't you?' Gabe said as he walked in, a sheaf of papers in his hands.

'I'm still part of the team, aren't I?' Matteo said obstinately. 'Even if I'm not allowed to race.'

Gabe rolled his eyes. 'You're on medical leave, Matteo.' He moved to push Matteo's feet from the desk before obviously remembering about his still-healing leg and resisting the urge.

Matteo kept his feet exactly where they were.

'My leg is fine,' he grumbled.

'Then you can get it off my desk.'

Rolling his eyes, Matteo stomped his feet onto the ground. 'Look, if I was well enough to be shipped off to Lake Geneva to show some random woman the sights, I'm well enough to drive, yeah?'

Taking his own seat on the other side of the desk, Gabe looked at him with interest. 'I've been waiting to hear all about your Swiss exploits. Are you ready to share with Uncle Gabe yet?'

Matteo shrugged. 'What's to share? It was a week in Lake Geneva taking in the tourist attractions and eating too much good food.'

'With a woman that M dating agency swears is your perfect match.' From the smirk on Gabe's face, he could tell that his manager wasn't taking that claim any more seriously than Matteo had, when he'd arrived at the villa.

Before he'd met Isabella.

'So, are you going to tell me about her?' Gabe pushed.

'What do you want to know?' Suddenly, he was strangely reluctant to share any details of his week. To give up any of the perfect, private experience that had been his week with Isabella.

The memories were his, and they were hers, and they didn't belong to anyone else.

Even when Madison Morgan herself had called to check in, post-date-week, and ask how it had gone, Matteo had kept his responses to a minimum. He'd confirmed that they'd had a great time, that the villa was perfect and they'd got on well, but left it at that. Madison had sounded faintly disappointed, but she was a professional, and she hadn't pushed him for gossip or sordid details.

Gabe, Matteo knew from experience, would *definitely* push him for both of those things.

'Was she as perfect for you as the agency promised?' Gabe asked, surprising him.

'Yes.' The word was out before he could stop it. 'In lots of ways, she was.'

Gabe beamed like a proud father. 'So, you'll be seeing her again?'

Matteo shook his head. 'I don't imagine so.'

'Why not?'

Gabe, Matteo knew, had been married to the love of his life since he was twenty-two, and never looked at another woman. He lived vicariously through his drivers, instead. For him, love was simple: you found it, you grabbed it, and you made damn sure never to let go.

He wouldn't understand that Isabella wasn't meant for him to hold onto, even if he wanted to.

What Isabella needed most in the world was to fly free; but what her position demanded of her was the opposite. That wasn't a fight Matteo intended to get in the middle of—not when she'd so clearly already made her choice.

'It wouldn't work between us,' Matteo said eventually. It had the benefit of being true, at least.

'How can you know if you don't try?'

When he didn't answer, Gabe sighed, and tossed the paperwork he clearly wasn't reading aside on his desk. Matteo wondered if he had enough time to run before the inevitable lecture Gabe was obviously building up to.

'Matteo...' Apparently not. 'You know I love you like a younger brother. A son, even.'

'Right down to the parental lectures and interfering in my love life, apparently.'

'You haven't *had* a love life until now,' Gabe pointed out. 'A sex life, sure. A dating life, for definite. But love?'

'I'm not looking for love,' Matteo pointed out.

'Why not?'

Because if I can't have Isabella, what's the point?

'Because love would slow me down.' That was a more acceptable, Matteo Rossi answer, right? 'You know how it goes. You fall in love and suddenly you have to change your whole life for them. Be more careful—on the track and off. Stop doing fun stuff.'

'*Dangerous* stuff,' Gabe countered.

'The stuff that makes me feel like I'm *living*.' Except he'd felt alive with Isabella. Calm, at peace—but alive. And now he'd crossed off everything on Giovanni's list, what was he going to do next, anyway? What risks were still out there to take? What heart-pulsing, blood-pumping things could he do to make the most of his life?

Possibly getting a princess pregnant is probably pretty risky, his mind added unhelpfully. *Her parents could probably have me assassinated.*

Okay, he wasn't thinking about that any more. Wasn't thinking about Isabella, either. Because whatever he thought he might have to give up for a chance of a relationship with her, it was nothing to what she would definitely have to sacrifice. Augustan princesses couldn't fall in love with Italian racing-car drivers. It was aristocracy or nothing.

He'd done a little research since he left Lake Geneva—and not just to look at photos of Isabella online, and curse the fact that he hadn't had the foresight to take any of her while they were together, if she'd have even let him. He'd found, buried in the depths of the Internet, the original coverage of the debacle she'd told him about with the reporter. And, with it, an interesting sidebar about the traditions of royal marriage in Augusta.

She'd have to give up her title, her place in the line of succession, not to mention probably a lot of money, to marry someone her family didn't approve of. Apparently her aunt had made the sacrifice before Isabella was even born. Augustan royalty took the rules seriously.

No wonder she didn't want to chance getting close to anyone that might make her want to risk it.

Across the desk, Gabe was watching him silently, as if he could see Matteo's thoughts ticking across his brain.

Matteo sincerely hoped that he couldn't, for any number of reasons.

'I'm not going to tell you that life without love isn't worth living,' he said slowly. 'But I would like you to think about one thing, Matteo. Will you do that for me?'

'Of course.' Gabe had been his mentor as much as his manager for most of his adult life. He always thought about the things Gabe told him—even though most often they were to do with how he took a corner, or the right mindset for an upcoming race.

'All the things you've done—the places you've been, the adventures you've had—you've done them alone. Ever since Giovanni died, it's just been you against the world, and every challenge it can throw at you.' Gabe got to his feet, the papers he'd walked in with long forgotten. 'Wouldn't it be nice to have someone to face those challenges with, again?'

He left before Matteo could marshal any arguments against his words, or point out that no one would ever be able to take his brother's place in his heart.

And as the door swung shut behind him Matteo used the sound of it crashing closed to ignore the voice inside his head that whispered: *Not replacing. Something new.*

Was it time for something new? Not Isabella, not love—there were still too many reasons that Gabe didn't understand why that wasn't an option.

But he'd completed Giovanni's list. He'd done everything his brother had ever dreamed of.

He was done. And that revelation felt like a weight off his shoulders, as if he were flying again, rather than held down by reality.

For so many years, ever since he'd made his promise to Giovanni, he'd been living by someone else's beliefs, following someone else's dreams. And it had brought him so far, given him so much, he couldn't regret it—especially not when he knew what it would have meant to his brother.

But still…

Now he had fulfilled his promise, that meant it was time for Matteo to live by his own beliefs, follow his own dreams. Set his own challenges and meet them.

Once he figured out what they should be.

He needed new adventures. Bigger, riskier ones. He needed to take life to the edge.

That was what he'd done when Giovanni died: filled the gaping hole where his brother had been with experiences. With reminders of everything the world had to offer.

With proof that he, at least, was still alive.

He needed to do the same thing again now. That was all.

Lost in thought, he reached across the desk to grab a blank piece of printer paper and a pen and started to write.

CHAPTER TEN

A WEEK LATER, Isabella stared at the diary on the desk in front of her and sighed.

'What's with the sighing?' Gianna peered over her shoulder at the blank boxes. 'It's a quiet week. I thought you'd be pleased.'

'I am. Mostly.' Her weeks at the palace didn't tend to be busy anyway, given her aversion to public events. But sometimes things snuck into her calendar when she wasn't there to stop them, and a few had definitely been added to her future diary while she was away in Switzerland. She'd struggled through the ones in her first week back and was already thinking of ways to get out of most of the others, even though they were weeks away.

But she'd asked for a quiet week this week, and she'd got it.

Except now she had no idea what to do with the free time.

Sitting alone with her thoughts simply wasn't an option, because her thoughts all revolved around one thing. Well, two, technically, although they both linked back to the same man.

Number one: she missed Matteo, with the kind of ache she'd never felt for Nate.

Number two: her period was late. Four days late, to

be precise, since she should have had it a week after her return from Switzerland.

She didn't need it circled in red in her official engagements diary or anything to know that; she'd been counting the days ever since she left Lake Geneva. Her period was normally like clockwork—the same as her schedule. She'd have assumed Gianna had organised it like the rest of her life, except that Gianna was all about Isabella's public persona, and nobody in Augusta wanted to think about the royals having bodily functions like that, surely?

Matteo had urged her to take risks, to get out there and live life while she had the chance, in Switzerland. But she was pretty sure he didn't mean this kind of risk.

Gianna was perched on the desk beside her, looking down at Isabella with concern.

'Is it still...him?' she asked softly. 'You're thinking about him again?'

'Yes.' There was no point lying about it. While she'd tried to keep the details about her time at the villa to a minimum, Gianna had organised the whole thing. She knew why she'd been there, and she'd seen the state she was in upon leaving.

'I should never have sent you there,' Gianna said now, shaking her head sadly. 'I never thought... I know they claim to find a perfect match, but I never imagined you could fall like this in just one week.'

Isabella looked up sharply. *A fallen woman.* How did she know? 'What do you mean? Fall?'

'In love,' Gianna replied. Her eyes were pitying. 'Your Highness, you have to believe I'd never have sent you there if I really thought you were going to fall in love. Not with someone you can't be with.'

'I'm not in love.' She wasn't. *But I could be.* If she let

herself fall, let herself spend more time with Matteo… she knew in her heart he was someone she could love, for real this time.

She just wouldn't let herself, because what good would that do them?

'Isabella—'

'You said it yourself,' she said sharply, cutting off her friend. 'Who falls in love in a week? Besides, whatever M claim, how could they find my perfect match without knowing the truth of who I am? You filled in those forms for me, and I didn't even know what that video interview was for. And since Matteo was in hospital with a broken leg when his application went in, I don't even think he did it all himself either. He said his manager set it up for him to keep him out of trouble.'

Gianna looked sceptical, but she didn't push it. Well, not too far. 'But you're still thinking about him.'

And the possibility he knocked me up.

She was going to have to talk to him, and soon. He deserved to know what was going on—and she could do with someone else to freak out about it with. If she told Gianna…her assistant was a friend, but she was also a royal employee. If she knew that the Princess was pregnant out of wedlock…and without even a romantic story to tell beyond a week-long Swiss booty call…she'd be obliged to tell the King and Queen.

Which was the absolute last thing that Isabella wanted.

Of course, then she'd have to confess her own part in the whole plan, Isabella supposed, but she liked Gianna too much to let her take the fall for that, anyway. No one had pushed her into Matteo's arms, or his bed. In fact, she'd stripped off in front of him and run there herself.

God, this was so much worse than anything Aunt Josephine had done. Especially if there was a baby…

She shook her head and forced a smile for Gianna. 'Well, then, I guess I need something to take my mind off things, don't you think? There must be something fun going on here at the palace, or some sort of royal trip that could benefit from a little bit of princessy sparkle, right?'

Anything to stop her wondering what would have happened if she hadn't run out on Matteo that last night. If they'd actually talked about what happened when they went back to reality, instead of trying to pretend it wasn't happening until the last minute.

If she was surprised at Isabella's sudden—and mostly unprecedented—interest in palace events, Gianna didn't show it. Probably because she knew how much she needed the distraction.

Instead, her assistant flipped through the giant paper organiser she insisted on using, even though the palace had invested in the latest technology for such things. 'There's a tea party for some of the country's most successful charitable fundraisers in the rose garden on Thursday. A visit from Augusta's greatest living novelist—'

Isabella groaned. 'Again? Why can't he just stay home and write more books?' She liked his novels far more than his company, and he always seemed to try and sit next to her at formal dinner, especially since he'd been appointed the Royal Writer last year. 'I definitely need something to get me away from the palace if he's visiting.'

'Well, Prince Leo is taking a trip to Rome at the weekend for a charity ball, if you *really* want to get away?'

Rome. 'Really?' She hadn't told Gianna that Matteo was Italian. Or that, according to his social media accounts—which she was only stalking under an anonymous account—he lived in Rome. Was there right now, in fact.

Why call, when she could talk to him face to face?

'Want me to ask your brother if there's space for one more on the trip?' Gianna asked, looking thrilled to have found something that distracted Isabella from her mysterious lover.

If only she knew...

'Well, I have been meaning to practise my Italian,' she said nonchalantly. 'Why don't you set it up, and I'll see if I have anything suitable to wear for a ball?'

And for seeing Matteo again, she hoped.

Matteo didn't know how Gabe talked him into stuff like this.

He was a racing driver, not some sort of wannabe philanthropist actor. Sure, he did what he could for causes that mattered to him—especially the cancer charity that had helped Giovanni in his last days. Most of his riskiest adventures were sponsored to raise money for them. But that was the point, wasn't it? He liked *doing* things for charity.

Showing up at some fancy ball in a tux and having his photo taken a lot really didn't count.

Still, it *was* for charity, and Gabe was right that his face was the most recognisable on the team. So Matteo had put on his tux jacket and bow tie and his best celeb smile and prepared himself for a dull evening.

If he'd seen the guest list earlier, he'd have known it would be anything but, he realised belatedly as a tall man with coal-black hair and dark eyes entered the room followed by a whole retinue and was announced.

'His Royal Highness Leonardo, the Crown Prince of Augusta.'

Matteo's chest tightened. So this was Isabella's brother, Leo.

There was no reason to think that he'd have brought his sister with him, but Matteo couldn't stop himself craning around to see if there was another royal hiding behind the Prince.

'Looking for someone?' Gabe asked, sounding amused.

It occurred to Matteo rather too late that his manager, in setting up the whole 'perfect week in paradise' thing, had probably got to see a lot of the paperwork, before and after the trip. Including the name of Matteo's perfect match.

Damn.

'Her Highness Princess Isabella of Augusta.'

Matteo's heart stopped at the herald's words, and he ceased caring about what Gabe knew or didn't know. Instead, he turned to face the doorway full on, and tried to remember how to breathe as Isabella walked through it.

She's here. She's really here.

He'd honestly thought he might never be in the same room as her again, and now here she was.

Her ball gown, a deep midnight blue, sparkled under the lights of the ballroom, caressing her curves as he wanted to do. Her dark curls were piled on the top of her head, the creamy skin of her neck and shoulders bare except for the glint of sapphires, and her lips red and kissable.

She looked every inch the Princess, and Matteo wanted her so much he could hardly breathe.

As he watched she surveyed the room, chin held high and her gaze cool and assessing. Her manner was as many light years away from the relaxing, laughing, smiling, *touching* Isabella he'd spent the week with as her ball gown was from the light sundresses she'd worn there.

Then her gaze landed on him, and he saw the Isabella he'd fallen for in Switzerland behind all of her jewels and her title.

If she was surprised to see him, she didn't show it. But her gaze turned warmer, and he felt his body respond to her smile the way it always did.

Then her brother motioned to her, and she turned away to follow him as he toured the room, being introduced to the rich and charitable gathered in Rome for the occasion.

Matteo knew he should be circulating too, having the sort of conversations that led to donations, or someone offering him the opportunity to go and risk his neck to raise money for causes that mattered to him. But it was hard to concentrate on anything except the Princess in the room. Gabe, obviously aware of his distraction, covered for him in most of their conversations, and Matteo made a mental note to thank him later, when he wasn't so distracted.

Eventually, though, the Crown Prince had been introduced to and conversed with all the people who actually mattered in the ballroom and, as the orchestra struck up again after a break in the entertainment, and people began to flood back onto the dance floor, Leo and Isabella finally reached Matteo and Gabe.

'Your Royal Highnesses,' their guide said, 'may I introduce Mr Matteo Rossi, the current world champion racing driver, and his team manager, Mr Gabriel Esposito.'

The Crown Prince probably said something, but whatever it was Matteo didn't hear it. Not when he was taking Isabella's hand in his and lifting it to his lips, kissing it and wishing he could hold on for ever.

Never mind cliff diving, bungee jumping or jungle trekking. Seeing Isabella again made him feel more whole than any of those risky adventures ever had.

Gabe, as so many times before, was his saviour. In seconds flat he'd diverted Isabella's brother with a deep and meaningful conversation about something or other, guiding the Crown Prince's attention away from his sister and the racing driver she had supposedly just met.

'Do you dance, Mr Rossi?' Isabella asked, her voice a touch more formal than he was used to. He'd *never* been Mr Rossi to her before.

'I can try,' he said honestly. Because while his mother might have instilled good manners in her boys, dance lessons hadn't exactly been included.

Isabella flashed him a smile that made her look much more like the woman he knew and wanted. 'Just follow my lead.'

'Anywhere you want to go,' he replied.

Because if it meant being with Isabella tonight, he'd follow her into hell.

Matteo might be fast on his feet when chasing her to the bedroom, but he was not a born dancer. Not that it mattered to Isabella, since dancing together was nothing more than an excuse to get him alone—and lead him away from Leo.

Oh, and maybe an excuse to have him hold her again. She definitely wasn't overlooking the benefits of that.

He knew where to put his hands, at least, and Isabella managed to half dance, half drag him across the dance floor, towards the balcony she'd spotted on an earlier tour of the room. If she was lucky, it would be empty—but even if not, it would still be dark and more private than a crowded ballroom with all eyes on her. And besides, they'd always had good luck with balconies.

'I didn't expect to see you again,' Matteo murmured as they attempted a sort of waltz. She half expected him to add 'so soon', but he didn't, and it made his words sit all the heavier in her heart. He hadn't expected to see her at all. He'd expected that they'd both go their separate ways and that would be it.

Was that what he wanted? She'd never know if she didn't ask. And she *had* to know, before she told him about the apparent consequences of their week together.

'Disappointed?' she asked, as lightly as she could.

'Amazed. And thrilled.' His hand at her waist gripped her tighter. 'And a little hopeful.'

That made her smile—even though she wasn't sure how his mood might change when she told him why she was here.

'I was surprised to find it so easy to see you,' she admitted. 'When I found out Leo was coming to Rome, I tagged along in the hope of finding you. But I hardly expected you to show up at an event on my first night in town.'

'Fate, perhaps,' Matteo said. 'Or luck. Or maybe M had it right with that soulmates thing…'

'You think we'll keep being drawn together for ever, now we've met?' They'd reached the balcony, at last, and stopped dancing. Isabella raised an eyebrow as she waited for his answer.

In a moment, she'd open the door and lead him outside and tell him that she might be pregnant. For these last few seconds, she just wanted to enjoy being the way they'd been together in Lake Geneva.

'I think I wouldn't complain if we were.'

'Good answer.' Because there was a solid chance they were bound together for life, now, by a small cluster of cells growing inside her womb.

Moving out of his arms, she reached for the door handle to the balcony and pushed it open. She glanced around the ballroom, ascertaining that Leo was still fully occupied in conversation with Matteo's manager, and a few other guests who had joined them, and was unlikely to notice her absence for a while.

'Come on,' she said, dragging him with her into the cooler evening air of the balcony. He followed easily, shutting the door silently behind them.

They were lucky; the balcony was deserted. Isabella let out a long, relieved breath, as she moved away from the ballroom and to the stone and metal barrier at the edge of the balcony.

Matteo moved behind her, his whole body pressed up against hers as they looked out over the city below them—ancient and modern by turn, lit up by the moon and the yellow streetlights as the summer evening passed into darkness. She could see the curve of the Coliseum in the distance, the remains of Trajan's market beyond. Traffic and chatter and laughter hung in the air; the city was very much still awake, despite the hour.

It was late. She'd been travelling all day, then rushed to prepare for the ball that night, and then she'd been introduced to so many people her head was spinning with names and information, not to mention the worries she'd brought with her. She was exhausted.

But when she stood with Matteo at her back, when she felt his warmth through her ball gown, his kiss against the bare skin of her neck, above her mother's sapphire necklace...all of that faded away.

She forgot about Leo, inside, probably wondering where she was. She pushed out of her mind the reason she'd come to Rome. And instead, she relaxed against her lover, and let him carry the weight of all her thoughts for a while.

Matteo, for his part, seemed content to stand in silence with her, just enjoying their closeness. Every few moments he'd press a kiss to her hair, her throat, even the swell of her breast over her ball gown. But that was enough.

Until, apparently, it wasn't.

'Isabella,' he murmured against her ear. 'Why did you come to Rome?'

Because I might be pregnant.

The truth, but not all of it. There was another truth she wanted him to know, too. So she gave him that, instead.

'Because I missed you.'

Matteo spun her round, pulling her tight against his chest as he kissed her soundly.

'You missed me too?' She laughed as he finally broke the kiss.

'More than I like to admit.' The truth of it was there in his eyes as she met his gaze.

She needed to tell him. And she would.

Just not yet.

Was it so wrong to want to enjoy this reunion just a little longer? To recapture everything she'd loved about being with him in Switzerland, before their situation got a lot more complicated?

'I dreamed about you,' she murmured, and watched his green eyes darken.

'Yeah? What did you dream?' His voice was gravelly and low, and it made her ache for him to touch her more.

'I dreamt of your hands on me.' At her words, Matteo slid his hands up from her waist, up to her breasts, rubbing his thumbs across her nipples through the thick fabric of her ball gown.

It wasn't enough; the fabric was too thick, she couldn't get the touch she needed. She whimpered her need to him, and it seemed Matteo understood. Without warning, he tugged it down just a couple of centimetres. Just enough to release her aching nipples. This time, when he brushed his thumbs across them, she moaned.

God, she hoped the music inside the ballroom was loud enough that no one heard her and came out to investigate.

'What else did you dream of?' Matteo's voice was rough with need, and Isabella thought longingly of the balcony at the villa in Lake Geneva, and how it conveniently led right to their bedrooms.

'Your mouth.' The words came out as a gasp, and Matteo flashed her a wicked smile before dipping his head lower.

His lips wrapped around first one nipple, then the other, giving each enough attention to make her squirm in his embrace.

'Anything else?' he asked, against her skin.

Time for some payback. Her hand snuck down to the front of his tuxedo trousers and pressed against the hardness she found there. 'I definitely dreamt about this, too. Inside me.'

Now it was Matteo's turn to let out a groan. 'Trust me, if I thought I could get away with making love to a princess here on a balcony, with the whole of Rome watching, I would.'

'Too much risk even for you, huh?' Isabella's smile faltered as she remembered what other risks they'd taken.

'Maybe I'm just worried I couldn't make it good enough for you, up here,' Matteo countered.

'I doubt that. You managed fine on the balcony in Lake Geneva.'

'True.' Matteo's smile turned wicked. 'Want to find out if I still have the magic touch?'

God, she did. So much.

But her real reasons for being in Rome were too heavy

in her mind—not to mention the risk of Leo coming out here to find her. That would be the end of her royal reputation for good.

She stepped away, tugging her dress back into position, as Matteo watched her, his eyes suddenly wary. And she knew she wouldn't be able to hide the truth from him any longer.

'Isabella, I'm going to ask you again. Why did you come to Rome?'

CHAPTER ELEVEN

MATTEO WASN'T ONE hundred per cent sure what the feeling thrumming through his body was, but he suspected it might be dread. Isabella bit down on her lower lip as she looked up at him, her warm brown eyes wide and guileless.

'I think I might be pregnant.'

All the dread that was bubbling through him gathered in his stomach, sinking it like a stone.

Pregnant. She might be pregnant. With his baby.

That last night. The broken condom. The risk that was so much greater than all the others he'd taken before.

Seeing Isabella again here in Rome…for a moment, he'd let himself get carried away, as he'd been able to do in Switzerland when it was just the two of them. For all of his protestations, he probably *would* have made love to her right there on the balcony if she'd let him.

She was a risk on a different level from any skydive or impossible climb. The Crown Prince could probably get him arrested, and if someone down below had spotted them and the Rome *polizia* were called, he'd *definitely* have been spending the night in the cells.

And yet she was a risk he couldn't resist. Not for the adrenaline, like all the others. Just for her.

He'd made a lifestyle of outrunning risk, of beating all the odds, every time.

But this time, it looked as if it had caught up with him.

'We need to get you back in there before you're missed.' He brushed down the back of her ball gown and hoped that no one would notice any specks of balcony dirt in amongst the embroidery and the sparkly bits. Her lipstick was mostly gone, but hopefully she could replace that. And he'd managed not to muss up her hair too much.

'Matteo, we need to talk about this.'

'I know! I know. And I want to. Just...' The door to the balcony opened for a brief moment, a laughing couple audible in the gap, until they obviously realised the space was occupied and closed the door again to seek another spot for privacy. 'Not here,' Matteo finished, redundantly.

'Okay.' She didn't look happy about it, but at least she seemed to understand.

He hoped so. It wasn't that he didn't want to discuss the situation. He just needed to get his head around it a bit first.

Having a baby *definitely* wasn't on his list of adventures. But it seemed that someone else was writing his bucket list, once again.

'I wish we had more time,' he said. 'How long are you in Rome for?'

'Another few days. Come and find me at my hotel tomorrow?' she suggested. 'You can show me the sights of Rome. And we can talk.'

She wanted to escape her security *and* her brother in a strange city, with him? He'd taught her the fun of taking risks well, it seemed.

'I will,' he promised. He knew he wouldn't be able to stay away, not as long as he knew Isabella was so close. 'But we need to get back in there now.'

The thought of leaving her, of having to deal with all this, was making him shake. He stumbled, his hand slipping on the door handle until it opened, and the sounds of the ballroom surrounded them.

'We'll...we'll talk tomorrow, yeah?' he managed, as he staggered back into the room. 'Wait here, then follow me in a few minutes. Okay?'

Isabella nodded, but he could see the fear in her eyes, even in the dim lights.

Matteo shut the door behind him and walked away. He needed to get away from the balcony before Isabella came out. He needed to be someone unsuspicious. To look as if he were having a perfectly ordinary evening—and his entire world hadn't been turned upside down.

He scanned the ballroom until he found Gabe—a solid, fixed point in his suddenly reeling world.

Gabe was a good manager and a better friend. While Matteo had no doubt Gabe knew where they were and what they were doing, he'd managed to keep Isabella's brother away from the balcony, holding him in conversation with a variety of people Matteo recognised by sight.

That was good. Taking off in the other direction, he headed for the bar, and a drink—making sure to keep the door to the balcony in his line of sight as much as he could. Leaning back against the bar, he watched Isabella reappear, slightly mussed, but still the most beautiful woman he'd ever seen. He saw the moment her brother spotted her and excused himself from Gabe. He saw Gabe clock Matteo on the other side of the room before he let him go.

And he heard the conversation between the royal siblings as they passed by him, heading towards the rest of their entourage.

'I just needed some air, Leo, that was all,' Isabella

said. But her eyes met his for a moment, and he couldn't stop his smile. Even with everything, just looking at his Princess made his day better.

Luckily, the Crown Prince was oblivious to his presence. But not his existence.

'I was starting to worry you'd run off somewhere with that racing driver,' Leo joked. 'Honestly, Bella, we really do need to stick together at these things. Who knows? I might want to introduce you to someone you might find...suitable.'

The emphasis on 'suitable' was almost innuendo, and Matteo's grip on his glass tightened at the sound of it.

Of course, *he* wasn't suitable for a princess. He'd known that from the start.

But that didn't change the fact that she might just be carrying his baby. And that as terrifying as that was...it didn't feel like the end of the world.

Matteo threw back the whisky in his glass and wondered how long he had to wait before he could get out of there.

And how long before he could steal Isabella away again, to start figuring out what the hell they did next.

Oh, he really hadn't ever prepared for *this* sort of risk. But as long as they figured it out together...maybe it would be okay.

Isabella didn't sleep that night.

She wished she'd managed to slip Matteo her mobile number, or something, so at least they could have kept in touch over the long hours before they saw each other again. But even if she had...they needed to have this conversation in person.

She just hated waiting for it.

Finally, the morning sun slipped through the curtains

of her hotel suite, and she allowed herself to get up and dressed. She chose a sundress more like the ones she'd worn in Switzerland, rather than one of the more formal outfits Gianna had packed for her; she didn't want to be Princess Isabella today. Not with Matteo.

Perhaps he had been unable to sleep, too, because when she snuck downstairs for the first breakfast serving, uncomfortably aware of her security team following her as she went, he was already seated at a table in the corner.

The hotel staff tried to usher her towards a private seating area, offering to bring her whatever breakfast foods she desired, but Isabella sent them away with a smile. She wanted to choose her own food, from the buffet, just as all the other guests would be doing; otherwise, she might as well have had breakfast alone in her room. Which, now she thought about it, was probably what the hotel staff—not to mention her security team and her brother—would have preferred.

Before Lake Geneva, that was exactly what she would have done. But things were different now.

Isabella motioned the bodyguard flanking her towards an unoccupied table in the corner, indicating that she'd follow shortly when she'd chosen her food. The buffet was in clear line of sight from the table, so he didn't object.

Helping herself to a plate, Isabella lingered by the watery scrambled eggs, and waited to see if Matteo would take the hint.

'You know, I could take you to about seven different cafés in walking distance of this hotel that would do you a better breakfast than this.' His voice, low and familiar by her ear, sent a warmth coursing through her that had nothing to do with summer.

'Then maybe you should,' she murmured back.

'Any suggestions on how I might get out of here alone, though?' She didn't risk a glance over her shoulder at her bodyguard, probably watching their every move.

Matteo didn't even pause to think; she suspected he'd been planning this all morning. 'The corner by the coffee station is hidden from sight, but there's another door out that way. Go get some coffee, and I'll distract your security guy. When you can see he's occupied, slip out the side door of the hotel and meet me there. I'll be as quick as I can; just stay out of sight.'

She nodded, to show that she'd heard him, then picked up her plate and headed for the coffee station, while Matteo walked away in the other direction. Giving her bodyguard a smile, she lifted a coffee cup from the stack to show her intention.

Her heart was racing at the idea of actually following through with the plan. But, she reminded herself, she wasn't just taking this risk for herself. It was for the baby that might be growing inside her right now.

That was most definitely worth taking risks for.

'Hey, aren't you Matteo Rossi?' she heard her bodyguard say as she ducked into the coffee area.

Smiling to herself, she listened to Matteo agreeing to sign an autograph, and getting into a deep discussion about his teammates' chances in the next Grand Prix, then slipped out of the promised door and headed for freedom.

She tucked herself behind a pillar just outside the hotel and waited. Matteo joined her not long after, grabbing her arm and taking off at a steady clip around the back of the hotel. 'Come on.'

Isabella wasn't even properly surprised when she found herself on the back of a motorcycle, a few moments later, a black helmet crammed over her head and her arms wrapped tight around Matteo's waist as he took off through the streets of Rome.

A wonderful sense of freedom, one she hadn't felt since she'd left Lake Geneva, rushed over her with the wind. This, this was what she'd been missing. Well, this and everything Matteo had given her on the balcony the night before…and everything else she wanted from him. Was it the motorcycle or him making her throb between her thighs?

Probably both, she decided as he swung around another corner and finally pulled to a halt.

'Where are we?' she asked, pulling off her helmet, and hoping her hair wasn't completely wrecked. She ran her fingers through her tangled curls and hoped for the best.

'Just around the corner from the Forum, and the Coliseum.' Matteo shrugged. 'I figured we can walk and talk, you can see a little history, and then we'll get pizza before I take you back. Sound okay?'

Isabella nodded. Leaving the bike parked in a side street, helmets attached, they headed out into the historical centre of Rome. Matteo held out a hand to her and she took it, conscious as they joined the streams of tourists wandering the ancient, excavated streets of the Forum that they could be any other couple, enjoying a summer's day in Rome.

The only thing that ruined the illusion was the tension in Matteo's shoulders, and the way she couldn't help but check over her shoulder for any sign of the palace security team catching up with them.

'So,' Matteo said, after a while of just wandering amongst the ruins. 'I guess we need to talk.'

He'd chosen a good place for it, she realised belatedly. Here in the open air, with so much conversation and chatter, and people moving past them all the time, who was there to listen in on such an intensely private conversation? And who would realise the consequences of it, even if they *did* listen?

In a restaurant, they might have been photographed together, or recognised by a waitress who later sold her story. Matteo was far more famous here than she was—her bodyguard had proved that—but with his cap pulled low over his face, hopefully no one would recognise him.

She took a deep breath. 'Yes, we do.'

'Are you sure?' he asked, and she looked at him with confusion until he shook his head and clarified. 'Not about talking. I mean, about…have you taken a test?'

'Not yet,' she admitted. 'It's not the easiest thing to do with the whole palace watching you.'

'Right. Do you…do you want to? I could find a pharmacy…'

Isabella sighed. 'I'll need to, soon. But for now… I'm over a week late, Matteo. I think we have to assume it's likely, given our last night together in Switzerland.'

That damn broken condom. Although, without it, would she even be here, in Rome, exploring with Matteo like a tourist? She doubted it. More likely, she'd be still locked up in the palace, itching to escape but not knowing where or how.

At least this had focused her. Shown her how much the freedom she'd found with Matteo had given her.

She'd already known how much she'd missed him.

'Yeah. So…assuming you are…'

'Pregnant,' she said, since it seemed that he couldn't.

'What do you want to do next?'

And wasn't that the million-euro question?

'I… If there's a baby, I want to keep it.' That part was easy. However hard it might be, however scandalised Augustan society, however furious her family. This was her baby, and no one could take that away from her. 'Is that a problem?'

Matteo looked horrified. 'I wasn't suggesting—I didn't mean—Isabella, *of course* I support you if you want to keep the baby. I guess all I meant was... I'll be guided by you on this. It's your body, your choice.'

Your reputation, he didn't add, but Isabella could hear it in the air between them, all the same.

She wouldn't have risked it for anything else, they both knew that. But a baby...that changed things.

'What about you?' she asked, to drive the thought away. 'Would you want to be involved? Or even acknowledged? I mean, nobody has to know, if you don't want to be part of this.'

Grabbing her hands, Matteo yanked her out of the path, against a crumbling ruin of a wall, and met her gaze with his own, intense green one.

'Bella. If you are pregnant with my child, of course I will be a part of that. I'll marry you in a heartbeat if you'll let me—or if the King and Queen will, I suppose. Having a family with you will be my next big adventure, I guess.' He flashed her a quick smile at that, but it did nothing to diminish the seriousness of what he was offering.

If she was pregnant, he would marry her. Because for all that he was a reckless, daredevil playboy, he was also a good man. He'd do the right thing.

Even if he didn't want to.

And that was the problem. There'd been no mention of love, in any of his grand declaration. If she hadn't come to Rome and told him about the possibility of the baby, would he have ever come to find her? She wasn't exactly difficult to locate—The Palace, Augusta would probably do it on a map search, or even a letter.

Matteo had given her a freedom she'd never experienced in her whole, pampered princess life. She wasn't going to take his away now, just to save a few shreds of her royal reputation.

So instead of the shock of an Italian racing-car driver stealing away their Princess, the Augustan crown and public might have to deal with having an unmarried single mother in the royal succession—if she was even allowed to keep her title, which was not a sure thing at all. Her stomach was cramping just thinking about her brother's reaction.

She knew she could lose everything, the same way Aunt Josephine had, and she might not even have true love to show for it.

'Let's find a pharmacy. Buy a test. Then we can plan. After pizza.'

Matteo *really* hoped nobody had recognised him buying a pregnancy test. But who else could he ask to do it? If he was recognised, at least no one would connect it to Isabella yet. If *she* was recognised, well… That was a whole different matter.

There was nothing to link him and the Princess of Augusta. Not until they announced their engagement, anyway.

Don't think about it.

It was the right thing to do, he knew that. For Isabella, and for their child. And for him, too, really. He wanted to be a part of his son or daughter's life, the way his own father never had, and if that child was Augustan royalty then the only way he was getting close was by living up to his responsibilities and marrying their mother.

He just didn't like the way his whole body clenched at the idea of being tied down as somebody's *husband*. Would he still be allowed to race? To live his life the way he wanted? He had a sneaky suspicion that his cliff-diving days would be limited, once he was inaugurated into the Augustan royal family.

If they'd even have him.

Would he cost Isabella her title by marrying her? It wasn't as if he couldn't afford to support her in the manner she was accustomed to—his billions would go a long way to providing compensation, as would, he hoped, the freedom they'd have to live their lives together unencumbered by the royal rules, if she was thrown out of the royal family.

But being a Princess of Augusta was her birthright. Giving up her country was something she wouldn't have even considered if it weren't for him. No, if it weren't for the baby.

They managed to sneak back into Isabella's hotel room by a similar distraction technique to earlier in the day. Matteo would have less respect for the security team for falling for it a second time except this time around Isabella was the distraction. With their apologetic wayward charge back in hand, all attention was on her explanation for her disappearance, leaving Matteo free to sneak into her room with the key card she'd given him.

She joined him a few minutes later, rolling her eyes as she shut the door to keep her latest bodyguard firmly outside the room.

'Okay?' Matteo asked softly as he emerged from his hiding place by the wardrobe.

'Fine. They just all think I'm still sixteen or something. I'm under orders to stay here for the rest of the evening.' She stalked towards him, a predatory grin on her face. 'Which shouldn't be a problem, since you're here with me.'

The pregnancy test burning a hole in his pocket was

totally forgotten when she smiled at him like that. But as she pushed his light summer jacket from his shoulders, it fell out onto the floor, a stark reminder to them both of why they were there.

'Do you want to take that now?' Matteo stepped away, giving her the space to decide.

He could see the warring thoughts fluttering across her face. She bent to pick up the box, pulled out the instruction leaflet, and scanned the text.

'It says it's best to do it first thing in the morning. I'll take it then. I mean, at this point, another few hours aren't going to make any difference. And I want—'

She broke off, and Matteo waited.

'I want to enjoy this last night. Before everything changes.'

He could hear the hesitancy in her voice. She wasn't any surer about this situation than he was, and who could blame her?

But the thing that had blossomed between them during their week on Lake Geneva was still as present and sure as it ever had been—hadn't he felt that last night, on the balcony?

Matteo knew what others might think and say. They'd believe that his actions the night before—attempting to seduce an honest-to-God princess in a semi-public setting—were all about the risk, the same as all of his other extra-curricular activities. But they'd be wrong. It hadn't been the risk that had him hard and desperate in the dark.

It was Isabella. Only ever Isabella.

And she was right; once she took that test and they knew for sure, everything would change. One of them would lose their dreams, their future. Either his racing career and adventurous lifestyle, or her title and her country.

But not yet. They had one last night together.

'You'll have to be very quiet,' he said, thinking of the security team waiting outside her hotel suite door. 'Do you think you can manage that?'

'I did last night, didn't I?' she asked, one eyebrow raised.

He took a step closer, and she echoed it, leaving the pregnancy test on the table behind her. 'Last night, I couldn't do half the things I wanted to do to you. Definitely not enough to make you scream.' And he'd dreamt all night of how different that might have been. If he'd been able to lift that heavy ballgown and kneel under the skirt and take his mouth to her...

'Well, maybe I'll need to fill my mouth with something to keep me quiet.' She kept her gaze trained on his as she dropped to her knees. 'Besides, I think it might actually be *you* who needs to try not to make any noise.'

There was no blood left in his brain, or anywhere except south of his belt. He didn't care about the inadequate thin curtains over the window, or the men outside the door who were trained to break him in two in a moment. All Matteo could concentrate on was Isabella's small hands unfastening his jeans, sliding them down his thighs with his boxers, until he kicked off his shoes and stepped out of them.

Then it wasn't just her hands on him. Shaking her long, dark curls away from her face, she nuzzled against the top of his thighs, pressing soft kisses against his hardness.

God. He was going to lose his mind. He was going to actually go insane with want—and if he didn't, if she did something about it, he was going to scream and get himself killed by her bodyguard.

He had to admit, it didn't sound like a bad way to go.

'You okay up there?' she murmured against his hardness, and he felt her words vibrate through him.

'More than,' he answered honestly.

'Good.' Then, with one last kiss against his thigh, she closed her mouth over the tip of him, and Matteo decided right there and then that this was *definitely* worth dying for.

Staggering back a couple of steps, he grabbed hold of the chair behind him for support, sinking into it as Isabella explored and tasted him to her heart's content. And his, for that matter. Finally, as his body started to tighten, he pulled her away before everything was over too soon for his liking.

'You don't want me to finish? Was it not okay?' She looked up at him, her mouth plump and slick and red but her eyes uncertain.

'It was perfect,' he assured her. 'I just don't want it to end so soon.'

She smiled at that, a catlike, satisfied smile. 'What would you like instead, then?'

He pulled her up into his lap, stripping her sundress over her head before letting her divest him of his shirt. 'I'd rather like to be inside you,' he whispered against her collarbone, and felt her shiver at his words.

She was wet and ready for him when he touched her, and it was only when she stood up to strip off her lingerie that his mind could work well enough to remember the essentials. 'Wait. Condoms.'

Isabella gave him a look as if to say, *Do you really think they're necessary at this point?*

He shrugged. 'No point taking unnecessary risks,' he said, which made her laugh. 'There are some in my wallet.'

She bent over to retrieve his wallet from his jeans

on the floor, and Matteo was happily enjoying the view when he heard the first noises outside. Voices. Then a bang on the door.

'Isabella!' The voice outside didn't sound patient. Or happy. 'Let me in this instant!'

CHAPTER TWELVE

Isabella spun around to face Matteo, still slumped in the chair watching her, his eyes wide. 'It's Leo!'

Because of course it was.

'Your brother?' Matteo kept his voice low, and she nodded in response.

'You need to hide!'

He'd hoped his days of hiding from angry older brothers were over when he became an actual adult, but apparently not. Scooping up his clothes, wallet and—in a brief flash of inspiration—the pregnancy test, Matteo let himself be bundled into the bathroom by Isabella.

'One moment!' she called out cheerily. 'I'm just changing.'

'Isabella, I swear to God—' Whatever Leo was swearing was cut off into a mumble, probably around the time the Crown Prince realised that *anyone* could be listening. Including the press—or at least people who'd sell the video or audio to the papers.

Isabella pulled her dress back over her head and surveyed the room.

'Bella,' Matteo whispered as she pushed the bathroom door closed. 'Remember, you're an adult. He might be a prince, but you're a princess. You get to make your own decisions. No crown can take that away from you, okay?'

Biting down on her lip, she nodded, but Matteo could tell she didn't fully believe him.

He sighed, and sat down on the toilet seat to wait, glad that the door hadn't closed all the way. He was still sitting in almost complete darkness, but at least there was that sliver of light from the bedroom. *And* it meant he could hear what Isabella and her brother were saying.

'Where were you today?' Leo asked, the moment Isabella opened the door.

Matteo hadn't spent much time with him at the ball the other night, and his attention had definitely been elsewhere, but he'd seen enough photos to be able to imagine the Crown Prince's face right then. Red, flustered and angry.

'You skipped out on your security, didn't leave word where you were going, wouldn't answer your phone—'

'I'm sorry.' The apology sounded automatic to Matteo's ears. As if she was so used to saying it, it was nothing more than a reflex.

Plus he happened to know that she really *wasn't* sorry for running out with him. Not if what they'd been doing before Leo banged on the door was any sign.

'My security team...they're not in any trouble, are they? Because I really didn't give them any choice. I just... I wanted to get outside, get some air. See a little of Rome, that was all. You know how rarely I leave the palace these days.' She was trying to mollify him, to earn his sympathy, but Matteo didn't know Leo well enough to guess whether it would work.

He *did* notice, however, that his habit of asking for forgiveness, not permission, seemed to be rubbing off on his Princess.

'And you know why that is,' Leo shot back. Matteo heard him sigh, then the sound of bed springs creaking, as if he'd sat down on the edge of the bed in exhaustion. 'Bella...people were worried. *I* was worried. You don't know this city, or anybody here. Anything could have happened to you. What if some brigand had recognised you and snatched you off the street?'

'Brigand?' Isabella asked, sounding amused.

'You know what I mean,' Leo snapped back. 'The point is, you weren't *safe*. And while you're here in Rome with me, it's my responsibility to keep you safe.'

'I know. I'm sorry. It's just...what if I didn't want to be safe, all the time?'

There, hidden in that question, was the Isabella *Matteo* knew. The one he wanted, more than any other woman he'd ever met before. The one who made him laugh and chase her and think.

The one who wanted to live a life that was more than being afraid all the time, or doing what other people wanted her to, rather than what she wanted herself.

The woman he might marry, soon. Might spend his whole life with.

It was just a glimmer, though. A brief flash of the woman he'd known in Lake Geneva, who he'd seduced on a balcony the night before. One that was soon smothered by her brother's next words.

'Of course you want to be safe, Isabella. Don't be stupid.'

'Yes. Right. Of course, I do. I'm sorry, Leo. I don't know what I was thinking.'

And with that, all of Matteo's hopes about who she could be if she was just willing to take the chance disappeared.

Maybe inside, Isabella wanted to be free, wanted to live her own life at last. But her family would always stomp out the first flames of rebellion, and she would always let them. She'd build up those walls brick by brick, all by herself, to hold onto her place in the royal family.

She didn't want to be pregnant with his child; her horrified reaction the night the condom had split had made that perfectly clear. She didn't want to have to marry him—it was just the least unacceptable option to her family, and their royal expectations.

He'd marry her, if she was pregnant, because he owed her that. But he had no illusions any more that it would be what either of them wanted. Now, they enjoyed each other's company, the sex was amazing and, yes, he knew he could fall for her. Hard.

But if they married…

He'd be tied into a life he didn't want to live. And she'd be embarrassed by him forever, even if marrying him didn't cost her the title of Princess. He wasn't what anyone wanted for her—even Isabella herself.

Outside, the royal siblings were still talking.

'Look, I know we can all seem a little overprotective at times, Bella,' Leo said. 'But you know why that is. You just don't understand the world outside the palace and, honestly, I'm not sure you want to. We just want to keep you safe, okay?'

'I know that,' Isabella replied, softly. 'I'm sorry.'

The bed springs creaked again. Leo was standing up. 'Don't cry, Bella. It's okay. Just…stay where we can keep you safe. Yeah?'

'Yeah.'

There was quiet for a long moment, before Matteo heard the door to the suite open and close again. He waited.

Isabella's eyes were red when she opened the door. 'I'm sorry you had to hear that.'

Maybe it was just as well that he had. At least it told him exactly what the future held for him.

He held out the pregnancy test. 'I think maybe you'd better take this now. Don't you?'

Negative.

How could it be negative?

'Could it be a false result?' Matteo's voice was tense as he sat beside her on the bed, but she was sure she heard relief in it, all the same.

Isabella shook her head. 'I mean, it *could,* but...'

She could feel it now, those telltale signs she'd been ignoring all day. The slight cramp in her lower back. The tiredness. The stupid tears when she'd been talking to Leo.

Her period was on its way.

She wasn't pregnant.

She might not have proof for another day or so, but she knew it, inside.

'I'm pretty sure it's right,' was all she said.

Matteo let out a long, relieved breath. 'Okay. Well, that's good. Right?'

'Absolutely.' She hadn't wanted to be pregnant—not now, not with a man she'd barely known a few weeks, with whom she had nothing in common outside the bedroom. A man her family would disapprove of on principle. A man who could cost her everything.

So why did she feel like crying?

Period hormones. That's all.

No, that *wasn't* all, and she wasn't going to pretend that it was.

'You okay?' Matteo asked. Of course, *he* looked fine. He didn't have stupid hormones. And he wasn't going back to a life trapped behind palace walls, never daring to reach out for what he wanted from the world, in case it turned on him. In case it destroyed his family, or his reputation.

Really, she'd had a narrow escape. She should be celebrating.

'I'm fine.' It came out as almost a sob. 'Happy tears,' she lied.

'Right.' He didn't look convinced. 'So...what now?'

'You're free,' she said, with a shrug. 'No need to worry about me.'

'And you're just going to go back to the palace as if nothing ever happened?' His tone was even, his expression blank. But Isabella could still feel the tension between them.

'What else can I do?' She was a Princess of Augusta. The privileges that gave her came with a cost—and a lot of expectation. 'I've already pushed about as far as I can coming here, especially so soon after my Switzerland trip. And it's a miracle nobody caught onto that, either.'

She shuddered at the thought of Leo bursting into her suite asking, 'What's this about you spending a week having sex with a racing-car driver in Lake Geneva?'

'I thought...' Matteo looked away, as if he wasn't going to finish his sentence. And suddenly it was vitally important to Isabella that she know *exactly* what he thought.

Because he was the first person in her life who had got to know her as a woman, not a princess. Who hadn't cared about titles or palaces or money. Who hadn't held expectations for what she should do and who she should be. Who loved risk enough to be with her anyway, even when it looked as if they might have been caught out by it.

His opinion mattered, more than almost anyone else's. She needed to hear it.

'What did you think?'

He sighed. Then he looked up from where his hands were clasped between his legs as he sat on the edge of the bed and met her gaze head-on.

'I thought that Lake Geneva had meant something. That coming here had meant something. To you, I mean. And not about me, particularly. I thought—I hoped—that it would be your first step out from under your family's thumb. That you might finally forgive yourself for what happened with that reporter and move on with your life.'

'I came here to tell you I might be having your baby.' Isabella swallowed, his words ringing in her ears. 'If that's not flying in the face of all my family's beliefs and expectations, I don't know what is.'

'And now that you're not? What are you going to do now that you're not pregnant, Isabella?'

She didn't know. She hadn't thought this far. Hadn't thought beyond finding him again, telling him about the baby.

Letting him figure out what she should do next, the way she'd always relied on her family to.

But he had no stake in her future now. No investment in what happened to her next.

She could go back to the palace, to her old life, but she already knew how stifling that felt, now she'd experienced something more. Last time, after everything had happened with Nate, she'd been so grateful for the safety of the palace, the security of her family around her, an impenetrable barrier against the real world outside that only seemed to want to hurt her.

This time...this time it was different. She was comparing her experience with Nate and her time with Matteo as if they were the same, but they weren't. Beyond the fact that they both included her having sex with a man the palace wouldn't approve of…the details were worlds apart.

Matteo didn't want to hurt her. Matteo could be trusted, even if his attitude to risk and opinions on suitable behaviour for a princess would scandalise the whole royal family. He was on *her* side; Nate had never been.

And she knew, now, that she'd never been truly in love with Nate. She wasn't a hundred per cent sure she could say the same about Matteo.

So what *was* she going to do now? What *could* she do?

'I need to go back to Augusta with Leo,' she said, thinking aloud. 'And obviously you don't now need to come with me. We don't need to go tell my parents I'm pregnant and they have to let us get married.' She flashed him a smile at that, ignoring the pang in her heart at the idea. He didn't smile back.

'So you just go back to your old life, and I go back to mine?'

'I guess.' Except that felt so wrong, Isabella knew it wouldn't work. Not for her, anyway. But maybe that was what Matteo wanted? His old life back—racing and risks and other women. 'Is that what you want?'

His smile was sad. 'I'm trying to find out what *you* want, Princess.'

When was the last time someone had asked her what she wanted and actually listened to the answer? Even the staff serving dinner at the palace brought her whatever dish the diet plan her mother's nutritionist had set her said she should eat, rather than what she actually fancied.

But Matteo was asking, and she knew he meant it.

What did she want? She wanted everything. He'd taught her the value of taking a risk, when it was the *right* risk. And maybe there was a way she could do it that wouldn't ruin everything else, too.

She took a breath, and a risk, and answered him honestly.

'I want to see you again. I want to *keep* seeing you. I don't want to say goodbye.'

Matteo's heart lurched in his chest as she spoke the words he'd been hoping—though not expecting—to hear. But before he could answer, she went on.

'I mean, we'd need to keep it a secret. God only knows what Leo would say if he found out. But we've managed this far, right? I think as long as I stay out of trouble at the palace, or when I'm with my family, nobody is going to mind if I take the odd weekend off. We can plan ahead, arrange to meet places where no one knows either of us. I might need to speak with Gianna about my security team…'

She had it all figured out, Matteo realised. Exactly how to have her cake and eat it.

Or have him, and not disappoint her family.

And it *should* be perfect. It should be exactly what he wanted. The freedom to live his life how he wanted and still see Isabella, without getting tied into her world and the expectations that went with it.

So why did his chest ache so much?

Because I'm not enough for her.

Ever since he was a teenager, he'd tried to live enough for two, to make up for everything Giovanni had lost. He'd done more, seen more, risked more than most people on the planet.

But he still wasn't enough for Isabella.

'Matteo?' She looked up at him, a tiny line forming between her eyebrows.

'I can't.' Pushing up off the bed, he paced across to the window. 'Isabella… I can't just be some dirty secret for you, the guy you're ashamed to bring home to your family.'

Her eyes widened at that, and she reached out towards him before sitting on her hands. 'That wasn't... I didn't mean it that way.'

'I know.' He sighed. 'But...when you told me you thought you were pregnant, I was scared, sure. But excited too. Because honestly? I've never felt anything like what I feel for you for any woman before now. I thought that maybe we could make this work. Until I heard you talking to your brother.'

'Leo? You can't... I just had to say whatever he needed to hear to get him out of here, before he found you hiding in my bathroom!'

'Yeah, but you meant it, too. And if I'd doubted it at all...you just confirmed it now.' God, he hated saying this. Hated thinking this. Realising it was true.

After so many years of pushing love away, of keeping it at arm's length to avoid the inevitable losses that came with it...now he found himself here. Wanting, wishing for a princess's love—and knowing that he couldn't take the loss that came with it when she didn't love him enough in return.

He'd been looking for an excuse to upend his whole life for her—to make her upend her life for him. But if she really wasn't pregnant, that excuse was gone. And he wasn't such a terrible human as to try again and bring a baby into a relationship they didn't have the courage to seek anyway.

He had honestly believed there was no risk he wouldn't take. Turned out that loving Princess Isabella of Augusta when she didn't love him was the line he couldn't cross.

'I'm not saying we *never* tell them,' she tried, but Matteo shook his head.

'It's okay, Isabella. We never—this wasn't ever the love match M wanted it to be. We weren't matched together because we were soulmates who were going to live happily ever after. We were put together because my manager wanted to keep me out of trouble and your assistant wanted to give you a week off from being a princess.'

'It was more than that,' she said softly.

'Was it?' Because it was hard to remember that right now.

'You know it was.'

'It was great sex, I'll give you that.' His heart was breaking, but he knew he couldn't give in. Couldn't let her say anything that would persuade him to stay. To hide away and follow her rules instead of his own.

For seventeen years he'd worked every day to fulfil his late brother's ambitions. To cross off every item on the bucket list he'd written before he died. And now, here he was, thirty-three years old and no idea what he wanted from his future for himself. Nothing except a half-scribbled list of adventures still to be had.

But he knew what he didn't want. And surely that was a pretty good place to start.

'Isabella, think about it. We sneak around, we have some fun, and, sure, I'm not denying I want that too—I want more time with you. But it wouldn't be enough. Not for me.' He'd never been the marrying type. Until he met Isabella. 'Eventually, the secrecy would break us. Or we'd get found out, and you'd have to choose. Your family, your title, or me. We dodged a bullet, this time. I won't put us in front of another one.'

'So what? We just never see each other again?' There were tears in her eyes. Matteo had to look away.

'I think it's for the best.' Even if it broke his heart. 'I can't live by your royal rules, even if they'd have me. I can't hide away my love for you, either. I need to go out there and live my life—not yours, not my brother's—just mine. I'm sorry.'

He didn't kiss her goodbye. Couldn't even meet her gaze.

Instead, he walked straight out of the hotel suite, and pretended not to see the astonished look from the bodyguard as he headed back to his old life once more.

CHAPTER THIRTEEN

Isabella slipped her sunglasses over her eyes as she stepped out of the car at the small airfield outside the city. She'd pretended to sleep during the short drive out there—believable, given the early start—but now she needed something else to hide her red-rimmed eyes from her brother.

Not that he was looking at her, of course. He had work to do: emails from the prime minister, or something. Leo was being groomed to take over the throne, possibly sooner rather than later if their father decided he'd like to step aside and retire to the country. It wasn't unprecedented in Augustan history, and King Leonardo *had* been looking tired recently.

Musing on royal successions distracted her brain from the only other topic it seemed able to hold until they were seated on the royal plane at last. But then, as they prepared for take-off, it occurred to her that once Leo became King her role would be even less clear.

Her brother had married three years ago in a royal pageant like none the country had seen before. His wife, Princess Serena, was still in Augusta with their adorable toddler son, pregnant with their next child already. The succession was secure, and Isabella was happy for it. The further she got from the throne, the less pressure on her to be perfect.

But since she *was* further from the throne...what was the point of her? As a princess, at least? Serena had happily taken over a lot of the public-facing duties; the daughter of an ex-prime minister and a famously beautiful duchess, she was used to the spotlight. She was also a huge favourite with the Augustan people, mostly for having cute babies, but also for her keen fashion sense and ability to look empathetic on demand.

Isabella just wore whatever Gianna told her to wear. And, having grown up in a palace, was generally seen as unable to empathise with the Augustan public, even more than a woman who'd also had nannies from birth and gone to the same boarding school.

The point was, there was no place for her in Leo's new palace. If her father *did* hand over the crown sooner rather than later, would she even be welcome to stay there? Or would she move to the country with her parents, a spinster princess for ever?

More likely, they'd marry her off to some duke or lord they needed support from for something. Because Augusta liked nothing more than tradition—and the tradition of using princesses as pawns was well established.

Are you just going to do what they tell you for ever? The words sounded in her head in Matteo's voice.

Suddenly, she had to know.

'Leo.'

Her brother looked up from his papers and his laptop, his reading glasses perched on the end of his nose, and irritation in his eyebrows. 'Yes?'

'When you become King, what happens to me?'

'What do you mean? You can carry on as you always have.' He looked back down at his papers.

'No, I mean… What role do I play in the country?' she pressed.

Sighing, Leo removed his glasses and rubbed his temples. 'You want to talk about this now?'

Isabella shrugged. 'We're not going anywhere. Why not now?'

'Because you haven't shown any interest in your future, or how you can support the country or the monarchy, in years. So I'll ask again, why now?'

'That's not true.' The words were automatic, but they didn't quite cover the sinking feeling in Isabella's stomach that, actually, it might be. 'I care about our country. I do the public appearances I have to. I smile for the cameras. I stay out of trouble… Just because I haven't married any of the titled idiots you keep throwing my way—'

Leo cut her off with a weary sigh. 'Bella… Do you really not get it? After everything that happened with that reporter chap—'

'None of you trust me to make my own decisions! Trust me, I get it. I have to follow The Rules, more than anyone else, because I can't be relied on to choose good people, to know who to trust. To fall in love responsibly.' As if she could ever have missed that.

Even after all the stories about Aunt Josephine, she might have had hope that Augusta was changing with the times.

If it hadn't been for everything that had happened with Nate, maybe she'd have had the courage to take Matteo home to meet her parents. To tell them that, while he might not be the Augustan lord they'd hoped she'd marry, she loved him, and she hoped she had their blessing—but she'd marry him without, if he'd have her.

If there'd been a baby, they'd have had to let her. But now…she knew they'd remind her of her past mistakes and steer her away from what she thought could make her happy.

'That's not... Bella, it's not that we don't trust you.' Leo sounded amazed that she could even think it, which, considering the number of lectures he'd given her over the years on the 'right sort', was a bit rich.

'Of course, it is—' she started, but Leo kept talking over her.

'It's that you don't trust *yourself*.'

She fell silent.

Oh. *Oh.* Leo's words resonated in her ribcage until she couldn't deny the truth of them.

All these years, she'd thought she was toeing the royal line for them. Because it was what she needed to do to have their love, their faith. To keep her position.

And Leo had torn that away with just one line.

She'd been using The Rules as an excuse, thinking she was protecting her reputation, her family—but in truth, she'd been protecting her heart.

'Do you blame me?' she asked, slumping down in her seat to consider the implications of this revelation. 'The last time I thought I was in love, I almost brought down the monarchy.'

Leo chuckled. 'I don't think it was quite *that* bad. Although at the time, I was a little worried that the prime minister was going to have a heart attack.'

'So why all the awful set-up dates with your friends and other lords?' Because she definitely hadn't imagined those.

'Because... Bella, after everything that happened, you sort of drew in on yourself. You shut yourself up in the palace, avoided as many public events as you could, and only spent time with people you'd known practically since birth—like Sofia, or Gianna. We were worried about you. So yes, we tried to get you back out there—to help you get some confidence back—by getting you to spend time with people we knew we could trust. And yes, I can't deny that we were hoping you'd find love with one of them. Because we want you to be *happy*, and you so obviously weren't.'

Isabella looked quickly out of the window, so her brother wouldn't see the tears in her eyes. 'I thought it was because you didn't trust me.'

'It was because we loved you. And we wanted you to trust yourself again. To find your way back to us.' Leo sighed. 'But apparently we only pushed you further away. Serena warned me...well, never mind that now. The important thing is, when I am King, the same as now, there will always be a place for you in my palace, if you want it.'

'Thank you, Leo,' she said softly. 'And...and I think that, maybe, I'm ready to do a little more for the family business, so to speak. If you want me?'

'If?' Leo laughed. 'Serena would *love* it if you could take some of her events and visits off her plate right now. This pregnancy is exhausting her even more than the last, and I've been worried about her trying to do so much.'

Guilt twinged in her chest. 'I'm sorry. I should have noticed—should have offered sooner.'

Reaching across the aisle between them, Leo took her hand. 'None of that. We're all at fault for not realising things sooner. Not talking about them. I know our parents...they're a different generation, and for them feelings are very private, not to be discussed. But it doesn't have to be like that for us, Bella. I'm always here if you want to talk.'

She smiled, although it felt weak on her lips.

Maybe she'd never be what Matteo wanted—she

couldn't stop being a princess, and she didn't *want* to walk away from her heritage, her country. Quite the opposite. She was finally ready to take her proper place and do her part—and it seemed that Leo would let her.

'You said "last time", before,' Leo said cautiously. 'The last time you fell in love. Does that mean…? Is there someone you think you might—?'

'No.' She cut him off quickly. 'That's not…don't worry about that.'

The lines on Leo's forehead told her that he *was* worrying. Isabella sighed.

'I met someone when I was in Switzerland I thought might…but he didn't want the royal life. Or me.' All the truth, even if Leo still believed her trip to Geneva was to visit their cousin Sofia. It was plausible that she might have met someone there, and she wasn't quite ready to confess *everything* to her brother, yet.

'Are you sure? Because, Bella, you put up walls. One day you're going to have to let someone in. And when you do, I'll support you. Whoever they are.'

But she had, hadn't she? That was the problem. She'd let Matteo all the way in. She'd been so afraid of falling in love again, and now it had happened she could see why.

Except that following The Rules meant she'd be heartbroken for ever, separated from the man she finally admitted to herself that she loved. Completely and totally.

She couldn't regret her time with him, even now he'd walked away from her because of who she was. Because loving Matteo had shown her that love was worth taking risks for.

'What about Aunt Josephine?' she asked suddenly, remembering all the stories that had swirled around the palace. 'You said "whoever they are" but that wasn't true for her, was it?'

Leo's brows met in a puzzled frown. 'Aunt Josephine… Bella, she left the palace before you were even born!'

'Was driven out, you mean. Because the King and Queen—our grandparents—didn't approve of who she fell in love with.' Everyone knew that.

'Bella, she *chose* to leave. She didn't want the life of pageantry at the palace. She wanted to run a racing stables with her husband, so they left.' He shook his head. 'I know there was a lot of gossip—I heard plenty of it myself. So I sought her out and asked her, and she told me the truth. I guess it didn't occur to you to do the same?' he asked, looking amused.

'Well…no.'

Leo sighed. 'But you're not entirely wrong. Josie knew that there'd be a lot of talk when she married her groom. I'm sure that weighed into her decision to step away from royal life. But I promise you that no one *made* her. And if you fell in love with someone…perhaps not entirely in keeping with royal expectation, we'd find a way to make it work. *I* would make it work for you, if he made you happy. Okay?'

'Okay,' she said, blinking away tears. 'Thank you, Leo.'

'So, with that in mind, are you *sure* there isn't a certain gentleman you'd like me to meet? I can have the pilot divert to Switzerland, if you want? Or return to Rome, perhaps…?' He left the suggestion hanging, and Isabella wondered how much he'd already guessed about the man she loved.

It was so tempting, to head back and find Matteo and tell him they could be together. But Leo was right about Aunt Josephine's decision, too. She'd chosen to move away from the royal life because there *would* be a scandal, and she didn't want to live it.

Whereas Isabella had only just reconfirmed to herself how much she wanted to step back *into* royal life. She loved Matteo, but she had to live her own life, too—just as he needed to live his. And she couldn't decide for him on this one. If he wanted to be part of her royal life, that would be up to him—and without the baby to bind them together, it didn't seem as if he would.

'I can't live by your royal rules, even if they'd have me.' His words echoed in her brain, and she knew there was no point turning around.

'I'm sure,' she replied to her brother.

Leo gave her a sad smile. 'I'm sorry, Bella. But one day, you'll find the right one.'

Isabella tried to smile, to look as if she believed him. But her heart was telling her that she already had.

She just hadn't been able to hold onto him.

Matteo slammed back into the team hotel, ignoring all the fans and press he passed on the way. No way he was talking to any of them—not after a race like that.

There was, unfortunately, one person he *couldn't* avoid, though.

Gabe slipped into his hotel room behind him, before Matteo could take out his rage on another door.

'So. That was quite a race.'

'It was a disaster.'

'It was definitely close,' Gabe admitted.

Throwing himself into the chair by the window, Matteo put an arm over his eyes, only to find those final moments of the race running behind his eyelids like a video. The way the barrier had seemed to rise up before him. The roar of the other car's engine, too close at his side.

The split second when he'd honestly believed that this could be it. The last risk he ever took.

He removed his arm and opened his eyes, to find Gabe perched on the edge of the bed across from him.

'What happened, Matteo?'

'It was a bad race, that's all.' Matteo shook his head. 'That idiot Rennard was too close.'

'There was no penalty given,' Gabe observed, mildly. 'There seemed to be room as he overtook.'

Except he shouldn't have been overtaking in the first place, should he? Matteo had never lost to *Rennard* of all people before now.

He'd lost his nerve, that had to be it. He'd seen that corner and, for the first time, thought about the risks.

Was this what love did to a person? If so, he needed to get over it, fast.

'Matteo…you've not been the same since you came back from Switzerland. I think everyone can see that. It's not just the race,' Gabe added quickly, when Matteo started to object. 'It's *you*. Before, you were happy, racing along through life, living it to the full. Ticking things off Giovanni's list.'

'How did you know about that?' Because Matteo was damn sure he'd never told him. He'd never told anyone except Isabella.

But Gabe just gave him a look. One of those, *When will you learn that I see everything and I know everything?* looks.

'The point is, you're not happy now,' Gabe said. 'Are you?'

'No.' It was hell to admit, but he wasn't.

How could he be unhappy? When he lived and Giovanni didn't? When he'd achieved everything his brother had ever set out to do?

He'd even started ticking things off his own bucket list—booking a trip to swim with sharks, during his next break. He had things to look forward to, a life to live. And, today's race notwithstanding, a career he loved and was great at.

'It's the Princess, isn't it? Isabella.' Because of course Gabe knew that too. He'd even kept her brother occupied while Matteo had whisked her out onto the balcony at the ball. 'You're in love with her.'

'I can't be.' Because she didn't love him back—not enough to go against her family, or her title.

She wouldn't take the risk to be with him. And he...he couldn't take the risk of trying to live someone else's life again. He'd done it for his brother, but once was enough.

'I don't think love works like that, son.' Gabe creaked to his feet—for all that he was only fifteen years older than Matteo—and pressed a hand against his shoulder. 'Trust me on this. If it's love that's the problem, there's only one way to fix it.'

'And that is?'

'Tell her. Talk to her.'

'Don't see how that fixes anything,' Matteo grumbled. All the reasons they weren't together would still be there, after all.

But Gabe gave him a knowing smile. 'You'd be surprised. I saw the way she looked at you in Rome, Matteo. So I don't think the problem here is unrequited love. Which means there's something else keeping you apart. And maybe that something else is insurmountable, I don't know. But what I *do* know is this: once you tell her? Then it's not just you against this thing. It's the two of you, together. And two people in love against the world? I'd back those odds every time.'

With one last squeeze to his shoulder, Gabe let himself out of the room, leaving Matteo thinking in his chair. After a moment, he pulled an already tattered piece of paper out of his pocket and stared at it.

His new bucket list. The one he'd started after Lake Geneva, to replace the one that Giovanni had left him with. He'd been adding to it piecemeal ever since, whenever a new adventure occurred to him.

Now, he read through it and realised something he'd never have believed if someone else had told him.

He didn't care about any of them.

If things had gone the wrong way on the track that day, in that split second when he'd believed it might, he wouldn't regret not having done any of the things on his bucket list. Hell, in that moment he wouldn't have even been able to remember what any of them were.

Because his mind had been filled with only one thought.

The thought that he'd never see Isabella again.

That would be his only regret.

Lurching to his feet, Matteo crushed the paper in his fist. He didn't need it any more. Didn't need a bucket list at all.

She was his list.

He'd been holding onto his freedom, his adventures, but ultimately, what did they matter if he didn't have her?

Maybe he'd never be enough for her, maybe she'd never love him enough to take the chances that were needed for them to be together. But he knew he had to try.

Until today, he'd always risked his body, freely, happily, loving that surge of adrenaline it gave him. The power over the universe he felt when he survived the odds. Every experience was proof that he'd outwitted the world. That he was *alive*, even if Giovanni wasn't.

But he'd only ever risked his body.
And now, he knew, it was time to risk his heart.

'Are you sure you're okay doing this?' Princess Serena lowered her very pregnant body into her chair and Isabella smiled at the obvious relief her sister-in-law immediately felt.

'Of course. I'm happy to. And at least it's only kids, right?' Some of the children Isabella would be talking to on their visit to the palace rose garden today had been barely walking when she'd embarrassed herself so horribly with Nate. Of course, their teachers would probably remember. But Leo had assured her that most of Augusta had moved on with their lives since then, and forgotten.

It was only Isabella who hadn't. Until now.

'Your Highness? When you're ready?' Gianna called her from the door, and Isabella nodded to tell her she was coming.

Her assistant seemed pleased that she was doing more, too. Isabella supposed it couldn't be much fun organising royal appointments for a princess who refused to do any beyond the odd video interview.

Of course, it was one of those video interviews that had led her here—via Lake Geneva, and Matteo.

As always, her heart twinged at the memory of him. Her period had come and gone as predicted, just two weeks later than planned. Apparently that could be due to stress, which Isabella supposed was possible. Whatever it was, with it the last piece of Matteo that she could have hoped to hold onto was gone too.

Time to start over.

A new life, new responsibilities.

She followed Gianna out along the endless hallways

to the rose garden door, taking care to keep her breathing even and her smile in place. Her hair was styled, her simple dress and cardigan polished but not overwhelming for a group of seven- and eight-year-olds. Apparently these were the children from the capital's schools who'd achieved the most over the school year and so, as a treat, they got to spend a day of their summer holidays in school uniform touring the palace—and meeting a real-life princess.

And this year, for the first time in years, that princess was Isabella.

'Ready?' Gianna asked, before she opened the door.

Isabella nodded, and stepped out into the August sunshine, smiling at the crowds of small children and teachers who clapped her appearance, even if she hadn't really done anything yet.

The speech she'd been asked to give had been written for Serena, but Isabella thought she gave it well enough all the same. Talking about doing your best, helping others and working hard—all the things the children were being commended for—reminded her a little too much of how many years she'd spent *not* doing those things. But she was changing that now, and that was something.

Once the speech was over, and cake and drinks were brought out for the children, Isabella spent her time chatting with them, and their teachers, individually—learning more about their lives, about how they viewed their country. It was only a start, but she felt closer to the people her family ruled over than she had in years.

She was so engrossed in her conversations that she only vaguely noticed when Gianna slipped away, after talking with one of the palace guards. And only realised she'd returned when she heard her clear her throat behind her and say, 'Your Highness? I'm sorry to interrupt, but there's someone here to see you.'

The teachers were already chivvying the children back towards their bus; the visit had gone on longer than planned, Isabella knew. She said her goodbyes to the group she was talking to, and turned to see who else wanted to speak with her—

And promptly lost the ability to speak.

'Wait! Aren't you Matteo Rossi? The racing-car driver?' One of the boys who'd been on the school visit had escaped his teacher's grasp and raced back across the grass, promptly followed by most of his friends.

Matteo smiled graciously and signed autographs on request. At least it gave her the chance to gather her thoughts and stop her heart from racing quite so fast at the sight of him.

Why was he here? Hadn't they said everything they needed to when they'd parted? Unless things had changed…but how could they?

She'd changed, though, hadn't she? One conversation with Leo on the plane home from Rome and she'd found a whole new path—and a better understanding of herself, her past, and maybe even her future.

Perhaps the same had happened to him.

Was it wrong of her to hope so?

Eventually, the teachers won the battle to get the children to go home, and the rose garden emptied of people. Even Gianna had found somewhere else to be, and the palace guard were back at their posts, studiously ignoring them.

And so it was just Isabella and Matteo again, as it had been at the start.

'You came,' she said. '*Here*. Why?'

'Because I couldn't go the rest of my life without seeing you again,' Matteo replied. 'In fact, I'm not sure I could go without seeing you every single day for the rest of my life, if it comes to that.'

'I'm not pregnant,' Isabella blurted. 'I mean, I know I said…but definitely. You don't have to marry me to save my honour or anything.'

'I know that.' Matteo's smile was half amused, half fond. 'What else?'

'I'm not going to stop being a princess. I mean, I only just remembered why it's important in the first place.' She couldn't let her hopes get too high, if that was still a deal-breaker.

But Matteo just asked, 'Which is?'

'Because I can do things that matter to me. Help people, raise awareness, support my country. That sort of thing.'

This time, his smile almost split his face. 'Doing things that matter to you is the *only* good reason, I've come to realise, to do anything. To risk everything.'

He stepped closer and she moved into his arms automatically, as if that was where she belonged. It felt as if she did, anyway.

'So…what now?' she asked.

'I can't be a secret,' Matteo said, his eyes serious. 'If we're together, I need to be able to tell the world. Because hiding it implies there's something wrong or bad about it, and there isn't. I love you, Isabella, and I don't ever want to hide that.'

'I don't, either,' Isabella admitted as the warmth of his words filled her. *He loves me.* 'I hadn't realised how much I'd hidden myself away, how afraid I was to trust my own instincts, to trust *anyone*. I was using my past as an excuse to put up walls. But I trust you, and I know how I feel about you.'

'What will your family think about that?' Matteo asked.

'My parents might be...not thrilled. Especially if you're planning to carry on racing?'

'I am.'

She nodded. Of course, he wouldn't give that up; it was who he was, not just for his late brother, but for himself. And she'd never want to stop him being himself—not when she was only just learning who she wanted to be herself.

'But I've come to see that actually my family do want me to be happy, more than anything else.' And some of the barriers to their relationship might have been in her own head rather than other people's. 'I can't promise it's going to be easy—I mean, a lot of the people in power here are old-school conservative. They'd be happiest if I married a second cousin or something, but...'

'But?'

It had taken a lot of courage to talk to Leo about her future. More to start putting herself back out there again. But this was the real test—and the only one she truly cared about passing.

Isabella took a deep breath. 'But I don't want to marry anyone but you. Because I love you, Matteo Rossi. And I'm willing to take any risk to keep you with me—if you're willing to submit to everything that comes with loving a princess.'

He swept her up into his arms until her toes barely touched the floor, kissing her passionately enough that she didn't need words any more to know how he felt. From behind the rose garden gate, she thought she might have heard a palace guard give a congratulatory whoop.

When she was finally back on solid ground again, she smiled up at him. 'So is that a yes, then?'

Matteo raised an eyebrow. 'Was there a question?'

'Matteo Rossi, will you marry me, and be my Prince?' She batted her eyelashes at him, and he laughed.

'Only if we can honeymoon in Lake Geneva.'

'Deal.'

'And have sex on the balcony again.'

'Definitely.'

'Then, yes, Princess Isabella of Augusta.' He pressed a light, chaste kiss to her lips. 'I'll marry you. Because life without you is one risk I'm just not willing to take.'

EPILOGUE

'I wasn't sure, you know,' Leo said as they stood at the front of the Cathedral of Augusta, listening to organ music and the buzz of excitement from the crowd behind them.

'About the outfits?' Matteo guessed, looking down at the traditional Augustan dress he'd been forced into for the occasion. Gabe had laughed out loud at the sight of it until he'd realised that, as Matteo's best man, he'd be required to wear it too.

'About *you*,' Leo clarified. 'I mean, after you stole my sister away at a public ball, then helped her escape her security team to roam about Rome with you…'

Matteo winced. 'She told you that?'

'No. I am just not an idiot.' Leo gave him a long, assessing look, and Matteo was very aware of Gabe not trying very hard to hide his smile beside him. 'I admit, I was not sure about you. But,' he went on, over Matteo's attempts to interrupt, 'I promised my sister that when she found the man she loved, I would support her. Whoever he was.'

'Well, thank you for that, anyway,' Matteo replied. He knew that her brother's support would have gone a way to giving Isabella the confidence she needed to take a chance on him.

'And having you here this week preparing for the wedding, I admit, has helped me change my mind.'

'It has?' Matteo asked, surprised. Especially since he and Isabella had, as much as possible, eschewed wedding prep in favour of getting to know one another all over again, away from that private villa on Lake Geneva. Which had mostly meant hiding away in her private rooms. In bed.

'You love my sister.' Leo shrugged. 'That's all I ever really wanted for her.'

'I do love her,' Matteo admitted. 'More than anything.' That part might have taken him a little while to realise, but now he had, he couldn't believe he'd ever thought otherwise.

They might be from different worlds, and have lived very different lives before they met, but they were a pair. He brought her out from behind her terrified walls, and she helped him find a way to live in the world that didn't mean risking his neck all the time, just to feel alive. To justify his existence.

Oh, he'd still have adventures, and she'd still have days where she needed to hide away. But mostly, they'd have adventures or hide together. Because together, they were so much stronger than they were apart.

And now he got to have that for the rest of his life.

'Good,' Leo said as the organ music changed. 'Because it's time to show the world that.'

Matteo turned as the huge doors to the cathedral creaked open. The pews were filled with the great and good of Augusta, as well as a couple of rows of schoolchildren, and another few of people in uniforms—nurses, soldiers, doctors, police, firefighters. Isabella had insisted on opening the wedding up to the people who really made a difference in her country—and Matteo had supported her.

His friends and teammates were in attendance too,

and Matteo sent a quick smile their way before turning his attention to the far end of the aisle. Past the camera crews, broadcasting the occasion live to the world. Past Madison Morgan, smiling with satisfaction in the final pew. To the vision in white appearing on the King's arm as the doors parted.

Isabella glided down the long aisle to sighs and gasps from the congregation. Matteo stared at her dark curls, pinned up to reveal her long, elegant neck, and the lace neckline of her gown. Below the lace, white silk clung to her curves, down past her hips, before flaring out into a train that was still entering the cathedral when she'd almost reached him at the altar.

Her dark red lips jumped into a nervous smile as she kissed her father on the cheek, then took the last couple of steps alone.

Steps towards *him*. Matteo Rossi—daredevil, racing driver, orphan, world champion. She had chosen *him*. And no race or accolade or adventure had ever made him feel so alive as knowing that Isabella would be at his side for the rest of their lives.

'You look so beautiful,' he whispered as she stood beside him. 'That dress is…'

She flashed him a wicked smile that really had no place in a cathedral. 'Just wait until you see what I'm not wearing under it.'

Beside him Leo made a choking noise, and Gabe stifled a laugh.

Matteo gave thanks for the ridiculous, but concealing, Augustan state dress, and smiled back at his soon-to-be wife. Yeah, being married to a princess was going to be a lot of fun.

* * * * *

THE PRICE OF SUCCESS

MAYA BLAKE

First and foremost for my dear sister, Barbara, who gave me the book that started this wonderful journey. For my husband, Tony, for his unwavering support and firm belief that this dream would become reality. For my HEART sisters – your incredible support kept me going right from the beginning – thank you! And finally for my darling MINXES! You are the best cheerleaders a girl can have and I'd be totally lost without you.

CHAPTER ONE

The moments before the crash played out almost in slow motion. Time paused, then stretched lethargically in the Sunday sun. And even though the cars were travelling at over two hundred and twenty kilometers an hour, there seemed an almost hypnotic, ballet-like symmetry in their movement.

Sasha Fleming stared, frozen, her heart suspended mid-beat, terrified to complete its task as Rafael's front wing clipped the rear tyre of the slower back marker. Hundreds of thousands of pounds' worth of carbon fibre bent backwards, twisted in on itself. Ripped metal tore through the left tyre, wrenching the car into a ninety-degree turn.

The world-renowned racing car launched itself into the air. For several brief seconds it looked more like a futuristic aircraft than an asphalt-hugging machine.

Inevitably, gravity won out. The explosion was deafening as sound erupted all around her. The screech of contorting metal rang through her head, amplified by the super-sized loudspeakers all around her. In the next instant the white concrete wall just after the Turn One hairpin bend was streaked with the iconic racing green paint of Rafael's car.

'He's crashed! He's crashed! The pole sitter and current world champion, Rafael de Cervantes, has crashed his Espiritu DSII. Only this morning the papers said this car was uncrashable. How wrong were they?'

Sasha ripped off her headphones, unable to stomach the frenzied glee in the commentator's voice or the huge roar that rose around the Hungaroring circuit.

Her heart, now making up for its sluggishness, was beating so hard and so fast it threatened to break through her ribcage. Her eyes remained glued to the bank of screens on the pit wall, and she and two dozen pit crew members watched the horrific events unfold.

'Turn up the sound,' someone yelled.

Curbing a wild need to negate that command, she clamped her lips together, arms folded tight around her middle. Memories of another time, another crash, played alongside the carnage unfolding on the screen. Unable to stem it, she let the memories of the event that had changed her for ever filter through to play alongside this appalling spectacle.

'Sometimes the only way to get through pain is to immerse yourself in it. Let it eat you alive. It'll spit you out eventually.'

How many times had her father told her that? When she'd broken her ankle learning to ride her bike. When she'd fractured her arm falling out of a tree. When she'd lost her mum when she was ten. When she'd suffered the desperate consequences of falling for the wrong guy.

She'd got through them all. Well...almost.

The secret loss she'd buried deep in her heart would always be with her. As would the loss of her father.

The commentator's voice scythed through her thoughts. *'There's no movement from the car. The race has been red-flagged and the safety car is on its way. So is the ambulance. But so far we haven't seen Rafael move. His engineer will be frantically trying to speak to him, no doubt. I must say, though, it's not looking good...'*

Sasha forced in a breath, her fingers moving convulsively to loosen the Velcro securing her constricting race suit. A shudder raked her frame, followed closely by another. She tried to swallow but she couldn't get her throat to work.

Alongside the thoughts zipping through her head, her last conversation with Rafael filtered through.

He'd been so angry with her. And the accusations he'd flung at her when she'd only been trying to help…

Ice clutched her soul. Was this *her* fault? Had *she* played a part in this carnage?

'The ambulance is there now. And there's Rafael's brother, Marco, the owner of Team Espiritu. He's on his way to the crash site…hopefully we'll get a progress report soon.'

Marco. Another fist of shock punched through her flailing senses. She hadn't even been aware he'd finally arrived in Hungary. In her two years as reserve driver for Team Espiritu, Marco de Cervantes hadn't missed a single race—until this weekend.

The whole paddock had been abuzz with his absence, the celebrities and royalty who jetted in from all over the world specifically to experience the de Cervantes lifestyle, visibly disappointed. From Rafael's terse response when she'd asked of his brother's whereabouts, Sasha had concluded the brothers had fallen out.

Her heart twisted tighter in her chest at the thought that Marco had finally arrived only to witness his brother's crash.

A daring cameraman broke through the flanking bodyguards and caught up with Marco. Tight-jawed, his olive skin showing only the barest hint of paleness, he kept his gaze fixed ahead, his set expression not revealing the slightest hint of his emotional state as he strode towards the courtesy car waiting a few feet away.

Just before he got into the car he turned his head. Deep hazel eyes stared straight into the camera.

Sasha's breath stilled. Icy dread flooded her veins at the banked fury in their depths. His features were pinched, his mouth a taut line, the lines bracketing his mouth deep and austere. Everything about him indicated he was reining in tight emotion. Not surprising, given the circumstances.

But, eerily, Sasha knew his emotion extended beyond the events unfolding now. Whatever emotion Marco was holding in, it went far beyond his reaction to his brother's horrific accident.

Another shiver raked through her. She turned away from the

screen, searching blindly for an escape. The back of the garage where the tyres were stacked offered a temporary sanctuary.

She'd taken one single step towards the opening when her heart sank. Tom Brooks, her personal press officer, broke away from the crew and made a beeline for her.

'We need to prep for an interview,' he clipped out, fingers flying over his iPad.

Nausea rose to join all the other sensations percolating inside her. 'Already? We don't even know how Rafael is.' Or even if he was still alive.

'Exactly. The eyes of the world will be on this team. Now's not the time to bungle our way through another disastrous soundbite,' he said unsympathetically.

Sasha bit her lip. Her heated denial of a relationship with Rafael only a week ago had fuelled media speculation, and brought unwanted focus on the team.

'Surely it's better to be well informed before the interview than to go on air half-cocked?'

His face darkened. 'Do you want to be a reserve driver for ever?'

Sasha frowned. 'Of course not—'

'Good, because I don't want to play press officer to a reserve driver for the rest of my career. You want to be one of the boys? Here's your chance to prove it.'

A wave of anger rose inside her. 'I don't need to be heartless to prove myself, Tom.'

'Oh, but you do. Do you think any of the other drivers would hesitate at the chance that's been presented?'

'What chance? We don't even know how Rafael is doing yet!'

'Well, you can sit on your hands until the moment's snatched from you. The handful of female X1 Premier Racing drivers who've gone before you barely made an impact. You can choose to become a meaningless statistic, or you can put yourself in the driver's seat—literally—and lay the paddock rumours to rest.'

She didn't need to ask what he meant. A wave of pain rolled through her. Pushing it back, she straightened her shoulders. 'I don't care about rumours. I'm a good driver—'

'You're also Jack Fleming's daughter and Derek Mahoney's ex. If you want to be taken seriously you need to step out of their shadows. Do the interview. Stake your claim.'

As his fingers resumed their busy course over his iPad, unease rose inside Sasha. As much as she disliked Tom's acerbic attitude, a part of her knew he was right. The move from reserve to full-time driver for Team Espiritu was a once-in-a-lifetime opportunity she couldn't afford to squander—not if she wanted to achieve her goals.

'I have a reporter ready to meet—'

'No.' Her gaze flicked to the screen and her resolve strengthened. 'I won't give an interview until I hear how Rafael is.'

Two ambulances and three fire engines now surrounded the mangled car. Sparks flew as the fire crew cut away the chassis.

Marco de Cervantes stood scant feet away, ignoring everyone, his impressive physique firmly planted, hands balled into fists, his unwavering gaze fixed on his brother's still form. Sasha's heart squeezed tighter.

Please be alive, Rafael. Don't you dare die on me...

Tom's stern look mellowed slightly as he followed her gaze. 'I'll prepare something while we wait. Find a quiet place. Get yourself together.' He glanced around, made sure he wasn't overheard and leaned in closer. 'This is the chance you've been waiting for, Sasha. *Don't blow it.*'

Marco de Cervantes stepped into the private hospital room in Budapest, sick dread churning through his stomach. He clenched his fists to stop the shaking in his hands and forced himself to walk to his brother's bedside. With each step the accident replayed in his mind's eye, a vivid, gruesome nightmare that wouldn't stop. There'd been so much blood at the crash site... *so much blood...*

His chest tightened as he saw the white sheet pulled over his brother's chest.

Absently, he made a note to have the staff replace the sheets with another colour—green, perhaps, Rafael's favourite colour. White hospital sheets looked...smelled...too much like death.

Rafael wasn't dead. And if Marco had anything to do with it this would be his last senseless brush with death. Enough was enough.

He drew level with the bed and stared down into his brother's pale, still face. At the tube inserted into his mouth to help him breathe.

Enough was enough.

Marco's throat closed up. He'd chosen to give Rafael time to come to his senses instead of forcing him to listen to reason. And by doing so he'd allowed his brother to take the wheel behind the world's most powerful car while still reeling from emotional rejection.

Unlike him, his brother had never been able to compartmentalise his life, to suppress superfluous emotions that led to unnecessarily clouded judgement. Rafael coalesced happiness, sadness, triumph and loss into one hot, sticky mess. Add the lethal mix of a seven hundred and fifty horsepower racing car, and once again *he* was left picking up the pieces.

His breath shuddered. Reaching out, he took Rafael's unmoving hand, leaned down until his lips hovered an inch from his brother's ear.

'You live—you hear me? I swear on all things holy, if you die on me I'll track you to hell and kick your ass,' he grated out, then swallowed the thickness in his throat. 'And I know you'll be in hell, because you sure as heck won't get into heaven with *those* looks.'

His voice caught and he forced back his tears.

Rafael's hand remained immobile, barely warm. Marco held on tighter, desperately infusing his brother with his own life force, desperately trying to block out the doctor's words…*his brain is swelling…there's internal bleeding…nothing to do but wait…*

With a stifled curse, he whirled away from the bed. The window of the ultra-private, ultra-exclusive, state-of-the-art hospital looked out onto a serene courtyard, with discreet fountains and carefully clipped flowers meant to soothe the troubled patient. Beyond the grounds, forests stretched as far as the eye could see.

Marco found no solace in the picturesque view. He found even less to smile about when his eyes lit on the paparazzi waiting beyond the hospital's boundaries, powerful lenses trained, ready to pounce.

Shoving a hand through his hair, he turned back to the bed.

A flash of green caught the corner of his eye. He focused on the flat-screen TV mounted on the wall and watched Rafael's accident replayed again in slow motion.

Bile rose to his throat. Reaching blindly for the remote, he aimed it at the screen—only to stop when another picture shifted into focus.

Anger escalated through him. Five minutes later he stabbed the 'off' button and calmly replaced the control.

Returning to Rafael's bedside, his sank onto the side of the bed. 'I know you'd probably argue with me, *mi hermano*, but you've had a lucky escape. In more ways than one.'

Jaw clenching, he thanked heaven his brother hadn't heard the interview just played on TV. Marco had first-hand knowledge of what people would sacrifice in their quest for fame and power, and the look of naked ambition in Sasha Fleming's eyes made his chest burn with fury and his skin crawl.

His fist tightened on the bed next to his brother's unmoving body.

If she wanted a taste of power he would give it to her. Let her acquire a taste for it the way she'd given Rafael a taste of herself.

Then, just as she'd callously shoved Rafael aside, Marco would take utter satisfaction in wrenching away everything she'd ever dreamed of.

'Excuse me, can you tell me which room Rafael de Cervantes is in?' Sasha infused her voice with as much authority as possible, despite the glaring knowledge that she wasn't supposed to be here.

The nurse dressed in a crisp white uniform looked up. The crease already forming on her brow caused Sasha's heart to sink.

'Are you a member of the family?'

'No, but I wanted to see how he was. He was…*is* my team

mate.' The moment the words left her lips she winced. *Way to go, Sasha.*

True to form, the nurse's frown dissolved as realisation dawned. 'His team mate…? You're Sasha Fleming!'

Sasha summoned her practised camera smile—the one that held the right amount of interest without screaming *look at me*, and lifted the oversized sunglasses. 'Yes,' she murmured.

'My nephew *loves* you!' The nurse gushed. 'He pretends not to, but I know he thinks you rock. Every time he sees you during Friday Practice his face lights up. He'll be thrilled when I tell him I met you.'

The tension clamping Sasha's nape eased a little. 'Thanks. So can I see Rafael?' she asked again. When the frown threatened to make a comeback, Sasha rushed on. 'I'll only be a moment, I promise.'

'I'm sorry, Miss Fleming. You're not on my list of approved visitors.'

Steeling herself against the nerves dragging through her, Sasha cleared her throat. 'Is Marco de Cervantes here? Maybe I can ask him?'

She pushed the mental picture of Marco's cold, unforgiving features to the back of her mind. She was here for Rafael. Surely, as his team mate, his brother wouldn't bar her from seeing him?

'No, he left half an hour ago.'

Shock slammed into her. 'He *left*?'

The nurse nodded. 'He didn't seem too happy, but considering the circumstances I guess it's to be expected.'

For a moment Sasha debated asking if the nurse would make an exception. Break the rules for her. But she dismissed it. Breaking her own rules, getting friendly with Rafael, was probably the reason he'd ended up in this situation. She refused to exacerbate it.

Plucking her sunglasses off her head, she slid them down to cover her eyes. In her jeans and long-sleeved cotton top, with a multi-coloured cheesecloth satchel slung across her body, she looked like every other summer tourist in the city. Her disguise had helped her evade the paparazzi on her way in. She prayed it would hold up on her way out.

With a heavy heart she turned towards the elevator doors, which stood open as if to usher her away from here as fast as possible.

'Wait.' The nurse beckoned with a quick hand movement and leaned forward as Sasha approached the desk. 'Maybe I can sneak you in for a few minutes,' she whispered.

Relief washed over Sasha. 'Oh, thank you so much!'

'If you don't mind signing an autograph for my nephew?'

A tinge of guilt arrowed through her, but the need to see Rafael overcame the feeling. With a grateful smile, Sasha took the proffered pen.

'What the hell are you doing in here?'

Sasha spun round at the harsh voice, and gasped at the dark figure framed in the doorway. A few minutes, the nurse had said. A quick glance at her watch confirmed her sickening suspicion. She'd been here almost an hour!

'I asked you a question.'

'I came to see Rafael. There was no one here—'

'So you thought you'd just sneak in?'

'Hardly! The nurse—' Sasha gulped back her words, realising she could be putting the nurse's job in jeopardy.

'The nurse what?'

Marco advanced into the room, his formidable presence shrinking the space. She scrambled to her feet, but she still had to tilt her head to see his face.

His cold-as-steel expression dried her mouth further.

She shook her head. 'I just wanted to see how he was.' She stopped speaking as he drew level with her, his hard eyes boring into her.

'How long have you been here?'

She risked another glance at her watch and cringed inwardly. Dared she tell him the truth or blag her way through? 'Does it really matter?'

'How long?' he gritted, his gaze sliding over his brother as if assessing any further damage.

'Why are you checking him over like that? Do you think I've harmed him in some way?' she challenged.

Hazel eyes slammed back to her. His contempt was evident as his gaze raked her face. 'I don't *think*! I *know* you've already harmed my brother.'

His tone was so scathing Sasha was surprised her flesh wasn't falling from her skin.

'Rafael told you about our fight?'

'Yes, he did. I can only conclude that your presence here is another media stunt, not out of concern for my brother?'

'Of course it isn't!'

'Is that why the media presence at the hospital gates has doubled in the last hour?'

Her gaze drifted to the window. The blinds were drawn against the late-afternoon sun, but not closed completely. She'd taken a step to look for herself when steely fingers closed on her wrist. Heat shot up her arm, the reaction so unfamiliar she froze.

'If you think I'm going to let you use my brother to further your own ends, you're sorely mistaken.'

Alarmed, she stared up at him. 'Why would you think I'd do that?'

A mirthless smile bared his teeth, displaying a look so frightening she shivered.

'That press conference you gave? About how much you cared for him? How your thoughts were with him and his family? *About how you're willing to step into his shoes as soon as possible so you don't let the team down?* What were your exact words? *"I've earned the chance at a full-time seat. I've proven that I have what it takes."'*

Sasha swallowed, unable to look away from the chilling but oddly hypnotic pull of his gaze. 'I…I shouldn't have….' The echo of unease she'd felt before and during the interview returned. 'I didn't mean it like that—'

'How *did* you mean it, then? How exactly have *you*, a mere reserve driver, earned your place on the team? Why do *you* deserve Rafael's seat and not one of the other dozen top drivers out there?'

'Because it's my time! I deserve the chance.' She wrenched at her captured arm. His hand tightened, sending another bolt of heat through her body.

Straight black brows clamped together. His arresting features were seriously eroding her thought processes. Even livid to the point where she could imagine heat striations coming off his body he oozed enough sex appeal to make her finally understand why his bodyguards were forever turning away paddock groupies from his luxury hospitality suite. Rumour had it that one particularly eager groupie had scaled the mobile suite and slipped into his bedroom via the skylight.

'*Your time?* Why?' he challenged again, stepping closer, invading her body space and her ability to breathe. 'What's so special about *you*, Sasha Fleming?'

'I didn't say I was special.'

'That's not what I got from the press junket. In fact I deduced something along the lines that the team would be making a huge mistake if you weren't given Rafael's seat. Was there even the veiled threat of a lawsuit thrown in there?'

The thought that this might be her only chance to find a decent seat had resonated in the back of her mind even as she'd felt sickened at the thought of how wrong the timing was.

'Nothing to say?' came the soft taunt.

She finally managed to wrench her wrist from his grasp and stepped back. 'Mr de Cervantes, this is neither the time nor the place to discuss this.'

Her glance slid to Rafael, her throat closing in distress at the tubes and the horrid beeping of the machines keeping him alive.

Marco followed her gaze and froze, as if just realising where he was. When his gaze sliced back to hers she glimpsed a well of anguish within the hazel depths and felt something soften inside her. Marco de Cervantes, despite his chilling words and seriously imposing presence, was hurting. The fear of the unknown, of wondering if the precious life of someone you held dear would pull through was one she was agonisingly familiar with.

Any thought of her job flew out of her head as she watched him wrestle with his pain. The urge to comfort, one human being to another, momentarily overcame her instinct for self-preservation.

'Rafael is strong. He's a fighter. He'll pull through,' she murmured softly.

Slowly he pulled in a breath, and any hint of pain disappeared. His upper lip curled in a mocking sneer. 'Your concern is touching, Miss Fleming. But cut the crap. There are no cameras here. No microphones to lap up your false platitudes. Unless you've got one hidden on your person?' His eyes slid down her body, narrowing as they searched. 'Will I go on the internet tomorrow and see footage of my brother in his sick bed all over it?'

'That's a tasteless and disgusting thing to say!' Spinning away, she rushed to the leather sofa in the suite and picked up her satchel. Clearly it was time to make herself scarce.

Careful not to come within touching distance of Marco de Cervantes, she edged towards the door.

'Any more tasteless than you vying for his seat even before you knew for certain whether he was alive or dead?' came the biting query.

Sasha winced. 'I agree. It wasn't the perfect time to do an interview.'

A hint of surprise lightened his eyes, but his lips firmed a second later. 'But you did it anyway.'

Blaming Tom would have been easy. And the coward's way out. The truth was, she *wanted* to be lead driver.

'I thought I was acting in the best interests of the team. And, yes, I was also putting myself forward as the most viable option. But the timing was wrong. For that, I apologise.'

That grim smile made another appearance. Her body shuddered with alarm. Even before he spoke Sasha had the strongest premonition that she wasn't going to like the words that spilled from his lips.

'You should've taken more time to think, Miss Fleming. Because, as team owner, *I* ultimately decide what's in the best interests of Team Espiritu. Not you.'

He sauntered to his brother's bedside and stood looking down at him.

Sasha glanced between the two men. This close, the resemblance between them was striking. Yet they couldn't have been more different. Where Rafael was wild and gregarious, his brother smouldered and rumbled like the deepest, darkest underbelly of a dormant volcano. The fear that he could erupt at any moment was a very real and credible threat. One that made her throat dry and her heart race.

Finally he turned to face her. Trepidation iced its way to her toes.

'My decision and mine alone carries. Your timing wasn't just wrong. It was detestable.' His voice could have frozen water in the Sahara. 'It also makes my decision incredibly easy.'

Her heart stopped. 'Wh—what decision?'

'Relieving you of your job, of course.' The smile widened. 'Congratulations. You're fired.'

CHAPTER TWO

'WHAT?'

'Get out.'

Sasha remained frozen, unable to heed Marco de Cervantes's command. Finally she forced out a breath.

'No. You—you can't do that. You can't fire me.' Somewhere at the back of her mind she knew this to be true—something about contracts…clauses—but her brain couldn't seem to track after the blow it had been dealt.

'I can do anything I want. I *own* the team. Which means I own you.'

'Yes, but…' She sucked in a breath and forced herself to focus. 'Yes, you own the team, but you don't *own* me. And you can't fire me. I haven't done anything wrong. Sure, the press interview was a little mistimed. But that isn't grounds to sack me.'

'Maybe those aren't the only grounds I have.'

Cold dread eased up her spine. 'What are you talking about?'

Marco regarded her for several seconds. Then his gaze slid to his brother. Reaching out, he carefully smoothed back a lock of hair from Rafael's face. The poignancy of the gesture and the momentary softening of his features made Sasha's heart ache for him, despite his anger at her. No one deserved to watch a loved one suffer. Not even Marco de Cervantes.

When his gaze locked onto her again Sasha wasn't prepared for the mercurial shift from familial concern to dark fury.

'You're right. My brother's bedside isn't the place to discuss this.' He came towards her, his long-legged stride purposeful and arrestingly graceful. His broad shoulders, the strength in his lean, muscled body demanded an audience. Sasha stared, unable to look away from the perfect body packed full of angry Spanish male.

In whose path she directly stood.

At the last second her legs unfroze long enough for her to step out of his way. 'It's okay. I'll leave.'

'Running away? Scared your past is catching up with you, Miss Fleming?'

She swallowed carefully, striving to maintain a neutral expression. Marco de Cervantes didn't know. He *couldn't*.

'I don't know what you're talking about. My past has nothing to do with my contract with your team.'

He stared into her face for so long Sasha wanted to slam on the shades dangling uselessly from her fingers.

'Extraordinary,' he finally murmured.

'What?' she croaked.

'You lie so flawlessly. Not even an eyelash betrays you. It's no wonder Rafael was completely taken with you. What I don't understand is why. He offered you what you wanted—money, prestige, a privileged lifestyle millions dream about but only few achieve. Isn't that what women like you ultimately want? The chance to live in unimaginable luxury playing mistress of a *castillo*?'

'Um, I don't know what sort of women *you've* been cavorting with, but you know nothing about me.'

Impossibly, his features grew colder. 'I know everything I need to know. So why didn't you just take it? What's your angle?' His intense gaze bored into her, as if trying to burrow beneath her skin.

It took every control-gathering technique she'd learned not to step back from him.

'I have no *angle*—'

'Enough of your lies. Get out.' He wrenched the door open, fully expecting her to comply.

Her eyes flicked to Rafael's still form. Sasha doubted she'd see him again before the team's month-long August break. 'Will you tell him I came to see him when he wakes up—please?' she asked.

Marco exhaled in disbelief. 'With any luck, by the time my brother wakes up any memory he has of you will be wiped clean from his mind.'

She gasped, the chill from his voice washing over her. 'I'm not sure exactly what Rafael told you, but you've really got this wrong.'

Marco shrugged. 'And you're still fired. Goodbye, Miss Fleming.'

'On what grounds?' she challenged, hoping this time her voice would emerge with more conviction.

'I'm sure my lawyers can find something. Inappropriate enthusiasm?'

'That's a reason you should be keeping me on—not a reason to fire me.'

'You've just proved my point. Most people know where to draw the line. It seems you don't.'

'I *do*,' she stressed, her voice rising right along with the tight knot in her chest.

'This conversation is over.' He glanced pointedly at the door.

She stepped into the corridor, reeling from the impact of his words. Her contract was airtight. She was sure of it. But she'd seen too many teams discard perfectly fit and able drivers for reasons far flimsier than the one Marco had just given her. X1 Premier Racing was notorious for its court battles between team owners and drivers.

The thought that she could lose everything she'd fought for made her mouth dry. She'd battled hard to hold onto her seat in the most successful team in the history of the sport, when every punter with a blog or a social media account had taken potshots at her talent. One particularly harsh critic had even gone as far as to debate her sexual preferences.

She'd sacrificed too much for too long. Somehow she had to convince Marco de Cervantes to keep her on.

She turned to confront him—only to find a short man wearing a suit and a fawning expression hurrying towards them. He handed Marco a small wooden box and launched into a rapid volley of French. Whatever the man—whose discreet badge announced him as Administrator—was saying, it wasn't having any effect on Marco.

Marco's response was clipped. When the administrator started in surprise and glanced towards the reception area, Sasha followed his gaze. The nurse who had let her in stood behind the counter.

The administrator launched into another obsequious torrent. Marco cut him off with an incisive slash of his hand and headed for the lifts.

Sasha hurried after him. As she passed the reception area, she glimpsed the naked distress in the nurse's eyes. Another wave of icy dread slammed into her, lending her more impetus as she rushed after Marco.

'Wait!'

He pressed the button for the lift as she screeched to a halt beside him.

Away from the low lights of the hospital room Sasha saw him—really saw him—for the first time. Up close and personal, Marco de Cervantes was stunning. If you liked your men tall, imposing and bristling with tons of masculinity. Through the gap in his grey cotton shirt she caught a glimpse of dark hair and a strong, golden chest that had her glancing away in a hurry.

Focus!

'Can we talk—please?' she injected into the silence.

He ignored her, his stern, closed face forbidding any conversation. The lift arrived and he stepped in. Sasha rushed in after him. As the doors closed she saw the nurse burst into tears.

Outraged, she rounded on him. 'My God. You got that nurse sacked, didn't you?'

Anger dissolved the last of her instinctive self-preservation and washed away the strangely compelling sensation she refused to acknowledge was attraction.

'I lodged a complaint.'

'Which, coming from you, was as good as ordering that administrator to sack her!'

Guilt attacked her insides.

'She must live with the consequences of her actions.'

'So there's no in-between? No showing mercy? Just straight to the gallows?'

Deep hazel eyes pinned her where she stood. 'You weren't on the list of approved visitors. She knew this and disregarded it. You could've been a tabloid hack. Anybody.'

His eyes narrowed and Sasha forced her expression to remain neutral.

'Or maybe she knew *exactly* who you were?'

She lowered her lids as a wave of guilty heat washed over her face.

'Of course,' he taunted softly. 'What did you offer her? Free tickets to the next race?'

Deciding silence was the best policy, she clamped her lips together.

'A personal tour of the paddock and a photo op with you once you became lead driver, perhaps?'

His scathing tone grated on her nerves.

Raising her head she met his gaze, anger at his high-handedness loosening her tongue. 'You know, just because your brother is gravely ill, it doesn't give you the right to destroy other people's lives.'

'I beg your pardon?' he bit out.

'Right now you're in pain and lashing out, wanting anyone and everyone to pay for what you're going through. It's understandable, but it's not fair. That poor woman is now jobless just because *you're* angry.'

'*That poor woman* abused her position and broke the hospital's policy for personal gain. She deserves everything she gets.'

'It wasn't for personal gain. She did it for her nephew. He's a fan. She wanted to do something nice for him.'

'My heart bleeds.'

'You do the same, and more, for thousands of race fans every year. What's so different about this?'

Dark brows clamped together, and his jaw tightened in that barely civilised way that sent another wave of apprehension through her. Again she glimpsed the dark fury riding just below his outward control.

'The difference, Miss Fleming, is that I don't compromise my integrity to do so. And I don't put those I care about in harm's way just to get what I want.'

'What about compassion?'

His brows cleared, but the volatile tinge in the air remained. 'I'm fresh out.'

'You know, you'll wake up one morning not long from now and regret your actions today.'

The lift doors glided open to reveal the underground car park. A few feet away was a gleaming black chrome-trimmed Bentley Continental. Beside it, a driver and a heavily muscled man whose presence shrieked *bodyguard* waited. The driver held the back door open, but Marco made no move towards it. Instead he glanced down at her, his expression hauntingly bleak.

'I regret a lot that's happened in the past twenty-four hours—not least watching my brother mangle himself and his car on the race track because he believed himself to be heartbroken. One more thing doesn't make a difference.'

'Your emotions are overwhelming you right now. All I'm saying is don't let them overrule your better judgement.'

A cold smile lifted one corner of his mouth. 'My *emotions*? I didn't know you practised on the side as the team's psychologist. I thought you'd ridden down with me to beg for your job back, not to practise the elevator pitch version of pop psychology. You had me as your captive audience for a full thirty seconds. Shame you chose to waste it.'

'Mock me all you want. It doesn't change the fact that you're acting like—' She bit her lip, common sense momentarily overriding her anger.

'Go on,' he encouraged softly. Tauntingly. 'Acting like what?'

She shrugged. 'Like…well, like an ass.'

His eyes narrowed until they were mere icy slits. 'Excuse me?'

'Sorry. You asked.'

Anger flared in his eyes, radiated off his body. Sasha held

her breath, readying herself for the explosion about to rain on her head. Instead he gave a grim smile.

'I've been called worse.' He nodded to his bodyguard, who took a step towards them. 'Romano will escort you off the premises. Be warned—my very generous donation to this hospital is contingent on you being arrested if you set foot anywhere near my brother again. I'm sure the administrator would relish that challenge.'

Despair rose to mingle with her anger. 'You can't do this. If you don't listen to me I'll...I'll talk to the press again. I'll spill everything!'

'Ah, I'm glad to finally meet the *real* you, Miss Fleming.'

'Ten minutes. That's all I want. Let me convince you to keep me on.'

'Trust me—blackmail isn't a great place to start.'

She bit her lip. 'That was just a bluff. I won't talk to the press. But I do want to drive for you. And I'm the best mid-season replacement you'll find for Rafael.'

'You *do* place a high premium on yourself, don't you?'

Unflinching, she nodded. 'Yes, I do. And I can back it up. Just let me prove it.'

His gaze narrowed on her face, then conducted a lazy sweep over her body. Suddenly the clothes that had served as perfect camouflage against the intrusive press felt inadequate, exposing. Beneath the thin material of her T-shirt her heart hammered, her skin tingling with an alien awareness that made her muscles tense.

As a female driver in a predominantly male sport, she was used to being the cynosure of male eyes. There were those who searched for signs of failure as a driver, ready to use any shortcomings against her. Then there were the predators who searched for weaknesses simply because she was a woman, and therefore deemed incapable. The most vicious lot were those who bided their time, ready to rip her apart because she was Jack Fleming's daughter. Those were the ones she feared the most. And the ones she'd sworn to prove wrong.

Marco de Cervantes's gaze held an intensity that combined

all of those qualities multiplied by a thousand. And then there was something else.

Something that made her breath grow shallow in her lungs. Made her palms clammy and the hairs bristle on her nape.

Recalling the sheer intensity of the look he'd directed into the camera earlier, she felt her heartbeat accelerate.

'Get in the car,' he bit out, his tone bone-chilling.

Sasha glanced into the dark, luxurious interior of the limo and hesitated. The feelings this man engendered in her weren't those of fear. Rather, she sensed an emotional risk—as if, given half a chance, he would burrow under her skin, discover her worst fears and use them against her. She couldn't let that happen.

'If you want me to hear you out you'll get in the car. Now,' he said, his tone uncompromising.

She hesitated. 'I can't.'

'*Can't* isn't a word I enjoy hearing,' he growled, his patience clearly ebbing fast.

'My bike.' He quirked one brow at her. 'I'd *rather* not leave it here.'

His glance towards the battered green and white scooter leaning precariously against the car park wall held disbelief. 'You came here on *that*?'

'Yes. Why?'

'You're wearing the most revolting pair of jeans I've ever seen and a scarf that's seen better days. Add that to the oversized sunglasses and I don't need to be a genius to guess you were trying some misguided attempt to escape the paparazzi. I am right?' At her nod, he continued. 'And yet you travelled on the slowest mode of motorised transport known to man.'

She raised her chin. 'But there's the beauty—don't you see? I managed to ride straight past the paparazzi without one single camera lens focusing on me. You, on the other hand… Tell me—how did they react when you rocked up in your huge, tinted-windowed monstrosity of a car?'

His jaw tightened and he glared at her.

'Exactly. I'm not leaving my bike.'

'Security here is—'

'Inadequate, according to you. After all, *I* managed to get through, didn't I?' She threw his words back at him.

One hand gripped the door of the car. 'Get in the car or don't. I refuse to argue with you over a pile of junk.'

'It's my junk and I won't leave it.'

With a stifled curse, Marco held out his hands. 'Keys?'

'Why?'

'Romano will return the scooter to your hotel.'

Sasha's eyes widened. Romano weighed at least two hundred and fifty pounds of pure muscle. The thought of what he'd put her poor scooter through made her wince.

'And before you comment on Romano's size I'd urge you to stop and think about his *feelings*,' Marco added mockingly.

Touché, she conceded silently.

Digging into her satchel, she reluctantly handed over her keys. Marco lobbed them to his bodyguard, then raised an imperious eyebrow at her.

With a resigned sigh, Sasha slid past his imposing body and entered the limo.

The door shut on them, enclosing them in a silent cocoon that threatened to send her already taut nerves into a frenzied tailspin.

As the car glided out of the car park it occurred to her that she had no idea where Marco was taking her. She opened her mouth to ask, then immediately shut it when she saw his gaze fixed on the small box.

Despite his bleak expression, his profile was stunningly arresting. The sculpted contours of his face held enough shadow and intrigue to capture the attention of any red-blooded female with a pulse—a fact attested to by the regular parade of stunning women he was photographed with.

His strong jaw bore the beginnings of a five o'clock shadow, and an even stronger, taut neck slanted onto impossibly broad shoulders. Under the discreetly expensive cotton shirt those shoulders moved restlessly. She followed the movement, her gaze sliding down over his chest, past the flat stomach that showed no hint of flab. Her eyes rested in his lap. The bulge beneath his zipper made heat swirl in her belly.

'Have you seen enough? Or would you like me to perform a slow striptease for you?'

Her cheeks burned. Her neck burned. In fact for several seconds Sasha was sure her whole body was on fire. Mortified, she hastily plucked her sunglasses from atop her head and jammed them onto her face.

'I… You didn't say where we were going.'

'I've called a meeting with Russell and the chief engineer. I'm handing over the reins temporarily so I can concentrate on making arrangements for Rafael to be evacuated home to Spain.'

'You're moving him?'

'Not yet, but the medical team is on standby. He'll be moved the moment it's deemed safe.'

'I see.'

Sharp eyes bored into her. 'Do you? You've talked your way into a last-chance meeting and yet you're wasting time exhibiting false concern for my brother.'

She sucked in a breath. 'My concern isn't false. I'd give anything for Rafael not to be in that place.'

Sasha watched, fascinated, as his hand tightened around the box. 'In my experience *anything* tends to arrive with a very heavy price tag and a carefully calculated catch. So be very careful with your choice of words.'

Sasha licked her lips, suddenly unable to breathe at the expression in his eyes. 'I'm sure I don't know what you mean.'

The look in his eyes hardened. 'You really should try a different profession. Your acting skills are highly commendable.'

'Driving suits me just fine, thanks. Where are we going, exactly?'

Keeping his gaze on her, he relaxed back in his seat. 'My hotel.'

'Your hotel?' she repeated dully. Her senses, still reeling after she'd been caught staring at Marco de Cervantes's man package, threatened to go into freefall. The thought of being alone with him—truly alone—made anxiety skitter over her skin. 'I don't think that's a good idea.'

'You don't have a choice. You wanted this meeting.'

Desperation lent her voice strength. 'The rest of the team will be wondering where I am. Maybe I should let them know.' Tom had asked where she was going after the press conference, but she'd been deliberately evasive.

'The team will be out doing what they do after every Sunday race. Bar hopping and trying it on with the local girls.'

'I don't think they'll be doing that tonight. Not with Rafael...' She bit her lip, unable to continue as she glimpsed the flash of pain in those hazel eyes.

But he merely shrugged. 'Call them if you want. Tell them where you're going. And why.'

Not expecting her bluff to be called, Sasha floundered. The circumstances of her past made it impossible to make friends with anyone on her team. The constant whispers behind her back, the conversations that stopped when she walked into a room, made it hard to trust anyone.

Tom only cared as far as her actions impacted upon his career. The only one who had cared—really cared—had been Rafael. A wave of pain and regret rushed through her. Until their row last night she'd foolishly let herself believe she could finally trust another human being.

Feigning nonchalance, she shrugged. 'I'll tell them later.'

Unable to stomach the mockery in Marco's eyes, she turned away.

Absently she stroked the armrest, silently apologising for calling the Bentley Continental a monstrosity. Amongst the luxury, sometimes vacuous, creations car manufacturers produced, the Bentley was one of the more ingenious styles. It had been her father's favourite non-racing car—his pride and joy until he'd been forced to sell it to defend himself.

'We're here.'

They were parked beneath the pillared portico of the Four Seasons. A liveried doorman stepped forward and opened the door on Marco's side, his bow of deference deep to the point of being obsequious.

Casting her gaze past him, Sasha felt her mouth drop open at the sheer opulence of the marbled foyer of the stunning hotel. The whole atmosphere glittered and sparkled beneath a super-sized revolving chandelier, which was throwing its adoring light on sleekly dressed patrons.

Sasha remained in her seat, super-conscious of how inappropriate her old hipster jeans and worn top were for the gold-leaf and five-star luxury spread before her. She was pretty sure she would be directed to the tradesman's entrance the moment the doorman saw her scuffed boots.

'Come out. And lose the glasses and the scarf. No one cares who you are here.'

She hesitated. 'Can't we just talk in the car?' she ventured.

He held out a commanding hand. 'No, we can't. We both know you're not shy, so stop wasting my time.'

She could argue, defend her personal reputation against the label Marco had decided to pin on her, but Sasha doubted it would make a difference. He, like the rest of the world, believed she was soiled goods because of her past and because she was a Fleming.

What good would protesting do?

The only weapon she had to fight with was her talent behind the steering wheel.

Her father's time had been cruelly cut short, stamped out by vicious lies that had destroyed him and robbed her of the one person who had truly loved and believed in her.

Sasha was damned if she would let history repeat itself. Damned if she would give up her only chance to prove everyone wrong.

Gritting her teeth, she ignored his hand and stepped out of the car.

Marco strode across the marble foyer, the box clutched firmly in his grip. Its contents were a vivid reminder, stamped onto his brain.

Behind him he heard the hurried click of booted heels as Sasha Fleming struggled to keep up with him.

He didn't slow down. In fact he sped up. He wanted this meeting over with so he could return to the hospital.

For a single moment Marco thanked God his mother wasn't alive. She couldn't have borne to see her darling son, the miracle child she'd thought she'd never have, lying battered and bruised in a coma.

It was bad enough that she'd had to live through the pain and suffering Marco had brought her ten years ago. Bad enough that those horrendous three weeks before and after his own crash had caused a rift he'd never quite managed to heal, despite his mother's reassurances that all was well.

Marco knew all hadn't been well because *he* had never been the same since that time.

Deep shame and regret raked through him at how utterly he'd let his mother down. At how utterly he'd lost his grip on reality back then. Foolishly and selfishly he'd thought himself in love. The practised smile of a skilful manipulator had blinded him into throwing all caution to the wind and he'd damaged his family in the process.

His mother was gone, her death yet another heavy weight on his conscience, but Rafael was alive—and Marco intended to make sure lightning didn't strike twice. For that to happen he had to keep it together. He *would* keep it together.

'Um, the sign for the bar points the other way.'

Sasha Fleming's husky voice broke into his unwelcome thoughts.

He stopped so suddenly she bumped into him. Marco frowned at the momentary sensation of her breasts against his back and the unsuspecting heat that surged into his groin. His whole body tightened in furious rejection and he rounded on her.

'I don't conduct my business in bars. And I seriously doubt you want our conversation to be overheard by anyone else.'

Turning on his heel, he stalked to the lift. His personal porter pushed the button and waited for Marco to enter the express lift that serviced the presidential suite.

Sasha shot him a wary look and he bit back the urge to let a feral smile loose. Ever since Rafael's crash he'd been pushing back the blackness, fighting memories that had no place here within this chaos.

Really, Sasha Fleming had chosen the worst possible time to make herself his enemy. His hands tightened around the box and his gaze rested on her.

Run, he silently warned her. *While you have the chance.*

Her eyes searched every corner of the mirrored lift as if danger lurked within the gold-filigree-trimmed interior. Finally she rolled her shoulders. The subtle movement was almost the equivalent of cracking one's knuckles before a fight, and it intrigued him far more than he wanted to admit.

'We're going to your suite? Okay…'

She stepped into the lift. Behind her, Marco saw the porter's gaze drop to linger on her backside. Irritation rose to mingle with the already toxic cauldron of emotions swirling through him. With an impatient finger he stabbed at the button.

'I see the thought of it doesn't disturb you too much.' He didn't bother to conceal the slur in his comment. The urge to attack, to wound, ran rampage within him.

Silently he conceded she was right. As long as Rafael was fighting for his life he couldn't think straight. The impulse to make someone pay seethed just beneath the surface of his calm.

And Sasha Fleming had placed herself front and centre in his sights.

He expected her to flinch. To show that his words had hit a mark.

He wasn't prepared for her careless shrug. 'You're right. I don't really want our conversation to feed tomorrow's headlines. I'm pretty sure by now most of the media know you're staying here.'

'So you're not afraid to enter a strange man's suite?'

'Are you strange? I thought you were merely the engineering genius who designed the Espiritu DSII and the Cervantes Conquistador.'

'I'm immune to flattery, Miss Fleming, and any other form of coercion running through your pretty little head.'

'Shame. I was about to spout some seriously nerd-tastic info *guaranteed* to make you like me.'

'You'd be wasting your time. I have a team specially selected to deal with sycophants.'

His barb finally struck home. She inhaled sharply and lowered her gaze.

Marco caught himself examining the determined angle of her chin, the sensual line of her full lips. At the base of her neck her pulse fluttered under satin-smooth skin. Against his will, another wave of heat surged through him. He threw a mental bucket of cold water over it.

This woman belonged to his brother.

The lift opened directly onto the living room—a white and silver design that flowed outside onto the balcony overlooking the Danube. Marco bypassed the sweeping floor-to-ceiling windows, strode to the antique desk set against the velvet wall and put the box down.

Recalling its contents, he felt anger coalesce once more within him.

He turned to find Sasha Fleming at the window, a look of total awe on her face as she gazed at the stunning views of the Buda Hills and the Chain Bridge. He took a moment to study her.

Hers wasn't a classical beauty. In fact there was more of the rangy tomboy about her than a woman who was aware of her body. Yet her face held an arresting quality. Her lips were wide and undeniably sensual, and her limbs contained an innate grace when she moved that drew the eye. Her silky black hair, pulled into a loose ponytail at the back of her head, gleamed like a jet pool in the soft lighting. His gaze travelled over her neck, past shoulders that held a hint of delicacy and down to her chest.

The memory of her breasts against his back intruded. Against him she'd felt decidedly soft, although her body was lithe, holding a whipcord strength that didn't hide her subtle femininity. When he'd held her wrist in Rafael's hospital room her skin had felt supple, smooth like silk…

Sexual awareness hummed within him, unwelcome and unacceptable. Ruthlessly he cauterised it. Even if he'd been remotely interested in a woman such as this, flawed as she was, and without a moral bone in her body, *she* was the reason his brother had crashed.

Besides, poaching had never been his style.

'So, what would it take to convince you to keep me on?' She addressed him without taking her eyes from the view.

Annoyance fizzled through him.

'You're known for having relationships with your team mates.'

Her breath caught and she turned sharply from the window. Satisfaction oozed through him at having snagged her attention.

Satisfaction turned to surprise when once again she didn't evade the question. 'One team mate. A very long time ago.'

'He also crashed under extreme circumstances and lost his drive, I believe?'

A simple careful nod. 'He retired from motor racing, yes.'

'And his seat was then given to you?'

Her eyes narrowed. 'Your extrapolation is way off base if you think it has any bearing on what has happened with Rafael.'

'Isn't it curious that you bring chaos to every team you join? Are you an unlucky charm, Miss Fleming?'

'As a former racer yourself, I'm sure you're familiar with the facts—drivers crash on a regular basis. It's a reality of the sport. In fact, wasn't a crash what ended *your* racing career?'

For the second time in a very short while the reminder of events of ten years ago cut through him like the sharpest knife. Forcing the memories away, he folded his arms. 'It's *your* circumstances that interest me, not statistics. You dumped this other guy just before a race. This seems to be your *modus operandi*.'

Her chest lifted with her affronted breath. He struggled not to let his gaze drop. 'I resent that. I thought you ran your team on merit and integrity, not rumour and hypothesis.'

'Here's your chance to dispel the rumours. How many other team mates have you slept with?'

'I had a *relationship* with one. Derek and I went out for a while. Then it ended.'

'But this…relationship grew quite turbulent, I believe? So much so that it eventually destroyed his career while yours flourished?'

She snorted. 'I wouldn't say flourished, exactly. More like sweated and blooded.'

'But you did start out being a reserve driver on his team. And you did dump him when his seat became available to you?'

Marco watched her lips tighten, her chin angling in a way that drew his eyes to her smooth throat.

'It's obvious you've done your homework. But I didn't come here to discuss my personal life with you—which, as it happens, is really none of your business.'

'When it relates to *my* brother and *my* team it becomes my business. And your actions in the past three months have directly involved Rafael.' He reached for the box on the table. 'Do you know what's in this box?' he asked abruptly.

A wary frown touched her forehead. 'No. How would I?'

'Let me enlighten you. It contains the personal effects that were found on Rafael's person when he was pulled out of the car.' He opened the box. The inside was smeared with blood. Rafael's blood.

Blood he'd spilled because of this woman.

He lifted a gold chain with a tiny crucifix at the end of it. 'My mother gave this to him on the day of his confirmation, when he was thirteen years old. He always wears it during a race. For good luck.'

A look passed over her face. Sadness and a hint of guilt, perhaps? He dropped the chain back into the container, closed it and set it down. Reaching into his pocket, he produced another box—square, velvet.

She tensed, her eyes flaring with alarm. 'Mr de Cervantes—'

His lips twisted. 'You're not quite the talented actress I took you for, after all. Because your expression tells me everything I need to know. Rafael asked the question he'd been burning to ask, didn't he?' he demanded.

'I—'

He cut across her words, not at all surprised when the colour fled her face. 'My brother asked you to marry him. And you callously rejected him, knowing he would have to race directly afterwards. *Didn't you?*'

CHAPTER THREE

SASHA clenched her fists behind her back, desperately trying to hold it together. Even from across the room she could feel Marco's anger. It vibrated off his skin, slammed around the room like a living thing.

Her heart thudded madly in her chest. She opened her mouth but no words emerged.

'Here's your chance to speak up, Miss Fleming,' Marco incised, one long finger flipping open the box to reveal a large, stunning pink diamond set within a circle of smaller white diamonds.

She'd never been one to run from a fight, and Lord knew she'd had many fights in her life. But, watching Marco advance towards her, Sasha yearned to take a step back. Several steps, in fact…right out through the door. Unfortunately she chose that moment to look into his eyes.

The sheer force of his gaze trapped her. It held her immobile, darkly fascinating even as her panic flared higher. She'd dealt with disrespect, with disdain, even with open slurs against her.

Seething, pain-racked Spanish males like Marco de Cervantes were a different box of frogs.

'Did you refuse my brother or not?' he demanded, and his low, dangerous voice scoured her skin.

Suppressing a shiver, she said, 'You've got it wrong. Rafael didn't ask me—'

'Liar.' He snapped the box shut. 'He sent me a text last night. You said no.'

'Of course I said no. He didn't mean—'

He continued as if she hadn't spoken. 'He thought you were just playing hard to get. He was going to try again this morning.'

Sasha knew the brothers were close, but Rafael hadn't given her any indication he was *this* close to his brother. In fact the reason she'd grown close to him, despite his irreverent antics with the team and his wildly flirtatious behaviour with every female he came into contact with, was because she'd glimpsed the loneliness Rafael desperately tried to hide. Loneliness she'd identified with.

She watched Marco's nostrils flare with ever deepening anger as he waited for her answer. She licked her lips, carefully choosing her words, because it was clear that Rafael, for his own reasons, hadn't given Marco all the facts.

'Rafael and I are just friends.'

'Do you take me for a fool, Miss Fleming? You really expect me to believe that you viewed the romantic dinners for two in London or the spontaneous trip to Paris last month as innocent gestures of a mere friend?'

Another stab of surprise went through her at the depth of Marco's knowledge. 'I went to dinner with him because Rav... his date stood him up.'

'And Paris?'

'He was appearing at some function and I was at a loose end. I tagged along for laughs.'

'For laughs? And you then proceeded to dance the night away in his arms? What about the other half a dozen times you've been snapped together by the paparazzi?' he demanded.

She frowned. 'I know you two are close, but don't you think you're taking an alarmingly unhealthy interest in your brother's private life?'

His head jerked as if she'd slapped him. His hazel eyes darkened and his shoulders stiffened as if he held some dark emotion inside. Again she wanted to step back. To flee from a fight for the first time in her life.

'It's my duty to protect my brother,' he stated, with a finality that sharpened her interest.

'Rafael's a grown man. He doesn't need protecting.'

His raised a hand and slowly unfurled his fingers from around the velvet box. 'Then what do you call this? Why did my brother, the reigning world champion, who rarely ever makes mistakes, deliberately drive into the back of a slower car?'

Her gasp scoured her throat. 'The accident wasn't deliberate.' She refused to believe Rafael would have acted so recklessly. 'Rafael wouldn't put himself or another driver in such danger.'

'I've watched my brother race since he was six years old. His skill is legendary. He would never have put himself into the slipstream of a slower car so close to a blind corner. Not if he'd been thinking straight.'

Sasha couldn't refute the allegation because she'd wondered herself why Rafael had made such a dangerous move. 'Maybe he thought he could make the move stick,' she pursued half-heartedly.

Long bronze hands curled around the box. Features tight, Marco breathed deeply. 'Or maybe he didn't care. Maybe it was already too late for him when he stepped into the cockpit?'

Horror raked through her. 'Of course it wasn't. Why would you say that?'

'He sent me a text an hour before the race to tell me he intended to have what he wanted. *At all costs.*'

Sasha's blood ran cold. 'I…no, he couldn't have said that! Besides, he didn't mean—' She bit her lip to stop the rest of her words. Although they'd rowed, she wasn't about to betray Rafael's trust. 'We're just friends.'

'You're poison.' His hand slashed through the denial she'd been about to utter. 'Whatever thrall you hold over your fellow team mates, it ends right now.'

Sliding the box containing the engagement ring into his pocket, he returned to the desk. Several papers were spread across it. He searched through until he found what he was looking for.

'Your contract is a rolling one, due to end next season.'

Still reeling from the force of his words, Sasha stared at him. 'My lawyers will hammer out the finer details of a pay-off in the next few days. But as of right now your services are no longer needed by Team Espiritu.'

With the force of a bucket of cold water, she was wrenched from her numbness.

'You're firing me because I befriended your brother?'

The hysterical edge to her voice registered on the outer fringes of her mind, but Sasha ignored it. She'd worked too hard, fought too long for this chance to let mere hysteria stand in her way. If she had to scream like a banshee she would do so to make Marco de Cervantes listen to her. After years of withstanding vicious whispers and callous undermining, she would not be dismissed so easily. Not when her chance to see her father's reputation restored, the chance to prove her own worth, was so close.

'Do you want to stop for a moment and think how absurd that is? Do you really want to carry on down that road?' she demanded, raising her chin when he turned from the desk.

'What road?' he asked without looking up.

'The sexist, discriminatory road. Or are you going to fire Rafael too when he wakes up? Just to even things up?'

His gaze hardened. 'I've been running this team for almost a decade and no one has ever been allowed to cause this much disruption unchecked before.'

'What do you mean, unchecked?'

'I warned Rafael about you three months ago,' he delivered without an ounce of remorse. 'I told him you were trouble. That he should stay away from you.'

Her anger blazed into an inferno. 'How dare you?'

He merely shrugged. 'Unfortunately, with Rafael, you only have to suggest there's something he can't have to make him hunger desperately for it.'

'You're unbelievable—you know that? You think you can play with people's lives!'

His face darkened. 'Believe me, I'm not playing. Five million.'

Confused, she frowned. 'Five million…for what?'

'To walk away. Dollars, pounds or euros. It doesn't really matter.'

Fire crackled inside her. 'You want to pay me to give up my seat? To disappear like some sleazy secret simply because I became friends with your brother? Even to a wild nut-job like me that seems very drastic. What exactly are you afraid of, Mr de Cervantes?'

Strong, corded arms folded over his chest. His body was held so tense she feared he would snap a muscle at any second. 'Let's just say I have experience with women like you.'

'Damn, I thought I was one of a kind. Would you care to elaborate on that stunning assertion?'

One brow winged upward. 'And have you selling the story to the first tabloid hack you find? I'll pass. Five million. To resign and to stay away from the sport.'

'Go to hell.' She added a smile just for the hell of it, because she yearned for him to feel a fraction of the anger and humiliation coursing through her. The same emotions her father had felt when he'd been thrown out of the profession that had been his life.

'Is that your final answer?' he asked.

'Yes. I don't need to phone a friend and I don't need to ask any audience. My final answer—*go to hell*!'

Sasha braced herself for more of the backlash he'd been doling out solidly for the last hour. But all he did was stare at her, his gaze once again leaving her feeling exposed, as if he'd stripped back a layer of her skin.

He nodded once. Then he paced the room, seemingly lost for words. Finally he raked both hands through his hair, ruffling it until the silky strands looked unkempt in a sexy, just-got-out-of-bed look that she couldn't help but stare at.

Puzzled by his attitude, she forced her gaze away and tried to hang on to her anger. She didn't deserve this. All she'd tried to be was a friend to Rafael, a team mate who'd seemed to be battling demons of his own.

After her experience with Derek, and the devastating pain of losing the baby she hadn't known she was carrying until it was too late, she'd vowed never to mix business with pleasure. Derek's jealousy as she'd risen through the ranks of the racing world had eroded any feelings she'd had for him until there'd been nothing left.

As if sensing her withdrawal, he'd tried to hang on to her with a last-ditch proposal. When she'd turned him down he'd labelled her a bitch and started a whispering campaign against her that had undermined all her years of hard work.

Thankfully Derek had never found out the one thing he could have used against her. The one thing that could have shattered her very existence. The secret memory of her lost baby was buried deep inside, where no one could touch it or use it as a weapon against her.

Even her father hadn't known, and after living through his pain and humiliation she'd vowed never to let her personal life interfere with her work ever again.

Rafael's easy smile and wildly charming ways had got under her guard, making her reveal a few careful details about her past to him. His friendship had been a balm to the lonely existence she'd lived as Jack Fleming's daughter.

The thought that Marco had poisoned him against her filled her with sadness.

'You know, I thought it was Rafael who told *you* about my past. But it was the other way round, wasn't it?' she asked.

She waited for his answer, but his gaze was fixed on the view outside, on the picturesque towers of the Royal Castle. A stillness surrounded him that caught and held her attention.

'For as long as I can remember I've been bailing Rafael out of one scrape or another.'

The words—low, intense and unexpected—jolted aside her anger.

'He's insanely passionate about every single aspect of his life, be it food, driving or volcano-boarding down the side of some godforsaken peak in Nicaragua,' he continued. 'Unfortunately the perils of this world seem to dog him. When he was eleven, he discovered mushrooms growing in a field at our vineyard in León and decided to eat them. His stomach had to be pumped or he'd have died. Two years later, he slipped away from his boarding school to run with the bulls at Pamplona. He was gored in the arm. Save for a very substantial donation to the school, and my personal guarantee of his reformation, he would've been thrown out immediately.'

His gaze focused on her. 'I can list another dozen episodes that would raise your hair.'

'He's a risk-taker,' Sasha murmured, wondering where the conversation was headed but deciding to go with it. 'He has to be as a racing driver; surely you understand that?' she argued. 'Didn't you scale Everest on your own five years ago, after everyone in your team turned back because of a blizzard? In my book that's Class A recklessness.'

'I knew what I was doing.'

'Oh, okay. How about continuing over half the London-Dakar rally with a broken arm?'

His clear surprise made her lips twist. 'How—?'

'Told you I had nerd-tastic info on you. You own the most successful motor racing team in the history of the sport. I want to drive for you. I've done my homework.'

'Very impressive, but risk-taking on the track is expected—within reason. But even before Rafael ever got behind the wheel of a race car he was…highly strung.'

'If he's so highly strung that you have to manage him, then why do you let him race? Why own the team that places him in the very sport likely to jeopardise his well-being?'

His eyes darkened and he seemed to shut off. Watching him, Sasha was fascinated by the impenetrable mask that descended over his face.

'Because racing is in our blood. It's what we do. My father never got the chance to become a racer. I raced for him, but because I had the talent. So does Rafael. There was never any question that racing was our future. But it's also my job to take care of my brother. To save him from himself. To make him see beyond his immediate desires.'

'Have you thought that perhaps if you let him make his own mistakes instead of trying to manage his life he'll wise up eventually?'

'So far, no.'

'He's a grown man. When are you going to cut the apron strings?'

'When he's proved to me that he won't kill himself without them.'

'And are you so certain you can save him every single time?'

'I can put safety measures in place.'

She laughed at his sheer arrogance. 'You're not omnipotent. You can't control what happens in life. Even if you could, Rafael will eventually resent you for controlling his life.'

Marco's lips firmed, his eyelids descending to veil his eyes.

She gave another laugh. 'He already does, doesn't he? Did you two fight? Was that why you weren't at the track this weekend?'

He ignored her questions. 'What I do, I do for his own good. And you're not good for him. My offer still stands.'

Just like that they were back to his sleazy offer of a buy-off. Distaste filled her.

She looked around the sleekly opulent room at the highly polished surfaces, the velvet walls, the bespoke furniture and elegant, sweeping staircases that belonged more in a stately home than in a hotel. Luxurious decadence only people like Marco de Cervantes could afford. The stamp of power and authority told her she wouldn't find even the smallest chink in the de Cervantes armour.

The man was as impenetrable as his wealth was immeasurable.

In the end, all she could rely on was her firm belief in right and wrong.

'You can't fire me simply to keep me out of Rafael's way. It's unethical. I think somewhere deep down you know it too.'

'I don't need moral guidance from someone like you.'

'I disagree. I think you need a big-ass, humongous compass. Because you're making a big mistake if you think I'm going to go quietly.'

His smile didn't quite reach his eyes. 'Rafael told me you were feisty.'

What else had Rafael told him? Decidedly uncomfortable at the thought of being the subject of discussion, she shrugged.

'I haven't reached where I am today without a fight or three. I won't go quietly,' she stressed again.

Several minutes of silence stretched. Her nerves stretched along with them. Just when she thought she'd break, that she'd have to resort to plain, old-fashioned, humiliating begging, he hitched one taut-muscled thigh over the side of the desk and indicated the chair in front of it.

'Sit down. I think a discussion is in order.'

Marco watched relief wash over her face and hid a triumphant smile.

He'd never had any intention of firing Sasha Fleming. Not immediately, anyway. He'd wanted her rattled, on a knife-edge at the possibility of losing what was evidently so precious to her.

The bloodthirsty, vengeance-seeking beast inside him felt a little appeased at seeing her shaken. He also wanted to test her, to see how far she would go to fight for what she wanted. After all, the higher the value she placed on her career, the sweeter it would be to snatch it away from her. Just as he'd had everything wrenched from *him* ten years ago.

He ruthlessly brushed aside the reminder of Angelique's betrayal and focused on Sasha as she walked towards him.

Again his senses reacted to her in ways that made his jaw clench. The attraction—and, yes, he was man enough to admit to it—was unwelcome as much as it was abhorrent. Rafael was in a coma, fighting for his life. The last thing Marco wanted to acknowledge was a chemical reaction to the woman in the middle of all this chaos. To acknowledge how the flare of her hips made his palms itch to shape them. How the soft lushness of her lower lip made him want to caress his finger over it.

'Regardless of the state of the team, I have a responsibility towards the sponsors.'

His office had already received several calls, ostensibly expressing concern for his brother's welfare. In truth the sponsors were sniffing around, desperate to find out what Marco's next move would be—specifically, who he would put in Rafael's place and how it would affect their bottom line.

She nodded. 'Rafael was scheduled to appear at several sponsored engagements during the August hiatus. They'll want to know what's happening.'

Once again Marco was struck by the calm calculation in her voice. This wasn't the tone of a concerned lover or a distraught team mate. Her mind was firmly focused on Team Espiritu. In other circumstances, her single-mindedness would have been admirable. But he knew first-hand the devastation ambition like hers could wreak.

Before he could answer a knock sounded on his door. One of his two butlers materialised from wherever he'd been stationed and opened the door.

Russell Latchford, his second-in-command, and Luke Green, the team's chief engineer, entered.

Russell approached. 'I've just been to see Rafael—' He stopped when he saw Sasha. 'Sasha. I didn't know you were here.' His tone echoed the question in his eyes.

Sasha returned his gaze calmly. Nothing ruffled her. Nothing except the threatened loss of her job. The urge to see her lose that cool once again attacked Marco's senses.

'Miss Fleming's here to discuss future possibilities in light of Rafael's accident.'

As team principal, it was Russell's job to source the best drivers for the team, with Marco giving final approval. Marco saw his disgruntlement, but to his credit Russell said nothing.

'Have you brought the shortlist I asked for?' Marco asked Russell.

Sasha inhaled sharply, and he saw her hands clench in her lap as Russell handed over a piece of paper.

'I've already been discreetly approached by the top five, but every driver in the sport wants to drive for us. It'll cost you to buy out their contracts, of course. If you go for someone from the lower ranking teams it'll still cost you, but the fallout won't be as damaging as poaching someone from the top teams.'

Marco shook his head. 'Our sponsors signed up for the package—Rafael and the car. I don't want a second-class driver.

I need someone equally talented and charismatic or the sponsors will throw hissy fits.'

Luke spoke up. 'There's also the problem of limited in-season testing. We can't just throw in a brand-new driver mid-season and expect him to handle the car anywhere near the way Rafael did.'

Marco glanced down at the list. 'No. Rafael is irreplaceable. I accept that the Drivers' Championship is no longer an option, but I want to win the Constructors' Championship. The team deserves it. All of these drivers would ditch their contract to drive for me, but I'd rather not deal with a messy court battle. Where do we stand on the former champion who retired last year? Have you contacted him?'

Russell shook his head. 'Even with the August break he won't be in good enough shape when the season resumes in September.'

'So my only option is to take on a driver from another team?'

'No, it isn't.' Sasha's voice was low, but intensely powerful, and husky enough to command attention.

Marco's eyes slid to her. Her stance remained relaxed, one leg crossed over the other, but in her eyes he saw ferocious purpose.

'You have something to add?'

Fierce blue eyes snapped at him as she rolled her shoulders. As last time, he couldn't help but follow the movement. Then his eyes travelled lower, to the breasts covered by her nondescript T-shirt. Again the pull of desire was strong and sharp, unlike anything he'd experienced before. Again he pushed it away and forced his gaze back to her face.

A faint flush covered her cheeks. 'You know I do. I know the car inside out. I've driven it at every Friday Practice since last season. The way I see it, I'm the only way you can win the Constructors' Championship. Plus you'd save a lot of money and the unnecessary litigation of trying to tempt away a driver mid-season from another team. In the last few practices my run-times have nearly equalled Rafael's.'

Marco silently admitted the truth of her words. He might not sit on the pit wall for every single minute of a race—the engineer and aerodynamicist in him preferred the hard facts of the telemetry reports—but he knew Sasha's race times to the last fraction.

He also knew racing was more than just the right car in the right hands. 'Yes, but you're yet to perform under the pressure of a Saturday practice, a pole position shoot-out and a race on Sunday. I'd rather have a driver with actual race experience.'

Russell fidgeted and cleared his throat. 'I agree, Marco. I think Alan might be a better option—'

'I've consistently surpassed Alan's track times,' she said of the team's second driver. 'Luke will confirm it.'

Luke's half-hearted shrug made Marco frown.

'Is there a problem?'

The other man cleared his throat. 'Not a problem, exactly, but I'm not sure how the team will react to…you know…'

'No, I don't know. If you have something to say, then say it.'

'He means how the team will react to a woman lead driver,' Sasha stated baldly.

Recalling her accusation of sexism, he felt a flash of anger swell through him. He knew the views of others when it came to employing women as drivers. The pathetically few women racers attested to the fact that it was a predominantly male sport, but he believed talent was talent, regardless of the gender that wielded it.

The thought that key members in his team didn't share his belief riled him.

He rose. 'That will be all, gentlemen.'

Russell's surprise was clear. 'Do you need some time to make the decision?'

His gaze stayed on Sasha. Her chest had risen in a sharp intake of breath. Again he had to force himself not to glance down at her breasts. The effort it took not to look displeased him immensely.

'I've requested figures from my lawyers by morning. I'll let you know my decision.'

His butler led them out.

'Mr de Cervantes—' Sasha started.

He held up a hand. 'Let me make one thing clear. I didn't

refuse you a drive because of your gender. Merely because of your disruptive influence within my team.'

Her eyes widened, then she nodded. 'Okay. But I want to—'

'I need to return to my brother's bedside. You'll also find out my decision tomorrow.' He turned to leave.

'Please. I…need this.'

The raw, fervent emotion in her voice stopped him from leaving the room. Returning to her side, he stared down at her bent head. Her hands were clenched tighter. A swathe of pure black hair had slipped its knot and half covered her face. His fingers itched to catch it back, smooth it behind her ear so he could see her expression.

Most of all, he wanted her to look at him.

'Why? Why is this so important to you?' he asked.

'I…I made a promise.' Her voice was barely above a whisper.

Marco frowned. 'A promise? To whom?'

She inhaled, and before his eyes she gathered herself in. Her spine straightened, and her shoulders snapped back until her whole body became poised, almost regal. Then her eyes slowly rose to his.

The steely determination in their depths compelled his attention. His blood heated, rushing through his veins in a way that made his body clench in denial. Yet he couldn't look away.

Her gaze dropped. Marco bit back the urge to order her to look at him.

'It doesn't matter. All you need to know is if you give me a chance I'll hand you the Constructors' Championship.'

Sasha heard the low buzzing and cursed into her pillow. How the blazes had a wasp got into her room?

And since when did wasps make such a racket?

Groaning, she rolled over and tried to burrow into a better position. Sleep had been an elusive beast. She'd spent the night alternately pacing the floor and running through various arguments in her head about how she would convince Marco to keep her on the team. In the end exhaustion had won out.

Now she'd been woken by—

Her phone! With a yelp, she shoved off the covers and stumbled blindly for the satchel she'd discarded on the floor.

'Huhn?'

'Do I take it by that unladylike grunt that I've disturbed your sleep?' Marco de Cervantes's voice rumbled down the line.

'Not at all,' she lied. 'What time is it?' She furiously rubbed her eyes. She'd never been a morning person.

Taut silence, then, 'It's nine-thirty.'

'What? *Damn.*' She'd slept through her alarm. Again.

Could anyone blame her, though? Being part of Team Espiritu meant staying in excellent accommodation, but this time management had excelled itself—the two thousand thread-count cotton sheets, handmade robes, the hot tub, lotions and potions, the finest technology and her personal maid on tap were just the beginnings of the absurd luxury that made the crew of Marco's team the envy of the circuit. But her four-poster bed and its mattress—dear Lord, the made-by-angels mattress—was the reason—

'Do you have somewhere else to be, Miss Fleming?'

'Yes. I have a plane to catch back to London at eleven.' Thankfully she didn't have a lot of things to pack, having put her restless energy to good use last night. And the airport was only ten minutes away. Still, she was cutting it fine.

'You might wish to revise that plan.'

She froze, refusing to acknowledge the thin vein of hope taking root deep within her. 'And why would I need to do that?'

'I have a proposition for you. Open your door.'

'What?'

'Open your door. I need to look into your eyes when I outline my plan so there can be no doubt on either part.'

'You're *here*?' Her eyes darted to her door, as if she could see his impressive body outlined through the solid wood.

'I'm here. But I'll soon be a figment of your imagination if you don't open your door.'

Sasha glanced down at herself. No way was she opening the door to Marco de Cervantes wearing a vampire T-shirt that declared *'Bite Me'* in blood-red. And she didn't even want to think of the state of her hair.

'I... Can you give me two minutes?' If she could get in and out of a race suit in ninety seconds, she sure as hell could make herself presentable in a fraction of that time.

'You have five seconds. Then I move on to my next call.'

'No. Wait!' Keeping the phone glued to her ear, she rushed to the door. Pulling it open, she stuck her head out, trying her best to shield the rest of her body from full view.

And there he stood. Unlike the casual clothes of yesterday, Marco was dressed in a bespoke suit, his impressive shoulders even more imposing underneath the slate-grey jacket, blue shirt and pinstriped tie, his long legs planted in battle stance. His hair was combed neatly, unlike the unruly, sexy mess it'd been yesterday. The strong desire to see it messy again had her pulling back a fraction.

Eyes locked on hers, he lowered his phone. 'Invite me in.'

'Why? Are you a vampire?' she shot back, then swallowed a groan.

Frown lines creased his brow. *'Excuse me?* Are you high?'

Sasha silently cursed her morning brain. 'Hah—I wish. Oh, never mind. I'm...I'm not really dressed to receive guests, but I didn't want you to leave, so unless you want to extend that five-second ultimatum this will have to do.'

His frown deepened. 'Are you in the habit of answering your hotel door naked?'

Heat crawled up her neck and stung her face. 'Of course not. I'm not naked.'

'Prove it' came the soft challenge.

'Fine. See?' Belatedly she wondered at her sanity as she stepped into his view and felt the dark, intense force of Marco's gaze as it travelled over her.

When his eyes returned to hers, the breath snagged in her lungs. His hazel eyes had darkened to burnt gold with dark green flecks; the clench of his jaw was even more pronounced. He seemed to be straining against an emotion that was more than a little bit frightening.

She stepped back. He followed her in and shut the door. The luxury hotel suite that had seemed so vast, so over the top, closed in on her. She took another step back. He followed, eyes locked on her.

Her phone fell from her fingers, thankfully cushioned by the shag-pile carpet. Mouth dry, she kept backing up. He kept following.

'I make it a point not to credit rumours, but it seems in this instance the rumours are true, Sasha Fleming.'

The way he said her name—slowly, with a hint of Latin intonation—made goosebumps rise on her flesh. Her nipples peaked and a sensation she recognised to her horror as desire raked through her abdomen, sending delicious darts of liquid heat to the apex of her thighs.

'What exactly do you think is true about me?'

'Sex is your weapon of choice,' he breathed, his eyes lingering on the telltale nubs beneath her T-shirt. 'The only trouble is you wield it so unsubtly.'

'I beg your pardon?' she squeaked as the backs of her legs touched the side of the bed. 'Did you just say—?'

'You need to learn to finesse your art.'

'What in heaven's name are you blathering about? Are you sure *you're* not the one who's high?' she flung back.

'No man likes to be bludgeoned over the head with sex. No matter how…enticing the package.'

'You're either loopy or you've got me confused with someone else. I don't bludgeon and I don't entice.'

He kept coming.

She leaned back on the bed and felt the hem of her shirt riding up her thighs. 'For goodness' sake, stop!'

He stopped, but his gaze didn't. It continued its destructive course over her, leaving no part of her untouched, until Sasha felt sure she was about to combust from the heat of it.

Desperate, she let her tongue dart out to lick her lips. 'Look… Derek—I presume that's where you got your little morsel from— said a lot of unsavoury things about me when we broke up. But I'm not who…whatever you think I am.'

'Even though I can see the evidence for myself?' he rasped in a low voice.

She scrambled over the side of the bed and grabbed the robe she'd dropped on the floor last night. With shaking fingers, and a mind scrambling to keep pace with the bizarre turn of the conversation, she pulled the lapels over her traitorous body.

Having pursued her profession in fast cars financed by billionaires with unlimited funds, Sasha knew there was a brand of women who found the whole X1 Premier Racing world a huge turn-on: women who used their sexuality to pursue racers with a single-mindedness that bordered on the obsessive.

She'd never considered for a second that she would ever be bracketed with them—especially by the wealthiest, most sought-after billionaire of them all. The idea would have been laughable if the sting of Derek's betrayal still didn't have the ability to hurt.

'Well, whatever it is you *think* you see, there's no truth to the rumour. Now, can we please get back to the reason you came here in the first place?'

Her words seemed to rouse him from whatever dark, edgy place he'd been in. He looked up from her thighs, slowly exhaled, and looked around the room, taking in the rumpled bed and the contents of her satchel strewn on the floor.

When he paced to the window and drew back the curtain she took the opportunity to tie the robe tighter around her, hoping it would dispel the electricity zinging around her body.

He turned after a minute, his face devoid of expression. 'I've decided not to recruit a new driver. Doing so mid-season is not financially viable. Besides, they all have contracts and sponsorship commitments to fulfil.'

Hope grew so powerful it weakened her legs. Sinking down onto the side of the bed, she swallowed. 'So, does that mean I have the seat for the rest of the season?'

He shoved his hands into his pockets, his gaze fixed squarely on her. 'You'll sign an agreement promising to honour every commitment the team holds you to. Half of the sponsors have agreed to let you fulfil Rafael's commitments.'

He hadn't given a definite *yes*, but Sasha's heartbeat thundered nonetheless. 'And the other half?'

'With nowhere to go, they'll come round. My people are working on them.'

Unable to stem the flood of emotion rising inside, she pried her gaze from his and stared down at her trembling hands. She struggled to breathe.

Finally. The chance to wipe the slate clean. To earn the respect that had been ruthlessly denied her and so callously wrenched from her father. Finally the Fleming name would be spoken of with esteem and not disdain. Jack Fleming would be allowed to rest in peace, his legacy nothing to be ashamed of any more.

'I…thank you,' she murmured.

'You haven't heard the conditions attached to your drive.'

She shook her head, careless of the hair flying about her face as euphoria frothed inside her. 'I agree. Whatever it is, I agree.' She wouldn't let this opportunity slip her by. She intended to grab it with both hands. To prove to anyone who'd dared to naysay that they'd been wrong.

His eyes narrowed. 'Yesterday you promised to give *anything* not to have Rafael in hospital. Today you're agreeing to conditions you haven't even heard. Are you always this carefree with your consent? Perhaps I need to rethink making you lead driver. I shudder to think what such rashness could cost me on the race track.'

'I… Fine—name your conditions.'

He quirked a mocking brow. '*Gracias*. Aside from the other commitments, there are two that I'm particularly interested in. Team Espiritu *must* win the Constructors' Championship. We're eighty points ahead of the next championship challenger. I expect those points only to go up. Understood?'

A smile lit up her face. 'Absolutely. I intend to wipe the floor with them.'

'The second condition—'

'Wait. I have a condition of my own.'

His lips twisted. '*Déjà vu* overwhelms me. I suppose I shouldn't be surprised.'

Sasha ignored him, the need to voice a wish so long denied making her words trip from her lips with a life of their own. 'If...*when* I secure you the Constructors' Championship, I want my contract with Team Espiritu to be extended for another year.'

When his eyes narrowed further, she rushed to speak again.

'You can write it into my contract that I'll be judged based on my performance during the next three months. If we win the Constructors' you'll hire me for another year.'

'Winning a Drivers' Championship means that much to you?'

His curiously flat tone drew her gaze, but his expression remained inscrutable. Her heart hammered with the force of her deepest yearning. 'Yes, it does.'

His eyelids descended, veiling his gaze. The tension in the room increased until she could cut the atmosphere with a butter knife. But when he looked back up there was nothing but cool, impersonal regard.

'Very well. Win the Constructors' Championship and I'll extend your contract for another year.'

She couldn't believe he'd agreed so readily. 'Wow, that was easy.'

'Perhaps it's because I don't believe in talking every subject to death. My time is precious.'

'Yes, of course...'

'As I was saying, before you interrupted, my second condition is more important, Miss Fleming, so listen carefully. You'll have no personal contact with any male member of the team; you will go nowhere near my brother. Any hint of a non-professional relationship with another driver or anyone within the sport, for that matter, will mean instant dismissal. And I'll personally make it my mission to ensure you never drive another racing car. Do we understand each other?'

CHAPTER FOUR

'IF YOU'VE finished your breakfast, I'll take you on the tour of the race track.'

Sasha looked up from her almost empty plate of scrambled eggs and ham to find Marco lounging in the doorway that connected the vast living room to the sun-drenched terrace of *Casa de Leon*.

She'd been here three days, and she still couldn't get her head round the sheer vastness of the de Cervantes estate. Navigating her way around the huge, rambling two-storey villa without getting lost had taken two full days.

With its white stucco walls, dark red slate roofs and large cathedral-like windows, *Casa de Leon* was an architect's dream. The high exposed beams, sweeping staircases and intricately designed marble floors wouldn't have been out of place in a palace. Every piece of furniture, painting and drape looked as if it cost a fortune. Even the air inside the villa smelled different, tinged with a special rarefied, luxurious quality that made her breath catch.

Outside, an endless green vista, broken only by perfectly manicured gardens, stretched as far as the eye could see… It was no wonder the countless villa staff travelled around in golf buggies.

Realising Marco was waiting for an answer, she nodded, drawing her gaze from the long, muscular legs encased in dark grey trousers. 'Sure. I'll just finish my coffee. Aren't you having anything?' She indicated the mouth-watering spread of seasonal fruit, pastries and ham slices on the table.

Disengaging himself from the doorway, he came towards her, powerfully sleek and oozing arrogant masculinity. 'I'll have a coffee, too.'

When he sat and made no move to pour it himself, she raised an eyebrow. 'Yes, boss. Three bags full, boss?'

His hazel eyes gleamed and Sasha had the distinct feeling he was amused, although not a smile cracked his lips. In fact he looked decidedly strained. Which wasn't surprising under the circumstances, she reminded herself.

Feeling the mutiny give way, she poured him a cup. 'Black?'

'*Sí*. Two sugars.'

She looked up, surprised. 'Funny, I wouldn't have pegged you for the two-sugars type.'

'And how *would* you have pegged me?'

'Black, straight up, drunk boiling hot without a wince.'

'Because my insides are made of tar and my soul is black as night?' he mocked.

She shrugged. 'Hey, you said it.' She added sugar and passed it over.

'*Gracias.*' He picked up a silver spoon and stirred his drink, the tiny utensil looking very delicate in his hand.

Sasha found herself following the movement, her gaze tracing the short dark hairs on the back of his hand. Suddenly her mouth dried, and her stomach performed that stupid flip again. Wrenching her gaze from the hypnotic motion, she picked up her cup with a decidedly unsteady hand.

'How are you settling in?' he asked.

'Do you really want to know?'

The speed with which Marco had whisked her from Budapest to Spain after she'd signed the contract had made her head spin. Of course his luxury private jet—which he'd piloted himself—had negated the tedium of long airport waits and might have had something to do with it. They'd flown to Barcelona, then transferred by helicopter to his estate in Leon.

He took another sip. 'I wouldn't have asked otherwise. You should know by now that I never say anything I don't mean.'

Now she felt surly. Her suite was the last word in luxury, complete with four-poster bed, half a dozen fluffy pillows and a deep-sunken marble bath to die for. Just across from where she sat, past the giant-sized terracotta potted plants and a barbecue area, an Olympic-sized swimming pool sparkled azure in the dappling morning light. She'd already sampled its soothing comfort, along with the sports gym equipped with everything she needed to keep her exercise regime on track. In reality, she wanted for nothing.

And yet...

'It's fine. I have everything I need. Thank you,' she tagged on waspishly. Then, wisely moving on before she ventured into full-blown snark, she asked, 'How is Rafael?'

Marco's gaze cooled.

Sasha sighed. 'I agreed to stay away from him. I didn't agree to stop caring about him.'

'The move from Budapest went fine. He's now in the care of the best Spanish doctors in Barcelona.'

'Since you'll probably bite my head off if I ask you to send him my best, I'll move on. How far away is the race track?'

'Three miles south.' Lifting his cup, he drained it.

'Exactly how big is this place?'

When Marco had announced he was bringing a skeleton team to Spain to help her train for her debut at the end of August, she'd mistakenly thought she would be spending most of her time in a race simulator. The half an hour it'd taken to travel from Marco's landing strip to his villa had given her an inkling of how immense his estate was.

His gaze pinned on her, he picked up an orange and skilfully peeled it. 'All around? About twenty-five square miles.'

'And you and Rafael own all of it?'

'*Sí.*' He popped a segment into his mouth.

Sasha carefully set her cup down, her senses tingling with warning. That soft *sí* had held a slight edge to it that made her wary. His next words confirmed her wariness.

'Just think, if only you'd said yes all this would've been yours.'

She didn't need to ask what he meant. Affecting a light tone, she toyed with the delicate handle of her expensive bone china cup. 'Gee, I don't know. The race track would've been handy, but what the hell would I do with the rest of the... What else is there, anyway?'

His gaze was deceptively lazy—deceptive because she could feel the charged animosity rising from him.

'There's a fully functioning vineyard and winery. And the stables house some of the best Andalucian thoroughbreds in Spain. There's also an exclusive by-invitation-only resort and spa on the other side of the estate.'

'Well, there you have it, then. My palate is atrociously common—not to mention that if I drink more than one glass of wine I get a raging headache. As for thoroughbreds—I couldn't tell you which end of the horse to climb if you put me next to one. So, really, you're way better off without me in your family. The spa sounds nice, though. A girl could always do with a foot rub after a hard day's work—although I have a feeling the amount of grease I tend to get under my nails would frighten your resort staff.'

A tiny tic appeared at his temple. 'Are you always this facetious, or do you practice?'

'Normally I keep it well hidden. I only show off when asked really, really nicely,' she flung back. Then she stood. 'From the unfortunate downturn of this conversation, I take it the offer of a tour is now off the table?' She tilted her chin, determined not to reveal how deep his barbs had stung.

'As much as I'm tempted to reward your petulance with time on the naughty step, that will only prove counterproductive.' Wiping his hands on a napkin, he rose to tower over her. 'You're here to train. Familiarising yourself with the race track is part of that training. I'll leave the naughty step for another time.'

Wisely deciding to leave the mention of the naughty step alone, Sasha relaxed her grip on the back of the chair. 'Thank you.'

Sasha followed him into the villa, staunchly maintaining her silence. But not talking didn't equate to not looking, and, damn it, she couldn't help but be intensely aware of the man beside her. His smell assailed her nostrils—that sharp tang of citrus coupled with the subtle undertones of musk that shifted as it flowed over his warmth.

Against the strong musculature of his torso his white polo shirt lovingly followed the superb lines of a deep chest and powerful shoulders. All that magnificence tapered down to a trim waist that knew not an ounce of fat.

Judging by his top-notch physicality, she wasn't surprised Marco had been the perfect championship-winning driver ten years ago.

'Why did you give up racing? You resigned so abruptly, and yet it's obvious you recovered fully after your crash.'

She saw his shoulders tense before he rounded on her. The icy, forbidding look in his eyes made her bite her lip.

Nice one, Sasha.

'That is not a subject up for discussion, Miss Fleming. And before you take it into your head to go prying I caution you against it. Understood?'

He barely waited for her nod before he wrenched open the front door.

Outside, two golf buggies sat side by side at the bottom of the steps. She headed towards the nearest one.

'Where are you going?' he bit out.

She stopped. 'Oh, I thought we were going by road.'

He nodded to the helipad, where a black and red chopper sat gleaming in the morning sun. 'We're touring by helicopter.'

It was a spectacularly beautiful machine—the latest in a long line of beautiful aircraft.

'Any chance you'll let me fly it?'

He flashed a mirthless grin at her. 'I don't see any pigs flying, do you?'

'Wow, this is incredible! How long have you had this race track?'

Marco glanced up from the helicopter controls, then immediately wished he hadn't. It was bad enough hearing her excitement piped directly into his headphones. The visual effects were even more disturbing.

When he'd offered her an aerial tour of the race track he hadn't taken into account how she was dressed. In most respects, her white shorts could be described as sensible—almost boyish. He'd been out with women who wore far less on a regular basis. Her light green shirt was also plain to the point of being utilitarian.

All the same, Marco found the combination of her excitement and her proximity...*aggravating*. Even more aggravating were the flashbacks he kept having of her leaning back on the bed in her hotel room, her T-shirt riding up to reveal skin so tempting it had knocked his breath clean out of his lungs...

Her naked ambition and her sheer drive to succeed were living things that charged the air around her. Marco knew only too well the high cost of blind ambition, and yet knowing the depths of Sasha Fleming's ambition and what she would do to achieve her goals didn't stop him from imagining how it would have felt to lift her T-shirt higher...just a fraction...

He was also more than a little puzzled that she'd made no attempt to gain his attention since that episode in her room. Women flaunted themselves at him at every opportunity—used every excuse in the book to garner his interest. Some even resorted to...*unconventional* means. Most of the time he was happy to direct them Rafael's way. He'd long outgrown the paddock bunny phase; had outgrown it even before Angelique, the most calculating of them all, had stepped into his orbit and turned his world upside down.

Marco sobered, seething at himself for the memories he suddenly couldn't seem to dispel so easily. Focusing on the controls, he banked the chopper and followed the straights and curves of the race track hundreds of metres below.

'I built it ten years ago,' he clipped out in answer to her question.

'After you retired?' she asked, surprised.

'No. Just before.' His harsh response had the desired effect of shutting her up, but when he glanced at her again, he noted the spark of speculation in her eyes. Before he could think about why he was doing so, he found himself elaborating. 'I thought I'd be spending more time here.' He'd woven foolish dreams about what his life would be like, how perfect everything had seemed. He'd had the perfect car; the perfect woman.

'What happened?'

The crushing pain of remembrance tightened around his chest. 'I crashed.'

She gave a sad little understanding nod that made him want to growl at her. What did she know? She was as conniving as they came.

Forcing his anger under control, he flew over the track towards the mid-point hill.

Sasha pointed to six golf buggies carrying mechanics who hopped out at various points of the track. 'What are they doing?'

'The track hasn't been used for a while. They're conducting last-minute checks on the moveable parts to make sure they're secure.'

'I can't believe this track can be reshaped to simulate other tracks around the circuit. I can't wait to have a go!'

Excitement tinged her voice and Marco couldn't help glancing over at her. Her eyes were alight with a smile that seemed to glow from within. His hands tightened around the controls.

'The track was built before simulators became truly effective. One concrete track would've served only to make a driver expert at a particular track, so I designed an interchangeable track. The other advantage is experience gained in driving on tarmac, or as close to tarmac—as you can get. Wet or dry conditions can make or break a race. This way the driver gets to practise on both with the right tyres. Electronic simulators and wind tunnels have their places, but so does this track.'

The helicopter crested another small hill and cold sweat broke out over his skin. Several feet to the side of the track a mound of whitewashed stones had been piled high in a makeshift monument. Marco's hand tightened on the lever and deftly swerved the aircraft away from the landmark he had no wish to see up close.

'Trust me, I'm not complaining. It's a great idea. I'm just surprised other teams haven't copied the idea. Or sold their firstborn sons to use your track.'

'Offers have been made in the past.'

'And?'

He shrugged. 'I occasionally allow them to use the track I designed. But for the whole package to come together they also need the car I designed.'

A small laugh burst from her lips. The sound was so unexpectedly pleasing he momentarily lost his train of thought, and missed her reply.

'What did you say?'

'I said that's a clever strategy—considering you own the team you design for, and the only other way anyone can get their hands on a Marco de Cervantes design is by shelling out…how much does the *Cervantes Conquistador* cost? Two million?'

'Three.'

She whistled—another unexpected sound that charged through his bloodstream, making him even more on edge than he'd been a handful of seconds ago.

She leaned forward into his eyeline. He'd been wrong about the shirt being functional. Her pert breasts pressed against the cotton material, her hands on her thighs as she peered down.

Marco swallowed, the hot stirrings in his abdomen increasing to uncomfortable proportions. Ruthlessly he pushed them away.

Sasha Fleming was bad news, he reminded himself.

Rafael had got involved with her to his severe detriment. Marco had no intention of following down the same road. His only interest in her was to make sure she delivered the Constructors' Championship. Now he knew what she really wanted—the Drivers' Championship—he had her completely at his mercy.

Control re-established, he brought the helicopter in to land, and yanked off his headphones. Sasha jumped down without his help and Marco caught the puzzled look she flashed him. Ignoring it, he strode towards Luke Green. His chief engineer had travelled ahead to supervise the initial training arrangements.

Sasha drew closer and her scent reached his nostrils. Marco's insides clenched in rejection even as he breathed her in. His awareness of her was becoming intolerable. Even her voice as she greeted Luke bit into his psyche.

'Is everything in order?' he asked.

Luke nodded. 'We're just about to offload the engine. The mechanics will check it over and make sure it hasn't been damaged during the flight.'

'It takes three hours max to assemble the car, so it should be ready for me to test this afternoon, shouldn't it?' Sasha asked, her attention so intent on the tarpaulin-covered engine Marco almost enquired if she yearned to caress it.

'No. You'll begin training tomorrow morning,' he all but growled.

Her head snapped towards him, her expression crestfallen. 'Oh, but if the car's here…'

'The mechanics have been working on getting things ready since dawn. This engine hasn't been used since last December. It'll have to go through rigorous testing before it's race-ready. That'll take most of the day—at least until sundown.'

He turned back to Luke. 'I want to see hourly engine readouts and a final telemetry report when you're done testing.'

'Sure thing, boss.'

Grabbing Sasha's arm, he steered her away from the garage. Several eyes followed them, but he didn't care. He was nothing like his brother. He had no intention of ever making a fool of himself over a woman again.

Opening the passenger door to his Conquistador, he thrust her into the bucket seat. Rounding the hood, he slid behind the wheel.

'Why do I get the feeling you're angry with me?' she directed at him.

Marco slammed his door. 'It's not a feeling.'

The breath she blew up disturbed the thick swathe of hair slanting over her forehead. 'What did I do?' she demanded.

He faced her and found her stunning eyes snapping fire at him. The blue of her gaze was so intense, so vivid, he wanted to keep staring at her for ever. The uncomfortable erotic heat he'd felt in her Budapest hotel room, when she'd strutted into view wearing that damned T-shirt that boldly announced *'Bite Me'*, rose again.

For days he'd been fighting that stupid recurring memory that strayed into his thoughts at the most inconvenient times.

Even here in Leon, where much more disturbing memories impinged everywhere he looked, he couldn't erase from his mind the sight of those long, coltish legs and the thought of how they would feel around his waist.

Nor could he ignore the evidence of Sasha's hard work and dedication to her career. Every night since her arrival in Spain he'd found her poring over telemetry reports or watching footage of past races, fully immersed in pursuing the only thing she cared about.

The only thing she cared about...

Grabbing the steering wheel, he forced himself to calm down.

'Marco?'

When had he given her permission to use his first name? Come to think of it, when had he started thinking of her as Sasha instead of Miss Fleming?

Dios, he was losing it.

With a wrench of his wrist the engine sprang to life, its throaty roar surprisingly soothing. Designing the Espiritu race cars had been an engineering challenge he'd relished. The *Cervantes Conquistador* had been a pure labour of love.

Momentarily he lost himself in the sounds of the engine, his mind picking up minute clicks and torsion controls. If he closed his eyes he would be able to imagine the aerodynamic flow of air over the chassis, visualise where each spark plug, each piston, nut and bolt was located.

But he didn't close his eyes. He kept his gaze fixed firmly ahead. His grip tightened around the wheel.

Her gaze stayed on him as he accelerated the green and black sports car out of the parking lot. The screech of tyres drew startled glances from the mechanics heading for the hangar. Marco didn't give a damn.

After a few minutes, when he felt sufficiently calm, he slowed down. 'It's not you.'

She didn't answer.

Shrugging, he indicated the rich forest surrounding them. 'It's this place.'

'This place? The race track or *Casa de Leon*?'

His jaw clenched as he tried in vain to stem the memories flooding him. 'This is where my mother died eight years ago.'

Her gasp echoed in the car. 'Oh, my God, I'm so sorry. I didn't know. You should've said something.'

He slowed down long enough to give her a hard look. 'It isn't common knowledge outside my family. I'd prefer it to remain that way.' He wasn't even sure why he'd told her. Whatever was causing him to act so out of character he needed to cauterise it.

She gave a swift nod. 'Of course. You can trust me.' Her colour rose slightly at her last words.

The irony wasn't lost on him. He only had himself to blame if she decided to spill her guts at the first opportunity. Flooring the accelerator, he sent the car surging forward as his *other* reason for wanting to escape the memories of this place rose.

Sasha remained silent until he pulled up in front of the villa. Then, lifting a hand, she tucked a strand of hair behind her ear. 'How did it happen?' she asked softly.

Releasing his clammy grip on the steering wheel, Marco flicked a glance at the villa door. He knew he'd find no respite within. If anything, the memories were more vivid inside. He didn't need to close his eyes to see his mother laughing at Rafael's shameless cajoling, her soft hazel eyes sparkling as she wiped her hands on a kitchen towel moments before rushing out of the villa.

'For his twenty-first birthday my father bought Rafael a Lamborghini. We celebrated at a nightclub in Barcelona. Afterwards I flew down here in the helicopter with my parents. Rafael chose to drive from Barcelona—five hours straight. He arrived just after breakfast, completely wired from partying. I tried to convince him to get some sleep, but he wanted to take my parents for a spin in the car.'

The familiar icy grip of pain tightened around his chest.

'Rafael was my mother's golden boy. He could do no wrong. So of course she agreed.' Marco felt some of the pain seep out and tried to contain it. 'My father insisted later it was the sun that got in Rafael's eyes as he turned the curve, but one eyewitness confirmed he took the corner too fast. I heard the crash from the garage.' Every excruciating second had felt like a lifetime as he sped towards the scene. 'By the time the air ambulance came my mother was gone.'

'Oh, Marco, *no*!'

Sasha's voice was a soft, soothing sound. The ache inside abated, but it didn't disappear. It never would. He'd lost his mother before he'd ever had the chance to make up for what he'd put her through.

'I should've stopped him—should've insisted he get some sleep before taking the car out again.'

'You couldn't have known.'

He shook his head. 'But I should have. Except when it comes to Rafael everyone seems to develop a blind spot. Including me.'

Vaguely, Marco wondered why he was spilling his guts. To Sasha Fleming, of all people. With a forceful wrench on the door, he stepped out of the car.

She scrambled out too. 'And your father? What happened to him?'

His fist tightened around the computerised car key. 'The accident severed his spine. He lost the use of his body from the neck down. He's confined to a wheelchair and will remain like that for the rest of his life.'

Sasha looked after Marco's disappearing figure, shocked by the astonishing revelation.

Now Marco's motives became clear. His overprotective attitude towards Rafael, his reaction to the crash, suddenly made sense. Watching his mother die on the race track *he'd* built had to be right up there with enduring a living hell every time he stepped foot on it.

So why did he do it?

Marco de Cervantes was an extraordinary engineer and aerodynamicist, who excelled in building astonishingly fast race cars, but he could easily have walked away and concentrated his design efforts on the equally successful range of exclusive sport cars favoured by Arab sheikhs and Russian oligarchs.

So what drove him to have anything to do with a world that surely held heart-wrenching memories?

She slowly climbed the stairs and entered the house, her mind whirling as she went into her suite to wash off the heat and sweat of the race track.

After showering, she put on dark jeans and a striped blue shirt. Pulling her hair into a neat twist, she secured it with a band and shoved her feet into pair of flat sandals.

She met Marco as she came down the stairs. The now familiar raking gaze sent another shiver of awareness scything through her. He stopped directly in front of her, his arresting face and piercing regard rendering her speechless for several seconds.

'Lunch won't be ready for a while, but if you want something light before then, Rosario can fix you something.'

The matronly housekeeper appeared in the sun-dappled hallway as if by magic, wiping her hands on a white apron.

'No, thanks. I'm not hungry.'

With a glance, he dismissed the housekeeper. His gaze returned to her, slowly tracing her face. When it rested on her mouth she struggled not to run her tongue over it, remembering how his eyes had darkened the last time she'd done that.

'I have a video call with Tom Brooks, my press liaison, in five minutes. Can I use your study?'

His eyes locked on hers. 'Why's he calling?'

'He wants to go over next month's sponsorship schedule. I can give you a final printout, if you like.'

She deliberately kept her voice light, non-combative. Something told her Marco de Cervantes was spoiling for a fight, and after his revelations she wasn't sure it was wise to engage him in one. Pain had a habit of eroding rational thought.

Being calmly informed by the doctor that she'd lost the baby she hadn't even been aware she was carrying had made her want to scream—loudly, endlessly until her throat gave out. She'd wanted to reach inside herself and rip her body apart for letting her down. In the end the only thing that had helped was getting back to the familiar—to her racing car. The pain had never left her, but the adrenaline of racing had eased her aching soul the way nothing else had been able to.

Looking into Marco's dark eyes, she caught a glimpse of his pain, but wisely withheld the offer of comfort on the tip of her tongue. After all, who was *she* to offer comfort when she hadn't quite come to terms with losing her baby herself?

Silently, she held his gaze.

For several seconds he stared back. Then he indicated his study. 'I'll set it up for you.'

She followed him into the room and drew to a stunned halt. The space was so irreverently, unmistakably male that her eyes widened. An old-style burgundy leather studded chair and footrest stood before the largest fireplace she'd ever seen, above which two centuries-old swords hung. The rest of the room was oak-panelled, with dusty books stretching from floor to ceiling. The scent of stale tobacco pipe smoke hung in the air. It wouldn't have been strange to see a shaggy-haired professor seated behind the massive desk that stood under the only window in the room. Compared to the contemporary, exceedingly luxurious comfort of the rest of the villa, this was a throwback to another century—save for the sleek computer on the desk.

Marco caught the look on her face and raised an eyebrow as he activated the large flat screen computer on the immense mahogany desk.

'Did your designer fall into a time warp when he got to this room?'

'This was my father's study—his personal space. He never allowed my mother to redesign it, no matter how much she tried.

He hasn't been in here since she died, and I…I feel no need to change things.'

A well of sympathy rose inside Sasha for his pain. Casting a look around, she stopped, barely suppressing a gasp. 'Is that a stag's head on the wall?' she asked, eyeing the large animal head, complete with gnarled, menacing antlers.

'A bull stag, yes.'

She turned from the gruesome spectacle. 'There's a difference?'

The semblance of a smile whispered over his lips. Sasha found she couldn't tear her gaze away. In that split second she felt a wild, unfettered yearning to see that smile widen, to see his face light up in genuine amusement.

'The bull stag is the alpha of its herd. He calls the shots. And he gets his pick of the females.'

'Ah, I see. If you're going to display such a monstrosity on your wall, only the best will do?'

He slanted her a wry glance. 'That's the general thinking, yes.'

'Ugh.'

He caught her shudder and his smile widened.

Warmth exploded in her chest, encompassed her whole body and made her breathless. Sasha found she didn't care. The need to bask in the stunning warmth of his smile trumped the need for oxygen. Even when another voice intruded she couldn't look away.

When Tom's voice came again she roused herself with difficulty from the drugging race of her pulse, carefully skirted a coffee table festooned with piles of books, and approached the desk as the screen came to life.

'Hello? Can you hear me, Sasha?' Tom's voice held its usual touch of impatience, and his features were pinched.

Marco's smile disappeared.

Sasha mourned the loss of it and moved closer to the screen. 'I'm here, Tom.'

He huffed in response, then his eyes swung over her shoulder and widened.

'Sit down,' Marco said from behind her, pushing the massive chair towards her.

She sat. He reached over her shoulder and adjusted the screen. Then he remained behind her—a heavy, dominating presence.

Tom cleared his throat. 'Uh, I didn't know you'd be joining us, Mr de Cervantes.'

'A last-minute decision. Carry on,' Marco instructed.

'Um…okay…'

She'd never seen Tom flounder, and she bit the inside of her mouth to keep from smiling.

'Sasha, you have a Q&A on the team's website next Friday. I've e-mailed the questions to you. I'll need it back by Wednesday, to proofread and get it approved by the lawyers. On Friday night you have the Children of Bravery awards in London. Tuesday is the Strut footwear shoot, followed by the Linear Watches shoot in Barcelona. On Sun— Is there a problem?' he asked testily when she shook her head.

'That's not going to work. I can't take all that time off just for sponsorship events.'

'This is the schedule I've planned. You'll have to deal with it.'

'Seriously, I think it makes more sense to group everything together and get it done in the shortest possible time—'

'*I'm* in charge of your schedule. Let *me* work out what makes sense.'

'Miss Fleming is right.' Marco's deep voice sounded from behind her shoulder. 'You have several events spaced out over the period of a week. That's a lot of time wasted travelling. Do you not agree?'

'But the sponsors—'

'The sponsors need to work around her schedule, not the other way round. They can have Thursday to Saturday next week. Otherwise they'll have to wait until the end of the month. Miss Fleming gets Sundays off. Your job is to manage her time properly. Make it happen.'

Marco reached past Sasha and disconnected the link. Although it was a rare treat to see Tom get his comeuppance, a large part of her tightened with irritation.

'I'm perfectly capable of arranging my own schedule, thank you very much.'

'It didn't seem that way.'

'Only because you didn't give me half a chance.' She craned her neck to gaze up at him, feeling at a severe disadvantage.

His head went back as he glared down his arrogant nose at her. 'I didn't like the way he spoke to you,' he declared.

Her heart lurched, then swung into a dive as a wave of warmth oozed through her. Sasha berated herself for the foolish feeling, but as much as she tried to push it away it grew stronger.

Despite the alien feeling zinging through her, she tried for a casual shrug. 'I don't think he likes me very much.'

A frown creased his forehead. 'Why not?'

Her bitter laugh escaped before she could curb it. Rising, she padded several steps away, breathing easier. 'Probably for the same reasons you don't. He doesn't think I have any business being a racing driver. He believes I've made him a laughing stock by association.'

'Because of your gender or because of your past indiscretions?'

'According to you they're one and the same, aren't they?' she retorted.

The hands gripping the back of the chair tightened. 'I told you in Budapest your gender had nothing to do with my decision to fire you. Your talent as a full-time racing driver is yet to be seen. Prove yourself as the talented racing driver you claim to be and you'll earn your seat. Until then I reserve my judgement.'

'You reserve your judgement professionally, but you're judge, jury and executioner when it comes to my personal life?'

A cold gleam had entered his eyes, but even that didn't stop her from staring into those hypnotising depths.

'We agreed that you will have *no* personal life until your contract ends, did we not? You wouldn't be thinking of reneging on that agreement so soon, would you?'

Sasha just stopped herself from telling him she already had no personal life. That she hadn't had one since Derek's lies and the loss of her baby had put her through the wringer. Rafael had been her one and only friend until that had headed south.

'Sasha.'

The warning in the way he said her name sent a shiver dancing down her spine. She glanced up at him and bit back a gasp.

When had he drawn so close? Within his eyes she could see the flecks of green that spiked from his irises. And the lashes that framed them were long, silky. Beautiful. He had beautiful eyes. Eyes that drew her in, wove spells around her. Tugged at emotions buried deep within her…

Eyes that were steadily narrowing, demanding an answer.

She sucked in a breath, her brain turning fuzzy again when his scent—lemony, with a large dose of man—hit her nostrils. 'No, Marco. No personal life. Not even a Labradoodle to cuddle when I'm lonely.'

A frown deepened. 'A what?'

'It's a dog. A cross between a Labrador and a poodle. I used to have one when I was little. But it died.'

'Pets have no place on the racing circuit.'

She glared at him. 'I wasn't planning on bringing one to work. Anyway, it's a moot point, since my schedule isn't conducive to having one. I detest part-time pet owners.'

Her phone buzzed in her back pocket. She pulled it out and activated it. Seeing the promised e-mail from Tom, she turned to leave.

'Where are you going?' he demanded.

She faked a smile to hide the disturbing emotions roiling through her body. 'Oh, I thought the inquisition was over. Only Tom has sent the Q&A and I want to get it done so I don't take up valuable race testing time.'

Her snarky tone didn't go unmissed. His jaw clenched as he sauntered over to her. She held her breath, forcing herself not to move back.

'The inquisition is over for now. But I reserve the right to pursue it at a later date.'

'And *I* reserve the right not to participate in your little witch hunt. I read the small print and signed on the dotted line. I know exactly what's expected of me and I intend to honour our agreement. You can either let me get on with it, or you can impede me and cause us both a lot of grief. Your choice.'

She sailed out of the room, head held high. Just before the door swung shut Sasha suspected she heard a very low, very frustrated growl emitted by a very different bull stag from the one hanging on the wall.

Her smile widened as she punched the air.

Marco didn't come back for dinner. Even after Rosario told her he'd gone to his office in Barcelona Sasha caught herself looking towards the door, half expecting him to stride through it at any second.

Luke had dropped off the engine testing results, which she'd pored over half a dozen times in between listening out for the sound of the helicopter.

Catching herself doing so for the umpteenth time, she shoved away from the table, ran upstairs to her suite and changed into her gym clothes.

Letting herself out of the side entrance, she skirted the pool and jogged along the lamplit path bordering the extensive gardens. Fragrant bougainvillaea and amaranth scented the evening air. She breathed in deeply and increased her pace until she spotted the floodlights of the race track in the distance. Excitement fizzed through her veins.

A few hours from now she'd start her journey to clear her father's name. To prove to the world that the Fleming name was not dirt, as so many people claimed.

Fresh waves of sadness and anger buffeted her as she thought of her father. How his brilliant career had crumbled to dust in just a few short weeks, his hard work and sterling dedication to his team wiped away by vicious lies.

The pain of watching him spiral into depression had been excruciating. In the end even his pride in her hadn't been enough...

Whirling away from her thoughts, and literally from the path, she jogged the rest of the way to the sports facility half a mile away and spent the next hour punishing herself through a strenuous routine that would have made Charlie, her physio, proud.

Leaving the gym, Sasha wandered aimlessly, deliberately emptying her mind of sad memories. It wasn't until she nearly stumbled into a wall that she realised she stood in front of a single-storey building. Shrouded in darkness, it sat about half a mile away from the house, at the far end of the driveway that led past the villa.

About to enter, she jumped as the trill of her phone rang through the silent night.

Hurriedly, she fished it out, but it went silent before she could answer it. Frowning, she returned it to her pocket, then rubbed her hands down her arms when the cooling breeze whispered over her skin.

Casting another glance at the dark building, she retraced her steps back to the villa. Her footsteps echoed on the marble floors.

'Where the hell have you been?'

Marco's voice was amplified in the semi-darkness, drawing her to a startled halt. He stood half hidden behind one of the numerous pillars in the vast hallway.

'I went to the gym, then went for a walk.'

His huge frame loomed larger as he came towards her. 'The next time you decide to leave the house for a long stretch have the courtesy to inform the staff of your whereabouts. That way I won't have people combing the grounds for you.'

There was an odd inflection in his voice that made the hairs on her neck stand up.

'Has something happened?' She stepped towards him, her heart taking a dizzying dive when he didn't answer immediately. 'Marco?'

'*Sí*, something's happened,' he delivered in an odd, flat tone.

He stepped into the light and Sasha bit back a gasp at the gaunt, tormented look on his face.

'Rafael... It's Rafael.'

CHAPTER FIVE

FEAR pierced through her heart but she refused to believe the worst. 'Is he…?' She swallowed and rephrased. 'How bad is it?'

Marco shoved his phone into his pocket and stalked down the hall towards the large formal sitting room. Set between two curved cast-iron balconies that overlooked the living room from the first-floor hallway, a beautifully carved, centuries-old drinks cabinet stood. Marco picked up a crystal decanter and raised an eyebrow. When she shook her head, he poured a healthy splash of cognac into a glass and threw it back in one quick swallow.

A fire had been lit in the two giant fireplaces in the room. Marco stood before one and raked a hand through his hair, throwing the dark locks into disarray. 'He's suffered another brain haemorrhage. They had to perform a minor operation to release the pressure. The doctors…' He shook his head, tightly suppressed emotion making his movements jerky. 'They can't do any more.'

'But the operation worked, didn't it?' She didn't know where the instinct to keep talking came from. All she knew was that Marco had come looking for her.

He sucked in a deep, shuddering breath. 'The bleeding has stopped, yes. And he's been put into an induced coma until the swelling goes down.'

She moved closer, her heart aching at the pain he tried to hide. 'That's good. It'll give him time to heal.'

His eyes grew bleaker. He looked around, as if searching for a distraction. 'I should be there,' he bit out. 'But the doctors think

I'm in their way.' He huffed. 'One even accused me of unreasonable behaviour, simply because I asked for a third opinion.'

The muttered imprecation that followed made Sasha bite her lip, feeling sorry for the unknown hapless doctor who'd dared clash with Marco.

She sucked in a breath as his gaze sharpened on her.

'Nothing to say?'

'He's your brother. You love him and want the best for him. That's why you've hired the best doctors to care for him. Maybe you need to leave them alone to do their jobs?' He looked set to bite her head off. 'And if he's in intensive care they probably need to keep his environment as sterile as possible. Surely you don't want anything to jeopardise his recovery?'

His scowl deepened and he looked away. 'I see you not only wear a psychologist's hat, you also dabble in diplomacy and being the voice of reason.'

Although Sasha did not enjoy his cynicism, she felt relieved that his voice was no longer racked with raw anguish. 'Yeah, that's me. Miss All-Things-To-All-People,' she joked.

Eyes that had moments ago held pain and anguish froze into solid, implacable ice. '*Si*. Unfortunately that aspect of your nature hasn't worked out well for my brother, has it? Rafael needed you to be *one* thing to him. And you failed. *Miserably.*'

'I tried to talk some sense into him…'

Rafael hadn't taken it well when she'd pointed out the absurdity of his out-of-the-blue proposal. He'd stormed out of her hotel in Budapest the night before the race, and she'd never got the chance to talk to him before his accident.

Marco turned from the mantel and faced her. 'Don't tell me… You were *conveniently* unsuccessful?' he mocked.

'Because he didn't mean it.'

He pounced. 'Why would any man propose to a woman if he didn't mean it?'

When she didn't answer immediately, his scowl deepened. In the end, she said, 'Because of…other things he'd said.'

'What *other* things?' came the harsh rejoinder.

'*Private* things.' She wasn't about to deliver a blow-by-blow account. It wasn't her style. 'I thought he was reacting to his last break-up.'

He dismissed it with a wave of his hand. 'Rafael and Nadia broke up two months ago. Are you suggesting this was a rebound?' Marco asked derisively. 'My brother's bounce-back rate is normally two *weeks*.'

Sasha frowned. 'Rafael's changed, Marco. To you he may have seemed like his normal wild, irreverent self. But—'

'Are you saying I don't know my own brother?' he demanded.

Slowly, Sasha shook her head. 'I'm just saying he may not have told you everything that was going on with him.'

Her breath caught at the derisive gleam that entered Marco's eyes.

'His text told me everything I needed to know. By refusing him, you gave him no choice but to come after you.'

'Of course I didn't!'

'Liar!'

'That's the second time you've called me a liar, Marco. For your own sake I hope there isn't a third. Or I'll take great pleasure in slapping your face. Contract or no bloody contract. Whatever Rafael led you to believe, I *didn't* set out to ensnare him, or encourage him to fall for me—which I don't think he did, by the way. And I certainly didn't get him riled up enough to cause his accident. Whatever demons Rafael's been battling, they finally caught up with him. I'm tired of defending myself. I was just being his friend. Nothing else.'

Heart hammering, she took a seat on one of the extremely delicate-looking twin cream and gold striped sofas and pulled in a deep breath to steady the turbulent emotions coursing through her. Emotions she'd thought buckled down tight, but which Marco had seemed to spark to life so very easily.

'I find it hard to believe your actions have taken you down the same path twice in your life.'

'An unfortunate coincidence, but that's all it is. I have to live with it. However, I refuse to let you or anyone else label me some sort of *femme fatale*. All I want is to do my job.'

He sat down opposite her. When his gaze drifted down her

body, she struggled to fight the pinpricks of awareness he ignited along the way.

'You're a fighter. I admire that in you. There's also something about you...'

His pure Latin shrug held a wealth of expression that made her silently shake her head in awe.

'An unknown quality I find difficult to pinpoint. You're hardly a *femme fatale*, as you say. The uncaring way you dress, your brashness, all point to a lack of femininity—'

Pure feminine affront sparked a flame inside her. 'Thanks very much.'

'And normally I wouldn't even class you as Rafael's type. Yet on the night before his accident he was fiercely adamant that *you* were the one. Don't get me wrong, he's said that a few times in the past, but this time I knew something wasn't quite right.'

Despite his accusation, sympathy welled inside her. 'Did you two fight? Was that why you didn't come to Friday's practice?'

His nod held regret. 'I lost it when he asked for the ring.'

'You had it?'

He pinched the bridge of his nose and exhaled sharply. 'Yes. It belonged to our mother. She didn't leave it specifically to either of us; she just wanted the first one of us to get married to give it to his bride.' He shook his head once. 'I always knew it would go to Rafael since I never intend—' He stopped and drew in a breath. 'Rafael has claimed to be in love with many girls, but this was the first time he'd asked for the ring.'

'And you were angry because it was me?'

His jaw clenched. 'You could have waited until the race was over,' he accused, his voice rough with emotion.

'Marco—'

'He'd have had the August hiatus to get over you; he would've mended his broken heart in the usual way—ensconced on a yacht in St Tropez or chasing after some Hollywood starlet in LA. Either way, he would've arrived back on the circuit, smiled at you, and called you *pequeña* because he'd forgotten your name. Instead he's in a hospital bed, fighting for his life!'

'But I couldn't lie,' she shot back. 'He didn't want me—not

really. And I'm not on the market for a relationship. Certainly not after—' She pulled herself up short, but it was too late.

He stood and pulled her up, caught her shoulders in a firm grip. 'After what?'

'Not after my poor track record.'

'You mean what happened with your previous lover?'

She nodded reluctantly. 'Derek proposed just before I broke up with him. I'd known for some time that it wasn't working, but I convinced myself things would work out. When I declined his proposal a week later he accused me of leading him on. He said I was only refusing him because I wanted to sell myself to the highest bidder.'

Derek had repeated that assertion to every newspaper and team boss who would listen, and Sasha's career had almost ended because of it. She pushed the painful memories away.

'Rafael knew there was no way I'd get involved with him romantically.'

Marco's grip tightened, his gaze scouring her face as if he wanted to dig out the truth. Sasha forced herself to remain still, even though the touch of his hands on her branded her—so hot she wanted to scream with the incredibly forceful sensation of it.

'Do you know the last thing I said to him?' he rasped.

Her heart aching for him, she shook her head.

'I told him to stop messing around and grow up. That he was dishonouring our mother's memory by treating life like his own personal playground.' His eyelids veiled his gaze for several seconds and his jaw clenched, his emotions riding very near the surface. 'If anything happens to him—'

'It won't.'

Without thought, she placed her hand on his arm. Hard muscles flexed beneath her fingers. His eyes returned to her face, then dropped to her mouth. Sharp sensation shot through her belly, making her breath catch.

Sasha felt an electric current of awareness zing up her arm—a deeper manifestation of the intense awareness she felt whenever he was near. *Comfort*, she assured herself. *I'm offering him com-*

fort. That's all. This need to keep touching him was just a silly passing reaction.

'He'll wake up and he'll get better. You'll see.'

Face taut and eyes bleak, he slowly dropped his hands. 'I have to go,' he said.

She stepped back, her hands clenching into fists behind her back to conceal their trembling. 'You're returning to the hospital?'

He shook his head. 'I'm going to Madrid.'

Her belly clenched with the acute sense of loss. 'For how long?' she asked lightly.

'For however long it takes to reassure my father that his precious son isn't dying.'

The state-of-the-art crash helmet was no match for the baking North Spanish sun. Sasha sat in the cockpit of the Espiritu DSI, the car that had won Rafael the championship the year before. Eyes shut, she retraced the outline of the Belgian race track, anticipation straining through her.

Sweat trickled down her neck, despite the chute pumping cold air into the car. When she'd mentally completed a full circuit she opened her eyes.

They burned from lack of sleep, and she blinked several times to clear them. She'd been up since before dawn, the start of her restless night having oddly coincided with the moment Marco's helicopter had lifted off the helipad. For hours she'd lain tangled up in satin sheets, unable to dismiss the look on Marcus's anguished face from her mind. Or the heat of his touch on her body.

Firming her lips, she forcibly cleared her mind.

She wrapped fireproof gloved hands around the wheel and pictured the Double S bends at Eau Rouge, and the exact breaking point at La Source. Keeping her breathing steady, she finally achieved the mental calm she needed to block out the background noise of the mechanics and the garage. She emptied every thought from her mind, the turmoil of the past few days reduced to a small blot. She welcomed the relief of not having to dwell on anything except the promise of the fast track in front of her.

Her eyes remained steady on the mechanic's *STOP/GO* sign, her foot a whisper off the accelerator.

When the sign went up, she launched out of the garage onto the track. Adrenalin coursed through her veins as the powerful car vibrated beneath her. Braking into the first corner, she felt G-forces wrench her head to the left and smiled. This battle with the laws of physics lent an extra thrill as she flew along the track, the sense of freedom making her oblivious to the stress on her body as lap after lap whizzed by.

'You're being too hard on your tyres, Sasha.'

Luke's voice piped into her earphones and she immediately adjusted the balance of the car, her grip loosening a touch to help manoeuvre the curves better.

'That's better. In race conditions you'll need them to go for at least fifteen laps. You can't afford to wear them out in just eight. It's early days yet, but things look good.'

Sasha blinked at the grudging respect in Luke's voice.

'How does the car feel?'

'Er…great. It feels great.'

'Good. Come in and we'll take a look at the lap times together.'

She drove back into the garage and parked. Keeping her focus on Luke as he approached her, she got out and set her helmet aside.

He showed her the printout. 'We can't compare it with the performance of the DSII, but from these figures things are looking very good for Spa in three weeks' time.'

Reading through the data, Sasha felt a buzz of excitement. 'The DSII is great at slow corners, so I should be able to go even faster.'

Luke grinned. 'When you have the world's best aerodynamicist as your boss, you have a starting advantage. We'll have a battle on the straight sections, but if you keep up this performance we should cope well enough to keep ourselves ahead.'

Again she caught the changed note in his voice.

Although she'd tried not to dwell on it, throughout the day, and over the following days during testing, Sasha slowly felt the changing attitude of her small team. They spoke to her with less condescension; some even bothered to engage her in conversation before and after her practice sessions.

And the first time Luke asked her opinion on how to avoid the under steering problem that had cropped up, Sasha forced herself to blink back the stupid tears that threatened.

Marco heard the car drive away as he came down the stairs. He curbed the strong urge to yank the door open and forced himself to wait. When he reached the bottom step he sat down and rested his elbows on his knees, his BlackBerry dangling from his fingers.

Light footsteps sounded seconds before the front door opened.

Sasha stood silhouetted against the lights flooding the outer courtyard, the outline of her body in tight dark trousers and top making sparks of desire shoot through his belly.

Clenching his teeth against the intensity of it, he forced himself to remain seated, knowing she hadn't yet spotted him in the darkened hallway. Her light wrap slipped as she turned to shut the door, and he caught a glimpse of one smooth shoulder and arm. Her dark silky hair was tied in a careless knot on top of her head, giving her neck a long, smooth, elegant line that he couldn't help but follow.

He found himself tracing the lines of her body, wondering how he'd ever thought her boyish. She was tall, her figure lithe, but there were curves he hadn't noticed before—right down to the shapely denim-clad legs.

Shutting the door, she tugged off her boots and kicked them into a corner.

She turned and stumbled to a halt, her breath squeaking out in alarm. 'Marco! Damn it, you *really* need to stop skulking in dark hallways. You nearly scared me to death!'

'I wasn't skulking.' He heard the irritation in his voice and forced himself to calm down. 'Where have you been? I called you several times.'

She pulled the wrap tighter around her shoulders, her chin tilting up in silent challenge. 'I went for a drink with the team.

They're all flying out tomorrow morning and I wanted to say goodbye. I know that wasn't part of the deal—me socialising with the team—but they kept asking and it would have been surly to refuse.'

Annoyance rattled through him. The last thing he wanted to discuss was his team, or the deal he'd made with Sasha Fleming. *Dios*, he wasn't even sure why he'd come back here. He should be by his brother's bedside—even if the doctors intended to keep him in his induced coma until the swelling on his brain reduced.

'And you were having such a great time you decided not to answer your phone?'

'I think it's died.'

'You *think*?'

'You're annoyed with me. Why?'

Sasha asked the question in that direct way he'd come to expect from her. No one in his vast global organisation would dare to speak to him that way. And yet…he found he liked it.

Rising, he walked towards her. A few steps away, the scent of her perfume hit his nostrils. Marco found himself craving more of it, wanting to draw even closer. 'Why bother with a phone if you can't ensure it works?'

'Because no one calls me.'

Her words stopped him in his tracks. For a man who commanded his multi-billion-euro empire using his BlackBerry, Marco found her remark astonishing in the extreme. 'No one calls you?'

'My phone never rings. I think *you* were the last person to call me. I get the occasional text from Tom, or Charlie, my physio, but other than that…zilch.'

Marco's puzzlement grew. 'You don't have any friends?'

'Obviously none who care enough to call. And, before you go feeling sorry for me, I'm fine with it.'

'You're fine with being lonely?'

'With being *alone*. There's a difference. So, is there another reason you're annoyed with me?'

She raised her chin in that defiant way that drew his gaze to her throat.

He shoved his phone into his pocket. 'I'm not annoyed. I'm tired. And hungry. Rosario had gone to bed when I arrived.'

'Oh, well, that's good. Not the tired and hungry part. The not annoyed part.' She bit her lip, her eyes wide on his as he moved even closer. 'And about Rosario...I hope you don't mind, but I told her not to wait up for me.'

Marco shook his head. 'So where did you go for this drink?' He strove to keep his voice casual.

'A bodega just off Plaza Mayor in Salamanca.'

He nodded, itching to brush back the stray hair that had fallen against her temple. 'And did you enjoy your evening out?'

Her shrug drew his eyes to her bare shoulder. 'Leon is beautiful. And I was glad to get out of the villa.'

Her response struck a strangely discordant chord within him. 'You don't like it here?'

'I don't mind the proximity to the track, but I was tired of knocking about in this place all by myself.'

Marco stiffened. 'Do you want to move to the hotel with the rest of the team?'

She thought about it. Then, 'No. The crew and I seem to be gelling, but I don't want to become overly familiar with them.'

Marco found himself breathing again. 'Wise decision. Sometimes maintaining distance is the only way to get ahead.'

'*You* obviously don't practise that dogma. You're always surrounded by an adoring crowd.'

'X1 Premier Racing is a multi-million-spectator sport. I can't exist in a vacuum.'

'Okay. Um...do you think we can turn the lights on in here? Only we seem to be making a habit of having conversations in the dark.'

'Sometimes comfort can be found in darkness.'

Facing up to reality's harsh light after his own crash ten years ago had made him wish he'd stayed unconscious. Angelique's smug expression as she'd dropped her bombshell had certainly made him wish for the oblivion of darkness.

Sasha gave a light, musical laugh. The sound sent tingles of pleasure down his spine even as heat pooled in his groin. His eyes fell to her lips and Marco experienced the supreme urge to kiss her. Or to keep enjoying the sound of her laughter.

'What's so funny?' he asked as she reached over his shoulder and flipped on the light switch.

'I was thinking either you're very hungry or you're very tired, because you've gone all cryptic on me.'

He *was* hungry. And not just for food. A hunger—clawing and extremely ravenous—had taken hold inside him.

Pushing aside the need to examine it, he followed her as she headed towards the kitchen. The sight of her bare feet on the cool stones made his blood thrum faster as he studied her walk, the curve of her full, rounded bottom.

'I could do with a snack myself. Do you want me to fix you something?'

Walking on the balls of her feet made the sway of her hips different, sexier. He tried to stop himself staring. He failed.

'You cook?' he asked past the strain in his throat.

'Yep. Living on my own meant I had to learn, starve or live on takeaways. Starving was a bore, and Charlie would've had conniptions if he'd seen me within a mile of a takeaway joint. So I took an intensive cookery course two years ago.'

She folded her wrap and placed it on the counter, along with a small handbag. Only then did he see that her top was held up by the thinnest of straps.

Opening the fridge, she began to pull out ingredients. 'Roast beef sandwich okay? Or if you want something hot I can make pasta carbonara?' she asked over her shoulder.

Marco pulled up a seat at the counter, unable to take his eyes off her. 'I'm fine with the sandwich.'

Her nod dislodged more silky hair from the knot on her head. 'Okay.' Long, luxurious tresses slipped down to caress her neck.

She moved around the kitchen, her movements quick, efficient. In less than five minutes she'd set a loaded plate and a bottle of mineral water before him. He took a bite, chewed.

'This is really good.'

Her look of pleasure sent another bolt of heat through him.

He waited until she sat opposite him before taking another bite. 'So, how long have you lived on your own?'

'Since…' She hesitated. 'Since my father died four years ago.'

She looked away, but not before he caught shadows of pain within the blue depths.

'And your mother? Is she not around?'

She shook her head and picked up her sandwich. 'She died when I was ten. After that it was just Dad and me.'

The sharp pain of losing his own mother surfaced. Ruthlessly, he pushed it away.

'The team are wondering how Rafael is,' Sasha said, drawing him away from his disturbing thoughts.

'Just the team?'

She shrugged. 'We're all concerned.'

'Yes, I know. His condition hasn't changed. I've updated Russell. He'll pass it on to the team.'

He didn't want to talk about his brother. Because speaking of Rafael would only remind him of why this woman who made the best sandwich he'd ever tasted was sitting in front of him.

'How is your father holding up?'

He didn't want to talk about his father either.

Recalling his father's desolation, Marco shoved away his plate. 'He watched his son crash on live TV. How do you think he's doing?'

A flash of concern darkened her blue eyes. 'Does he…does he know about me?' she asked in a small voice.

'Does he know the cause of his son's crash is the same person taking his seat?' He laughed. 'Not yet.'

He wasn't sure why he'd kept that information from his father. It certainly had nothing to do with wondering if his brother's version of events was completely accurate, despite Rafael's voice ringing in his head… *She's the one, Marco.*

Sasha's gaze sought his, the look into them almost imploring. 'I didn't cause him to crash, Marco.'

Frustrated anger seared his chest. 'Didn't you?'

She shook her head and the knot finally gave up its fight. Dark, silky tresses cascaded over her naked shoulders and everything inside Marco tightened. It was the first time he'd seen it down, and despite the fury rolling through him the sudden urge to sink his fingers into the glossy mass, feel its decadent luxury, surged like fire through his veins.

'Then what did? Something must have happened to make him imagine that idiotic move would stick.'

Her lips pursed. The look in her eyes was reluctant. Then she sighed. 'I saw him just before the race. He was arguing with Raven.'

Marco frowned. 'Raven Blass? His physio?'

She nodded. 'I tried to approach him but he walked away. I thought I'd leave him to cool off and talk to him again after the race.'

Marco's muttered expletive made her brows rise, but he was past caring. He strode into the alcove that held his extensive wine collection. 'I need a drink. White or red?'

'I shouldn't. I had a beer earlier.' She tucked a silky strand behind one ear.

Watching the movement, he found several incredibly unwise ideas crowding his brain. Reaching out, he grabbed the nearest bottle. 'I don't like drinking alone. Have one with me.'

Her smile caused the gut-clenching knot to tighten further. 'Is the great Marco de Cervantes admitting a flaw?'

'He's admitting that his brother drives him *loco*.' He grabbed two crystal goblets.

'Fine. I was going to add another twenty minutes to my workout regime to balance out the incredible *tapas* I had earlier. I'll make it an even half-hour.'

Marco's gaze glided over her. 'You're hardly in bad shape.'

Another sweet, feminine laugh tumbled from her lips, sparking off a frenzied yearning.

'Charlie would disagree with you. Apparently my body mass index is *way* below acceptable levels.'

Marco uncorked the wine, thinking perhaps Charlie needed his eyes examined. 'How long is your daily regime?'

'Technically three hours, but Charlie keeps me at it until I'm either screaming in agony or about to pass out. He normally stops once I'm thoroughly dripping in sweat.'

His whole body froze, arrested by the image of a sweat-soaked Sasha, with sunshine glinting off her toned body.

Dios, this was getting ridiculous. He should not be feeling like this—especially not towards the woman who was the every epitome of Angelique: ruthlessly ambitious, uncaring of anything that got in her way. Sasha had nearly destroyed his brother the way Angelique had destroyed Marco's desire ever to forge a lasting relationship.

And yet in Barcelona he'd found himself thinking of Sasha... admitting to himself that his sudden preoccupation with her had nothing to do with work. And everything to do with the woman herself. The attraction he'd felt in Budapest was still present... and escalating.

Which was totally unacceptable.

He took a deep breath and wrenched control back into his body. While his brother was lying in a coma, the only thing he needed to focus on was winning the Constructors' Championship. And teaching Sasha Fleming a lesson.

He poured bold red Château Neuf into one glass and set it in front of her. 'I've seen the testing reports. You'll need to find another three-tenths of a second around Eau Rouge to give yourself a decent chance or you'll leave yourself open to overtaking. Belgium is a tough circuit.'

She took a sip and his gaze slid to the feline-like curve of her neck. Clenching fingers that itched to touch, he sat down opposite her.

'The DSII will handle the corners better.'

His eyes flicked over her face, noting her calm. 'You don't seem nervous.'

Another laugh. A further tightening in his groin.

Madre di Dios. It had been a while since he'd indulged in good, old-fashioned, no-holds-barred sex. Sexual frustration had a habit of making the unsavoury tempting, but this...this yearning was insane.

Mentally, he scanned through his electronic black book and

came up with several names. Just as fast he discarded every one of them, weariness at having to disentangle himself from expectation dampening his urge to revisit old ground.

Frustration built, adding another strand of displeasure to his already seething emotions.

'Believe me, I get just as nervous as the next racer. But I don't mind.'

'Because winning is everything, no matter the cost?' he bit out.

Her eyes darkened. 'No. Because nerves serve a good purpose. They remind you you're human; they sharpen your focus. I'd be terrified if I wasn't nervous. But eighteen years of experience also helps. I've been doing this since I was seven years old. Having a supportive father who blatantly disregarded the fact that I wasn't a boy helped with my confidence too.'

'Not a lot of parents agree with their children racing. You were lucky.'

She smiled. 'More like pushy. I threw a tantrum every time he threatened to leave me with my nanny. I won eventually. Although I get the feeling he was testing me to see how much I wanted it.'

'And you passed with flying colours.' He raised his glass to her. 'Bravo.'

Unsettlingly perceptive blue eyes rested on him. 'Oops, do I detect a certain cynicism there, Marco?'

He clenched his teeth as his control slipped another notch. 'Has anyone told you it's not nice to always go for the jugular?'

Her eyes widened. 'Was that what I was doing? I thought we were having a get-to-know-each-other conversation. At least until you went a little weird on me.'

'*Perdón*. Weird wasn't what I was aiming for.' He took a large gulp of his wine.

'First an admission of a flaw. Now an apology. Wow—must be my lucky night. Are you feeling okay? Maybe it would help to talk about whatever it is that spooked you?'

Perhaps it was the mellowing effect of the wine. Perhaps it was the fact that he hadn't had an engaging conversation like this in a while. Marco was surprised when he found himself laughing.

'I have no memory of ever being spooked. But, just for curiosity's sake, which hat will you be wearing for this little heart-to-heart? Diplomat or psychologist?'

Her gaze met his squarely. 'How about friend?' she asked.

His laughter dried up.

She wanted to be his friend.

Marco couldn't remember the last time anyone had offered to be his friend. Betrayal had a habit of stripping the scales from one's eyes. He'd learnt that lesson well and thoroughly.

He swallowed another gulp of wine. 'I respectfully decline. Thanks all the same.'

A small smile curved her lip. 'Ouch. At least you didn't laugh in my face.'

'That would have been cruel.'

One smooth brow rose. 'And you don't do cruel? You've come very close in the past.'

'You were a threat to my brother.'

'*Were?* You mean you're not under that impression any more?'

Realising the slip, he started to set her straight, then paused. *You can't control what happens in life...Rafael will resent you for controlling his life...* 'I'm willing to suspend my judgement until Rafael is able to set the picture straight himself.'

Her smile faded. 'You don't trust me at all, do you?'

He steeled himself against his fleeting tinge of regret at the hurt in her voice.

'Trust is earned. It comes with time. Or so I'm told.'

So far no one had withstood the test long enough for Marco to verify that belief. Sasha Fleming had already failed that test. She was only sitting across from him because of what he could give her.

She hid her calculating nature well, but he knew it was there, hiding beneath the fiercely determined light in her eyes.

'Well, then, here's to earning trust. And becoming friends.'

Marco didn't respond to her toast because part of him regretted the fact that friendship between them would never be possible.

CHAPTER SIX

'THIS way, Sasha!'
'Over here!'
'Smile!'

The Children of Bravery awards took place every August at one of the plushest hotels in Mayfair. Last year Sasha had arrived in a cab with Tom, who had then gone on to ignore her for the rest of the night.

Tonight flashbulbs went off in her face the moment Marco helped her out of the back of his stunning silver Rolls-Royce onto the red carpet.

Blinking several times to help her eyes adjust, she found Tom had materialised beside her. Before he could speak, Marco stepped in front of him.

'Miss Fleming won't be needing you tonight. Enjoy your evening.'

The dismissal was softly spoken, wrapped in steel. With a hasty nod, a slightly pale Tom dissolved back into the crowd.

'That wasn't very nice,' she murmured, although secretly she was pleased. Her nerves, already wound tight at the thought of the evening ahead, didn't need further negative stimulus in the form of Tom. 'But thank you.'

'De nada,' he murmured in that smooth deep voice of his, and her nerves stretched a little tighter.

When he took her arm the feeling intensified, then morphed into a different kind of warmth as another sensation altogether enveloped her—one of feeling protected, cherished...

She applied mental brakes as her brain threatened to go into meltdown. Forcing herself away from thoughts she had no business thinking, she drew in a shaky breath and tried to project a calm, poised demeanour.

'For once I agree with the paparazzi. *Smile*. Your face looks frozen,' Marco drawled, completely at ease with being the subject of intense scrutiny.

He seemed perfectly okay with hundreds of adoring female fans screaming his name from behind the barriers, while she could only think about the ceremony ahead and the memories it would resurrect.

Pushing back her pain, she forced her lips apart. 'That's probably because it is. Besides, you're one to talk. I don't see you smiling.'

One tuxedo-clad shoulder lifted in a shrug. 'I'm not the star on show.' He peered closer at her. 'What's wrong with you? You didn't say a word on the way over here and now you look pale.'

'That's because I don't *like* being on show. I hate dressing up, and make-up makes my face feel weird.'

'You look fine.' His gaze swept over her. 'More than fine. The stylist chose well.'

'She didn't choose this dress. I chose it myself. If I'd gone with her choice I'd be half naked with a slit up to my cro—' She cleared her throat. 'Why did you send me a stylist anyway?'

When she'd opened the door to Marco's Kensington penthouse apartment to find a stylist with a rack of designer gear in tow, Sasha had been seriously miffed.

'I didn't want to risk you turning up here in baggy jeans and a hippy top.'

'I'd never have—!' She caught the gleam of amusement in his eyes and relaxed.

Another photographer screamed her name and she tensed.

'Relax. *You* chose well.' His gaze slid over her once more. 'You look beautiful.'

Stunned, she mumbled, 'Thank you.'

She smoothed a nervous hand over her dress, thankful her new contract had come with a lucrative remuneration package that meant she'd been able to afford the black silk and lace floor-length Zang Toi gown she wore.

The silver studs in the off-the-shoulder form-fitting design flashed as the cameras went off. But even the stylish dress, with its reams of material that trailed on the red carpet, couldn't stem the butterflies ripping her stomach to shreds as the media screamed out for even more poses. Nor could it eliminate the wrenching reason why, on a night like this, she couldn't summon a smile.

'Stop fidgeting,' he commanded.

'That's easy for you to say. Anyway, why are you here? I don't need a keeper.' Nor did she need the stupid melting sensation in her stomach every time his hand tightened around her arm.

'I beg to differ. This event is hosting many sport personalities, including other drivers from the circuit. Your track record—pardon the pun—doesn't stand you in good stead. The one thing you *do* need is a keeper.'

'And you're it? Don't you have better things to do?'

When he'd pointed out after they'd landed this morning that it was more time-efficient for her to stay with him in London, than to come to the ceremony from her cottage in Kent, she hadn't bargained on the fact that he'd appoint himself her personal escort for the evening.

His rugged good looks lit up in sharp relief, courtesy of another photographer's flash, but he hardly noticed how avidly the media craved his attention. Nor cared.

'The team has suffered with Rafael's absence. It'll be good for the sponsors to see me here.'

The warmth she'd experienced moments ago disappeared. She felt his sharp gaze as she eased her arm from his grasp.

'How long do we have to stay out here?' The limelight was definitely a place she wasn't comfortable in. However irrational, she always feared her deepest secret would be exposed.

'Until a problem with the seating is sorted out.'

She swivelled towards him. 'What problem with the seating?'

Relief poured through her as he steered her away from the

cameras and down the red carpet into the huge marble-floored foyer of the five-star hotel.

The crowd seemed to pause, both men and women alike staring avidly as they entered.

Oblivious to the reaction, Marco snagged two glasses of champagne and handed one to her. 'Some wires got crossed along the line.'

Sasha should have been used to it by now, but a hard lump formed in her throat nonetheless. 'You mean I was downgraded to nobody-class because my surname is Fleming and not de Cervantes?'

He gave her a puzzled look. 'Why should your name matter?'

'Come on. I may have missed school the day rocket science was taught, but I know how this works.' Even when the words weren't said, Sasha knew she was being judged by her father's dishonour.

'Your surname has nothing to do with it,' Marco answered, nodding greetings to several people who tried to catch his eye. 'When the awards committee learned I would be attending, they naturally assumed that I would be bringing a plus one.'

A sensation she intensely disliked wormed its way into her heart. 'Oh, so I was bumped to make room for your date. Not because…?'

He raised a brow. 'Because?'

Shaking her head, Sasha took a hasty sip of her bubbly. 'So why didn't you? Bring a date, I mean?' When his brow rose in mocking query, she hurried on. 'I know it's certainly not for the lack of willing companions. I mean, a man like you…' She stumbled to a halt.

'A man like me? You mean The Ass?' he asked mockingly.

Heat climbed into her cheeks but she refused to be cowed. 'No, I didn't mean that. The other you—the impossibly rich, successful one, who's a bit decent to look at….' Cursing her runaway tongue, she clamped her mouth shut.

'*Gracias*…I think.'

'You know what I mean. Women scale skylights, risk life and limb to be with you, for goodness' sake.'

'Skylight-scaling is a bit too OTT for me. I prefer my women to use the front door. *With* my invitation.' His gaze connected with hers.

Heat blazed through her, lighting fires that had no business being lit. His broad shoulders loomed before her as he bent his head. As if to… As if to… Her gaze dropped to his lips. She swallowed.

Chilled champagne went down the wrong way.

She coughed, cleared her throat and tried desperately to find something to say to dispel the suddenly charged atmosphere. His eyelids descended, but not before she caught a flash of anguish. Stunned, she stared at him, but when he looked back up his expression was clear.

'To answer your question, this is a special event to honour children. It's not an event to bring a date who'll spend all evening checking out other women's jewellery or celebrity-spotting.'

'How incredibly shallow! Oh, I don't mean you date shallow women—I mean… Hell, I've put my foot in it, haven't I?'

The smile she'd glimpsed once before threatened to break the surface of his rigid demeanour. 'Your diplomatic hat is slipping, Sasha. I think we should go in before you insult me some more and completely shatter my ego.'

'I don't think that's possible,' she murmured under her breath. 'Seriously, though, you should smile more. You look almost human when you do.'

The return of his low, deep laugh sang deliciously along her skin, then wormed its way into her heart. When his hand arrived in the small of her back to steer her into the ballroom a whole heap of pleasure stole through her, almost convincing her the butterflies had been vanquished.

The feeling was pathetically short-lived. The pictures of children hanging from the ceiling of the chandeliered ballroom punched a hole through the euphoric warmth she'd dared to bask in. Her breath caught as pain ripped through her. If her baby had lived she would have been four by now.

'Are you sure you're okay?' Marco demanded in a low undertone.

'Yes, I'm fine.'

Unwilling to risk his incisive gaze, she hurried to their table and greeted an ex-footballer who'd recently been knighted for his work with children.

Breathing through her pain, it took a moment for her to realise she was the subject of daggered looks and whispered sniggers from the other two occupants of the table.

Feeling her insides congeal with familiar anger, she summoned a smile and pasted it on her face as the ex-footballer's trophy wife leaned forward, exposing enough cleavage to sink a battleship.

'Hi, I'm Lisa. This is my sister, Sophia,' she said.

Marco nodded in greeting and introduced Sasha.

Sophia flashed Marco a man-gobbling smile, barely sparing Sasha a glance.

A different form of sickness assailed Sasha as she watched the women melt under Marco's dazzling charisma. Eager eyes took in his commanding physique, the hard beauty of his face, the sensual mouth and the air of authority and power that cloaked him.

He murmured something that made Sophia giggle with delight. When her gaze met Sasha's, it held a touch of triumph that made Sasha want to reach out and pull out her fake hair extensions. Instead she kept her smile and turned towards the older man.

If fake boobs and faker lashes were his thing, Marco was welcome to them.

Marco clenched his fist on his thigh and forced himself to calm down. He'd never been so thoroughly and utterly ignored by a date in his life.

So Sasha wasn't technically his date. So what? She'd arrived with him. She would leave with him. Would it hurt her to try and make conversation with *him* instead of engaging in an in-depth discussion of the current Premier League?

Slowly unclenching his fist, he picked up his wine glass.

Sasha laughed. The whole table seemed to pause to drink it in—even the two women who had so rudely ignored her so far.

By the time the tables were cleared of their dinner plates he'd had enough.

'Sasha.'

She smiled an excuse at the older man before turning to him. 'Yes?'

At the sight of her wide, genuine smile—the same one she'd worn when she'd offered her friendship at *Casa de Leon*—something in his chest contracted. He forced himself to remember the reason Sasha Fleming was here beside him. Why she was in his life at all.

Rafael. The baby brother he'd always taken care of.

But he isn't a child any more…

Marco suppressed the unsettling voice. 'The ceremony's about to start. You're presenting the second award.'

Her eyes widened a fraction, then anxiety darkened their depths.

'Yes, of course. I…I have my speech ready. I'd better read it over one more time, just in case…' Her hands shook as she plucked a tiny piece of paper from her bag.

Without thinking, he covered her hand with his. 'Take a deep breath. You'll be fine.'

Eyes locked onto his, she slowly nodded. 'I… Thanks.'

The MC took to the stage and announced the first award-giver. Sasha smiled and clapped but, watching her closely, Marco caught a glimpse of the pain in her eyes. Forcing himself to concentrate on the speech, he listened to the story of a four-year-old who'd saved her mother's life by ringing for an ambulance and giving clear, accurate directions after her mother had fallen down a ravine.

The ice-cold tightening his chest since he'd stepped from the car increased as he watched the little girl bound onto the stage in a bright blue outfit, her face wreathed in smiles. Forcing himself not to go there, not to dwell in the past, he turned to gauge Sasha's reaction.

She was frozen, her whole body held taut.

Frowning, he leaned towards her. 'This is ridiculous. Tell me what's wrong. *Now.*'

She jumped, her eyes wide, darkly haunted with unshed tears. Her smile flashed, only this time it lacked warmth or substance.

'I told you, I'm fine. Or I would if I'd remembered to bring a tissue.'

Wordlessly, he reached into his tuxedo jacket and handed her his handkerchief, a million questions firing in his mind.

Accepting it, she dabbed at her eyes. 'If I look a horror, don't tell me until I come back from the stage, okay?' she implored.

It was on the tip of his tongue to trip out the usual platitudes he gave to his dates. Instead he nodded. 'Agreed.'

Marco watched her gather herself together. A subtle roll of her shoulders and a look of determination settled over her features. By the time she rose to present the award her smile was fixed in place.

Watching the lights play over her dark hair, illuminate her beautiful features and the generous curve of her breasts, Marco felt the familiar tightening in his groin and bit back a growl of frustration.

'As most of you know, Rafael de Cervantes was supposed to present this award to Toby this evening. Instead he's skiving off somewhere in sunny Spain.'

Laughter echoed through the room.

'No, seriously, just as Toby said a prayer before rushing into his burning home to save his little sister and brother, so we should all take a moment to say a prayer for Rafael's speedy recovery. Toby fought for his family to live. Not once did he give up. Even when the rescuers told him there was no hope for his little brother he ignored them and rescued him. Why? Because he'd promised his mother he'd take care of his siblings. And he never once wavered from that promise. There are lessons for all of us in Toby's story. And that's never to give up. No matter how small or big your dreams, no matter how tough or impossible the way forward seems, never give up. I'm delighted to present this award to Toby Latham, for his outstanding bravery against all odds.'

Sasha's voice broke on the last words. Although she tried to hide it, Marco caught the strain in her face and the pain behind her smile even as thunderous applause broke out in the ballroom.

Automatically Marco followed suit, but inside ice clenched his heart, squeezing until he couldn't breathe. It was always like this when he allowed himself to remember what Angelique had taken from him. What his weakness had cost him. He'd failed to take care of his own.

Never again, he vowed silently.

Sasha stepped down from the stage and made her way back to her seat. Despite the rushing surge of memories, he couldn't take his eyes off her. In fact he wanted to jump up, grab her hand and lead her away from the ballroom.

She reached the table and smiled at him. 'Thank God I didn't fall on my face.'

Sliding gracefully into the seat, she tucked her hair behind one ear. In that moment Marco, struggling to breathe and damning himself to hell, knew he craved her.

Impossibly. Desperately.

Sasha caught the expression on Marco's face and her heart stopped.

'What's the matter? Oh, my God, if you tell me I have food caught in my teeth I'll kill you!' she vowed feverishly.

Desperately blinking back the threatening tears, she tried to stem the painful memories that looking into Toby Latham's face had brought. She couldn't afford to let Marco see her pain. The pain she'd let eat her alive, consume her for years, but had never been able to put to rest.

She heard sniggers from across the table but ignored them, her attention held hostage by the savagely intense look in Marco's eyes.

'Your teeth are fine,' he replied in a deep, rough voice.

'Then what? Was my speech that bad?' Caught in the traumatising resurgence of painful memories, she'd discarded her carefully prepared notes and winged it.

'No. Your speech was...*perfecto*.'

Her heart lurched at his small pause. Before she could question him about it the MC introduced the next guest. With no choice but to maintain a respectful silence, she folded her shaking hands in her lap.

Frantically, she tried to recall her speech word for word. Marco was obviously reacting to something she'd said. Had she been wrong to mention Rafael? Had her joke been too crass? A wave of shame engulfed her at the thought.

She waited until the next award had been presented, then leaned over. 'I'm sorry,' she whispered into his ear.

His head swivelled towards her. His jaw brushed her cheek, sending a thousand tiny electric currents racing through her.

'What for?' he asked.

'I shouldn't have made that crack about Rafael skiving off. It was tasteless—'

'And exactly what Rafael himself would've done had the situation been reversed. Everyone's been skirting around the subject, either pretending it's not happening or treating it with kid gloves. You gave people the freedom to acknowledge what had happened and set them at ease. I'm no longer the object of pitying glances and whispered speculation. It is I who should be thanking you.'

'Really?'

'Sí,' he affirmed, his gaze dropping to her mouth.

'Then why did you look so...*off*?'

His eyes darkened. 'Your words were powerful. I was touched. I'm not made of stone, Sasha, contrary to what you might think.'

The reproach in his voice shamed her.

'Oh, I'm sorry. It's just... I thought...'

'Forget it.'

He gave a tight smile, turned away and addressed Sophia, who flashed even more of her cleavage in triumph.

As soon as the last award was given, Sophia turned to Marco. 'We're going clubbing.' She named an exclusive club frequented by young royals. 'We'd love you to join us, Marco,' she gushed.

Sasha gritted her teeth but stayed silent. If Marco wanted

to party with the Fake Sisters it was his choice. All the same, Sasha held her breath as she waited for his answer, hating herself as she did so.

'Clubbing isn't my scene, but thanks for the offer.'

'Oh, we don't have to go clubbing. Maybe we can do something...*else*?'

Sasha stood and walked away before she could hear Marco's response.

She'd almost reached the ballroom doors when she felt his presence beside her. The wave of relief that flooded her body threatened to weaken her knees. Sternly, she reminded herself that Marco's presence had nothing to do with her personally. He was here for the team's sake.

'Are you sure you'd rather not be out with the Fa... Sophia? She seemed very eager to show you a good time. Seriously, I can take a taxi back.'

His limo pulled up. He handed her inside, then slid in beside her. 'I prefer to end my evening silicone-free, *gracias*.'

She laughed. 'Picky, picky! Most men wouldn't mind.'

Perfect teeth gleamed in the semi-darkness of the limo. 'I am not most men. No doubt you'll add *that* to my list of flaws?'

His eyes dropped to her chest, abruptly cutting off her laughter.

'You had better not be examining me for silicone. I'll have you know these babies are natural.'

'Trust me, I can tell the difference,' he said, in a low, intense voice.

She swallowed hard. The thought that she was suddenly treading unsafe waters descended on her. Frantically, she cast her mind around for a safe subject.

'So you don't like clubbing?'

'It's not how I choose to spend an evening, no.'

'Let me guess—you're the starchy opera type?'

'Wrong again.'

She snapped her fingers. 'I know—you like to stay indoors and watch game shows.'

Low laughter greeted her announcement. Deep inside, a tiny part of Sasha performed a freakishly disturbing happy dance.

Encouraged, she pressed on. 'Telemetry reports and aerodynamic calculations?'

'Now you're getting warm.'

'Ha! I knew you were a closet nerd!'

He cast her a wry glance. 'I prefer to call it passion.'

She shrugged. 'A passionate nerd who surrounds himself with a crowd but keeps his distance.'

He stiffened. 'You're psychoanalysing me again.'

'You make it easy.'

'And *you* make baseless assumptions.'

'Good try, but you can't freeze me out with that tone. You're single-minded to the point of obsession. I wiki-ed you. You have more money than you could ever spend in ten lifetimes and yet you don't let anyone close. You have the odd liaison, but nothing that lasts more than a few weeks. According to your girlfriends, you never stay over. And there's a time limit on every relationship.'

'You shouldn't believe everything you read—especially in the tabloid press.'

'Tell me which part is false,' she challenged.

His gaze hardened. 'I'll tell you which part is right—every relationship ends. For ever is a concept made up to sell romance novels.'

'Didn't you have a long liaison once, when you were still racing? What was her name…? Angela? Ange—?'

'Angelique,' he bit out, his face frozen as if hewn from rock. 'And she wasn't a liaison. We were engaged.'

'She must be the reason, then.'

Cold eyes slammed into her. 'The reason?'

'For the way you are?'

'Did Derek Mahoney turn you into the intrusive woman you are today?' he fired back, his tone rougher than sandpaper. 'Because I'd like to find him and throttle the life out of him.'

Sasha knew she should let it go. But somehow she couldn't.

'Yes. No.' She sighed and looked out of the window at Kensington's nightlife. 'Damn, I wish I smoked.'

An astounded breath whistled from his lips. 'Why would you wish that?'

'Because trying to have a conversation with you is exhausting enough to drive anyone to drink. But since I have to be up at the crack of dawn tomorrow, and I've reached my one-glass drink limit, smoking would be the other choice—if I smoked.' Abandoning the view, she turned back to him. 'Where was I?'

A mirthless smile lifted one corner of his mouth. 'You were dissecting my life and finding it severely deficient.'

'Mockery? Is that your default setting?'

He lowered his gaze to her lips and her insides clenched so hard she feared she'd break in half. The limo turned a sharp corner. She grabbed the armrest to steady herself. Too late she realised the action had thrust her breasts out. Marco's gaze dropped lower. Heat pooled in her belly. Her breasts ached, feeling fuller than they'd ever felt.

He leaned closer. Her heart thundered.

'No, Sasha,' he said hoarsely. '*This* is my default setting.'

Strong hands cupped her cheeks, held her steady. Heat-filled eyes stared into hers, their shocking intensity igniting a fire deep inside her.

Sasha held her breath, almost afraid to move in case…in case…

He fastened his mouth to hers, tumbling her into a none-too-gentle kiss that sent the blood racing through her veins. He tasted of heat and wine, of tensile strength and fiery Latin willpower. Of red-blooded passion and intoxicating pleasure. And he went straight to her head.

Sasha felt a groan rise in her throat and abruptly shut it off. She wasn't *that* easy. Although right now, with Marco's mouth wreaking insane havoc on her blood pressure, *easy* was deliciously tempting.

His tongue caressed hers and the groan slipped through, echoing in the dim cavern of the moving car. One hand slipped to her nape, angling her head. Although he didn't need to. She was willingly tilting her head, all the better to deepen the pressure and pleasure of his kiss. Her mouth opened, boldly inviting him in.

His moan made her triumphant and weak at the same time. Then she lost all thought but of the bliss of the kiss.

Lost all sense of time.

Until she heard the thud of a door.

Their lips parted with a loud, sucking noise that arrowed straight to the furnace-hot apex of her thighs.

Marco stared down at her, his breath shaking out of his chest. *'Dios,'* he muttered after several tense, disbelieving seconds.

You can say that again. Thankfully, the words didn't materialise on her lips. Her eyes fell to his mouth, still wet from their kiss, and the heat between her legs increased a thousandfold.

Get a grip, Sasha. She reined herself in and pulled away as reality sank in. She'd kissed Marco de Cervantes—fallen into him like a drowning swimmer fell on a life raft.

'We're here,' he rasped, setting her free abruptly to spear a hand through his hair.

'Y-yes,' she mumbled, cringing when her voice emerged low and desire-soaked.

With one last look at her, he thrust his door open and helped her out.

They entered the exclusive apartment complex in silence, travelled up to the penthouse suite in silence. Sasha made sure she placed herself as far from him as possible.

After shutting the apartment door he turned to her. Sasha held her breath, guilt rising to mix with the desire that still churned so frantically through her.

'I have an early start—'

'Sasha—'

Marco gestured for her to go first.

Sasha cleared her throat, keeping her gaze on his chest so he wouldn't see the conflicting emotions in her eyes. 'I have an early start tomorrow. So…um…goodnight.'

After a long, heavy pause, he nodded. 'I think that's a good idea. *Buenos noches.*'

All the way down the plushly carpeted hallway she felt his

gaze on her. Even after she shut the door behind her his presence lingered.

Dropping her clutch bag, she traced her fingers over her lips. They still tingled, along with every inch of her body. Resting her head against the door, she sucked in a desperate breath.

One hand drifted over her midriff to her pelvis, where desire gripped her in an unbearable vice of need. A need she had every intention of denying, no matter how strong.

Wanting Marco de Cervantes was a mistake. Even if there was the remotest possibility of a relationship between them it would be over in a matter of weeks. And she knew without a shadow of a doubt that it would also spell the end of her career.

And her experience with Derek had taught that no man—no matter how intensely charismatic, no matter how great a kisser—was worth the price of her dreams.

CHAPTER SEVEN

'Coffee...I smell coffee,' she mumbled into the pillow, the murky fog of her brain teasing her with the seductive aroma of caffeine. 'Please, God, let there be coffee when I open my eyes.'

Carefully she cracked one eye open. Marco stood at the foot of her bed, in a dark green T-shirt and jeans, a steaming mug in his hand.

'If I demand to know what you're doing in my bedroom so early, will you withhold that coffee from me?'

There was no smile this morning, just an even, cool stare, but awareness drummed beneath the surface of her skin nonetheless.

'It's not early. It's eight o'clock.'

With a groan, she levered herself up, braced her back against the headboard. 'Eight o'clock is the crack of dawn, Marco.' She held out her hand for the cup. He didn't move. 'Please,' she croaked.

With an uncharacteristically jerky movement he rounded the bed and handed it to her. Sasha tried not to let her eyes linger on the taut inch of golden-tanned skin that was revealed when he stretched. Her brain couldn't handle anything so overwhelming. Not just yet.

She took her first sip, groaned with pleasure and sagged against the pillow.

'You're not a morning person, are you?'

'Oops, my secret is out. I think whoever decreed that anything was important enough to start before ten o'clock in the morning should be hung, drawn and quartered.' She cradled the warm mug in her hand. 'Okay, I guess now I'm awake enough to ask what you're doing in my room.'

'I knocked. Several times.'

She grimaced. 'I sleep like the dead sometimes.' She took another grateful sip and just stopped herself from moaning again. Moans were bad. 'How did you know to bring me coffee?'

'I know everything about you,' he answered.

Her heart lurched, but she managed to keep her face straight. Marco didn't know about her baby. And she meant to keep it that way.

'I forgot. You have mad voodoo skills.'

His eyes strayed up from where he'd been examining the vampire on her T-shirt. 'No voodoo. Just mad skills. As to why I'm here—I have a meeting in the city in forty-five minutes—'

'On a Saturday?' She caught his wry glance. 'Oh, never mind.'

'I wanted to discuss last night before I left.'

Her breath stalled in her chest. 'Yes. Last night. We kissed.'

A sharp hiss issued from his lips. Then, '*Sí*, we did.'

She bravely met his gaze, even as her heart hammered. 'Before you condemn me for it, you need to know I don't make a habit of that sort of thing.'

His very Latin shrug drew her eyes to the bold, strong outline of his shoulders. 'And yet it happened.'

'We could blame the wine? Oh, wait, you barely touched your glass all evening.'

'How would you know? You were neck-deep in discussing the Premier League.'

She sighed. 'What can I say? I love my footie. Which club do you support?'

'Barcelona.'

She grimaced. 'Of course. You seem the Barcelona type.'

He shook his head. 'I don't even want to know what that means.'

Silence encased them. She took a few more sips of her coffee, instinctively sensing she'd need the caffeine boost to withstand what was coming.

Marco raised his head and looked at her. The tormented gleam in his eyes stopped her breath. 'What happened last night will not happen again.'

Despite telling herself the very same thing over and over last night, she felt a sharp dart of disappointment and hurt lance through her. She feigned a casual tone. 'I agree.'

'You belong to my brother,' he carried on, as if she hadn't spoken.

'I belong to no one. I'm my own person.'

His gaze speared hers. 'It can't happen again.'

Again the uncomfortable dart of pain. 'And I agreed with you. Are you trying to convince me or yourself?'

He shook his head. 'You know, I've never met anyone so forthright.'

'I believe in being upfront. I'm nobody's yes-woman. You need to know that right now. I kiss whomever I want. But kissing you was a mistake. One that I hope will not jeopardise my contract.'

His gaze hardened. 'You value being a racing driver more than personal relationships?'

'I haven't had a successful run with relationships but I'm a brilliant driver. I think it's wise to stick to doing what I do best. And I'd prefer not to lose my job because you feel guilty over a simple kiss. I also understand if you have some reservations because of your brother. Really, it's no big deal. There's no need to beat yourself up over it.'

Running out of oxygen, she clamped her mouth shut.

This was yet another reason why she hated mornings. At this time of day the natural barrier between her brain and her mouth was severely weakened.

Throw in the fruitless soul-searching she'd done into the wee hours, and the resultant sleep-deprivation, and who knew what would come of out her mouth next?

He shoved a forceful hand through his hair. '*Dios*, this has nothing to do with your contract. If you were mine to take I'd have no reservations. None. The things I would do to you. *With* you.'

He named a few.

Her mouth dropped open.

Lust singed the air, its fumes thick and heavy. Her fingers clenched around her mug. Silently, desperately, she willed it away. But her body wasn't prepared to heed her. Underneath her T-shirt her nipples reacted to his words, tightening into painful, needy buds.

'Wow! That's…um…super, *super*-naughty.'

Hazel eyes snapped pure fire at her. 'And that's just for starters,' he rasped.

Her breath strangled in her chest.

In another life, at another time…

No! Even in a parallel universe having anything to do with Marco would be bad news.

'I hear a *but* somewhere in there. Either you still think I'm poison or it's something else. Tell me. I can take it.'

He gave a jerky nod of his head in a move she was becoming familiar with. 'Last night, at the awards, you spoke of Rafael like a friend.'

'Because that's what he is. Just a friend.'

His jaw clenched. 'You're asking me to take your word over my brother's?'

'Not really. I'm saying give us both the benefit of the doubt. See where it takes you.'

He shook his head. 'As long as Rafael sees you as his there can be nothing between us.'

Despite the steaming coffee in her hand, she felt a chill spread through her. 'The message has been received, loud and clear. Was there something else?'

For a full minute he didn't answer. Then, 'I don't want you to think that the kiss has bought you any special privileges.'

'You mean like expecting you to bring me coffee every morning?' she replied sarcastically, a surprisingly acute pain scouring its acidic path through her belly.

'My expectations from you as a driver haven't changed. In fact nothing has changed. Understood?'

Setting down her mug on the bedside table, she hugged her

knees. 'All this angst over a simple kiss, Marco?' The need to reduce the kiss to an inconsequential blip burned through her, despite her body's insistence on reliving it.

He prowled to the window and turned to face her. 'Women have a habit of reading more into a situation than there actually is.' His raised hand killed her response. 'While taking pains to state the contrary. But I want to be very clear—I don't *do* relationships.'

Her breath fractured in her lungs. 'I'm not looking for one,' she forced out.

His whole body stiffened. 'Then it stands to reason that there shouldn't be a problem.'

She hugged her knees tighter. 'Again I sense a *but*.'

'*But*…for some reason you're all I think about.'

The statement was delivered with joyless candour. Yet her heart leapt like a puppet whose string had been jerked. And when his eyes met hers and she saw the heat in them something inside her melted.

He strode back towards the bed, shoving clenched fists into his pockets. She stared up at him, her pulse racing. 'And you're annoyed about that?'

His gaze raked her face slowly. Then slid to her neck, her breasts, and back up again. Molten heat burned in his eyes. 'Livid. Frustrated. Puzzled. Intensely aroused.'

Of their own volition her eyes dropped below his belt-line. Confronted with the evidence, she felt a deep longing melt between her legs. She swallowed as heat poured through her whole being.

Looking away, she muttered, 'Don't do that.'

A strained sound escaped his throat. 'I was just about to demand the same of you.'

'I'm not doing anything. You, on the other hand—you're…' She sucked in a desperate breath.

'I'm what?' he demanded, his voice low, ferocious.

'You're all brooding and…and fierce…and angry…and… aroused. You're cursing your desire for me and yet your eyes are promising all sorts of rampant steaminess.' Her eyes darted back to the bulge in his trousers and a lump clogged her throat. 'I...I think you should leave.'

'You don't sound very sure about that.'

'*I am.* I don't want you. And even if I did you're off-limits to me, remember? So you can't...can't present me with...*this*!'

A pulse jerked in his jaw. 'I never said the situation wasn't without complications.'

'Well, the solution is easy. You hired me to do a job so let me get on with it. We don't have to see each other until the season ends and we win the Constructors' Championship. We'll stand on the top podium and douse ourselves in champagne. Then we'll go our separate ways until next season starts.'

'And you will have fulfilled this promise you made?'

Surprise zapped through her. He remembered. 'Partly, yes,' she replied, before thinking better of it.

His gaze turned speculative. 'To whom did you make the promise?'

She dragged her eyes from his, the sudden need to spill everything shocking her with its intensity. But she couldn't. Marco didn't trust her. And she wasn't prepared to trust him with the sacred memory of her father.

She shook her head. 'It's none of your business. Are you going to leave me alone to get on with it?'

His mouth firmed into a hard line. 'The team has too much riding on this for me to take my eye off the ball at this juncture. So do our sponsors. Once you have proved yourself—'

'Yes, I've heard it all before.' She couldn't stop the bitterness from spilling out. 'Prove myself. Don't bewitch anyone on the team. *Especially* not the boss. Message received and understood. Perhaps you could take your frustrations elsewhere, then, and spare me the thwarted lust backlash?'

He stiffened with anger. '*Dios.* Has no one ever told you that the difference between attractive feistiness and maddening shrew is one bitchy comment too many?'

'No one has dared,' she threw back.

'Well, take it from me. You need to stop throwing blind punches and learn to pick your fights.' He strode towards the door. 'Romano will drive you to your appointment and bring you back here.'

'That's not necessary. I've hired a scooter.'

He whirled to face her. 'No. Romano will drive you.' His tone brooked no argument.

'Seriously, Marco, you need to dial back the caveman stuff—'

'And *you* need to take greater responsibility for your welfare. If you come off your scooter and break an arm or a leg the rest of the season is finished. I thought you wanted the drive? Or do you think you're invincible on those little piles of junk you like to travel on?'

She bit back a heated retort. Marco was right. All her hard work and sacrifice would amount to nothing if she couldn't ensure she turned up to her races with her bones intact.

'Fine. I'll use the car.'

Pushing back the covers, she slid her feet over the edge and stood. The air thickened once more as Marco tensed.

Sasha refused to look into his face. His brooding, tempting heat would weaken her sorely tested resolve.

'I need to get ready for the shoot.'

He made a sound she couldn't decipher. She squeezed her thighs together and fingered the hem of her T-shirt.

'Your breakfast will be delivered in half an hour.' He moved towards the door. 'Oh, and Sasha…?'

Unable to stop herself, she looked. Framed in the doorway, his stature was impressively male and utterly arresting. 'Yes?' she rasped.

'Unless you want things to slide out of control, don't wear that T-shirt in my presence again. You may not be mine, but I'm not a saint. The next time I see you in it I may feel obliged to take advantage of its instruction.'

His words hit her with the force of a tsunami. By the time he shut the door, a hundred different images of Marco using his teeth on her had short-circuited her brain.

The photo shoot was horrendously tedious. Several hours of sitting around getting her hair and make-up done, followed by a frenzied half-hour of striking impossible poses, then back to repeating the whole process again.

Sasha returned to the hotel very near exhaustion, but she had gained a healthy respect for models. She also now understood why men like Marco dated them. The sample pictures the photographer had let her keep showed an end result that surprised her.

After pressing the button for the lift, she fished the pictures out of her satchel, shocked all over again by how different she looked—how a few strokes of a make-up brush could transform plain to almost...*sexy*. Or was it something else? All day she'd been unable to dismiss last night's kiss from her mind. Her face burned when she reached the picture of her licking her tingling lips. She'd been recalling Marco's moan of pleasure as he'd deepened their kiss.

So really it was Marco's fault...

Opening the door to the suite, she stopped in her tracks as strains of jazz music wafted in from the living room. Following the sound, she entered the large, opulent room to find Marco lounging on the sofa, an electronic tablet in his hand and a glass of red wine on a table beside him.

'I thought you were going to be late?' The words rushed out before she could stop them. Her suddenly racing pulse made her dizzy for a few seconds.

His gaze zeroed in on her. 'I wrapped things up early.'

'And you couldn't find anyone in your little black book to spend the evening with?'

The thought that he hadn't gone out and vented his sexual frustration on some entirely willing female sent a bolt of elation through her, which she tried—unsuccessfully—to smash down.

She couldn't read the hooded look in his eyes as he set aside the gadget.

'It's only seven-thirty. The night is still young,' he replied.

Something crumpled into a small, tight knot inside her, and the sharp pang she'd felt that morning returned. 'That's just typical. You're going to call some poor woman out of the blue and expect her to be ready to drop everything to go out with you, aren't you?' she mocked.

One corner of his mouth quirked. 'Luckily, the women I know are kind enough to *want* to drop everything for me.'

She snorted. 'Come off it. We both know kindness has nothing to do with it.'

As she'd seen first-hand at the awards ceremony, women would crawl over hot coals to be with Marco. And many more would do so regardless of his financial status or influence. With a body and face like his, he could be penniless and still attract women with a snap of his fingers. As for that lethal, rarely seen smile, and the way he kissed—

Her thoughts screeched to a halt as he stood and came towards her.

'Maybe not,' he conceded, with not a hint of arrogance in sight. 'How was the shoot?'

The question wrenched her from her avid scrutiny of his body. 'Aside from the free shoes, it was a pain in the ass,' she replied.

'Of course,' he agreed gravely. Then without warning he reached out and plucked the pictures from her fingers. 'Maybe you'll even get around to wearing them instead of going barefoot or wearing those hideous boots—'

He stopped speaking as he stared at the pictures. Awareness crawled across her skin as he slowly thumbed through them, lingering over the one where she was draped over the bonnet of the not-yet-released prototype of his latest car, the Cervantes Triunfo. Eventually he returned to *that* one. And looked as if he'd stopped breathing.

'Marco…'

She stretched out her hand to retrieve the pictures. He ignored her, his attention fixed on the picture, his skin drawn tight over the chiselled bones of his face.

'Marco, I don't want to keep you. I have plans of my own.'

His head snapped up. 'What plans?' he demanded, his tone rough and tight.

Sasha couldn't think how to answer. Her whole mind was

paralysed by the way his eyes blazed. Shaking her head, she tried to turn away. He grabbed her arm in a firm hold.

No! Too hot. Too irresistible. Too much.

'Let me go,' she murmured, her voice scraped raw with desire.

'What plans?' he gritted out.

'Are you sure you want to know? You may not approve.'

His hand tightened on her arm, his eyes darkening into storm clouds that threatened thunder and lightning. 'Then think carefully before you speak.'

She sighed. 'Fine. You've busted me. I was going to beg your chef to make me that T-bone steak and salad he made for us yesterday, followed by chocolate caramel delight for dessert—I'll think about the calories later. Afterwards I intend to have a sweltering foursome with Joel, LuAnn and Logan.'

The hand that had started to relax suddenly tightened, harder than before.

'Excuse me?' Marco bit out, his voice a thin blade of ice slicing across her skin.

Reaching into the handbag slung over her shoulder, she pulled out the boxed set of her favourite TV vampire show.

He released her and reached for it. After scrutinising it, he threw it down onto the sofa along with the pictures.

'Take a piece of advice for free, *pequeña*. It's a mistake to keep goading me. The consequences will be greater than you ever bargained for.' His voice was soft. Deadly soft.

Sasha felt a shiver go through her. Most people mistakenly assumed partaking in one of the most dangerous sports in the world meant X1 Premier Racing drivers were fearless. Sasha wasn't fearless. She had a healthy amount of fear and respect for her profession. She knew when to accelerate, when to pull back the throttle, when to pull over and abandon her car.

Right now the look on Marco's face warned her she was skidding close to danger. She heeded the warning. Lashing out because of the maelstrom of emotions roiling inside her would most likely result in far worse consequences than she'd endured with Derek.

'Understood. Let me go.'

Surprise at her easy capitulation lit his eyes. Abruptly he released her.

'I need a shower. I guess you'll be gone when I come out. Enjoy your evening.'

Shamelessly, she fled.

Marco watched her go, frustration and bewilderment fighting a messy battle inside him.

He prided himself on knowing and understanding women. After Angelique, his determination never to be caught out again had decreed it. Women liked to think they were complicated creatures, but when it came down to it their needs were basic, no matter how much they tried to hide it. Hell, some—like Angelique—even spelled it out.

'I want fame, Marco. I want excitement! I can't be with a man who's a has-been.'

The memory slid in, reminding him why he now ensured the women he associated with knew there was no rosy future in store for them and had no surprises waiting to trap him.

A reality devoid of surprises suited him just fine.

His eyes followed Sasha's tall, slim figure down the hallway.

She surprised him, he admitted reluctantly. She also infuriated him. She made his blood boil in a way that was so basic, so...*sexual*—even without the benefit of those pictures...

Dios! With a growl, he whirled towards the window. When he'd gone to her room to set things straight this morning the last thing he'd expected was for her to reassure him that it had been no big deal.

Despite being totally into the kiss—as much as he'd been— she'd walked away from him last night. A situation he'd never encountered before.

Was it because she didn't really want him? Or was she merely waiting for his brother to wake up so she could resume where they'd left off?

Acid burned through his stomach at the thought. But even the corrosive effect couldn't wash away the underlying sexual need that seared him.

He'd rushed through his meeting with every intention of calling one of the many willing female acquaintants on his BlackBerry. But once he'd returned, his need to go out again had waned. He withdrew from examining why too closely.

He turned back from the window and his eyes fell on the pictures on the sofa. To the one of her draped all over his car...

Blindly he stumbled towards his jacket and dug around for his phone. Two minutes later reservations were made. By the time his Rolls collected him from the foyer, Sasha Fleming had been consigned to the furthest corner of his mind.

Marco stood outside the door ninety minutes later, caught himself listening for sounds from inside, and grimaced in disbelief. He'd spent the last hour or so wining and dining a woman whose name he couldn't now remember.

He'd stared at his date's in-your-face scarlet lips and thought of another set of lips. Plump, freshly licked lips, captured in perfect celluloid. Lips that had responded to his kiss in a way that had sent the most potent pulse of excitement through him.

Forbidden lips.

In the end he'd thrown down his napkin and extracted several large notes. 'You'll have to forgive me. I'm terrible company tonight. I shouldn't have disturbed your evening.'

The practised pout had reappeared. 'You know I'll forgive you anything, Marco.'

Candy? Candice? had leaned forward in another carefully calculated pose, designed to showcase her body to its best advantage.

'Listen, I have an idea. I know how much you like your coffee. When I was filming in Brazil last month I absolutely fell in love with the coffee and brought some back with me. Why don't we skip dessert and go back to my place and I'll give you a taste?'

Barely containing rising distaste, he'd shaken his head. 'Sorry, I'll take a rain check.'

He'd led her out amid soft protests and further throaty promises of the delights of her cafetière. But coffee, or sex with Candy/Candice had been the last thing on his mind.

His sudden hunger for chocolate caramel had become overpowering.

'Take my car. I'll walk,' he'd said.

And now here he stood, skulking outside his own apartment like a hormonal teenager on his first date.

He entered and approached the living room.

She was curled up on the sofa, a bowl of popcorn in her lap. Her head snapped towards him. As if she'd been listening out for him too. The thought pleased him more than it should have.

The striking blue of her eyes paralysed him.

'You're still awake.' *Excelente, Marco. First prize for stating the obvious.*

She blinked. 'It's only nine-fifteen.' Her eyes followed him as he shrugged off his jacket and dropped it on the sofa. When her gaze lingered on his chest he felt the blood surge stronger than before.

He watched her fingers dance through the bowl of popcorn, the movement curiously erotic. His heart hammered harder. 'You didn't have the chocolate caramel after all?'

'Charlie's disapproving face haunted me. Popcorn is healthier.' She looked away. 'So, how was your date?' she asked, her voice husky.

He wrenched his gaze from her fingers. 'You really want to know?'

Her sensual lips firmed and she shook her head.

The need to gauge her true feelings drew him closer. 'Jealous?'

She inhaled sharply. 'I thought we weren't doing this?'

His eyes fell to her lips. 'Maybe I've changed my mind.'

'Well, change it back. Nothing has changed since this morning. I can't handle your…baggage. And I don't want a relationship. Of any sort.'

Marco opened his mouth to tell her he didn't want anything from her either. But he knew he was lying. His very presence in this room belied that.

Forbidden or not, he wanted her with a compulsive need that unnerved and baffled him. But the fact that he wanted her didn't mean he would have her. He was known for his legendary control. He sat down next to her, caught her scent, and simply willed himself not to react.

Forcing his body to relax, he nodded towards the television. 'You have a thing for vampires?'

'Doesn't everyone?' she replied breathlessly.

He wanted to look at her. But he denied himself the urge and kept his gaze fixed ahead. 'What's the story about?'

She hesitated, fidgeted and sat forward. From the corner of his eye he saw her lick her lips. Fiery heat sang through his veins.

'Oh, you know—it's the usual run-of-the-mill storyline. Two brothers in love with the same girl.'

Something tightened in his chest and his stomach muscles clenched. 'I see.'

'You don't have to watch it.' She shifted backwards, out of his periphery.

'Why not? I'm intrigued.' The two male protagonists faced off on the screen, fangs bared. 'What are they doing now?'

Again she hesitated. 'They're about to fight to the death for her.'

His muscles pulled tighter. Blood surged through his veins and he forcibly relaxed the clenched fist on his thigh.

'Which one are you rooting for?' he asked, the skin on his nape curiously tight as he waited for her answer.

It occurred to him how absurd the conversation was. How absurd it was to be so wound up by a TV show. But every second he waited for her answer felt like an eternity.

'Neither.'

Illogically, his insides hollowed. 'You don't care if either one of them dies?' The words grated his throat.

'That's not what I said. I said neither because I know they won't kill each other. They might tear chunks out of each other, but ultimately they love each other too much to let a woman come between them. No matter how difficult, or how heart-wrenching it is to watch, I know they'll work it out. That's why I love the show. Popcorn?'

The bowl appeared in front of him.

He declined and nodded at the screen as a female character walked on. 'Is she the one?'

Sasha laughed. 'Yep. LuAnn—*femme fatale extraordinaire*. With those huge brown eyes and that body she can have any man she wants. On *and* off the screen.'

'She may look innocent onscreen but off-screen is another matter.'

It was her gasp that did it. That and her scent, mingled with the strangely enticing aroma of popcorn.

Control failed and his eyes met Sasha's stunning blue. Marco wondered if she knew how enthralling they were. How captivating. How very easily she could give LuAnn a run for her money.

'You've met her?'

'Briefly. At one of Rafael's parties.'

Her eyes returned to the screen. 'As much as I'm dying to know the details of your no-doubt salacious meeting, I don't really want the illusion spoiled. Do you mind?'

Again Marco was struck by Sasha's contrast to the other women he'd dated. They would have been bowled over by his mention of a celebrity, dying to know every single detail. Her refreshingly indifferent attitude made him relax a little more.

When he found himself munching on popcorn another bolt of surprise shot through him.

When was the last time he'd relaxed completely like this? Shared an enjoyable evening with a woman that hadn't ended in sex if he'd wanted it to?

He glanced at Sasha. Her eyes were glued to the screen, her lower lip caught between her teeth. Heat ratcheted through him. Correction—an evening that wasn't going to end in sex because sex was forbidden?

He reached for another mouthful of popcorn and his hand brushed hers. Her breath caught but she didn't look away from the screen. When he reluctantly forced his gaze away from her, he saw LuAnn caught in a heated clinch with Joel.

As a thirty-five-year-old man, who knew that sex onscreen was simulated, he shouldn't have found the scene erotic. Especially not with those damned fangs thrown in.

Nevertheless, when Sasha's breath caught for a second time he turned to her, his heart pounding so loudly in his ears he couldn't hear anything else.

'You should be watching the screen, not me.'

Her husky murmur thrummed along his nerve-endings and made a beeline for his groin.

'I was never much of a spectator. I prefer to be a participant.'

Dios! He was hard—so hard it was a toss-up as to whether the feeling was pain or pleasure. The logical thing to do was to get up, walk away.

Yet he couldn't move. Couldn't look away from this woman his body ached for but his mind knew he couldn't have.

Her eyes found his. 'Marco…'

Again it was a husky entreaty.

His fingers brushed her cheek. 'Why can't I get you out of my head? I took a beautiful woman to dinner but I can barely remember what she looked like now. I ate but hardly tasted the food. All I could think about was you.'

'Do you want me to apologise?'

'Would you mean it?'

Her pink tongue darted out, licked, darted back in. He groaned in pain.

'Probably not. But I may have an explanation for you.'

A few feet away the TV belted out the closing sequence of the show. Neither of them paid any attention. His forefinger traced her soft skin to the corner of her mouth, the need to taste her again a raging fever flaming through his veins. 'I'm listening.'

She shrugged. 'Maybe you share a trait with your brother after all. Deny you something and you want it more?'

Marco didn't need to think about it to answer. 'No. The difference between Rafael and me is that he wouldn't have hesitated to take—consequences be damned. He sees something he wants and he takes it.'

'Whereas you agonise about it endlessly, then deny yourself anyway? It's almost as if you're testing yourself—putting yourself through some sort of punishment.'

Her eyes darkened when he froze. She moved her head and

her lips came closer to his finger. Marco couldn't speak, needing every single ounce of self-control to keep his shock from showing. He *deserved* to put himself through punishment for what he'd done. He'd lost the most precious thing in life—a child—because he'd taken his eye off the ball.

'Maybe you should learn to bend a little...take what is being offered? What is being offered freely.'

An arrow of pain shot through the haze of desire engulfing him. He gave a single shake of his head and inhaled. 'I stopped believing in *free* a long time ago, Sasha. There are always consequences. The piper always expects payment.'

'I don't believe that. Laughter is free. Love is free. It's hate that eats you up inside. Bitterness that twists feelings if you let them. And, no, I'm not waxing philosophical. I've experienced it.'

'Really?' he mocked, dropping his hand. When his senses screeched in protest he merely willed the feeling away. 'To whom did you make your promise?' he asked, the need to know as forceful as the need raging through his veins.

Wariness darkened her eyes. Then her shoulders rolled. 'My father.'

'What did you promise him?'

'That I'd win the Drivers' Championship for him.'

'Out of some misguided sense of duty, no doubt?' he derided.

Anger blazed through her eyes. 'Not duty. *Love.* And it's about as misguided as your bullheaded need to coddle Rafael.'

'There's a difference between responsibility and your illusionary love,' he rebutted, irate at this turn of the conversation.

'I suffer no illusions. My father loved me as unconditionally as I loved him.'

Tensing, he sat back in the seat. 'Then you were lucky. Not everyone is imbued with unconditional love for his or her child. Some even use their unborn children as bartering tools.'

Her breath caught. 'Did you...? Are you saying that from experience?'

A cold drench of reality washed over him at how close he'd come to revealing everything.

Surging to his feet, he stared into her face. 'I was merely making a point. As much as I want you, Sasha, I'll never take you. The consequences would be too great.'

CHAPTER EIGHT

The consequences would be too great.

Sasha tried to block out the words as she adjusted the traction control on her steering wheel. The tremor in her fingers increased and she clenched her fists tighter around the wheel.

Shears, Marina Bay, Raffles Boulevard. Watch out for Turn Ten speed bump—Padang, pit lane exit, look after the tyres...

Her heart hammered, excitement and adrenaline shooting through her as she went through the rigorous ritual of visualising every corner of the race. At her third attempt, fear rose to mingle with her emotions.

She'd secured pole position for the first time in her racing career, but despite the team's euphoria afterwards she'd sensed a subtle waning of their excitement as speculation as to whether she could do the job trickled in. Sasha had seen it in their faces, heard it in Luke's voice this morning when he'd grilled her over race strategy for the millionth time. Even Tom had weighed in.

Consequences...responsibility...last chance...

Sweat trickled down her neck and she hastily sipped at her water tube. She couldn't afford dehydration. Couldn't afford to lose focus. In fact she couldn't afford to do anything less than win.

Beyond the bright lights of the circuit that turned night into day at the Singapore Grand Prix thousands of fans would be watching.

As would Marco.

He hadn't spoken to her since that night on his sofa in London, but he'd attended every race since the season had resumed and Sasha knew he was somewhere above her, in the exclusive VIP suite of the team's motor home, hosting the Prime Minister, royalty and a never-ending stream of celebrities.

Some time during the sleepless night, when she'd been looking down at the race track from her hotel room, she'd wondered whether he'd even bother to grace the pit with his presence if she made it onto that final elusive step on the podium. Or whether he would be too preoccupied with entertaining his latest flame—the blonde daughter of an Italian textile magnate who never seemed far from his side nowadays.

She tried desperately to block him from her mind. Taking pole position today—a dream she'd held for longer than she could remember—should be making her ecstatic. She was one step further towards removing the dark stain of her father's shame from people's minds. To finally removing herself from Derek's malingering shadow.

Yet all she could think about was Marco and their conversation in London.

She clenched her teeth in frustration and breathed in deeply.

Luke's voice piped through her helmet, disrupting her thoughts.

'Adjust your clutch—'

She flicked the switch before he'd finished speaking. The sheer force of her will to win was a force field around her. Finally she found the zen she desperately craved.

Focusing, she followed the red lights as they lit up one by one. Adrenaline rushed faster, followed a second later by the drag of the powerful car as she pointed it towards the first corner.

She made it by the skin of her teeth, narrowly missing the front wing of the number two driver. Her stomach churned through lap after gruelling lap, even after she'd established a healthy distance between her and the car behind.

What seemed like an eternity later, after a frenzied race, including an unscheduled pitstop that had raised the hairs on her arms, she heard the frenzied shouts of her race engineer in her ear.

'You won! Sasha, you won the Singapore Grand Prix!'

Tears prickled her eyes even as her fist pumped through the air. Her father's face floated through her mind and a sense of peace settled momentarily over her. It was broken a second later by the sound of the crowd's deafening roar.

Exiting the car, Sasha squinted through the bright flashes of the paparazzi, desperate to see familiar hazel eyes through the sea of faces screaming her name.

No Marco.

A stab of disappointment hollowed out her stomach. With a sense of detachment, she accepted the congratulations of her fellow drivers and blinked back tears through the British national anthem.

Dad would be proud, she reminded herself fiercely. *He* was all that mattered. Plastering a smile on her face, she accepted her trophy from the Prime Minister.

This was what she wanted. What she'd fought for. The team—*her* team—were cheering wildly. Yet Sasha felt numb inside.

Fighting the alarming emptiness, she picked up the obligatory champagne magnum, letting the spray loose over her fellow podium winners. Brusquely she told herself to live in the moment, to enjoy the dream-come-true experience of winning her first race.

Camera flashes blinded her as she stepped off the podium. When it cleared Tom stood in front of her, a huge grin on his face.

'I *knew* you could do it! Prepare yourself, Sasha. Your world's about to rock!'

The obligatory press conference for the top three winning drivers took half an hour. When she emerged, Tom grabbed her arm and steered her towards the bank of reporters waiting behind the barriers.

'Tom, I don't really want—'

'You've just won your first race. *"I don't really want"* shouldn't feature in your vocabulary. The world's your oyster.'

But I don't want the world, she screamed silently. *I want Marco. I want not to feel alone on a night like this.*

Feeling the stupid tears build again, Sasha rapidly blinked them back as a microphone was thrust in her face.

'How does it feel to be the first woman to win the Singapore Grand Prix?'

From deep inside she summoned a smile. 'Just as brilliant as the first man felt when he won, I expect.'

Beside her she heard Tom's sharp intake of breath.

Behave, Sasha.

'Are you still involved with Rafael de Cervantes?' asked an odious reporter she recognised from a Brazilian sports channel.

'Rafael and I were never involved. We're just friends.'

'So now he's in a coma there's nothing to stop you from switching *friendships* to his brother, no?'

Tom stepped forward. 'Listen, mate—'

Sasha stopped him. 'No. It's fine.' She faced the reporter. 'Marco de Cervantes is a world-class engineer and a visionary in his field. His incredible race car design is the reason we won the race today. It would be an honour for me to call him my friend.' She tagged on another smile and watched the reporter's face droop with disappointment.

Tom nodded at a British female reporter. 'Next question.'

'As the winner of the race, you'll be the guest of honour at the rock concert. What will you be wearing?'

Mild shock went through her at the question, followed swiftly by a deepening sense of hollowness. The X1 Premier Rock Concert had become a fixture on every A-List celebrity's calendar. No doubt Marco would be there with his latest girlfriend.

'It doesn't matter what I'll be wearing because I'm not going to the concert.'

Sasha dashed into the foyer of her six-star hotel, grateful when the two burly doormen blocked the chasing paparazzi. She heaved in a sigh of relief when she shut her suite door behind her.

The ever-widening chasm of emptiness she couldn't shake threatened to overwhelm her. Quickly she stripped off her clothes and showered.

The knock came as she was towelling herself dry. For a second she considered not answering it.

A sense of *déjà vu* hit her as she opened the door to another perfectly coiffed stylist, carting another rack of clothes.

'I think you've got the wrong suite.'

The diminutive Asian woman in a pink suit simply bowed, smiled and let herself in. Her assistant sailed in behind her, clutching a large and stunningly beautiful bouquet of purple lilies and cream roses.

'For you.' She thrust the flowers and a long oblong box into Sasha's hand.

Stifling a need to scream, Sasha calmly shut the door and opened the box. On a red velvet cushion lay the most exquisite diamond necklace she'd ever seen. With shaking fingers, she plucked the card from the tiny peg.

Pick a dress, then they'll leave. Romano is waiting downstairs.

Sasha stared at Marco's bold scrawl in disbelief. When she looked up, the women smiled and started pulling clothes off the hangers.

'No—wait!'

'No wait. Twenty minutes.'

'But...where am I going?' she asked.

The stylist shrugged, picked up a green-sequinned dress barely larger than a handkerchief, and advanced towards her. Sasha stepped back as the tiny woman waved her hand in front of her.

'Off.'

With a sense of damning inevitability...and more than a little thrill of excitement...she let herself be pulled forward. 'Okay, but definitely not the green.'

The stylist nodded, trilled out an order in Mandarin, and advanced again with another dress.

Twenty minutes later Sasha stepped from the cool, air-conditioned car onto another red carpet. This time, without

Marco, she was even more self-conscious than before. On a warm, sultry Singapore night, the cream silk dress she'd chosen felt more exposing than it had in the safety of her hotel room. At first glance she'd refused to wear the bohemian mini-dress because…well, because it had no back. But then the stylist had fastened the draping material across her lower back and Sasha had felt…*sexy*—like a woman for the first time in her life.

Her hair was fastened with gold lamé rope, her nails polished and glittering. The look was completed with four-inch gold stilettos she'd never dreamt she'd be able to walk in, but she found it surprisingly easy.

Romano appeared at her side, his presence a reminder that somewhere beyond the wild flashes of the paparazzi's cameras Marco was waiting for her.

All the way from her hotel she'd felt the emptiness receding, but had been too scared to acknowledge that Marco had anything to do with it. Now she couldn't stop a smile from forming on her face as the loud boom of fireworks signalled the start of the rock concert.

The VIP lounge teemed with rock stars and pop princesses. She tried to make small talk as she surreptitiously searched the crowd for Marco. Someone thrust a glass of champagne in her hand.

Half an hour later, when a Columbian platinum-selling songstress with snake hips asked who her designer was, Sasha started to answer, then stopped as an ice-cold thought struck her. Was Marco even here? Had she foolishly misinterpreted his note and dressed up only to be stood up?

The depths of her hurt stunned her into silence.

She barely felt any remorse as the pop star flounced off in a huff. Blindly she turned for the exit, humiliation scouring through her.

'Sasha? You're heading for the stage, right?' Tom grabbed her arm and stopped her.

'The…the stage?'

'Your favourite band is about to perform. Marco had me fly them out here just for you.'

'He *what*?' A different kind of *stun* stopped her heart.

'Come on—you don't want them to start without you.'

A thousand questions raced through her brain, but she didn't have time to voice a single one before she was propelled onto the stage and into the arms of the band's lead singer.

Torn between awe at sharing the stage with her favourite band, and happiness that she hadn't misinterpreted Marco's note after all, Sasha knew the next ten minutes were the most surreal of her life. Even seeing herself super-sized on half a dozen giant screens didn't freak her out as much as she'd imagined.

She exited the stage to the crowd's deafening roar. Tom beamed as he helped her down the stairs.

'Have you seen Marco?' Sasha attributed her breathlessness to her onstage excitement—not her yearning to see Marco de Cervantes.

Tom's smile slipped and his gaze dropped. 'Um, he was around a moment ago…'

She told herself not to read anything into Tom's answer. 'Where is he?'

'Sasha…' He sighed and pointed towards the roped-off area manned by three burly bodyguards.

At first she didn't see him, her sight still fuzzy from the bright stage lights.

When she finally focused, when she finally saw what her mind refused to compute, Sasha was convinced her heart had been ripped from her chest.

Each step she took out of the concert grounds felt like a walk towards the opening mouth of a yawning chasm. But Sasha forced herself to keep going, to smile, to acknowledge the accolades and respect she finally had from her team.

Even though inside she was numb and frozen.

The knock came less than ten minutes later.

Marco leaned against the lintel. The buttons of his shirt were *still* undone; his hair was unkempt. As if hands—*female hands*—had run through it several times. He stood there, arrogantly imposing, larger than life.

She hated him more than she could coherently express. And yet the sight of him kicked her heart into her throat.

'What do you want?' she blurted past the pain in her throat.

His gaze, intense and unnerving, left her face to take in the bikini she'd changed into. 'Why did you leave the concert?'

'Why aren't you back there, being pawed by your Italian sexpot?'

'You left because you saw me with Flavia?'

'You know what they say—two's company, three's a flash mob. Now, if you'll excuse me...' She grabbed her kaftan from the bed and the box containing the diamond necklace.

'Here—take this back. I don't want it.'

'It's yours. Every member of the team receives a gift for the team's win. This is yours.'

Her mouth dropped open. 'You're kidding me?'

'I'm not. Where are you going?'

She stared at the box, not sure how to refuse the gift now. 'For a swim—not that it's any of your business.'

'A swim? At this hour?'

'Singapore is the longest race on the calendar. It's even longer when you're leading and trying to defend your position. If I don't warm up and do my stretching exercises my muscles will seize up. That's what I'd planned to do before... Whatever—will you please get out of my way?'

His gaze dropped to her legs. A hoarse sound rumbled from his throat. A look entered his eyes—one that made her excited and afraid at the same time.

'Marco, I said—'

'I heard you.' Still, he didn't move away. Instead, he extracted his phone and issued a terse command in Spanish, his gaze on her the whole time.

Sasha dropped the box on the bed and took a deep calming breath, willing her skin to stop tingling, her heartbeat to slow down. Her senses were too revved up, ready to unleash the full power of her conflicted feelings for this man.

'Let's go.' He finally moved out of the doorway.

'I'm not going anywhere with you until you tell me what you're doing here,' she responded.

He speared a hand through his hair, mussing up the luxurious strands even more. 'Does it matter why I'm here, Sasha? Are you happy to see me?' he demanded in a low, charged tone.

She hated the fire that raced through her veins, stinging her body to painful life in a way even her first race win hadn't been able to achieve.

'Less than half an hour ago you had another woman all over you. Last time I checked, my name wasn't Sloppy Seconds Sasha.'

He swore under his breath. 'You know, you're the most difficult, infuriating woman I know.'

Despite the raspy vehemence in his tone, she smiled. 'Thank you.'

He took her arm and led her to the lift. 'It wasn't a compliment.'

'I know. But I'll take it as one.' She tried not to breathe too deeply of his scent as he stepped in beside her.

The lift whisked them upwards. From the corner of her eye she saw him turn his phone off and shove it into his pocket.

The doors opened onto a space that was so beautiful Sasha couldn't speak for several seconds. In the soft breeze potted palm trees swayed. Strategically placed lights gave the space an exotic but intimate feel that just begged to be enjoyed. Several feet away an endless, boomerang shaped infinity pool poised over the tip of the hotel's tower glimmered blue and silver.

Then she noticed what was missing. 'It's empty.' There wasn't a single soul on the sixtieth-floor skydeck.

'Sí.'

The way he responded had her turning to face him.

'You had something to do with it?'

A simple nod.

'Why?'

His shook his head in disbelief. 'That's the hundredth question you've asked since I knocked on your door. I didn't want your swim to be interrupted.'

She kicked away her slippers, her temperature rising another notch when his gaze dropped to her bare feet. 'This pool is three times the size of an Olympic pool. It's hardly cramped.'

His gaze turned molten. 'I wanted privacy.' He released the last button on his shirt and it fell open to reveal a golden washboard torso.

Heat piled on. Beneath the Lycra bikini, her nipples tightened, and her stomach muscles quivered with a need so strong she could barely breathe. 'I see. Will you snarl at me if I ask why?'

'Yes,' he snarled.

Striding to her, he drew the hem of her kaftan over her head and tossed it over his shoulder. Then he took her hair tie, raked his fingers through the strands and secured her hair on top of her head.

Fresh waves of desire threatened to drown her. 'Marco...'

'How many laps do you need to be less tense?'

'Tw—twenty.' She couldn't drag her eyes from the beauty of his face, from the sensual, inviting curve of his mouth.

'Twenty laps it is, then.' He shrugged off his shirt, then released his belt.

Her eyes widened. 'What are you doing?'

'What does it look like?'

'Um...'

Without warning he leaned forward and sniffed the skin between her neck and shoulder. 'You're covered in *eau de* Sleazy Rock Star. I smell of cloying Italian perfume. What say we wash the scent of other people off our skin, and then we'll talk, *sí*?

'Marco...'

He swore under his breath. 'Go, Sasha. I need to cool off, or *Dios* help me, I won't be responsible for my actions.'

She went, with the heaviness of his hot gaze scorching her skin.

Pausing at one end of the pool, she stretched her arms over her head. At his sharp intake of breath, she let a sensual smile curve her lips.

The water was a welcome but temporary relief from the sensations arcing between them. He dived in after her a second later, quickly caught up with her and matched her stroke for stroke. When she swam faster, to escape the frenzied need clawing inside, he kept up with her.

His presence made every stroke of water against her skin feel like a caress. At the last lap he increased his pace and heaved himself out of the water. She clung to the side, her lungs heaving, and watched the play of water on his magnificent body as he returned to the poolside.

'Out,' he commanded tersely, his hand holding out a towel like a bull-baiting matador.

She rose out of the pool, careful not to look at the wet clinginess of his boxers. He folded the towel around her, his movements brisk as he rubbed the moisture off her. Then he swung her into his arms and carried her to the enclosed cabana a few feet away.

Two silk-covered loungers stood side by side, separated by a table laid out with several platters of food, from local delicacies to caviar on blinis. In a sterling silver tub a linen-draped bottle of vintage champagne chilled on ice.

Marco set her down on the lounger and picked up the bottle.

Sasha forced her gaze from the play of muscles and looked at the table. 'There's enough here to feed an army.' Reaching for a small plate, she dished out grilled prawns and fragrant rice.

'You don't like caviar?'

She grimaced. 'It smells funny and tastes disgusting. I don't know why people eat the stuff.' She took a mouthful of her food and felt the explosion of textures on her tongue. Thankfully she managed to swallow without choking. 'Now, *this* is heavenly.' She took another mouthful and groaned.

Marco took his seat across from her and held out one glass of champagne, his gaze never leaving hers. What she glimpsed in the heated depths made her heart quicken.

'Marco—'

'Eat. We'll talk when you're done.'

How can I eat? she wanted to ask. Especially when his eyes followed her every move. But words refused to form on her lips.

It was as if he'd cast some sort of spell on her. Maybe he was a vampire after all, she thought hysterically.

The thought should have lightened her mood, made it easier for her to cope, but all it did was cause a fevered shudder to race down her spine.

Clawing in a desperate breath, she set the plate aside. 'Let's talk now. You invited me to the concert, then ignored me to make out with your girlfriend. What else is there to talk about?'

'Flavia's not my girlfriend, and I wasn't making out with her. She was congratulating me on the team's win, just like a lot of people have done tonight.'

'She was *all* over you. And you didn't seem to mind.'

'I was…preoccupied.'

She snorted. 'Evidently.'

'*Para el amor de Dios!* I was waiting in the VIP room for *you*! The Prime Minister turned up when I was about to come and meet you. I tried to get away as quickly as possible, only to find you were more interested in plastering yourself all over your favourite rock star. It was very evident you didn't have a bra on, but tell me—were you even wearing panties under that dress?'

A harsh flush of anger tinged his cheekbones. This was the angriest she'd ever seen Marco. The reason why stopped her breath.

'You were jealous?'

His jaw clenched. 'Do you mean was that what I expected when I had the band flown over for you? No. Did I want to break every bone in his pathetically thin body? *Sí.* For starters.'

The air thickened around them.

A thousand different questions rushed into her mind. One emerged.

'I'm not stupid, Marco, I know where this is going. But what about the consequences? The ones that made you avoid me for the past three weeks?'

He abandoned his glass and rested his hands on his knees, his eyes never leaving hers. 'Seeing you in another man's arms has simplified my decision. For the sake of my sanity, and to avoid murder charges, no more staying away,' he rasped.

'Right. Well, I'm happy for you and your sanity. But what about what *I* want?'

His eyes dropped to her lips. 'If you know where this is going then you know how badly I want to kiss you. Come here.'

Her mouth, the subject of his very intense scrutiny, tingled so badly she had to curb the urge to bite it. 'I meant what I said in London. I don't want a relationship.'

A hard look passed through his eyes. 'I don't want a relationship either.'

'What about *your* clause?'

'I'm not a racing driver and I don't work for the team so I'm exempt. Come here, Sasha.'

'No. Aren't you twisting the rules?'

'No. I can quote them verbatim for you later. Right now I want you to come over here and kiss me.'

Her breath shortened. 'What if I don't want to?'

His gaze darkened. 'Then I'll return to the concert, find your reedy rock star and decorate the VIP lounge with him.'

A roar went up a few miles away. The throb of the rock concert echoed superbly the blood surging through her veins as Marco continued to watch her.

'I hope you won't expect me to bail you out of jail.'

He shrugged. 'I live in hope for a lot of things, *querida*. At this moment I'm hoping you'll stop arguing and crawl into my lap. Would it help if I said that not a day went by these past three weeks when you didn't feature in my thoughts?' He lifted a winged brow.

'Maybe that helps. A little…'

Without warning he reached across the table and scooped her up. Settling her in his lap, he freed her hair and sighed in pleasure as the heavy tresses spilled into his hands. Then he lowered her until her back rested on the upraised lounger.

Despite her bikini's relative modesty, Sasha had never felt more exposed in her life. Especially when Marco took his time to trail his fierce gaze over her, missing nothing as he scoured her body, and followed more slowly with one long, lazy finger.

'You're doing it again.' Her voice was smoky with lust, her flesh alight wherever he touched.

'What?' he murmured, his eyes resting at the apex of her thighs.

Beneath her bottom the hard ridge of his erection pressed into her flesh, its heat making her skin tighten in feverish anticipation.

'The thing with your eyes. And your hands. And your body.'

'If you want me to stop you'll have to kiss me.'

'Maybe I don't want you to stop. Maybe this is what I'll allow before I decide this is a very bad idea.'

His finger paused on her belly. 'You think this is a bad idea?'

A thread of uncertainty wheedled through her desire. 'My last involvement left a lot of bruises.'

He tensed. 'Derek physically hurt you?'

'No, but he influenced a lot of people against me. You included.'

He shook his head. 'I make up my own mind. If you truly don't want this, say the word and I'll stop.'

The thought of denying herself made her heart lurch painfully.

Her body moved closer of its own volition. He hissed out a breath, the skin around his mouth tightening as he visibly reined in control. 'If you intend to stop that's not a great idea, *querida*.'

Sasha had had enough. Marco had spent far too much of his life controlling everything. For once she yearned to see him lose his cool, to crack the shell of tightly reined-in emotion. She wriggled again.

His gaze connected with hers. The dark hunger in its depths made her breath catch. Giving in to the urge, she slipped her hand over his nape and urged his head down.

He took control of her lips in a kiss so driven, so desperate, she cried out against his mouth. He fisted one hand in her hair to hold her still, his other hand sliding over her bottom to drag her closer.

Sasha went willingly, her body a fluid vessel of rampant desire that craved only him. Every single doubt that crowded in her brain drowned under ever-increasing waves of sensation.

She might be risking everything to experience a few hours of pleasure, but Sasha could no more push Marco away than she could voluntarily stop breathing. She would deal with regret in the morning.

Losing herself in the kiss, she boldly thrust her tongue against his. His body jerked, making a tiny fizz of pleasure steal through her.

When his fingers squeezed her buttock, she moaned.

He pulled back. 'You like that?' he rasped, his gaze heavy and hooded.

She nodded and licked her lips, already missing the feel of his mouth against hers.

'Tell me what else you'd like, *mi tentación*.' He released the tie of her bikini top and trailed his mouth over her skin.

'You…not to be so overdressed…' she gasped out.

Another roar from the concert ripped through the night air. Momentarily she remembered where they were.

'On the other hand, maybe that's not so bad—'

'We won't be disturbed.'

The finality of the statement, along with the graze of his teeth over one Lycra-clothed nipple, melted the last of her reservations. Giving her feelings free rein, she slid her hand over his shoulders, touching the smooth skin of his nape before exploring his damp, luxurious hair.

Her urgency fed his. With renewed vigour he kissed her again, pulling off the wet cloth and tossing it aside. Reversing their positions, he eased her onto the lounger, then tugged off her bikini bottoms.

In the soft, ambient light of the enclosed cabana his skin gleamed golden, the dark silky hairs on his chest making her fingers tingle to touch.

'I want to touch you all over.' The heated words had slipped out before she could stop them.

His face contorted in a pained grimace. Tugging off his boxers, he stretched out next to her. Leaning down, he ran his tongue over her mouth. 'I believe I mentioned the near insanity that has plagued me these past weeks? Touching me all over is not a good idea right now.'

Her breath rasped through her chest. Breathing had become increasingly difficult. 'Oh. Then I guess it's not a good time to mention I also intend biting a few strategic places?'

A heartfelt groan preceded a few heated Spanish words muttered against her lips. 'Do me a favour, *mi tentadora*. Keep your thoughts to yourself for the time being. You have my word. I'll let you vocalise your every want later.'

Swooping down, he captured one exposed nipple in his mouth, his fierce determination to shut her up working wonders. Words deserted her as sensation took over. Liquid heat pooled at the apex of her thighs, the flesh of her sex swelling and pulsating with the strength of her need. By the time he transferred his attention to her other nipple Sasha was incoherent with desire.

Marco traced his lips lower, ruthlessly turning her inside out with pleasure, but when she felt his mouth dip below her navel she froze.

Sensing her withdrawal, he raised his head. 'You don't want this?'

'I *do*.' So much so the force of her need shocked her. 'I do... But you don't have to if...' Her words fizzled out at the searing heat in his eyes.

'I've spent endless nights imagining the taste of you, Sasha.' He parted her legs wider, licked the sensitive skin inside her thigh, his eyes growing darker at her breathless groan. 'But I've always preferred reality to dreams.'

He put his mouth on her, slowly worked his tongue over the millions of nerve-endings saturated with pleasure receptors. Sasha screamed, and came in a rush of pleasure so intense her whole body quivered with it.

Before the last of her orgasm had faded away Marco was surging over her. His kiss was less frantic but no less demanding. And, just like the engine of a finely tuned car, her body responded to his demands, anticipation firing her blood like nothing had ever done in her life.

Tension screamed through Marco's body as he raised himself from the intoxicating kiss. The sound of Sasha's orgasm echoed in his head like a siren's call, promising him pleasure beyond measure. He couldn't remember ever being so fired up about sex—so impatient he'd nearly forgotten protection.

Luckily sanity prevailed just in time.

Sasha moved restlessly beneath him, her sultry gaze steady on his as he parted her thighs.

Every single night of the past three weeks he'd woken with an ache in his groin and a sinking sensation that he was fighting a losing battle. He'd congratulated himself on staying away, but he'd known deep down it was a hollow victory.

Truth was he'd never wanted a woman as much as he wanted Sasha. He'd stopped trying to decipher what made her so irresistible. She just *was*. He'd also made discreet enquiries and verified that she'd spoken the truth—she hadn't been involved with Rafael.

So just this once he was going to take. Sasha Fleming had worked her way under his skin like no other woman had and now this was the inevitable conclusion. Her underneath him, her thighs parted, her sultry gaze steady on his. Just as he'd dreamed…

With a groan he sank into her.

'Thank God!' she cried. 'For a second there I thought you were about to change your mind.'

As if to stop him taking that route, her muscles clamped tight around him.

Another groan tore from his throat. 'I thought I told you to shut up?' He pulled back and surged into her once more, pleasure such as he'd never known rocking through him.

'I am… I will… Just please don't stop.' Raking her nails down his back, she clamped her hands around his waist.

As if he could even if he wanted to. He was past the point of no return, his need so great he was almost afraid to acknowledge its overwhelming scope. Instead he lost himself in her pleasure, in the hitched sounds and feminine demands of her body as she welcomed him into her sweet warmth.

'*Dios*, you feel incredible,' he rasped as sensation piled upon sensation.

Inevitably the bough broke. Ecstasy rode through him, blinding him to everything else but the glorious satisfaction of unleashed passion.

With her cry of bliss he followed off the peak, the muscles in his body tightening with the force of his orgasm as he emptied himself into her.

He collapsed on top of her, her soft, sweat-slicked body a cushion to his hardness. He remained there until their breathing calmed then, rolling onto the lounger, he tucked her against his side.

As the last of the haze faded away he felt the first inevitable twinge of regret. He'd succumbed to temptation. Now the piper would expect payment. And for the first time in his life Marco was afraid at just how much he was willing to pay.

CHAPTER NINE

'What—?' Sasha jerked awake.

The solid body curved around hers and the arm imprisoning her kept her from falling off the lounger. Opening her eyes, she encountered Marco's accusing gaze.

'You fell asleep.'

The wide expanse of muscled chest scrambled her brain for a few seconds, before a few synapses fired a thought. She'd had sex with Marco. Wild, unbelievable, pleasure-filled sex. After which—

'You fell *asleep*,' he incised a second time, affront stamped all over his face.

'Uh…I'm sorry…'

'I get the feeling you don't mean that.'

'And I get the feeling I'm not following this conversation at all.' Before she could stop it a wide yawn broke through.

His glare darkened.

'Did I not please you?' He seemed genuinely puzzled, and a little unsure. One hand curved under her nape to tilt her face up to his.

Thoughts of their lovemaking melted her insides. 'Of course you did,' she said, struggling to keep from blushing at recalling her cries of pleasure. Lifting her hands, she framed his face. 'I've never felt more pleasure than I did with you.'

'It was so good you fell asleep straight after?'

'Take it as a compliment. You wore me out.'

His lids veiled his eyes. 'This is a first, I admit.'

'Wearing a woman out?' she asked, stunned.

'Of course not. The falling asleep part.'

Laughter bubbled up from deep within her, delight filling her. Leaning up, she pressed her lips against his in a light kiss.

Marco took over and turned it into a long, deep kiss.

By the time he was done with her she struggled to breathe. And he...he was fully engorged, his erection a forceful presence against her belly. Emboldened by the thought that she could arouse him again so quickly, she caressed her fingers down his side, eliciting a shuddered groan from him that released a wanton smile from her.

'Like I said, I'm sorry. How can I make it up to you?' She slid her hand between them and gripped him tight. His lips parted on another groan. She caressed up and down, marvelling at the tensile strength of him.

His mouth trailed over her face to the juncture between her neck and shoulder. Erotic heat washed through her.

When her grip tightened, his breath shuddered out. '*Sí, mi querida*, that's the right way to make it up to me.'

His hips bucked against her hold, heat and strength pulsing through her fingers. Liquid heat gathered between her thighs. She was unbelievably turned on by the pleasure she gave him.

At yet another caress he suddenly reared up and flipped her over. 'You're getting carried away.'

She slid her thighs either side of him and lowered herself until her wet heat touched him. The feel of his strong hands sliding down her back to capture her bottom made her shiver with delight.

'Then me being on top wasn't the best idea, was it?'

His predatory gaze swept over her, lingering on her breasts, making them peak even more painfully.

'It's time you learned that I can control you from whichever position I'm in,' he breathed.

He surged into her, filling her so completely stars exploded behind her closed lids. He captured her nape, forced her down and took her mouth in a scorching kiss. His tongue seeking the deep cavern of her mouth, he took her over completely, escalating the desire firing through her until Sasha was aflame with a pleasure so intense it frightened the small part of her brain that could still function.

Sasha hung on as he clamped one hand in the small of her back to hold her still. His pace was frantic, frightful in its demand and exquisite in its delivery of pleasure. She whimpered when he freed her mouth, only to blindly seek his for herself before she could draw another breath. Sensation spiralled out of control as bliss gathered with stunning speed.

'Open your eyes. Let me see your eyes when you come for me.'

She obeyed. Then wished she hadn't when the heat in his eyes threatened to send her already flaming world out of control.

'Marco…'

'*Sí*, I feel it too.'

She believed him. The sheen of sweat coating his skin, the unsteady hand that caressed down her face before recapturing her nape, the harsh pants that escaped his lungs all attested to the fact that he was caught in this incredible maelstrom too.

Pleasure scythed through her heart, arrowed down into her pelvis, forcing her to cry out one last time as her orgasm exploded through her.

Beneath her, still controlling their pleasure, Marco thrust into her release, groaning at the sensation of her caressing convulsions, then found his own satisfaction.

Their harsh breaths mingled, hearts thundering as the breeze cooled their sweat-damp skin. Far away, another burst of fireworks lit up the sky.

Inside the cabana, the intensity of their shared pleasure sparked a threat of fear through her.

To mask her feelings, she hid her face in his shoulder. 'I'd love to compose a sonnet to you right now. But I have no words.'

A short rumble of laughter echoed through his heated chest. 'Sonnets are overrated. Your screams of pleasure were reward enough.'

Sasha sighed, put her head on his chest and tried to breathe. The alarm that had taken root in that small part of her brain grew. Something had happened between their first and second lovemaking.

Then she'd felt safe enough to fall asleep in Marco's arms.

Now... Now she felt exposed. Her emotions felt raw, naked. Unbidden, tears prickled her eyes. She scrambled to hide her composure but Marco sensed her feelings.

Pushing her head gently off his shoulder, he stared into her face. 'You're crying. Why?'

How could she explain something she had no understanding of?

When she tried to shrug he shook his head. 'Tell me.'

'I'm just feeling a little overwhelmed. That's all.'

After a second he nodded and brushed a hand down her cheek. '*Sí*. This is your first victory. That feeling can never be equalled.'

For several heartbeats Sasha didn't follow his meaning. When she realised he was talking about the race, and not the roiling aftermath of their lovemaking, her heart lurched.

Panic escalating, she grasped the lifeline. 'I wish my father had been there.'

Marco nodded. 'He would've been proud of you.'

Surprise widened her eyes. 'You knew my father?'

'Of course. He was the greatest driver never to win a championship. I've seen every single race of his. Clearly you inherited his talent.'

The unexpected compliment made her feel even more tearful. She tried to move away but he caught her back easily, lowered his head and kissed his way along her arm. When she shivered, he shook out a cashmere throw and pulled it over them, one muscular leg imprisoning both of hers.

She was grateful for the cover—not least because the familiar feeling of humiliation had returned. 'You know what happened to him, then?'

'He bet on another car to win and deliberately crashed his car.' The cold conviction in his voice sent an icy shiver down her spine, bleeding away the warmth she'd felt in his arms.

This time she moved away forcefully. Standing, she grabbed

her kaftan and slid it over her head, even though it did little to cover her nakedness.

'The allegations were false!'

Marco folded his arms behind his head. 'Not according to the court that found him guilty.'

'He never managed to disprove the claims. But *I* believed him. He would *never* have done that. He loved racing too much to crash deliberately for money.'

'I was on the board that reviewed the footage, Sasha. The evidence was hard to refute.'

Shock and anger twisted in her gut. '*You* were one of those who decided he was guilty?'

He lowered his feet to the floor. 'He didn't do much to defend himself. It took him weeks to even acknowledge the charges.'

'And that makes him automatically guilty? He was devastated! Yes, he should have responded to the allegations earlier, but the accusations broke his heart.'

Her voice choked as memories rushed to the fore. Her father broken, disgraced by the sport he'd devoted his life to. It had taken Sasha weeks to convince her father to fight to clear his name. And in those precious weeks his reputation in the eyes of the public had been sullied beyond repair. By the time Jack Fleming had taken the stand his integrity had been in tatters.

'So he gave up? And let you carry the weight of his guilt?'

'Of course not!'

'Why did you promise him the championship?'

Sasha floundered, pain and loss ripping through her. 'He started drinking heavily after the trial. The only time he stopped was when I had a shot at the Formula Two Championship. When I crashed and had to stay a while in hospital he started drinking again.'

'You were in hospital? And the father you claim loved you *unconditionally* wasn't there for you?'

Hazel eyes now devoid of passion taunted her.

Tears prickled her eyes but she refused to let them fall. In her darkest, most painful moments after losing her baby she'd asked herself the same question.

Blinking fiercely, she raised her chin. 'Whatever point you're trying to make, Marco, make it without being a total bastard.'

He sighed and ran a hand over his chin.

She stayed at the other end of the cabana, her arms curved around her middle.

'Did you hire another lawyer to appeal?'

'Of course we did. He… Dad died before the second trial.'

His gaze softened a touch. 'How did he die?'

'He drove his car off a bridge near our cottage.' Pain coated her words. 'Everyone thinks he did it because he was guilty. He was just…devastated.'

'And you feel guilty for this?'

She plucked at the hem of her kaftan. 'If I hadn't got involved with Derek I'd have won a championship earlier. Maybe that would've saved my father…'

Marco's hand slashed through her words. 'Your life is your own. You can't live it for someone else. Not even your father.'

'Who's got their psychoanalysing hat on now?'

His brow lifted. 'You can dish it out but you can't take it?'

Sasha tried to stem the wave of guilt that rose within her. After his trial she'd suggested her father not come to her races, because she'd watched him slide deeper into depression after attending every one.

'Whatever he was, he wasn't a cheat. And I intend to honour his memory.'

Marco rose from the lounger, completely oblivious to his sheer masculine beauty and the effect it had on her tangled emotions. Sasha wanted to burrow into him, to return to the warm cocoon of his arms. But she forced herself to stay where she was.

'Come here.'

She shook her head. 'No. I don't like you very much right now.'

His smile made a mockery of her words as he strolled towards her. 'That's not true. You can't keep your eyes off me. Just like I can't take mine off you.'

'Marco…'

He cupped her jaw and lifted her face to his. Her heart stuttered, then thundered. 'You made your promise out of guilt—'

'No, I want to win the Championship.'

'Sometimes the best deal is to walk away.'

'I don't intend to. So don't stand in my way.'

He brought his mouth within a whisper of hers. Sasha swayed towards him, her willpower depleting rapidly.

'Determination is a quality I admire, *querida*. But remember I won't tolerate anything that stands in the way of *my* desires.'

Tugging her firmly into his arms, he proceeded to make her forget everything but him. Including the fact that he'd never believed her father's innocence.

Marco attended the next two races, flying back each time from Spain, where Rafael was still in a coma. When she won in Japan he took the whole team to celebrate, after which he took Sasha to his penthouse for a private celebration of their own.

After a tricky, hair-raising start, Korea secured her yet another victory. But one look at Marco's taut expression when she emerged from the press conference told her there would be no team celebrations this time.

'Marco?'

'We're leaving. Now.'

He whisked her away from the Yeongam Circuit in his helicopter, his possessive fingers tense around hers all through the flight to a stunning beach house on the outskirts of Seoul City, where he proceeded to strip off her race suit and her underclothes.

'You know that by dragging me away like that in front of the team you've blown this thing between us wide open, don't you?' she asked, in the aftermath of another pulse-melting session in his bed.

His lovemaking had been especially intense, with an edge that had bordered on the frenzied. And, as much as she'd loved it, he'd left her struggling for breath, in danger of being swept away by the force of his passion.

He brushed a damp curl from her cheek and studied her face. 'Does it bother you?'

She gave the matter brief thought. 'There was speculation even before we were together. Paddock gossip can make the tabloid press look like amateurs.'

He pulled back slightly, his earlier tension returning. 'That doesn't answer my question.'

'They knew I was a good driver before I started sleeping with you. They just didn't want to acknowledge it because of who I am. I only care about what they think of me as a driver. What they think of me personally doesn't matter. It never has.'

'You're a fighter,' he said, his expression reflective.

'I've had to fight for what I've achieved.' She cast him a droll look. 'As you well know.'

When he didn't smile back, a cloud appeared on the horizon of her happy haze. 'It bothers you that I don't care what other people think about me?'

'Single-mindedness has its place.'

'I smell a *but* in there somewhere.'

His gaze because suspiciously neutral. 'Following a single dream is risky. When it's taken from you you'll have nothing.'

'*When?* Not *if*? Are you trying to tell me something?'

'Nothing lasts for ever.'

'You must be jet-lagged again, because you've gone all cryptic on me. I'm three races away from securing the Constructors' Championship for you. Unless I don't finish another single race, and our nearest rival wins every one, it's pretty much a done deal.'

He got out of bed and pulled on his boxer shorts. For a man who embraced nudity the way Marco did, the definitive action sent a shiver of unease down her spine.

'Done deals have a way of coming undone.'

Her anxiety escalated. 'Enough with the paradoxes. What's going on, Marco?'

Marco strode to the champagne chilling in a monogrammed silver bucket, filled up a glass and brought it back to her.

Returning to the cabinet, he poured a whisky for himself and downed it in one go.

He slammed the glass down and spun towards her. '*Madre di Dios*, you nearly crashed today!'

Her fingers tightened around the delicate stem of her glass as the full force of his smouldering temper hit her. Her car had stalled at the start of the race, leaving her struggling to retain pole position. Her rivals hadn't hesitated in trying to take advantage of the situation. She'd touched tyres with a couple of cars and nearly lost a front wing.

'I found myself in a slightly hairy situation. I dealt with it.' She glanced at him. 'Were you worried?'

'That my lover would end up in a mangled heap of metal just like my brother did mere weeks ago? What do you think?' he ground out.

She trembled at the harshness in his tone even while a secret part of her thrilled that he'd been worried about her. 'I know what I'm doing, Marco. I've been doing it almost all my life.'

He speared a hand into her hair, tilting her face up to his. 'Rafael knew what he was doing too. Look where he ended up. You can't do it for ever. You do realise that, don't you?'

The question threw her, for Sasha had been deliberately avoiding any thoughts of the future. Even the end of the racing season didn't bear thinking about. If by some sheer stroke of bad luck she lost the Constructors' Championship then she was out of a job.

If she won her professional future would be secured for another year. But what about her personal future?

The reality was that she'd fallen into Marco's bed expecting little more than a one-night stand. But with each day that passed she was being consumed by the magic she experienced there. With no thought to the future…

'Yes,' she finally whispered. 'I realise nothing lasts for ever.'

'*Bueno*,' he breathed, as if her answer had satisfied him.

He shucked his boxers in one smooth move. 'Are you going to drink that? Only, after watching you nearly crash, I feel an urgent need to re-affirm life with you again. Repeatedly.'

She passed him the glass and opened her arms.

It wasn't until their breaths were gasping out in the aftermath of soul-shattering orgasms that she tensed in disbelief.

'Marco!'

'What?' He raised his head, a swathe of hair falling seductively over one eye.

'We didn't… We forgot…' Frantically she calculated dates.

He let loose a single epithet. '*Dios*. Please tell me you're on the Pill?' he rasped.

His voice was a choked sound that chilled her.

Reassured with the dates, she nodded, then noticed his pallor. 'Hey, it's okay. Even if the Pill doesn't work it's the wrong time of the month.'

'Are you sure?' he demanded.

Frowning, Sasha laid a hand on his cheek, which had grown cold and clammy. 'I'm sure. Relax.'

Marco eased away from Sasha, steeling himself against her throaty protest as he left the bed. Pulling on a robe, he went into his study. His laptop was set up on his desk, his folders neatly arranged by his assistant. He bypassed it, threw himself into the leather sofa and scrubbed a hand down his face.

He hadn't meant to lose it with Sasha like that earlier.

But seeing her come within a whisker of crashing had set him on a knife-edge of fear and rage he hadn't been able to completely dismiss. Now his loss of control had made him forget his one cardinal rule—contraception. *Always*.

He hadn't slipped once in ten years. Until tonight. Thank goodness Sasha was as against accidentally conceiving a child as he was…

Grimly reining in the control that seemed to be slipping from him, he strode to his desk and picked up the top folder. A sliver of guilt rose inside him but he quashed it.

Enough. He'd done what needed to be done. He refused to feel guilty for protecting what was important to him. Nothing mattered except keeping his family safe.

He picked up the phone and called his brother's doctors. Once he'd been updated on Rafael's condition, he placed another call.

Fifteen minutes later he slammed down the lid of his laptop and pushed away from the desk, at peace with his decision.

Feeling a sense of rightness, he returned to the bedroom and slid into bed, his need for Sasha overcoming the wish to let her rest. With a soft murmur she wound her supple body around his. The sense of rightness increased, making his head spin.

'I missed you. Where have you been?'

Another wave of guilt hit him—harder than before. Inhaling the seductive scent of her, he pushed away the disturbing feeling. 'I needed to take care of something.' Bending his head, he placed his lips against the smooth skin of her neck. His body stirred, transmitting its persistent message.

'Um. And have you?' she murmured.

'Sí.' His voice emerged gruffer than he wished. 'It's all taken care of.'

CHAPTER TEN

SASHA watched Marco turn the page of his newspaper, a frown creasing his brow before it smoothed out again. Watching him had become something of a not-so-secret pleasure in the last few weeks. On cue, she experienced the slow drag of desire in her belly as her gaze drifted over the sensual curve of his lips, the unshaven rasp of his jaw and the strong column of his throat to the muscled bare torso which she'd caressed to her heart's content last night and this morning.

As if sensing her gaze, his eyes met hers over the top of the paper. One brow lifted. 'You want to go back to bed?'

He laughed at her less-than-convincing shake of the head. The remnants of breakfast lay scattered on the table, long forgotten as they basked in the South Korean sun.

'I didn't know you could read Korean,' she said, eager for something to distil the suffocating heat of the desire that was never far from the surface.

Marco smiled and folded away the paper. 'It's Japanese. I never quite mastered Korean.'

'Wow. You're freely admitting *another* flaw? Shocking!'

He shrugged. 'It was down to a choice of which was the most useful.'

She wrinkled her nose. '*Useful?* Do you ever do anything just for pleasure?'

His droll look made her colour rise higher.

'Besides sex,' she mumbled.

'Sex with you is all the pleasure I crave, *mi corazón*.'

'You have other interests, surely? Everyone does.'

His throaty laugh made her pulse pound harder. 'What did you have in mind?'

'Some culture. An exhibition. Something other than…' Flustered, she waved her hand towards the severely rumpled bed beyond the sliding doors leading into the master suite, trying not to think of all the *other* places—the highly polished teak floor, the wooden bench in his outdoor bathroom, the hammock overlooking the stunning beach—where Marco had pleasured her during the long night.

Leaning over, he slid a hand around her nape and pulled her in for a hot kiss. 'I'd much rather spend the day with you in my bed. But if you insist—'

'I insist.'

Because Sasha had woken up this morning with a fearful knowledge deep in her heart. She was in danger of developing feelings for Marco de Cervantes. Feelings that she dared not name. Feelings that threatened to overwhelm her the more time she spent locked in his embrace.

At least away from this place, real life would impede long enough to knock some sense into her. To remind her that she couldn't afford to lose her head over a man like Marco—a man whom she knew deep down grappled with his guilt for being attracted to her. After all, hadn't it taken him three weeks to decide he could be with her?

He was also a man who believed her father to be guilty of fraud, a small voice added.

A sharp pang pierced through the concrete she'd packed around her pain. She hadn't been able to raise the subject with Marco since that night in Singapore. Somehow knowing he'd painted her father with the same brush of guilt as everyone else hurt so much more. Which made her a fool. Why should he believe any differently? Just because they were sleeping together it didn't mean the taint of her name had disappeared.

'You have fifteen minutes to get ready.'

She roused herself to find Marco ending a call. 'Ready for what?'

He tossed his phone on the table and brushed his knuckle along her jaw. Sparks of pleasure lit along her skin.

'You want culture, *mi encantadora*. Korea awaits.'

'Oh, my God,' Sasha whispered as her bare feet touched the wet flagstones that led to the ancient lake temple, unable to tear her gaze away from the magnificent vista before her.

'I'm finding that I don't like you using that expression unless it relates directly to me, *pequeña*,' Marco complained, releasing her hand as she leapt onto the next flagstone.

'Are you jealous?' she asked on a laugh.

He raised a mocking brow. 'Of your insane adoration of old temples and ancient monuments?' He rolled up his trouser cuffs and stepped on to the flagstones, bringing his warmth and addictive body up close and personal. 'Not a chance. But I suggest you alter your phraseology, because every time you say *Oh, my God* in that sexy tone I want to flatten you against the nearest surface and have my way with you.'

He grinned at her gasp and his head started to descend.

'No.' She pulled away reluctantly.

He frowned. *'Qué diablos?'*

'Shh, we're in a holy place,' she whispered. 'No kissing. And no swearing.'

She giggled at his muted growl and skipped over the rest of the flagstones until she stood in front of the temple.

'Wow.'

'*Wow* I can live with.'

'You'll have to. I have no other words.'

From where they stood the small temple seemed to float on the water, its curved eaves reminiscent of a bird in flight. In the light of the dying sun huge pink water lilies glowed red, their rubescent petals unfurled to catch the last of the sun's rays.

'It's all so beautiful. So stunning.' With reverent steps Sasha approached the temple doors. 'Can we go in?'

He nodded. 'It's not normally open to visitors. But on this occasion…'

Unbidden, a lump rose to her throat. 'Thank you.'

'*De nada.* Go—explore to your heart's content.'

With legs that felt shaky, and a heart that hammered far too hard to be healthy, Sasha paused to wipe her feet, then entered the temple.

Like every single place Marco had taken her to since he'd summoned his car after breakfast, the temple was breathtakingly exquisite. The *shoji* scrolls lining the walls looked paper-thin and fragile, causing her to hold her breath in case she damaged the place in any way. Examining one, she wished she had a translator to explain the three lines of symbols to her.

'"Peace through wisdom. Wisdom through perspicacity,"' Marco murmured from behind her. 'This temple was originally Japanese. It changed owners a few times before the Shaolin monks took over in the fourth century.'

'It puts everything into perspective, doesn't it?'

'Does it?'

'You said nothing lasts for ever. This temple proves some things do.'

For a long moment he didn't answer. His hooded gaze held hers, but in the gathering dusk she couldn't read the expression in his eyes.

'Come, it is time to leave. Romano will think you've kidnapped me.'

'What? Little ol' me?'

He laughed—a sound she was finding she liked very much. 'Romano knows you have a black belt in Jujitsu.'

'I'd still think twice before I tried to drop-kick a man of his size. So you're safe with me.'

'*Gracias.*' He threaded his fingers through hers, then signalled to Romano to bring the car round.

She waited until they were in the car before leaning over to press her lips to his. 'Thank you for showing me Seoul.'

His hand tightened around her waist and pulled her closer. 'The tour isn't over yet. I have one last treat for you.'

Pleasure unfurled through her. 'Really?'

'The night is just beginning. I know a little place where, if you're really nice to the staff, they'll name a dish after you.

Will you allow me to show it to you?' He picked up her hand and kissed the back of it.

Watching the dark head bent over her hand, Sasha experienced that irrational fear again. Only this time it was ten times worse. Her heart hammered and her pulse raced through her veins as the reason for her feelings whispered softly through her mind.

No. She *wasn't* falling for Marco de Cervantes. Because that would be stupid.

And reckless.

Marco didn't do relationships. And she'd barely survived being burned once.

His lips caressed the sensitive skin of her wrist.

At her helpless sigh, he smiled. 'On second thoughts, a Michelin-star-chef-prepared meal on the beach sounds very appealing.'

Resisting temptation was nearly impossible. But Sasha forced herself to speak. 'It's not fair to dangle the opportunity to have a dish named after me and then withdraw it. Now it's on my lust-have list.'

He reached out and cupped her breast. 'I have only one thing on *my* lust-have list.'

'You're insatiable,' she breathed, unable to stop her moan when his thumb passed over her nipple.

Bending his head, he brought his lips close to hers. 'Only for you do I have this need,' he muttered thickly. 'And, *por favor*, I won't have it denied.' He drew closer until their breaths mingled.

'What about dinner…the dish…?' she whispered.

'You'll have it,' he vowed. 'Just…later.'

With a muted groan, he closed the gap, sealing them in a hot cocoon of fevered need so intense it stopped her breath.

The cocoon held them intimately all the way through their torrid lovemaking in Marco's bed and in the shower afterwards, where he explored every inch of her body as if seeing it for the first time.

His phone rang as they dressed for dinner. At first she thought it was a business call. Then she noticed his ashen pallor.

Their cocoon had been shattered.

'Who was that?' she asked, even though part of her knew the answer.

'It was the hospital. Rafael's suffered another bleed.'

'What the hell are you doing under there? Freebasing engine oil?'

Sasha froze at the voice she hadn't heard in six long sleepless nights and forced herself to breathe. 'Hand me the wrench.'

'Didn't the staff tell you no one's allowed in here?' The harsh censure in his voice grated on her already severely frayed nerves.

'They probably *tried*.'

'You didn't listen, of course?'

'I don't speak Spanish, remember? Are you going to hand me the wrench or not?'

His designer-shod feet moved, then a wrench appeared underneath the body of the 1954 Fiat 8V Berlinetta.

'Not that one. The retractable.'

The right wrench reappeared. 'Thanks.'

She hooked the wrench on to the bolt and pulled. Nothing happened.

'Come out from under there.'

'No.'

'Sasha…' His voice held more than a hint of warning.

Her mouth compressed. She didn't want to see his face, didn't want to breathe his scent. In fact she wanted to deny herself everything to do with Marco. To deny that every single atom of her being yearned to wheel herself from under the car and throw herself into his arms.

She gripped the wrench and yanked harder, reminding herself of how almost a week ago he'd ordered Romano to bring her to *Casa de Leon* and walked away.

As if Seoul had never happened.

'We need to talk.'

Her heart clenched. 'So talk.'

An expensively cut suit jacket landed a few feet from her head, followed a millisecond later by Marco's large, tightly packed frame.

'What are you doing?' she squeaked, holding herself rigid as his shoulder brushed hers.

He ignored her, taking his time to study the axle she'd been working on. 'Hand me the wrench and move over.'

'Why? Because you think you're bigger and stronger than me?'

'I *am* bigger and stronger than you.'

'Sexist pig.'

'Simple truth.'

'I see you still live in the Dark Ages.'

'Only when it comes to protecting what's mine.'

Realising he wasn't going to go away, she shrugged. 'Fine. Knock yourself out.'

His gaze sharpened. 'No arguments, *querida*? That's how it works between us usually, isn't it? I say something, then you argue my words to death until I kiss you to shut you up?'

'I don't crave arguments—or your kisses, if that's what you're implying. In fact I'd love nothing better than for you to leave me alone,' she suggested. 'You've managed it quite successfully for almost a week.'

Silently he held out his hand. She slapped the wrench into his palm. With a few firm twists he loosened the bolt on the axle.

'Show-off,' she quipped. 'What do you want?'

'I thought you'd want an update on Rafael.' His gaze stayed intense on hers.

'I thought he was off-limits?'

'If I still believed you and he were involved I wouldn't have taken you to my bed.'

'Okay. So how is he?'

'He's doing better. The doctors managed to stop the bleed. They expect him to wake up any day now.'

Licking her lips carefully, she nodded. 'That's great news.'

'*Sí.*'

The intensity in his eyes sent a bolt of apprehension through her. Without warning, his gaze dropped to her lips. Belatedly Sasha realised she was licking them. She stopped. But the quickening was already happening. The cramped space underneath the car became smaller. The air grew thinner.

'You didn't have to come back here to tell me that. A simple phone call would've sufficed. I'll pack my things and leave this afternoon.'

He stiffened. 'Why would you do that?'

'Rafael will need you when he comes home. I can't be here.'

'Of course you can. I want you here.'

Despite the thin hope threading its way through her, she forced herself to speak. 'That wasn't the impression I got from your six-day silence.'

He sucked in a weary breath and for the first time she noticed the lines of strain around his eyes.

'I didn't expect to be away this long. I'm sorry.'

When her mouth dropped open in surprise at the ready apology he grimaced.

'I know. I must be losing my touch.' He glanced around, his strained look intensifying. 'How did you get in here? The door is combination locked.'

'Rosario let me in. She recognises stir-craziness when she sees it. So—twenty-five vintage cars locked away in a garage? Discuss.'

He inhaled sharply, then flung the wrench away. 'I refuse to have this conversation underneath a car, with grease dripping on me.'

'You should've thought of that before you crawled down here.'

'*Dios*, I've missed your insufferable attitude.' He paused. 'This is your chance to tell me you've missed me too.'

The stark need to do just that frightened her. 'Are you sure you don't want me to leave? I can go home for a few days before the team leaves for Abu Dhabi next week. Maybe it's for the best.'

'And maybe you need to shut up. Just for one damn moment,' he snarled, then grabbed her arm and turned her into his body.

The heat of his mouth devoured hers. Fiery sensation was instantaneous. Sasha held nothing back. Her fingers gripped his nape, luxuriating in the smooth skin before spearing upward to spread through his hair. His deep groan echoed hers. Willingly, she let her mouth fall open, let his tongue invade to slide deliciously against hers.

His hand snaked around her waist and veered downwards, bringing her flush against his heated body. Need flooded her. To be this close again with him, to feel him, to be with him, made her body, her heart sing.

She wanted to be close. Closer. Physically and emotionally. Because… Because…

Infinitely glad he'd shed his jacket, she explored the large expanse of his shoulders.

When the demands of oxygen forced them apart his gaze stayed on her. One hand cupped her bottom. Against her belly she felt the ripe force of his erection.

'You do realise we're making out under a car, don't you?' she asked huskily.

'It's the only thing stopping me from pulling you on top of me and burying myself inside you. Tell me you missed me.'

'I missed you.'

'Bueno.' He fastened his mouth to hers once more.

By the time he freed her and pulled them from underneath the car her brain had become a useless expanse seeking only the pleasure he could provide. When he undressed her, led her to the back door of a 1938 Rolls-Royce, she was a willing slave, ready to do his every bidding.

Snagging an arm around her waist, he speared a hand through her hair and tilted her face to his. 'You have no idea how long I've wanted to do this.'

'What?' she breathed.

His mouth swooped, locked on the juncture where her shoulder met her neck, where her pulse thundered frantically.

Her blood surged to meet his mouth. When his teeth grazed her skin she cried out. The eroticism of it was so intense that liquid heat pooled between her legs, where she throbbed, plumping up for the studied and potent possession only he could deliver.

He took his time, tasted her, his mouth playing over the delicate, intensely aroused skin. Just when she thought it couldn't get any more pleasurable his tongue joined in. Ecstasy lashed at her insides, creating a path of fire from her neck to her breasts, to her most sensitive part and down to her toes. Nowhere was safe from the utter bliss rushing through her.

Finally, satisfied, he lifted his head. He took a step forward, then another, until the edge of the car seat touched her calves. With his gentle push she fell back onto the wide seat.

He followed immediately, his warmth surrounding her. In his arms she felt delicate, cared for, as if she mattered. As if she was precious. Which was silly. For Marco this was just sex. But for her…

She shut her mind off the painful train of thought. 'I thought you wanted me on top?'

His teeth gleamed in a slow, feral smile. 'In good time, *mi tentación*. We have a long way to go. Now, don't move.'

He cupped her breasts, toying with the nipples, torturing her for so long she wriggled with pleasure.

'I said don't move,' he gritted through clenched teeth, the harsh stamp of desire tautening his face.

'You expect me to just lie here like a ten-dollar hooker?'

Despite the intense desire threatening to swallow them whole, laughter rumbled through his chest. 'Never having been graced with the attentions of a ten-dollar hooker, I can't answer that. But if you don't stop tormenting me with your body I won't be responsible for my actions.'

'Oh, *now* you're just threatening me with a good time.'

'*Dios*, woman. Your mouth…'

'You want to kiss it?' It was more of a plea than a question. Her head rose off the seat in search of his.

He pulled away. 'It's a weapon of man's destruction.'

She groaned. 'You can always kiss me to shut me up. I can't promise I won't blow you away, though.'

He mumbled something low and pithy under this breath. And then he kissed her.

A long while later, stretched out alongside Marco's warm length on the back seat of the car, she finally acknowledged her feelings.

She was happy. It was a happiness doomed to disaster and a short lifespan, but no matter how delusional she wanted it to last a little while longer.

Glancing down, she noticed Marco's wallet had dropped onto the floor of the car. Spying a picture peeking out, she picked up the wallet and peered closer.

The long, unruly hair was unfamiliar, as was the small go-kart in the background. But the determination and fierce pride in those hazel eyes looked familiar.

'This picture of you is adorable. Now I know what your children will look like.' She tried not to let the pain of that thought show on her face. 'I bet they'll be racers just like you and Rafael.'

Marco stiffened, his eyes growing cold and bleak. 'There won't be any children.'

The granite-like certainty in his voice chilled her soul. 'Why do you say that?'

For a long, endless moment he didn't answer. Then he took the wallet from her. Reaching for his trousers, he opened the car door, stepped out and pulled them on.

'Come with me.'

Despite already missing his arms around her, she sat up. 'Where are we going?'

The look in his eyes grew bleaker. 'Not far. Put your clothes on. I don't want to get distracted.'

She was all for distracting him if it meant he wouldn't look so cold and forbidding. But she did as he said.

Marco led her to the far side of the garage. Keying in a security code, he threw open the door and stepped inside, pulling her behind him.

With a flick of a switch, light bathed the room. Sasha looked around and gasped at the contents of many glass cabinets.

'These are all yours?' she whispered. Walking forward she opened the first cabinet and lifted the first trophy.

'*Sí.*' Marco's voice was husky with emotion. 'I started racing when I was five.'

There were more trophies than she could count, filling four huge cabinets. 'I know.'

He walked to the farthest cabinet and picked up the lone trophy standing in a case by itself. 'This was my last trophy.'

'You never told me why you gave up racing,' she murmured.

When he tensed even more, she went to him and grasped his balled fists.

'Tell me what happened.'

His eyes bored into hers, as if judging her to see if he could trust her with his pain. After an eternity his hand loosened enough to grasp hers.

'I got my first contract to race when I was eighteen. By twenty-one I'd won two championships and acquired a degree in engineering. I was on the list of every team, and I had the choice of picking which team to drive for. A week after I signed for my dream team I met Angelique Santoro. I was twenty-four, and foolishly believed in love at first sight. And even by then I'd had my fill of paddock bunnies. She was…different. Smart, sexy, exciting—far older than her twenty-five years. All I wanted to do was race and be with her. She convinced me to sack my manager and take her on instead. Six months later we were engaged and she was pregnant.'

A shiver of dread raced over Sasha. Deep inside her chest a ball of pain, buried but not forgotten, tightened.

There won't be any children.

'You didn't want the baby?' she whispered in horror.

He laughed. A harsh, tortured sound that twisted her heart. 'I wanted it more than I'd ever wanted anything in my life.'

Sasha frowned. 'But…what happened?'

'I rearranged my whole life around that promise of a family. I designed the *Casa de Leon* track so I could train there, instead of going away to train at other tracks. My parents moved here. My mother was ecstatic at becoming a grandparent.'

The note of pain through his voice rocked her.

'Angelique wasn't satisfied?'

'She wholeheartedly agreed with everything. Until I crashed.'

Her hand tightened around his. 'I don't understand. Your crash was serious, yes, but nothing you couldn't come back from.'

'I was in a coma for nine days. The team hired someone else to replace me when the doctors told my parents and Angelique it was unlikely I'd race again.'

'They must have been devastated for you.'

'My parents were.'

Sadness touched her soul. 'I'm sorry. I can't imagine what you must have gone through.'

He slid a finger under her chin and lifted her face to his, an echo of pain in his eyes. 'Nor would I want you to. But this…' he pulled her closer, his gaze softening a touch '…this helps.'

With a smile, she lifted her mouth to his. 'I'm glad.'

Their kiss was gentle, a soothing balm on his turbulent revelations.

When they parted, she glanced again at the trophies. 'Is that why you don't let anyone in here? Because it reminds you that your racing career is over?'

'When I accepted that part of my life was over I locked them away.' He pulled her away from the cabinet.

'Wait. You said your parents were devastated? What about Angelique?'

He stiffened again, his gaze turning hooded as he thrust his hands into his pockets. 'When it turned out I was destined for a job designing cars instead of racing them, she lost interest,' he said simply, but his oblique tone told a different story.

'That's not all, is it?'

Pain washed over his face before he could mask it. 'Before I crashed Angelique was almost three months pregnant. When I woke from my coma she was no longer pregnant.'

Sasha's horrified gasp echoed through the room. 'She had an abortion?'

His eyes turned almost black with pain. '*Sí*. Two months later she married my ex-team boss.'

A wave of horror washed over her. 'Are you even sure she was pregnant in the first place?' Considering how heartless the woman had been, Sasha wouldn't be surprised if she'd faked the pregnancy.

Marco's movements were uncharacteristically jerky as he

reached for his wallet. Beneath the photo, a small grey square slid out. In the light of the trophy room Sasha saw the outline of a tiny body in a pre-natal scan.

Tears gathered in her eyes and fell before she could stop them. With shaking hands she took the picture from him, the memory of her own loss striking into her heart so sharply she couldn't breathe.

'I was there the day this was taken. The thing was, all along I suspected Angelique was capable of that. She was extremely ruthless—driven to the point of obsession. But since she channelled all that into being my manager I chose to see it as something else.'

'Love?' she suggested huskily.

His jaw tightened. 'I blinded myself to her true colours. My mother tried to warn me, but I wouldn't listen to her. I almost cut her out of my life because of Angelique.' He sucked in a harsh breath. 'I lost my child…she lost her grandchild…because I chose to bury my head in the sand. She was devastated, and I don't think she really got over the damage I did to our family.'

Brushing a hand across her cheek, she asked, 'Why do you keep this?'

Marco took the scan and placed it back in his wallet. 'I failed to protect my daughter. This reminds me never to fail my family again.'

CHAPTER ELEVEN

MARCO left again the next day and didn't return for another two. When he returned Sasha met him in the hallway. His dragged her into his study and proceeded to kiss her with brutal need.

His confession in the garage had afforded her a glimpse into the man he was today. She now truly understood why he was so ferociously protective of Rafael. And why she couldn't afford for him to find out the true depth of her feelings.

Taking a deep breath, she forced herself to vocalise what she'd been too afraid to say over the phone the night before.

'Marco, I think I should leave. You can stay in Barcelona and not keep flying back here to see me. I can use the race track back home to train.'

His face clouded in a harsh frown. 'What the hell are you talking about?' Roughly he pulled her into his arms and kissed her again. 'You're not going anywhere.'

She tried to pull back but he held her easily. 'But—'

His smile was strained through tiredness. 'Rafael woke briefly last night. Only for a few minutes. But he appeared lucid, and he recognised me.' The relief in his voice was palpable.

Sasha smiled. 'I'm glad. But I think that's even more of a reason for you to stay in Barcelona. What if he wakes again when you're not there?'

Setting her free, he stabbed a hand through his hair. 'He's been moved to a private suite and I've set up video conferencing so I have a live feed into his room. Nothing will happen to him without my knowledge. I've also hired extra round-the-clock staff for when he comes home—including that nurse who was fired from the hospital in Budapest. So, you see, I'm not a total ass.'

'I know you're not. But you're splitting yourself in two when it's really Rafael who needs you most now.'

'Maybe I want to put my needs ahead of Rafael's for once in my life.' He threw his hands up in the air. 'What exactly do you want from me, Sasha?'

She was unprepared for the question. But she had one of her own burning at the back of her mind.

'What do *you* want from *me*? What is the real reason you want me to stay here? Am I here just so you can have sex on tap or is this something more…?' She faltered to a halt, too afraid to voice the words traipsing through her mind.

His eyes narrowed. 'I hardly think this is the time to be having a *where is this relationship going?* conversation.'

'Is there ever a right time? Besides, you don't *do* relationships, remember?'

He shrugged off his jacket and flung it onto a nearby chair. 'I want you here with me. Isn't that enough?' he rasped.

Another question she wasn't prepared for. Not because she didn't know the answer. It was because she knew the answer was *no*. Wanting was no longer enough. She was in love with Marco: with the boy whose heart had been shredded by a heartless woman and the formidable man who'd loved his unborn child so completely he'd closed his heart to any emotion.

She loved him. And it scared the hell out of her. The urge to retreat stabbed through her. Marco's obvious reluctance to discuss their relationship frightened her. But looking at him, his face haggard, his hands clenched on the desk in front of him, she knew she couldn't leave. Not just yet. Not when he was so worried about Rafael.

'I'll stay,' she said.

Naked relief reflected in his eyes. *'Gracias.'* He pulled her into his arms. 'Don't mention leaving again. Even the mere thought makes me want to hurl something.'

She hated herself for the thrill of pleasure that surged through her. 'It was for your own good—even if you don't want to see it.' And not just for Marco's sake. She had to find the strength to walk away. Because the longer she stayed, the more she risked losing everything.

'If you want suggestions on what's good for me, I have several ideas—' He stopped and cursed when his phone started ringing.

'Before you start hurling things, I'll remove myself to the garage. Your '65 Chevelle Impala's chrome finish needs polishing.'

'It also has extra wide front seats, if I recall.'

Desire weakened her. 'Marco…'

'Fine. But before you go—'

He plastered his lips against hers and proceeded to show her just how foolish her decision to leave had been.

By the time Sasha stumbled from the study she knew her heart was in serious trouble.

Marco threw himself into his seat two days later and barely stopped himself from punching a hole in the wall behind him.

Even though she'd changed her mind about leaving, Marco had sensed a withdrawal in Sasha he couldn't shake. It was almost as if Rafael's impending emergence from his coma had put a strain between them.

But why? If there was nothing between them Sasha should be happy that Rafael was recovering. Unless…? The thought that Sasha had feelings for Rafael after all sent a wave of anger and jealousy through him.

No. He dismissed the thought.

She'd listened to him bare his soul, held him in her arms as he'd relived Angelique's betrayal. Sasha had shed tears for him; he refused to believe the raw pain he'd seen in her eyes wasn't real.

But he couldn't deny something was wrong.

Only when they made love, when he held her afterwards, did he feel he had the real Sasha back. Even now, mere hours before she was due to leave for London, she'd locked herself away in his garage, hell-bent on restoring his vintage cars to even more pristine condition than they'd originally been in. While he sat here, grappling with confusion and a hunger so relentless he was surprised he didn't spontaneously combust from want.

No. It was more than want. This craving for Sasha, whether she was within arm's reach or he was in Barcelona, went beyond anything he'd ever known. The few times he'd contemplated whether it would be better if she wasn't at the villa at all he'd felt a wrench so deep it had shaken him.

Angelique had never made him feel like this, even though at the time he'd thought he would never yearn for another woman the way he'd yearned for her.

What he felt for Sasha was different…deeper…purer…

Marco stiffened, the breath trapped in his chest as he tried to get to grips with his feelings. But the more he tried to unravel the unfamiliar feeling, the more chaotic and frantic it grew.

He glanced out of his study window towards his garage. The feeling that she was slipping through his fingers wouldn't fade. But he couldn't deal with it now. There were too many loose ends left to tie up.

As if on cue, his phone rang. With a muttered curse, he picked it up.

All the way to his suite Sasha forced herself to breathe. Despite the cold lump of stone in her stomach, she needed to do this. She couldn't continue to string things along any longer.

She entered the suite and heard the shower running. Without pausing, she crossed the room and slid open the door.

Water streamed off Marco's naked, powerful body. The need that slammed through her threatened to weaken her resolve. It took several seconds before she could speak.

'Marco, I…I've decided…I'm not coming back here after the next race.'

He whirled about, looked stricken for a moment, then his jaw clenched. 'I thought we had this conversation already.'

Even now, with the wrenching pain of losing him coursing through her, she couldn't resist the intense pull of desire that watching the water cascade over his body brought.

She steeled herself against it. 'I tried to talk. You laid down the law.'

He snapped a towel off the heated rack and stepped from the shower. 'You timed it perfectly, didn't you?'

'Excuse me?'

'Your exit strategy. At first I didn't want to believe it, but now it makes perfect sense.'

She frowned. 'Perfect sense… What are you talking about?'

'You can drop the pretence. I had a call twenty minutes ago. From Raven Blass.'

Her eyes widened in surprise. 'Raven? Why—?'

'She's in Barcelona. She wants to see Rafael. I gave the hospital permission to let her see him, but funnily enough she was more worried about how *you* would feel about her visit.'

'Marco—'

'Apparently you're very *territorial* about Rafael. She said something about warning Rafael to stay away from her the day he crashed?'

'That wasn't how it was—'

He tied the towel around his trim waist. 'What was the plan? Use me as a stopgap until Rafael was on his feet, then go back to him?'

'Of course not!'

'You started withdrawing from me the moment I told you Rafael was about to wake up. Well, I'm glad to have been of service. But if you have any designs on my brother, kill them now. He won't like soiled goods.'

She flinched and bit back her gasp. For a moment he appeared to regret his words, then his expression hardened again.

'Wow. Okay, I guess your mind's made up.'

'I mean it, Sasha. Come anywhere near Rafael and I'll crush you like a bug.'

Pain congealed into a crushing weight in her chest. 'I suspected this, and I see I was right. Rafael will always come first with you—no matter how much you protest about putting yourself first. I just hope you don't have to give up something you really want one day.'

He frowned. 'There's nothing I want more than my family safe.'

'Well, that says it all, doesn't it?'

Whirling, she hurried from the room, cursing the stupid tears that welled up in her eyes.

In her room, she grabbed her suitcase and stuffed her belongings into it. She was snapping it shut when her door flew open.

'What are you doing?'

'Leaving. *Obviously.*'

'Your flight is not for another four hours.'

She picked her case off the bed. 'Oh? And what? You want one last shag for old times' sake?'

His eyes darkened in a familiar way even as his jaw clenched.

A stunned laugh escaped her. 'Let me get this straight. You want more sex with me even though I'm "soiled goods" you wouldn't let your own brother touch?'

Dull colour swam into his cheeks. 'Don't put it like that.'

'You know when I said you weren't an ass? I was stupendously wrong! You're the biggest ass in the universe.' She stalked towards the door.

'Sasha—'

'And to think I fooled myself into thinking I was in love with you. You don't deserve love. And you certainly don't deserve mine!'

Had she looked back as she sped through the door, pleased with herself for not breaking down in front of him, she would have seen his stunned face, his ashen pallor.

Sasha flew home to Kent after the Indian Grand Prix, one step closer to cementing the Constructors' Championship.

Returning home for the first time in months felt bittersweet. Glancing round the familiar surroundings of the home she'd grown up in, she wanted to burst into tears. Pictures of her father graced the mantel. A wooden cabinet in the dining room held their trophies. They weren't as numerous as Marco's, but she was proud of every single one of them. Unlike Marco, who'd chosen to hide his away the way he'd chosen to close off his heart…

But had he? He'd shown her that he would fight to the death to protect his family. Didn't that prove it was *her* who wasn't worth fighting for? The thought hurt more than she could bear.

With an angry hand she dashed away the tears. She refused to dwell on him. Her only goal now was finishing the season. She couldn't summon the appropriate enthusiasm for next year.

Wearily, she trudged to the kitchen and put on the kettle. Mrs Miller, her next door neighbour, had texted to let her know the fridge was fully stocked.

Sasha opened the fridge, caught a whiff of cheese and felt her stomach lurch violently. She barely made it to the bathroom seconds before emptying the contents of her stomach. Rinsing her mouth, she decided to forgo the tea in favour of sleep. Dragging herself to the shower, she washed off the grime of her transatlantic flight and fell into bed.

The stomach bug she suspected she'd caught in India, along with half of the team, didn't go away immediately, but by the time she arrived in Brazil three and a half weeks later she was in full health.

And three points away from securing the championship.

São Paolo was vibrant and exhilarating. The pit was abuzz with the excitement of the season's final race, and Team Espiritu even more so with a potential championship win only a few short hours away.

Sasha had taken the coward's way and hidden in her hotel room until the last minute, in case she bumped into Marco. In Abu Dhabi she'd declined his invitation to an after-race party on his sprawling yacht. It seemed he was back to entertaining dignitaries and A-list celebrities with barely a blink in her direction.

Whereas she…she just wanted the season to be over.

The joy had gone out of racing.

With a sharp pang she realised Marco had been right—her guilt about her father had blinded her to the fact that she didn't need to prove to anyone that she was good enough. Nor did she need to defend Jack Fleming's integrity. With her deeper integration and final acceptance into the team she'd discovered that most people remembered Jack Fleming as the great driver he'd been. Her guilt lingered, but she would deal with that later.

First she had to get through the press interviews before and after the race.

She spotted Tom heading her way as she was pulling on her jumpsuit. She winced at the sensitivity of her breasts as the Velcro tightened over them.

She paused, then suddenly was scrambling madly for dates, calculating frantically and coming up short every time. Panic seized her.

'Are you all right? You've gone pale. Here—have some water.'

Tom poured water into a plastic cup and handed it to her. His attitude had undergone a drastic change since she'd become involved with Marco. Snarkily, Sasha wondered whether he'd go back to being insufferable once he found out she and Marco were no longer together.

'It's the heat,' she replied, setting the cup aside. 'I'm fine,' she stressed when he continued to peer at her in concern.

'Okay. Your last interview is with local TV.' He rolled his eyes. 'It's that smarmy one who interviewed you in Singapore. I'd cut him out of the schedule, but since we're on his home turf we don't have any choice. Don't worry. If he looks as if he's straying into forbidden territory I'll stop him.'

He went on to list the other interviewers, but Sasha was only half listening. She'd finally worked out her period dates and breathed a sigh of relief. She'd had her last albeit brief period just before she'd left Leon. And her cycle was erratic at the best of times.

Reassured, she followed Tom around to the paddock and spoke to the journalists.

The race itself was uneventful. With her eight-second lead unchallenged after the first six laps she cruised to victory, securing the fastest lap ever set on the Interlagos circuit. She managed to keep a smile plastered on her face all through the celebrations and the myriad interviews that followed, sighing with relief as she entered the team's hospitality suite for her last interview.

Despite having done dozens of interviews, she still suffered an attack of nerves whenever a camera was trained on her. And, unlike nerves during a race, interview nerves never worked to her advantage.

'Don't worry, Miss Fleming. It will be all right.'

The note of insincerity in the interviewer's thick accent should have been her first warning.

The first few questions were okay. Then, 'How does it feel to be dating the team boss? Has it earned you any advantages?'

From the corner of her eye she saw Tom surge from his seat. Her 'no comment' made him relax a little.

'After winning the Constructors' Championship, surely your seat for next year is secured?'

'No comment.'

He shrugged. 'How about your ex, Derek Mahoney? Have you heard he's making a comeback to racing?'

Sasha tensed. 'No, I haven't heard.'

'He gave us an interview this morning. And he mentioned something quite interesting.'

Icy dread crept up her spine. 'Whatever it is, I'm sure it has nothing to do with me.'

'On the contrary, it has everything to do with you.'

Her interviewer rubbed his chin in a way that was probably supposed to make him appear smart. It only confirmed the slimeball he really was.

'You see, Mr Mahoney claims you were pregnant with his child when you broke up, and that you deliberately crashed to lose the baby because you didn't want a child to hamper your career. What's your response to that?'

The room swayed around her. Vaguely she heard Tom shouting at the cameraman to stop filming. Inside she was frozen solid, too afraid to move. The buzz in the room grew louder. Someone grasped her arm and frogmarched her into another room. The sole occupant, a waitress cleaning a table, looked from her to the TV and quickly made herself scarce.

'Sasha… I… God, this is a mess,' Tom stuttered. 'Will you be all right? I need to secure that footage…'

'Please, go. I…I'll be fine,' she managed through frozen lips.

He hurriedly retreated and she was alone.

Dropping her head between her thighs, she tried to breathe evenly, desperately willing herself not to pass out. The TV hummed in the background but she didn't have the strength to walk over to turn it off.

Oh, God, how had Derek found out? Not that it mattered now. Her secret was out. Out there for the whole world to pore over…

Tears welled in her eyes. Derek was all about causing maximum damage. But she'd never dreamed he'd sink this low.

The door flew open and Marco walked in.

Her gaze collided with his, and every single thing she'd told herself over the last three weeks flew out of the door.

He'd lost weight. The gap at the collar of his light blue shirt showed more of his collarbones and his jacket hung looser. But he was just as arresting, just as breathlessly beautiful, and her heart leapt with shameless joy at the sight of him.

'I need to talk to you,' he said tautly, his gaze roving intensely over her before capturing hers again.

She licked her dry lips. 'I…I need to tell you…' How could she tell him? She'd never vocalised her pain, never told another human being.

'What is it?' He came over and took her hands. 'Whatever it is, tell me. I can handle it.'

That gave her a modicum of strength. 'You promise?'

'*Sí*. I have a few things I need to tell you too, *mi corazón*. The things I said in Leon…' He paused and shook his head, a look of regret in his eyes. 'You were right. I'm an ass.'

'I didn't…' *I didn't mean it*, she started to confess, but her eyes had strayed to the TV. There, like a vivid recurring nightmare, her interview was being replayed.

Seeing her distraction, Marco followed her gaze.

Just in time to hear the interviewer's damning question.

Marco dropped her hands faster than hot coals and surged to his feet. '*No!* It's a lie. Isn't it, Sasha? *Isn't it?*' he shouted when she couldn't speak.

'I…'

He paled, his cheekbones standing out against his stark face as he stepped back from her.

'Marco, please—it wasn't like that.' She finally found her voice. But it was too late.

He'd taken several more steps backwards, as if he couldn't stand to breathe the same air as her.

'Did you race knowing you were pregnant?' he insisted, his voice harsh.

'Not the day Derek's talking about—'

'But you *did* race knowing you were pregnant?'

'I suspected I was—'

'Dios mío!'

'I'd already lost the baby when I crashed. That was *why* I crashed! Racing was all I knew. After the doctor told me I'd lost the baby I didn't know what else to do.'

'So you got straight back in your car? You didn't even take time to mourn the loss of your child?' he condemned in chilling tones.

Somehow she found the strength to stand and face him. 'The doctor said it wasn't my fault. The pregnancy wasn't viable to begin with. But I still cried myself to sleep every night for years afterwards. If you're asking if I carry a picture of a scan to punish myself with, or as an excuse to push people away, then no, I don't. She lives in my heart—'

"*She?*" His voice was a tortured rasp, his fists clenching and unclenching and his throat working as he paled even more.

Tears spilled from her eyes and she nodded. 'Mine was a girl too. She lives in my heart and that's where I choose to remember her. You say you don't live in the past, but that's exactly what you're doing. You're judging *me* by what happened to you ten years ago.'

He inhaled sharply. 'And you've proved to me just how far you'll go. I told you about Angelique, about my child, and you said nothing. Because a small thing like a lost pregnancy is less important to you than your next race, isn't it?'

She swayed as pain clamped her chest in a crushing vice. 'You know why I wanted to race!'

'I was a fool to believe you were trying to preserve the memory of your father. You were really just seeking to further your own agenda.'

Pain arrowed through her. 'Don't pretend you don't think he was guilty.'

'I said he was *found* guilty. I didn't say I agreed with the verdict.'

'But—'

He slashed a hand through her words. 'I had my lawyers investigate the case. Some of the testimony didn't add up. If your father had spent less time feeling sorry for himself and more time getting his lawyers to concentrate on his case he'd have realised that. That's one of the things I came here to tell you.'

Tears stung the backs of her eyes, her throat clogging with unspoken words. 'Marco, please—can't we talk about this?'

He gave a single, finite shake of his head. 'I'm not interested in anything you have to say. I'm only grateful I never made you pregnant. I don't think I could survive another child of mine being so viciously denied life for the sake of ruthless ambition.'

Her insides froze as his words cut across her skin.

With one last condemning look he headed towards the door. Panic seized her. 'Marco!'

He stilled but didn't turn around, one hand on the doorknob.

'What else did you come to say to me?'

The cold malice in his eyes when he turned around made her heart clench.

'I sold the team six weeks ago. In Korea. The paperwork was finalised today. As of one hour ago your contract is null and void.'

CHAPTER TWELVE

She was pregnant with Marco's child. Sasha had been certain of it almost as soon as Marco had walked out on her in São Paolo. Taking the pregnancy test once she'd returned home had only established what she'd known in her heart.

There was no doubt in her mind that she would tell him he was about to become a father. The only problem was when.

He'd made his feelings clear. Her own emotions were too raw for her to face another showdown with Marco. She doubted he would believe whatever she had to tell him anyway.

Gentle fingers stroked over her belly. The doctor had confirmed today that she was almost three months pregnant. Her fingers stilled. Angelique had terminated Marco's child at three months. Sadness welled inside her as she recalled Marco's face when he'd shown her his scan.

Making up her mind before she lost the courage, she dug out her phone. Her fingers shook as she pressed the numbers.

'*Sí?*' came the deep voice.

'Marco, it's me.'

Taut silence.

'I know you don't want to speak to me…but there's something I need to tell you.'

'I'm no longer in the motor racing business, so you're wasting your time.' The line went dead.

Sasha stared at the phone, anger and pain churning through her. '*Ass.*'

She threw the phone down, vowing to make Marco beg before she let him anywhere near his child.

Two days later Sasha was standing at her fridge stacking groceries when she heard the agonisingly familiar sound of helicopter rotorblades. The aircraft flew directly over her small cottage before landing in a field half a mile away.

Even though she forced herself to finish her task, every sense was attuned to the knock that came less than five minutes later.

Heart hammering, she opened her door to find Marco standing there, tall, dark and windswept.

'You know you'll have my neighbours dining out on your spectacular entrance for years, don't you? What the hell are you doing here anyway? I recall you wanting nothing to do with me.'

Hazel eyes locked on hers, the look in them almost imploring. 'Invite me in, Sasha.'

'I don't invite heartless bloodsuckers into my home. You can stay right where you are. Better yet, jump back into your vampire-mobile and leave.'

'I'm not leaving until you hear what I have to say. I don't care what your neighbours think, but I get the feeling *you* do. There's a blue-haired one staring at us right now.' Brazen, he waved at Mrs Miller, who shamelessly waved back and kept right on staring at them.

Firming her lips, Sasha stepped back and waved him in. 'You think you're very clever, don't you?'

Expecting a quick comeback, she turned from shutting the door to find him staring at her, a tormented grimace on his face.

'No, I don't think I'm clever at all. In fact, right now, I'm the stupidest person I know.'

Her mouth dropped open.

His grimace deepened. 'Yes, I know. Shocker.'

'Marco…' She stopped and finally did what she'd been dying to do since he knocked on her door. She let her eyes devour him. Let her heart delight in the sheer magnificent sight of him. He went straight to her head. Made her sway where she stood.

He stared right back at her, a plethora of emotions she was

too afraid to name passing over his face. He opened his mouth a couple of times but, seemingly losing his nerve to speak, cast his gaze around her small living room, over the pictures and racing knick-knacks she and her father had accumulated over the years.

Finally he dug into his jacket pocket. 'This is for you.'

Sasha took the papers. 'What are these?'

'Signed affidavits from two former drivers who swear your father wasn't involved in the fraud. He was the fall guy.'

Hands shaking, she read through the documents. 'How…? Why…?' Tears clogged her throat, making the words difficult to utter. Finally she could clear her father's name.

'The how doesn't matter. The why is because you deserve to know.'

She didn't realise she was crying until the first teardrop landed on her hand. Sucking in a sustaining breath, she swiped at her cheeks. 'I…I really don't know what to say. After what happened…' She glanced down at the papers again and swallowed. 'Thank you, Marco,' she said huskily.

'De nada,' he replied hoarsely.

'You didn't have to deliver it in person, though.'

His watchful look intensified. 'I didn't. But I needed the excuse to see you.'

'Why?' she whispered, too afraid to hope.

He swallowed. 'Rafael woke up—really woke up yesterday.'

Her heart lurched. 'Is he okay?'

Marco nodded. 'I went to see him this morning. He told me what happened in Budapest.'

Sasha sighed. 'I know it was stupid, but I lost it when I found out what Rafael was doing.'

'You mean deliberately using your friendship to make Raven jealous?'

She nodded. 'I think she was smitten with Rafael when she first joined the team. That changed when she found out he'd dated most of the women in the paddock. She refused to have anything to do with him after that.'

Marco pursed his lips. 'And he, of course, found it a challenge when she kept refusing him. Why didn't you tell me?' he demanded.

'You told me the significance of your mother's ring. I didn't think you needed to know Rafael was intending to use it to…'

'Get lucky?' He grimaced, then sobered. 'He's over that now, I think. He's seems different—more…mature. I think the accident was a wake-up call for him.'

His eyes locked on her, their expression so bleak it broke her heart.

'For me too. You were right.'

'I was?'

He moved towards her suddenly. '*Sí*. I was living in the past. I knew it even before you left Leon. I knew it when I came to see you in São Paolo. Hearing Rafael tell me what I already knew—how great you are, how much of a friend you'd been to him…' He stopped and swallowed. 'Did I mention I'm the stupidest person I know right now?'

'Um, you may have.'

'What I said in São Paolo was unforgivable…' His anxious gaze snared hers. 'I was in shock, but I never should've said what I did. I'm sorry you lost your baby. I think you would've made a brilliant mother.'

'You do?'

'*Sí*. I saw how the Children of Bravery Awards affected you. You held it together despite your pain. Watching you on stage with the kids made me wish my child had had a mother like you. At least then she would've had a chance.'

Tears filled her eyes. 'Oh, Marco…' She could barely speak past the lump in her throat.

Another grimace slashed his face. 'I've made you cry again.' He sat next to her and gently brushed away her tears. 'This wasn't what I intended by coming here.'

'Why did you come here, Marco?'

He sucked in a huge breath. 'To tell you I love you. And to beg your forgiveness.'

'You love me?'

He gave a jerky nod. 'It ripped me apart to learn I'd had your love and lost it because I'd been so stupid. When you called two days ago—'

'When you hung up on me?'

'I panicked. The hospital had just called about Rafael. I thought you knew and were calling to ask to see him.' He frowned. 'Why *did* you call?'

'I had something to tell you. When you hung up on me I wrote a letter instead.'

'A letter?'

'Well, it was more like a list.'

She'd done it to stop herself from crying—something she couldn't seem to stop doing lately.

Reaching into her pocket, she pulled it out and held it towards him. 'Here.'

He stared at the paper but didn't take it, his face ashen. 'Is forgiveness anywhere on that list, by any chance?'

Her gaze sharpened on him. 'Forgiveness?'

'Yes. Forgiveness of judgemental bastards who don't know the special gift of love and beauty and goodness when it's handed to them.'

'Er...' She glanced down at the list, her thundering heartbeat echoing loudly in her ears. 'No. But then I've only had two days to work on it.'

Dropping down on his haunches, he cupped her face in his hands. 'Then consider this a special request, *por favor*. I know I have a lot of grovelling to do for judging you harshly from the beginning.'

'You were hurting. And you were right. I *was* acting out of guilt.'

'No. You were doing whatever it took for you to move on—whereas I let one stumbling block shatter me. I resented you for that.'

'The blows you were dealt were enough to knock anyone sideways.'

'But I let it colour my judgement. I told myself I had recovered, that I didn't care, but I did. Do you know that until you came to Leon I hadn't entered that garage in over ten years? You opened my eyes to what a barren life I'd led until then.'

'Look at the letter, Marco.'

He inhaled sharply and stood. 'No. If you're going to condemn me I'd rather hear it from you.'

'You might want to sit down.'

He stuffed his fingers into his coat pockets, but not before she caught the trembling of his hands.

'Just tell me.'

'Fine. But if you faint from shock don't expect me to help you. You're too big—'

When he made an incoherent sound racked with pain, she unfolded the paper.

Anxiety coursed through her. He'd said he loved her, but what if Marco truly didn't want another child? What if the loss of his unborn child had been too great a pain for him ever to move on from?

'Sasha, *por favor*.'

'That's the second time you've said please in the last five minutes,' she whispered.

When his eyes grew dark, she read aloud. *'"Marco, you were an ass for hanging up on me but I think you should know—"'* She looked up from the sheet. *'"You're going to become a father."'*

For a full minute he didn't move. Didn't breathe, didn't blink. Then he stumbled into the chair. His hands visibly shook when he reached out and cupped her cheek. 'Sasha. Please tell me this isn't a dream,' he rasped.

'This isn't a dream. I'm pregnant with your child.'

A look of complete reverence settled over his face before his eyes dropped to her still-flat stomach.

'Are you okay? Is everything all right?' he demanded.

'You mean with the baby?'

'With both of you.'

'Yes. I saw the doctor. Everything is fine. Does that mean you want the baby?'

'*Mi corazón*, you've given me a second chance I never would've been brave enough to take on my own. I may have burned my bridges with you, but, yes, I want this baby.' His eyes dropped to her stomach, and lingered. '*Por favor*, can I touch?'

Sweet surprise rocked through her. 'You want to touch my belly?'

'If you'll allow me?'

'You know the baby isn't any larger than your thumb right now, don't you?'

'*Sí*, but my heart wants what it wants. Please?'

Renewed tears clogged her throat as she nodded and unbuttoned her jeans.

Warm fingers caressed her belly. Watching his face, she felt the breath snag in her chest at the sheer joy exhibited there. Then his eyes locked on hers and his fingers slid under her sweater, heating her bare flesh.

Her heart kicked, the fierce love she felt for this man and for her baby making her throat clog with tears. Reluctantly she withdrew from his seductive warmth. 'Marco, I haven't finished reading the letter.'

A look of uncertainty entered his eyes. 'I know what a hard bargain you can drive. Is there any room for negotiation?'

'You need to hear what's in it first.'

He gave a reluctant nod, his joy fading a little.

'"*If it's a boy I would like to name him after my father. One of his names, at least.*"'

A quick nod met her request. 'It will be so.'

'"*I want our child to be born in Spain. Preferably in Leon.*"'

He swallowed hard. 'Agreed.'

She looked up from the paper. '"*I'd like to stay there after the baby's born. With you.*"'

His eyes widened and he stopped breathing. 'You want to stay in Leon? With me?'

Her heart in her throat, she nodded. 'Our child deserves two parents who don't live in separate countries.'

Disappointment fleeted over his face. 'You're right.'

'Our child also deserves parents who love each other.'

Pain darkened his eyes. 'I intend to do everything in my power to earn your love again, Sasha.'

She shrugged, her heart in her throat. 'You'll need to focus your energies on other things, Marco. Because I love you.'

He sucked in a breath. 'You...love me...?'

'Yes,' she reiterated simply. 'I knew in Leon, even though I'd convinced myself it wouldn't work.'

'I didn't exactly make it easy. I felt my life unravelling and I got desperate.'

Shock rocked through her. 'Was that why you sold the team?'

He grimaced. 'Rafael's accident and your near-collision in Korea convinced me it was time to get out of racing. But I managed to bulldoze my way through that too. I also may have left a tiny detail out regarding your firing.'

'Oh?'

'The sale contract included a stipulation that you were to have first refusal of the lead driver's seat. If you wanted it.'

Lifting loving hands, she cradled his face. 'Didn't you read Tom's press release last week?'

'What press release?'

'I've retired from motor racing.'

He frowned. 'What about your promise to your father?'

'He would've been proud that I helped you win the Constructors' Championship. But what he really wanted was for me to be happy.'

'And are you?'

'Tell me you love me again and I'll let you know.'

'I am deeply, insanely in love with you, Sasha Fleming, and I can't wait to make you mine.'

She flung the letter away and slid her arms around his neck. 'Then, yes, I'm ecstatically happy.'

EPILOGUE

'Happy birthday, *mi preciosa*.'

Sasha turned from where she'd been watching another stunning Leon sunset and tucked the blanket around their two-month-old baby.

'*Shh*. You'll wake him.'

Marco joined her at the crib. With a look of complete adoration on his face, he brushed a finger down his son's soft cheek. 'Jack Alessandro de Cervantes can sleep through a hurricane—just like his mother.' He pressed a kiss on his son's forehead, then held out his hand to her. 'Come with me.'

'Marco, you're not giving me another present? You've already given me six—oh, never mind.' By now she knew better than to dissuade her husband when he was on a mission. Today his mission was to shower her with endless gifts.

'*Sí*, now you're learning.'

As Marco led her to their bedroom she glanced down at the large square diamond ring he'd slid next to her seven-month-old wedding ring this morning. Not a week went by without Marco giving her a gift of some sort. Last week he'd presented her with the most darling chocolate Labradoodle puppy, and then grumbled when she'd immediately fallen in love with the dog.

'I hope it's not another diamond. There's only so much bling a girl can wear before she's asking for a mugging.'

'It's not a diamond. This present is much more...personal.'

He shut the door behind them, settled his hands on her hips and pulled her closer, his hazel eyes growing dramatically darker. 'The kind of *personal* that happens when you wear this T-shirt.'

'Why do you think I'm wearing it?'

He gave a low, sexy laugh. '*Dios*, you're merciless.'

'Only when it comes to you. Turning you on gives me a huge buzz.'

Stretching up, she wrapped her arms around his neck, luxuriating in their long kiss until she reluctantly pulled away.

At his protest, she shook her head. 'I have something to show you before we get too carried away.'

Reaching towards her bedside table, she handed him a single piece of heavily embossed paper.

He read through the document before glancing up at her. 'It's finalised?'

Happiness burst through her chest. 'Yes. The mayor's office sent over confirmation this afternoon. I'm officially patron of the De Cervantes Children's Charity. My programme to help disadvantaged kids who're interested in racing is a go!'

His devastating smile held pride even as he sighed. 'Between that and you being spokeswoman for women motor racers, I see my cunning plan to keep you busy in my bed having babies fast disappearing.'

Her smack on his arm was rewarded with a kiss on her willing mouth.

He sobered. 'Are you sure you don't want to go back to racing? You know you'd have my support in that too.'

Sasha blinked eyes prickling with tears and pressed her mouth against his. 'Thank you, but that part of my life is over. The chance to work with children is another dream come true. As for making more babies with you—it's my number one priority. Right up there with loving you for ever.'

His eyes darkened. 'I love you too, *mi corazón*.'

'Enough to take advantage of the instruction on my T-shirt?' she asked saucily.

With a growl, he tumbled her back onto the bed and proceeded to demonstrate just how good he was at taking instruction.

* * * * *

COMING SOON!

We really hope you enjoyed reading this book.
If you're looking for more romance
be sure to head to the shops when
new books are available on

Thursday 19th June

To see which titles are coming soon, please visit
millsandboon.co.uk/nextmonth

MILLS & BOON

MILLS & BOON

THE HEART OF ROMANCE

A ROMANCE FOR EVERY READER

MODERN — Prepare to be swept off your feet by sophisticated, sexy and seductive heroes, in some of the world's most glamourous and romantic locations, where power and passion collide.

HISTORICAL — Escape with historical heroes from time gone by. Whether your passion is for wicked Regency Rakes, muscled Vikings or rugged Highlanders, awaken the romance of the past.

MEDICAL — Set your pulse racing with dedicated, delectable doctors in the high-pressure world of medicine, where emotions run high and passion, comfort and love are the best medicine.

True Love — Celebrate true love with tender stories of heartfelt romance, from the rush of falling in love to the joy a new baby can bring, and a focus on the emotional heart of a relationship.

HEROES — The excitement of a gripping thriller, with intense romance at its heart. Resourceful, true-to-life women and strong, fearless men face danger and desire - a killer combination!

afterglow BOOKS — From showing up to glowing up, these characters are on the path to leading their best lives and finding romance along the way – with plenty of sizzling spice!

To see which titles are coming soon, please visit

millsandboon.co.uk/nextmonth

FOUR BRAND NEW BOOKS FROM
MILLS & BOON MODERN

The same great stories you love, a stylish new look!

Conveniently ARRANGED
LYNNE GRAHAM · LORRAINE HALL

WANTED: HIS HEIR
MAYA BLAKE · DANI COLLINS

DEFIANT Brides
Tara Pammi · Michelle Smart

ABBY GREEN · NATALIE ANDERSON
THE BILLIONAIRE'S LEGACY

OUT NOW

Eight Modern stories published every month, find them all at:

millsandboon.co.uk

LET'S TALK
Romance

For exclusive extracts, competitions and special offers, find us online:

- **f** MillsandBoon
- **X** @MillsandBoon
- **◉** @MillsandBoonUK
- **♪** @MillsandBoonUK

Get in touch on 01413 063 232

For all the latest titles coming soon, visit
millsandboon.co.uk/nextmonth

afterglow BOOKS

Afterglow Books is a trend-led, trope-filled list of books with diverse, authentic and relatable characters, a wide array of voices and representations, plus real world trials and tribulations. Featuring all the tropes you could possibly want (think small-town settings, fake relationships, grumpy vs sunshine, enemies to lovers) and all with a generous dose of spice in every story.

@millsandboonuk
@millsandboonuk
afterglowbooks.co.uk
#AfterglowBooks

For all the latest book news, exclusive content and giveaways scan the QR code below to sign up to the Afterglow newsletter:

SCAN ME

afterglow BOOKS

He's on track to win her heart...
KAREN BOOTH
NOT SO FAST

They're enemies at work...but can love write their happy ending?
Much Ado About Hating You
Sarah Echavarre Smith

- Sports romance
- Enemies to lovers
- Spicy
- Workplace romance
- Forbidden love
- Opposites attract

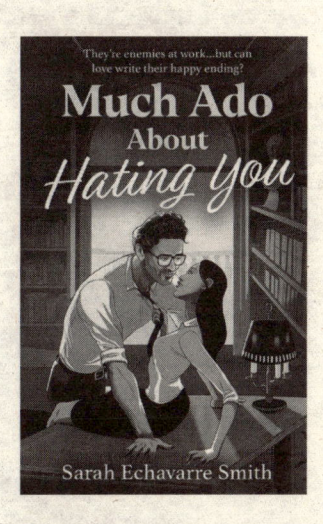

OUT NOW

Two stories published every month. Discover more at:
Afterglowbooks.co.uk

OUT NOW!

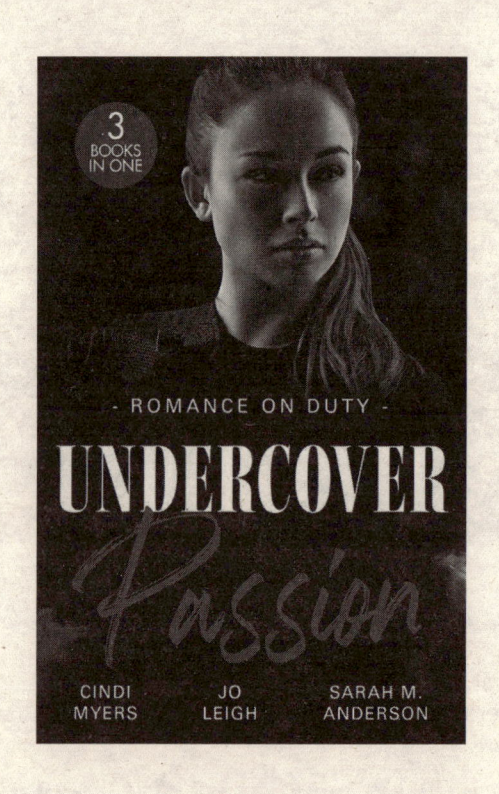

ROMANCE ON DUTY
UNDERCOVER Passion

CINDI MYERS   JO LEIGH   SARAH M. ANDERSON

3 BOOKS IN ONE

Available at
millsandboon.co.uk

MILLS & BOON

OUT NOW!

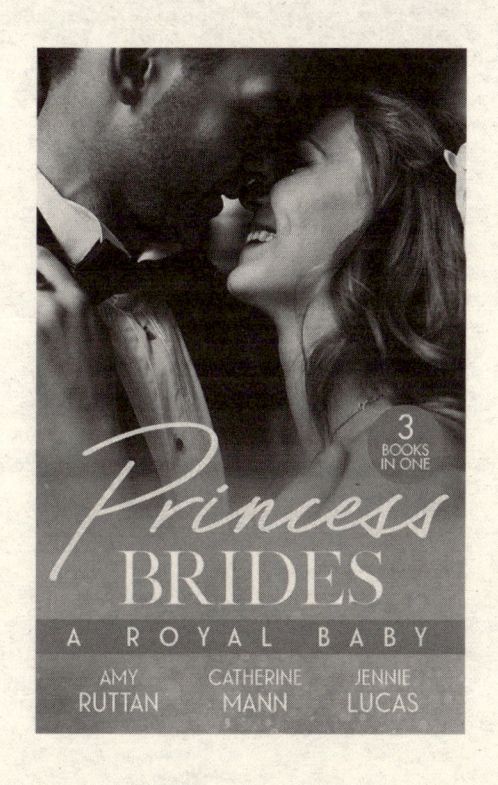

Princess BRIDES
A ROYAL BABY

3 BOOKS IN ONE

AMY RUTTAN
CATHERINE MANN
JENNIE LUCAS

Available at
millsandboon.co.uk

MILLS & BOON

OUT NOW!

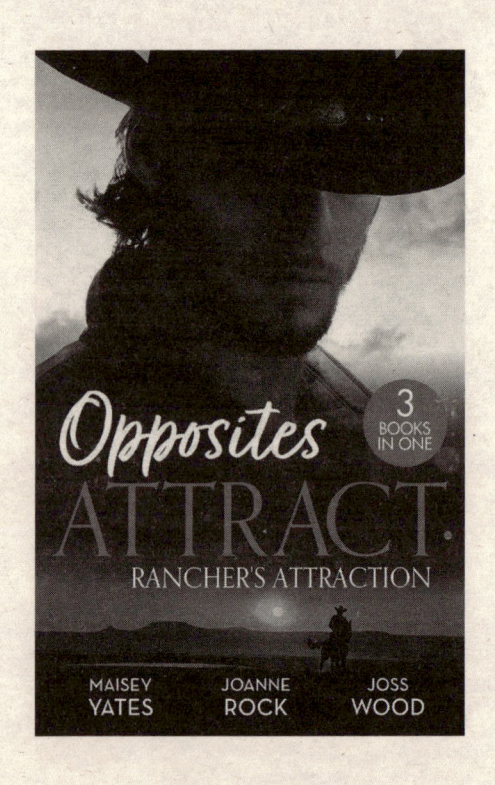

Opposites Attract: Rancher's Attraction

3 BOOKS IN ONE

MAISEY YATES · JOANNE ROCK · JOSS WOOD

Available at
millsandboon.co.uk

MILLS & BOON

MILLS & BOON
A ROMANCE FOR EVERY READER

- **FREE** delivery direct to your door
- **EXCLUSIVE** offers every month
- **SAVE** up to 30% on pre-paid subscriptions

SUBSCRIBE AND SAVE

millsandboon.co.uk/Subscribe

MILLS & BOON
MODERN
Power and Passion

Prepare to be swept off your feet by sophisticated, sexy and seductive heroes, in some of the world's most glamorous and romantic locations, where power and passion collide.

Eight Modern stories published every month, find them all at:

millsandboon.co.uk

MILLS & BOON
HEROES
At Your Service

Experience all the excitement of a gripping thriller, with an intense romance at its heart that will keep you on the edge of your seat. Resourceful, true-to-life women and strong, fearless men face danger and desire – a killer combination!

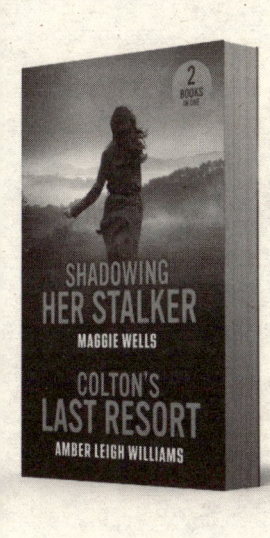

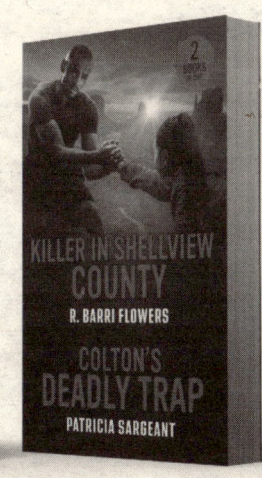

SHADOWING HER STALKER
MAGGIE WELLS

COLTON'S LAST RESORT
AMBER LEIGH WILLIAMS

KILLER IN SHELLVIEW COUNTY
R. BARRI FLOWERS

COLTON'S DEADLY TRAP
PATRICIA SARGEANT

FUGITIVE HARBOR
CASSIE MILES

MISTAKEN IDENTITIES
TARA TAYLOR QUINN

Eight Heroes stories published every month, find them all at:
millsandboon.co.uk

MILLS & BOON
True Love
Romance from the Heart

Experience the rush and intensity of falling in love! Be prepared to be swept away to international destinations along with our strong, relatable heroines and intensely desirable heroes.

Four True Love stories published every month, find them all at:

millsandboon.co.uk/TrueLove

MILLS & BOON
MEDICAL
Pulse-Racing Passion

Set your pulse racing with delectable doctors, hot-shot surgeons and fearless first resonders. Escape to a world where life and love play out against a high-pressured medical backdrop, where emotions and passion run high.

Six Medical stories published every month, find them all at:

millsandboon.co.uk

GET YOUR ROMANCE FIX!

Get the latest romance news, exclusive author interviews, story extracts and much more!

blog.millsandboon.co.uk